FREEDOM'S CROSSROAD

RAMONA K. CECIL

BARBOUR
PUBLISHING

Sweet Forever © 2008 by Ramona K. Cecil
Everlasting Promise © 2008 by Ramona K. Cecil
Charity's Heart © 2008 by Ramona K. Cecil

ISBN 978-1-60260-803-0

All scripture quotations are taken from the King James Version of the Bible.

This book is a work of fiction. Names, characters, places, and incidents are either products of the author's imagination or used fictitiously. Any similarity to actual people, organizations, and/or events is purely coincidental.

Cover design: Kirk DouPonce, DogEared Design

Published by Barbour Publishing, Inc., P.O. Box 719, Uhrichsville, Ohio 44683, www.barbourbooks.com

Our mission is to publish and distribute inspirational products offering exceptional value and biblical encouragement to the masses.

ecpa Member of the
Evangelical Christian
Publishers Association

Printed in the United States of America.

Dear Readers,

I hope you enjoy *Freedom's Crossroad*. As a native Hoosier, I am proud and excited to bring you this collection of novels set in Indiana's rich past. Crafting tales of romance is my passion, and sharing the truths of God's Word is my joy. These particular stories each focus on different members of the Hale/Morgan family and span the years from 1845 to 1867.

I believe every reader can relate to the emotions my characters experience in *Sweet Forever*, *Everlasting Promise*, and *Charity's Heart*. Like Rosaleen, who at some point in their life has not questioned how God could love them—as the old hymn says "A sinner, condemned, unclean"? When prayers seem to go unanswered, we, like Susannah, sometimes wonder if God is even listening. And like Charity and Daniel, we, too, can find our faith tested by Christ's command to forgive.

My aim is to weave stories that thrill both the hearts and souls of my readers. Here in *Freedom's Crossroad*, I hope you will find sweet love stories that tug at your heartstrings while reaffirming that only with God's help can we deal successfully with life's problems, and that all human relationships are enhanced when He is included.

I love to hear from my readers. I invite you to visit my Web site at www.ramonakcecil.com and sign my guest book. I look forward to reading your thoughts on *Freedom's Crossroad*.

Blessings,
Ramona K. Cecil

SWEET
FOREVER

Dedication

"There's a land beyond the river,
That we call the sweet forever—"
from *When They Ring Those Golden Bells*
by Daniel de Marbelle

Special thanks to the local history and genealogy department of the Madison Jefferson County Public Library; Historic Madison, Inc., Madison, Indiana; Jefferson County Historical Society; Verdin Company and the Verdin Bell and Clock Museum of Cincinnati, Ohio; Kim Sawyer and Staci Wilder for their invaluable critique work on this project; and my husband, Jim, and daughters, Jennifer and Kelly, whose encouragement and support make what I do possible.

Chapter 1

Tap, tap, tap.

Rosaleen Archer fixed her attention on the silver tip of Bill McGurty's walking stick.

Tap, tap, tap.

Its hypnotic cadence against the floor of her riverboat cabin held her in a terrified trance.

"You'll be a good girl this evening, won't you, Rosaleen?" The corner of his black clipped mustache twisted in a tiny sneer.

Rosaleen nodded, swallowing hard past the wad of fear in her throat.

"There's my good girl." The reflection of the wall sconce taper's flame danced in his small black eyes. "I'd hate to have to punish you again."

Tap, tap, tap.

He reached his hand out toward her, and Rosaleen moved away, pressing her back against the cabin wall. Shivering, she turned her face from the cold touch of his fingers on her cheek.

"You know what to do." The silky sweetness left his voice as he glanced at his silver watch then slipped it back into the pocket of his scarlet brocade vest. "Wait about an hour, till we're well into the game and they're well into their cups, then you can join us."

Again she nodded. Anything to make him leave her alone.

He pinched her chin hard between his forefinger and thumb.

Rosaleen fought nausea as he pressed a whiskey-laden kiss on her lips.

"Make me some money tonight." He lifted his dark beaver hat from the wrought iron hook beside the door to the Grand Saloon. With a parting wink, he set the hat at a jaunty angle atop his slicked-down black hair.

Long moments after her cabin door closed, Rosaleen sat trembling on the little bunk affixed to one wall of the cramped room. She looked around the dimly lit, white-washed cabin that was, for all practical purposes, her prison cell. The bunk and a tiny washstand against the opposite wall were the only comforts afforded by the five-by-six-foot area.

Tonight marked exactly six months since her husband's death aboard the steamboat *River Queen*. Shivering, she relived the sight of Bill McGurty accusing

Donovan of cheating at cards. She'd watched Bill pull out the wicked little derringer, heard the shot, and saw Donovan jerk back then fall forward.

As awful as that sight had been, what followed eclipsed it in terror. Bill McGurty declared the act self-defense since Donovan also carried a derringer. No one at the table dared dispute his claim. Pronouncing himself Rosaleen's "protector," he quickly became the opposite, forcing her to move with him from riverboat to riverboat.

For Rosaleen, the months since had amounted to a swift descent into a horrible existence. The shame of how Bill had used her night after night burned inside her like a spirit-consuming flame.

I'll die before I let him touch me again.

In an act of defiance, she snatched her little black velvet reticule from the bedside table, fished out the gold ring Donovan had placed on her hand eight months ago, and slipped it back on her finger. She would leave the cabin tonight—but not to help Black Jack Bill McGurty. Her plan of escape had begun when they'd boarded the *Cortland Belle* two days ago in Cincinnati and she'd learned Arthur Ellis piloted the boat.

During their short marriage, Donovan had mentioned Mr. Ellis, a fellow riverboat pilot, as a friend. If she could only manage a moment alone with him, perhaps he'd protect her and make Bill answer for his crimes when they docked at Louisville, Kentucky. Somehow she must make her way to the pilot's cabin on the Texas deck at the top of the boat.

Rosaleen glanced at the two doors on either side of her cabin. One led to the outer deck, the other to the Grand Saloon. Their first night on the *Cortland Belle*, she'd attempted an escape through the door to the outer deck. But a couple of Bill's gambling cronies had caught her on the promenade deck and returned her to her captor. She pressed her fingers against her ribs, still sore from the beating the thwarted attempt had elicited. Tonight she would try again. But this time she had a different strategy in mind.

It had been no more than a half hour, she guessed, since Bill had left her cabin. Yet if she waited longer, he would be expecting her to appear beside him at the gambling tables. Gathering her courage along with the purple silk folds of her skirts, she stood and walked to the door that opened to the Grand Saloon.

The beginnings of a prayer withered inside her as the scowling visage of her former guardian assembled itself in her mind. Reverend Wilfred Maguire, the elder brother of her late adoptive father, had made it quite clear—because of her illegitimacy God wanted nothing to do with her.

She must depend upon the gambler's luck of Rory Maguire, the man who'd raised her as his own and who in her heart would always be "Papa."

"All that's required is but a little smile from Lady Luck."

Remembering her father's frequent maxim, Rosaleen hoped Lady Luck would beam tonight.

She touched her mother's brooch pinned to the bodice of her dress. A gift from her father on her tenth birthday, the bejeweled cameo had always helped Rosaleen feel closer to the mother she'd never known. . .and the adoptive father she still missed.

Rosaleen blinked back hot tears. *Oh Papa, how I wish you were here to help me.*

The strong odors of cigar smoke and whiskey assailed her nostrils as she entered the Grand Saloon. A lively banjo tune blended with the cacophony of conversation and hearty laughter.

A Persian carpet of maroon, gold, and blue covered the entire floor area, stretching over two hundred feet long and nearly twenty feet wide. A row of brass and crystal chandeliers hanging along the center of the ceiling lit the opulent expanse. Rosaleen thought the saloon, richly decorated with silk upholstered chairs, horsehair sofas, and ornately carved marble-topped tables, one of the nicer ones she'd seen during her life aboard the steamboats.

As she moved along the wall of cabin doors, her heart pounded. She shot quick glances across the room where Bill sat laughing at a gambling table, chewing on an unlit cigar. Perhaps Lady Luck would continue smiling and Bill would not notice her.

"Rosaleen!"

Her heart dropped. Managing a shaky smile, she made her way toward Bill McGurty and the half dozen other men around the table.

"A bit early, ain't ya?" Bill's smile never reached his black eyes.

"Sorry." She remembered the sting of his ebony walking stick against her back, and a cold shiver slithered through her.

"Here's a V-spot. Be a good girl and go get us another couple of bottles of whiskey from the bar." He tucked the five-dollar note into the bodice of her dress.

Rosaleen nodded, realizing Lady Luck had just begun smiling like crazy. The bar was at the front end of the Grand Saloon, next to the door that led to the outer deck. With just a bit more luck she might be able to steal away without Bill's seeing her.

Just a few more steps.

When she slipped through the door, a fresh breeze welcomed her at the outside promenade of mid-deck. She rubbed her bare arms in the chill night air of early spring.

With a nervous glance over her shoulder at the door to the Grand Saloon, Rosaleen stepped toward the short stairway to the Texas deck. There, just below the pilothouse, were the cabins of the crew, including that of pilot Arthur Ellis. Pausing at the bottom step, she rehearsed the petition she would present to her late husband's friend.

Suddenly, the night exploded in a deafening flash of orange and yellow. The deck bucked like an unbroken colt, sending her flying against the rail.

Bruised and stunned, Rosaleen pulled herself up by the rail. In shock, she looked around at her altered surroundings. The pilothouse and much of the steamboat's stern no longer existed. All her life, she'd heard horror stories of boiler explosions. *Is that what just happened?*

Fire engulfed the back half of the boat. Its hungry crackle mixed with the screams and trampling sounds from the boatful of hapless humanity. The conflagration brightened the night as if it were day.

A stiff breeze blew searing heat and smoke into her face, causing Rosaleen to cough. Earlier, she'd decided she would die before she allowed Bill and his gambling cronies to have their way with her another night. Now, death seemed a distinct possibility. She glanced at the spreading flames behind her then down at the dark cold waters of the Ohio River beneath her. Grasping the riverboat's rail, she wondered which would be the easier way to die.

"Rosaleen! Rosaleen!"

The sound of Bill's voice barking from somewhere in the darkness sealed her decision. Gulping a lungful of smoke-laced air, she vaulted over the rail.

Hitting the cold water, she gasped, the enveloping river causing her to lose precious oxygen. The heaviness of her clothes pulled her down farther into the dark depths of the Ohio River.

Black. Pitch-black.

Her burning lungs felt as if they might explode. How easy to just open her mouth and surrender to the death she'd contemplated only an hour earlier. Yet as fear wrapped her heart in its crippling grasp, panic sprang from deep within her, bursting into a determined resolve. She wanted to live.

The terror in her heart turned to anger. She wouldn't let the river take her. Given this chance of escape, she'd not surrender to death without a fight.

Her arms flailing, she kicked out her legs bound by the heavy wet folds of her skirt and petticoats. Her head emerged from the water, and she sucked in grateful gulps of air. Blinking water from her eyes, she continued to kick her legs while pushing and pulling her arms, treading water just as Papa had taught her years ago.

She looked through the darkness at the blazing riverboat, now several yards away. The orange flames licked at the night sky. Unearthly screams filled the air. Curses blended with prayers, causing her to wonder if she really had died and this was hell.

She could hear splashes that indicated other passengers were also abandoning certain death on the *Cortland Belle*, choosing to seek dubious refuge in the river. Was Bill McGurty among them?

Rosaleen's shivers had little to do with the cold water. She pushed her arms harder, attempting to put more distance between herself and the boat. Her legs fought the strong current as the undertow threatened to pull her beneath the surface.

As frightening and uncertain as the dark abyss of death seemed, Black Jack Bill McGurty was far more terrifying.

Donovan had been a good man. If heaven existed, surely Donovan had gone there. Maybe if she begged God—if there *was* a God—He'd take her to Donovan. Even if she was undeserving, they'd been married. Didn't that mean they belonged together?

A sob tore from her smoke-filled throat. *Oh God, if You're really out there somewhere and can hear me, if I die, please take me to Donovan.*

❧

Oh Lord, I can only wonder how many died without knowing You.

The prayer rose from Jacob Hale's heavy heart. Standing at the corner of Broadway and Second Street, he gazed through the early morning mist toward the Ohio River. There, in the dark of the previous night, unnumbered souls had glimpsed this world for the last time, propelled into the next by the explosion of the steamboat's boiler and subsequent blaze.

Sighing, he set his toolbox in the shade of the old willow. Its supple green tresses of new spring foliage were bent as if in sorrowful benediction.

It bothered him to think that bodies still lay beneath the river with nothing to mark their watery graves. Hopefully, all could be recovered, identified, and given Christian burials. But sadly he knew that often, after such accidents, bodies remained trapped under debris or were swept downriver by the current.

He looked down at the modest, flat stone caressed by the willow's tender branches. "At least, my old friend, *you* have a marker."

Rev. Orville Whitaker, b.1782 d.1845.

Two months ago, Jacob had buried his friend and mentor on the plot they'd planned for the new church. His gaze swept over the nearly completed foundation. "It should be finished by the end of the summer, Orville."

Jacob liked to imagine his friend looking down from heaven and smiling upon his efforts.

The congregation Orville had established still met on Sunday mornings in Opal Buchanan's boardinghouse parlor to hear Jacob's sermons. But God willing, they'd be listening to them this fall from pews in this church he was helping to build with his own hands.

Jacob's gaze drifted back to the river, his thoughts turning once more to the steamboat accident. The sound of the explosion had jolted him awake. Although he'd hurried to join others from the Fair Play Fire Company, he'd soon returned home, realizing nothing could be done to save the doomed steamboat.

Compelled to be nearer to the scene of last night's tragedy, he walked a block down Broadway to Ohio Street and the river's edge. A lingering smell of wood smoke clung to the morning air, competing with the odors of Madison, Indiana's pork-packing industry.

He looked across the river's surface glinting in the morning sun to the charred remains of what had been the steamboat *Cortland Belle*. Listing hard starboard, it lay snagged on a sandbar near the Kentucky shore. Blackened, jagged pieces of the boat, along with unidentifiable debris, littered the water.

Jacob said a prayer for the souls of those who'd died in the accident then blew out a long, deep sigh. *Many others are still alive and could hear the Word before it's too late—*

His musings were cut short when he caught sight of an odd-looking object a few yards to his left down a sandy embankment. Curious, he made his way toward what looked like a purple bundle. As he drew nearer, his heart sank.

The body of a woman lay half hidden amid a cluster of sapling willows. He could see she was only partially out of the river with her legs still in the water, swathed in the wet folds of her purple dress. She lay facedown, her hair splayed out around her head, covering her features. The sun shone on the wavy, mahogany-colored strands, revealing tinges of burnished copper.

What beautiful hair.

The thought pricked Jacob's conscience the moment it formed in his mind. This had been a person. Someone's daughter. Perhaps someone's wife. Most probably, a victim of the riverboat explosion. She would need a Christian burial. He reached a tentative hand out toward her shoulder.

Oh Lord, I don't want to do this.

He'd seen several dead bodies in his twenty-six years of life, but it never got any easier. Jacob grasped her shoulder to turn her over.

She groaned, causing him to jump back in surprise.

As the morning sun touched her features, he detected a faint blush of pink staining her pale cheeks and full lips. This was no dead body!

Heart pounding, he dropped to his knees beside the woman. Taking her cool hands into his, he began rubbing warmth into her long, delicate fingers.

Her eyelids, fringed by thick dark lashes, fluttered open.

Slipping his left arm beneath her back, Jacob lifted her head and upper torso from the riverbank. "It's all right. You're going to be all right," he assured her, brushing hair and sand from her face with his free hand.

Her lips parted to emit another soft groan.

Jacob wrenched his attention from the arresting beauty of the woman to focus upon her plight. "You'll be all right now," he repeated. "I'm going to take care of you."

She blinked several times before squinting blue green eyes against the morning sun. "Donovan? Is that you, Donovan?" It was all she managed to mumble before her eyes closed again.

Lowering her to the riverbank, he anxiously pressed his fingers against her throat just below her jaw. A strong pulse beneath his touch brought him a measure of relief.

Ephraim. I need to get her to Ephraim.

Hurrying back up Broadway, he fetched his mule-drawn wagon full of lumber down to Ohio Street then returned to the woman, lifted her in his arms, and carried her up to his wagon.

Dear Lord, please just let her live.

As gently as possible, Jacob laid her on the two-by-sixes in the wagon bed. He climbed to the wagon seat and slapped the reins down hard onto the mules' backs. "Heyaa!" he yelled, urging the animals to a quickened pace up Broadway toward Main-Cross Street.

Chapter 2

A strong smell of camphor caused Rosaleen to jerk awake. She blinked and the image of a man came into focus.

"Ah, there you are." The tall, dark-haired man smiled as he waved the offensive-smelling bottle in front of her nose.

Where was she? How had she gotten here? Confused, she cast quick glances around the room. A large green cabinet sat against one wall. Corked bottles holding varying colors of liquids and powders crowded on four shelves behind the cabinet's glass doors.

The man picked up a trumpet-shaped object from a sideboard. "I am Dr. Morgan and, with your permission, I'd like to check the strength of your heartbeat."

Rosaleen nodded her assent, and he pressed the broader end of the instrument against her chest while holding the small, ivory-colored end to his ear.

"Well," he said, laying aside the instrument, "other than some bruising and exhaustion, I can find no injuries."

"Wh–where am I?" Disoriented, Rosaleen attempted to rise from a large, leather-upholstered chair.

A woman she hadn't noticed before gently restrained her. Dark brown curls peeked from beneath the white cotton cap framing the woman's pleasant face. "You're all right, dear. You're in Madison, Indiana, in Dr. Ephraim Morgan's office. I'm his wife, Becky Morgan." The kindness in the woman's soothing voice helped to quell Rosaleen's anxiety.

Sinking back into the chair, she submitted to the pressure of Mrs. Morgan's gentle grasp on her shoulders.

"You've been through an awful ordeal, but you are safe now." The woman's bright blue eyes conveyed assurance above an encouraging smile as she smoothed the white starched apron covering her blue calico day dress.

Still trying to make sense of it all, Rosaleen paid scant attention when the doctor's wife walked to a side door. Opening it, Mrs. Morgan spoke quiet, unintelligible words in a summoning tone.

"How did. . . How did I get. . . ?" Rosaleen murmured. Suddenly, it all flooded back into her consciousness with dizzying speed. The explosion. The fire. Bill.

She remembered the sun's warmth on her face and a man with light hair. Donovan? No. Donovan was dead. Had she been visited by an angel? *Do angels really exist?*

"I found you on the riverbank. Thought you. . .hadn't made it." The voice that answered her fractured question belonged to the figure of a second man who'd just entered the room.

Following the sound of his voice, Rosaleen blinked again as the man moved from the glare of the window.

Dressed as a common laborer, he wore a pair of black wool work trousers and a white work shirt. The shirt's sleeves, rolled above his elbows, revealed tanned, muscular arms. His vivid blue eyes, so like those of the woman who'd comforted her, peered intently into her face. It was his hair, however, that helped untangle her snarled memories. A shock of thick, light hair framed his tanned features.

Her "angel."

"Do you have any family we should contact?" The man took a step nearer.

For a moment she sat mute, gazing at her rescuer. "Family?" The stern features of Wilfred and Irene Maguire swam before her eyes. "No." She heard the word leave her lips on a sad whisper. "I have no family who cares for me."

"No husband?" The blond young man shot a quizzical glance at her gold wedding ring on her left hand.

"Dead." Tears sprang to Rosaleen's eyes at the awful memory of Donovan slumping over the card table, his blood spreading a maroon stain across its green felt top.

"Others survived the explosion," the doctor interjected with an encouraging lilt. "Most survivors were rescued on the Kentucky side of the river, but I treated a few last night. What was your husband's name?" He turned to his wife. "Becky, love, would you please get the record book?"

Mrs. Morgan stepped toward a large mahogany desk at the end of the room.

"No." Rosaleen's definitive tone arrested the woman's slight, energetic form. "He's dead. I watched him die." Caving beneath the weight of all that had happened to her in the past months, Rosaleen pressed her hands to her face and wept.

"Oh, you poor dear." The doctor's wife rushed to Rosaleen's side, gathering her in a lye-soap-and-verbena-scented embrace.

Allowing her body to sway with the woman's rocking, Rosaleen sobbed, eagerly embracing the genuine caring she'd craved since Donovan's death.

When her tears subsided, Rosaleen twisted in Mrs. Morgan's arms, sniffed, and gazed up at her "angel."

"I'm so sorry for your loss, ma'am. Jacob Hale, at your service." He dipped a quick bow. "I'm Mrs. Morgan's brother," he added. "And you are. . ."

"Rosaleen. Rosaleen Archer."

"Well, you'll need somewhere to stay." Mrs. Morgan's tone solidified. "You must stay with us."

Dr. Morgan turned to his wife with a rueful shake of his head. "Darling, you

15

know I would normally encourage such a philanthropic notion, but think, there is nowhere at the moment we could comfortably situate a houseguest."

His wife's sigh conveyed her regret. "Of course you're right, my dear. With the upstairs being renovated, we do well to manage accommodations for ourselves and the children."

"I wouldn't want to intrude. I'm sure there must be somewhere. . ." Without the prospect of a roof over her head, Rosaleen battled a resurgence of panic.

"Mrs. Buchanan has a spare attic room at the boardinghouse at the moment. She's also been looking for an extra hired girl now that Patsey is in the family way." The corner of Jacob Hale's mouth quirked in an encouraging smile. "I'm sure I could work something out."

At his steady gaze, Rosaleen's heart quickened. She scolded herself sternly. *I can't make attachments. I must get away from here as soon as I can. I must get away from the river.*

⁂

Riding on the wagon seat beside Jacob Hale, Rosaleen took in the town of Madison. Cradled between the Ohio River to the south and steep, stony hills to the east and north, the "Porkopolis" seemed focused on the river to which it owed its prosperity.

She'd passed the place many times on riverboats yet had never disembarked here. Once, Donovan had pointed out the town to her from the pilothouse of a stern-wheeler. He'd explained that most of the pork in the country was packed at Madison, Indiana.

As they traveled down a street marked Main-Cross, the smooth gravel paving the extraordinarily wide thoroughfare crunched beneath the wagon's iron-rimmed wheels. A couple of blocks beyond the doctor's house, the neat two-story brick houses lining the street gave way to bustling shops—all brick.

"Is everything made of brick here?" she asked, voicing her thoughts.

"Almost." His lips curved in a grin. "Five years ago the town adopted an ordinance requiring all new buildings be bricked in order to cut down on fires."

As they turned left onto a much narrower street, panic clenched her insides as tightly as her laced fingers whitening in her lap. What if the Buchanan woman didn't accept her? *What if—*

"Opal Buchanan is a good woman," Jacob Hale said with a kind smile as if he'd read her thoughts. "Her husband, a coffee merchant, died of dropsy six years ago. After George's death, she sold the business and opened her home as a boardinghouse. Well, here we are." He pulled the mules to a halt in front of a two-story home.

The brick facade of the boardinghouse looked unpretentious in its coat of gray paint. It seemed warm and homey. Its white-pillared porch reached out a welcoming greeting.

Rosaleen felt safe—a feeling that had been absent in her life during the six months since Donovan's murder.

A small brass bell at the top of the front door jingled as Jacob Hale ushered her into a front hall brightened by the opaque glass of a transom window.

The warm, comforting aroma of freshly baked bread greeted them, causing Rosaleen's stomach to grind with hunger. She soon heard the sound of quick footsteps, and a tall, large-boned woman appeared, smoothing back her graying blond hair.

Jacob Hale glanced from the woman to Rosaleen. "Mrs. Buchanan, may I introduce Mrs. Rosaleen Archer. She's a survivor from last night's riverboat explosion."

Feeling Jacob Hale's reassuring hand against her back, Rosaleen watched the woman's curious smile fade to a look of sympathy.

Mrs. Buchanan's kind green gaze seemed to flit over Rosaleen. "You poor soul, please come in and sit." The woman reached out her substantial arm and encircled Rosaleen's waist, quickly whisking her into a sunny parlor.

Stunned by Mrs. Buchanan's swift action, Rosaleen glanced back at her rescuer, left standing in the front hall.

Jacob Hale met her look with an amused grin.

Entering the parlor, Rosaleen took in the room. Larger than she would have expected for this size of house, the parlor testified to the success of the late Mr. Buchanan's business. Rich India carpets of green and gold hues dotted the floor. The room showcased several pieces of nice furniture, including a horsehair sofa, carved mahogany tables, as well as silk- and velvet-upholstered chairs and settees.

"You must be starving, poor thing. I'll bring you a nice big glass of milk and some thick buttered slices of Patsey's fresh bread." The woman seemed adept at taking charge and obviously relished the position. "You sit right down here." Mrs. Buchanan guided her toward a green velvet settee, pooh-poohing Rosaleen's concerns about her skirt soiled with river mud.

"Mrs. Archer lost her husband in the accident and has no other family or place to stay," Jacob said as he entered the parlor. "You'd mentioned you were looking for another hired girl. Mrs. Archer is willing to take the job in exchange for the use of the attic room."

Rosaleen didn't correct the man. Perhaps it would be better for them to think that Donovan had died in the explosion.

Opal Buchanan gave a sympathetic gasp and pressed her hand to her heart. "A widow, and so young. Why, you can scarcely be out of your teens."

"Twenty," Rosaleen supplied.

Opal glanced up at Jacob. "Yes, of course she can have the attic, but that little room is hardly more than a closet with only a straw mattress on the floor." She turned back to Rosaleen. "I wish I could do better for you, dear, and you shall be paid besides. That is, as soon as you feel up to any work." The woman clasped Rosaleen's hands in her large ones, giving them a quick, warm squeeze.

Rosaleen's helpless gaze traveled from one to the other as she wiped grateful tears from her cheeks with the lace handkerchief Mrs. Buchanan pressed into her hand. "I don't know how to thank you both. I—"

"Now, now, dear." Opal Buchanan patted her shoulder. "We are doing no more than what our Lord has asked of us. Isn't that right, Reverend Hale?"

A preacher?

Dread knotted Rosaleen's insides, and her heart raced. She let the kerchief drop to her lap. Her eyes widening, she raised her face to Jacob Hale's.

"That's right, Opal." He smiled and dipped a bow. "Mrs. Archer, I shall leave you in Opal's capable hands and see you at supper." When his eyes—the color of an October sky—gazed deeply into hers, Rosaleen caught her breath.

"And don't you be late, Reverend." Rosaleen heard a measure of affection in Opal Buchanan's teasing tone. "A preacher, and he's the only one of my boarders who's ever late for supper." With a soft chuckle, Opal left the room shaking her head.

While she waited on the settee for Mrs. Buchanan's promised bread and milk, a thread of disappointment embroidered the trepidation wrapping around Rosaleen's heart. Reverend Wilfred Maguire's disapproving countenance floated before her eyes. Her gaze dropped to the rose-patterned rug in the parlor doorway vacated only moments before by her handsome rescuer.

A preacher! Why does he have to be a preacher?

Chapter 3

"Reckon this oughta 'bout do it, Rev'rend." Freedman Andrew Chapman stood near the parlor door and mopped at his dark, sweaty forehead with a tattered kerchief.

Jacob straightened after helping Andrew place the last of a dozen two-by-eights across rows of low trestles. His slow gaze swept Mrs. Buchanan's re-arranged parlor. The sofa and settee made up the first row, followed by an odd collection of five chairs. Behind the chairs came the rows of plank seating. "Actually, Andrew, my fervent prayer is that it *won't* be enough." Jacob met the tall young black man's wide grin with one of his own.

In the year since he and Orville Whitaker had begun holding services in Opal Buchanan's boardinghouse, their congregation had doubled from an average of ten to twenty. "I've planned the sanctuary of the new church to accommodate over one hundred. Orville always told me to never limit God. 'Think big, build big, and He will fill it big.' "

Andrew nodded. "Amen to that, Rev'rend. The Lord'll provide the crop. It's up to us to do the harvestin'."

The resurgence of a nagging concern caused Jacob's smile to sag with his heart. The relentless doubt that constantly gnawed at his confidence whispered its insidious charge. *You've not had one convert since Orville's death. Perhaps this is not your calling. Perhaps God has not anointed you.*

Adding to his uncertainty, the one person he'd worked the hardest to bring into the fold continued to resist his efforts. Rosaleen Archer always seemed to find something else she needed to do on Sunday mornings rather than attend his services.

Andrew's chest puffed out with pride. "Well, reckon me and Patsey are doin' our part to add another soul to our church up at Georgetown. The babe oughta be comin' along in the fall, 'bout the time we get your church built."

"Be fruitful and multiply, Andrew." Jacob chuckled, giving his friend a slap on the back.

How wonderful it would be to have a helpmate. Before, thoughts of marriage had conjured little more than a vague idea in Jacob's mind—a faceless lady offering support, love, and an equal commitment to winning souls for the Lord as she worked tirelessly by his side. Three weeks ago, that image had been given a face.

The fact that Rosaleen showed no sign of interest in the Lord, or His work,

19

caused a painful tug-of-war inside Jacob. He understood her pain and respected her loss. But living in the same boardinghouse, exposed to her beauty and industry day after day, he could not deny his attraction to the lovely young widow.

The words of 2 Corinthians 6:14 tortured Jacob's mind and heart: *"Be ye not unequally yoked together with unbelievers."*

If only she'd come once and hear the Word. *If only. . .*

"Patsey says she needs more wood for the kitchen stove, Andrew."

Jacob's head jerked with his heart. Heat spread from his neck to his face. The subject of his thoughts stood in the parlor doorway. Rich brown tendrils had escaped her snowy daycap and curled appealingly against her rosy cheeks.

Laughing, Andrew shook his head and walked toward the kitchen. "That woman ain't content 'less I'm either choppin' or fetchin' wood."

Rosaleen turned to follow Andrew.

"Rosaleen. . ." His heart thumping, Jacob managed her name, stopping her at the threshold between the door and hallway.

She turned back and faced him with a questioning look.

"I'm hoping that maybe you could put aside time tomorrow morning to attend services. I've prepared a sermon dealing with God's peace and love in times of grief. I thought if you're ready, it might help. . . ." Fearing he was completely botching the invitation, Jacob's heart lifted when she rewarded his attempt with a sad, sweet smile.

"Reverend Hale, I'm sure it is a very fine sermon." The touch of her hand on his forearm sent shivers racing to Jacob's shoulder. "I just don't see any sense to it. I mean, I don't see what good the scriptures could do *me*."

"Oh, Rosaleen, just open your heart. God wants to comfort you. All of us here want to comfort you, too."

The tears welling in her beautiful blue green eyes ripped at his heart. *Please, Lord, give me the words.* "Won't you just come and listen?"

"I don't know," she answered just above a whisper.

He watched her lovely lips tremble as a tear slipped down her cheek. It took all his strength to not pull her into his arms. Instead, he clasped her hands in his. "I hope you will consider it." He forced a smile. "I'd love to see you in the congregation."

Disappointment twanged inside him when she pulled her hands from his, turned, and left the parlor.

⸰⸾⸰

In the darkness of her tiny attic room, Rosaleen sat bolt upright on her straw mattress. A cold sweat beaded on her forehead, and her breath came in painful puffs. Someone had screamed. She hugged the voluminous nightdress against her shaking body and realized her own throat had made the awful sound.

"Rosaleen? Rosaleen, are you all right?" Jacob Hale's frantic plea came from just outside her door.

"I—I'm all right." She fought to keep her voice steady. "Just a night terror."

"Would you like to talk?"

"No, thank you. I'm all right."

All right in no way described how Rosaleen felt. Yet she couldn't bring herself to share with Jacob Hale the horrors that had caused her screams. He considered her a respectable widow. She loathed the thought of shattering that image. However, just hearing his voice and knowing he stood outside her door helped to chase away the terror lurking in the dark corners of her mind.

"If you're sure you're all right. . ." The hesitancy in his voice caused a sweet ache deep inside her.

She heard a flurry of footfalls on the steps leading to her attic room, followed by Opal Buchanan's concerned voice. "What's wrong?"

"Just a nightmare, Mrs. Buchanan. Everything is all right." Rosaleen could hear Jacob's quiet voice reassuring Opal, interrupted by Tobias Stilwell's surly tone.

"Can't get a decent night's sleep around this place. Thought somebody'd been murdered." The salesman's deep-throated grumble faded down the creaking stairway.

"Rosaleen, dear. If there's anything you need. . ."

"No, thank you, Opal. I'm well. I'm sorry I bothered everyone's sleep."

"Nonsense, dear. You've been through an awful experience. The steamboat. . . your husband. . ." Opal's voice faltered with her attempt at consolation.

Quiet, unintelligible whispers preceded the sound of Opal's slow, heavy footsteps on the stairs.

"Any time you need to talk, I'm here."

"Thank you, Reverend. I'm sorry I—"

"Any time, Rosaleen." She heard a smile creep into his voice. "Please call me Jacob. I much prefer it."

"Thank you. . .Jacob."

Long after the sound of his footsteps had faded away, she shifted on her mattress, sleep eluding her. She'd tried to ignore her attraction to the handsome young minister, but with each passing day, his grasp on her heart grew tighter.

Didn't he know she was irretrievably beyond the realm of salvation? Reverend Wilfred Maguire had called her "irredeemable—the wicked by-blow of a harlot." Surely, he—the minister of a huge church in Natchez, Mississippi—knew the scriptures better than a poor, young backwoods preacher.

If God rejects me, then I shall reject God!

Rosaleen squeezed her eyes shut tight against the tears oozing through her lashes. For all she knew, nothing but oblivion awaited her beyond this life. So she must make the best of it—find what happiness she could while she lived.

She patted the place in the mattress where she'd made a small slit and pushed in the calico pouch holding her three-week earnings. The reassuring *clink* of coins rubbing against one another lent a measure of hope to her heart.

When she'd earned enough money, she must make her way to Maestro Levitsky in New York and her dream of becoming a concert pianist.

Besides, she had no way of knowing for sure if Bill McGurty had survived the accident or gone down with the steamboat. Perhaps he was looking for her on the Kentucky side of the river—or he could be in Madison this very minute. A shudder wriggled through her.

Anyway, the last place he'd expect to find me would be in the company of church-going people.

Calmed by the thought, she reached into the slit in the mattress. Feeling through the prickly straw, she wrapped her fingers around the sack that held her hope.

Chapter 4

T hat man o' mine sure outdid hisself with this mess of squirrels." Patsey beamed at the two large crocks filled with butchered squirrel parts covered in brine.

From the first day Jacob brought her to Opal Buchanan's boardinghouse, Rosaleen had found a true friend in Patsey Chapman. In fact, Mrs. Buchanan's pretty hired girl with skin the color of rich cocoa had welcomed her with open arms. About her own age, with an unquenchable, bubbly personality, Patsey had helped Rosaleen reclaim the joy of being young.

"I've never eaten squirrel." Rosaleen lobbed a spoonful of lard into the hot cast-iron skillet on the stove, unsure of how she felt about the supper entrée.

"Then you're in for a real treat. I growed up on squirrel down where I come from. It's gener'ly my favorite. But right now"—she laughed as she patted the mound beneath her calico apron—"I cain't even abide the smell of meat."

"You're not from here?"

"No." A dusty white cloud rose as Patsey dumped a handful of squirrel into another crockery bowl filled with flour and seasoning. Her bright, dark eyes grew round, and her voice dropped to a conspiratorial whisper. "My mammy an' me 'scaped from Williamsburg, Kentucky, and come up here on the Railroad a couple years ago."

Rosaleen realized she wasn't talking about any sort of conveyance that moved on rails. She'd heard whispers of the Underground Railroad in the month she'd been in Madison and suspected the town was a stop on escaped slaves' routes north to Canada. She'd learned that the Georgetown district where Patsey and Andrew lived, just two blocks east of the boardinghouse, was the free-black section of town. There, men like the barber, George de Baptiste, and the blacksmith, Elijah Anderson, were leaders in the work of the Underground. She also suspected that Mrs. Buchanan actively helped in the humanitarian effort.

"When we got here to the Georgetown district, Andrew was one of 'em helpin' to find us places to stay and food to eat." Her teeth flashed like pearls amid the grin stretching her rosy brown cheeks. "He was the finest-lookin' man I ever did see."

Rosaleen grinned. "Then it was love at first sight?"

"Was for me." Patsey smiled. "And I reckon I'd have pined the rest of my life for him if I hadn't took sick with a fever, keepin' me and Mammy from movin' on to the next station. We stayed a month with Andrew and his folks till my fever passed."

"And you and Andrew fell in love?"

Patsey nodded, her smile quirking into a grin. "Andrew wouldn't admit it, but I think he was feared o' lovin' me, knowin' I'd be movin' on."

"But you didn't."

"No." Her brow creased, and Rosaleen could see she was remembering the emotional struggle. "Mammy begged me to go on with her up north to Indianapolis. Said this was way too close to the line."

Rosaleen knew that along this stretch of the Ohio, the river itself was the line between slave and free country. Many whites here were more than willing to turn blacks over to their slaveholders for the bounty.

"But when Andrew got up the nerve and asked me to stay and jump the broom with him, I couldn't say no." Patsey's face lit and her eyes sparkled with love. "Never been sorry. He's as purty inside as out," she said, grinning. Handing Rosaleen the crock of floured squirrel, she shot her a curious glance. "Did you love your man?"

Unprepared for the question, Rosaleen allowed a long moment of silence while she busied herself positioning the sizzling meat in the skillet with extra care. "No." She felt a pang of guilt at the whispered word.

The question had been one she'd shied away from for a long time. She glanced at Patsey's face, still glowing at the mere mention of Andrew.

Rosaleen thought of the man thirteen years her senior to whom she'd been wed for six short weeks. Although he had been a kind and gentle husband, thoughts of Donovan Archer had never quickened her heart. Since her father's death, the short time she'd spent with Donovan had been the one brief splash of contentment in her life. But in her heart she knew she'd never felt true love for him.

"You're young. You got plenty of time." The kind, almost pitying tone of Patsey's voice caused Rosaleen to blink away tears.

Nodding, Rosaleen felt a stab of envy.

Patsey's voice took on a teasing lilt. "I done seen the way Rev'rend Hale looks at you. His eyes goin' all mooncalflike. Done seen the way you look at him, too." She danced around the little kitchen in an exaggerated sashay, holding out the sides of her calico skirt with dusty hands. "Jis a few winks and nods, and you'd have him askin' you to jump the broom."

"Patsey Chapman!" Heat that had nothing to do with the frying pan rushed to Rosaleen's face. Had she been so transparent about her feelings for Jacob? Could Patsey be right about Jacob? It didn't matter. Unlike Patsey, she couldn't stay. "I have no designs on Reverend Hale, and I'm sure he has no interest in me that way either."

Patsey gave an indelicate snort and laughed. "Well, you have it your way, but I jis know what I done seen, that's all." Then, with a low moan, she waved her hand at the gamy meat and sage-laced steam rising from the skillet. Holding her stomach with one hand, she pressed the other against her mouth. "Lord, help me! I cain't abide another minute of that smell," she mumbled through her hand. "I best peel these taters outside." Snatching a wooden bowl full of potatoes from the table, she retreated toward the kitchen door.

Gazing through the open door, Rosaleen watched the young woman settle herself on a stool beneath an oak tree to pare the potatoes. She told herself that Patsey's notion sprang simply from her romantic imagination, yet there was a part of her that hoped it hadn't.

≈

"Mmm, squirrel." Jacob inhaled deeply when Rosaleen brought the platter heaped with the golden brown pieces of meat to the supper table. "I've been looking forward to this since Andrew told me what luck he'd had hunting."

Rosaleen's heart quickened beneath Jacob's lingering gaze.

"Smells like you've done a wonderful job with them," Jacob commented to her.

"And how do you know Patsey didn't cook these?" His bright blue eyes fixed on hers drained the strength from her arms, and she hurried to set down the platter.

"Because Andrew told me he was afraid he might not get any as the smell of meat makes Patsey ill now."

"Then I suppose I'm the one to blame if they are not cooked well," Rosaleen said with a grin. She was finding it increasingly difficult to disavow Patsey's claim.

"Squirrel! I haven't had squirrel since—Well, I can't remember when I last had squirrel." Rosaleen gave an inward groan when Tobias Stilwell dropped his lanky frame onto a dining room chair.

A look of dismay replaced the smile on Jacob's face.

Since his appearance two weeks ago, the cookstove salesman had not ingratiated himself to anyone at the boardinghouse. His habits rivaled the worst Rosaleen had seen during her years aboard the steamboats. Except at mealtime, he perpetually kept a wad of chewing tobacco in his jaw. He'd continually spit the foul-smelling brown juice in the general direction of the nearest spittoon, seemingly unconcerned whether he hit the mark. Worse, the looks he raked over Rosaleen gave her cold chills and caused her to lock her attic room door at night.

Good-hearted Opal Buchanan couldn't seem to bring herself to send the unsavory character on his way, even though his promised payment for room and board had yet to materialize.

"Rosaleen, do you remember how many squirrels you fried up?" Jacob's tone sounded benign, but Rosaleen caught a mischievous glint in his eyes.

She'd learned in the past month that Jacob Hale had a penchant for practical jokes. She remembered how Opal had laughed, recounting that she'd once

25

made the mistake of teasing him about always being the preacher and never taking a day off. Later that day, she'd discovered all her candles missing from their holders. After searching the house over, she'd found them under a bushel basket turned upside down on the back porch. Opal told her Jacob later confessed to the prank, saying he was attempting to make a point about a verse in the Gospel of Matthew. Rosaleen couldn't remember the scripture Opal quoted, but it had something to do with not hiding a light under a bushel basket but putting it on a candlestick so it would light the house.

"No, I never actually counted the squirrels," Rosaleen answered Jacob, unsure of his intention but keen to play along.

"Andrew said he killed six squirrels, but that sure looks like more. Hmm," he said thoughtfully. "By the way, have you seen that tortoiseshell cat that's been bedeviling Mrs. Buchanan? I heard her tell Andrew she wanted him to get rid of that thing one way or another."

"Now that you mention it, I haven't seen it at all today." Rosaleen fought to keep a straight face, realizing what Jacob was up to. She'd learned that the one thing Opal Buchanan and Tobias Stilwell had in common was their mutual disdain for the feline species.

"One, two, three—" His face wearing a deadly serious expression, Jacob poked a fork at the golden brown pieces of fried squirrel.

Tobias had become very still. Rosaleen ventured a glance in his direction and was forced to press a napkin to her mouth. The salesman's eyes began growing large, and his pinched features took on a greenish pallor all the way up to his balding pate.

"Andrew must have counted wrong, because I'm counting legs and back pieces for seven animals," Jacob concluded.

Tobias Stilwell practically leaped from his chair, causing it to fall backward with a thud. "I–I'm not really hungry. I—I just remembered I have an appointment in Cincinnati day after tomorrow." His hand shook as he righted the chair and mumbled, "Please give Mrs. Buchanan my regrets and tell her I'll be sending my payment."

"What's gotten into him?" Opal Buchanan carried a plateful of corn bread into the dining room just in time to see Tobias race out.

"Suddenly remembered an important engagement," Jacob told her with a poker face as good as any Rosaleen had ever witnessed. He gave a deep, soulful sigh. "Alas, I'm afraid we will no longer be enjoying Mr. Stilwell's stellar company."

"Thank the Lord! I've been praying for this for two solid weeks." Opal sank to a chair, relief blooming on her face.

"Prayer works, Opal. All it takes is a little faith." Jacob's eyes lit as a sudden thought seemed to ignite behind them. He turned an impish grin toward Rosaleen. "I just decided on my theme for Sunday's sermon. 'Faith without works is dead.'"

Rosaleen allowed her gaze to meet Jacob's, dancing with fun. As they shared a secret grin, she acknowledged the truth screaming from her heart.

How am I going to leave now that I know Patsey is right?

Chapter 5

R osaleen."

Jacob's quiet voice caused Rosaleen's heart to thump. She turned toward the parlor doorway, her feather duster poised in midair.

She'd been careful not to enter the parlor until she felt sure he'd gone to the church building site. If she were to squelch her blossoming feelings for the preacher, Rosaleen knew she must avoid him whenever possible.

"I was wondering if you might like to accompany me to my sister's home for a visit this afternoon."

A small burst of panic flared inside her. How could she trust her heart to behave during an entire afternoon in Jacob's company? "I—I have chores to do. Opal expects—"

"Opal agrees you should go." His blue eyes twinkled into hers. "She says you've been cooped up in this house for the last month and need to get out more. I agree."

Rosaleen had to admit it would be nice to get away from the boardinghouse for a while. Her self-imposed confinement here had ceased to feel as much like protection as incarceration. But she needed to stay detached from Madison—from Jacob. She must find some excuse. Any excuse.

She glanced down at the patched calico dress Patsey had loaned her. "I have nothing decent to wear for a social call."

"And that is precisely the reason you need to visit Becky. She told me she's found a few of her dresses from last summer that are a little too snug since the birth of my niece, Lucy. She's sure they will fit you perfectly."

Rosaleen stiffened. She didn't like being considered a charity case. Worse, she did not want to feel beholden to Jacob's sister. "From what I remember, your sister looked very trim. I'd think with a small alteration. . ."

Jacob's grin suggested he had no plans to cede the argument. "My guess is Becky's glad for an excuse to buy new dresses." His smile softened with his tone. He took her hand in his. Rosaleen's heart raced at his touch.

"Rosaleen, Becky wants to help you. We all want to help you. We believe that helping others is the same as helping our Lord. Jesus tells us in Matthew 25:40, 'Inasmuch as ye have done it unto one of the least of these my brethren, ye have done it unto me.' "

The kind look in his eyes eroded her resolve.

"Please, Rosaleen, allow Becky to help you. Allow us all to help you."

Rosaleen swallowed hard and blinked back tears. Kindness, charity, and generosity were qualities she'd rarely encountered. She returned to dusting the cherry table that no longer needed it. "I still have nothing fit to wear."

"Mrs. Buchanan was able to salvage that purple frock you were wearing when I found you." His gaze held hers in a tender embrace and her heart stood still. "Whatever you wear, you will look fetching."

A half hour later, Rosaleen stood in Opal Buchanan's bedchamber, the yards of purple silk rustling as she shook out the dress. Though water stained and with a bodice cut far too low to be proper for day wear, it was the best she had.

After donning the dress, Rosaleen stood before the dresser mirror, her heart aflutter. Opal had managed to brush away all visible remnants of river mud. Rosaleen had to admit, aside from its inappropriate style and damaged condition, the dress did flatter her coloring.

Three times she twisted her auburn locks into a figure-eight bun without complete satisfaction. Grimacing her dismay, she covered her unruly hair with the gray silk bonnet Opal had loaned her.

It's only Jacob. I see him every day.

The silent admonitions did little to calm Rosaleen's palpitating heart. What she saw in the cherrywood-framed mirror only added to her unease. The image of a saloon girl mocked her from the glass.

"Soiled dove."

Rosaleen's face burned with grief and shame. *Not because I wanted it. Never, never. . .*

She choked back a sob and felt the tentative grasp she'd had on her nerve slip.

During her time with Bill McGurty, the looks she'd gotten from respectable people had stung. Their furtive glances had seemed a mixture of disgust and morbid curiosity. Aboard the steamboats, mothers had nervously shooed their children past her while gentlemen openly ogled her when their wives were not looking.

It had brought back all the cruel taunts and snide comments she'd endured from upper-class girls at Mrs. Griswold's Academy after they learned of her illegitimacy. Those hurtful jeers blended with Wilfred and Irene Maguire's disparaging description of her as "the filthy little spawn of a harlot."

Rosaleen drew a deep breath and, with trembling hands, wrapped Opal's black lace shawl around her shoulders left bare by the dress's revealing bodice. Her heart pounding, she headed down the stairs.

"You look lovely." At the bottom step, Jacob greeted her with a deep bow, a bell-crowned white beaver hat in his hand. He looked every inch a gentleman in his maroon claw-hammer coat over a buff waistcoat, satin neckerchief, and close-fitting black trousers. Yet the eager anticipation sparkling in his blue eyes lent an irresistible boyish charm to his features. Even the thin scar running parallel to his left cheekbone added to, rather than detracted from, his good looks.

As they strolled along the boardwalk edging Main-Cross Street, Rosaleen's gaze took in the beauty of the little river town. Graceful oaks, sycamores, and maples lined the street, shading its broad expanse of smooth gravel.

"Ah, here we are." Jacob's smile widened when they neared a two-story brick home.

A fragrant greeting wafted their way from phlox, larkspurs, and petunias growing beneath the two tall, narrow windows. Left of the windows, two white-painted pillars supported a corniced portico jutting out from a recessed doorway.

"You're sure we are not intruding upon your sister's time?" Rosaleen's stomach felt the flutter of nervous butterflies as the wrought iron gate creaked a tiny protest against Jacob's hand.

"Nonsense. Becky has been pestering me about you for the past month. And since you refuse to attend Sunday services," he teased with a quirk of his mouth, "I decided an afternoon visit was in order."

Rosaleen's heart quickened at the reassuring touch of his hand on her back, guiding her up the two stone steps to the little enclosed portico.

"Mrs. Archer." A bright smile lit Becky Morgan's face when she met them at the door.

Accepting the woman's warm hug, Rosaleen noticed the same scent of verbena she remembered from her first day in the doctor's office.

"I'm so glad Jacob succeeded in convincing you to come for a visit," the doctor's wife said as she took Jacob's hat and Rosaleen's bonnet before ushering them into the parlor.

Far smaller than the one at Opal Buchanan's boardinghouse, the Morgans' little parlor seemed cozy and inviting. The leaves of a large maple in the side yard dappled the afternoon sun onto the rose-patterned carpet. An early summer breeze fluttered the lace curtains at the tall, narrow open window.

Rosaleen's gaze roamed the room until it fixed on an object between the window and hearth. Suddenly, she felt her heart leap and her fingers itch. All other thoughts were swept away at the sight of the square piano.

"Rosaleen, do you play the piano? Rosaleen?"

"Yes," Rosaleen finally answered Becky Morgan's question with a breathless whisper. "I learned while employed at Mrs. Griswold's Academy for Young Ladies in Jackson, Mississippi. Mrs. Griswold insisted that every girl under her roof learn at least the basic skills and social graces." Rosaleen experienced a bittersweet pang, remembering how her natural talent for the instrument had won her teacher's praise but scorn from the woman's other students. She turned a wobbly smile toward Becky. "I loved playing and discovered I have a talent for it."

Beaming, Jacob's sister clapped her hands. "Wonderful! Perhaps after refreshments we could prevail upon you to play something."

Offered the one temptation she could not resist, Rosaleen's desire for an abbreviated visit vanished. She felt herself being pulled deeper into the world of Madison—deeper into the world of Jacob Hale.

As his sister served them lemon cake and tea, Jacob had to admit the afternoon outing had not been entirely unselfish on his part. Beyond the joy he derived from spending time in Rosaleen's company, he'd hoped to learn more about the beauty who'd wrapped her lovely fingers around his heart. And if he could grow their friendship, he might persuade her to attend worship services.

Now, something as unexpected as his sister's new piano promised a glimpse into Rosaleen Archer's carefully guarded past. Becky's request for her to play the piano had lit Rosaleen's eyes with a brightness Jacob had never seen in them. At his sister's urging, Rosaleen reminded him of a filly prancing in its carriage traces, eager to be off. As she was already on her feet, he suspected he'd have to physically restrain her in order to keep her from the piano.

For the better part of an hour, Jacob sat enthralled while Rosaleen worked through Becky's stack of sheet music, treating them to one beautiful piano piece after another. His sister's parlor rang with ballads and sonnets, as well as classical pieces.

The afternoon sun shimmered copper lights over Rosaleen's lovely dark auburn tresses as she swayed with the melodies. Her eyes closed, her features held a beautiful tranquillity. Somewhere in the midst of Beethoven's "Ode to Joy," Jacob knew he'd lost his heart.

Later that afternoon, as he strolled with Rosaleen along the streets of Madison, Jacob tried to keep his heart in check. He was still reeling from the discovery of her musical talent. *What other wondrous facets of this intriguing woman remain to be disclosed?*

"It's as beautiful as the finest plantation houses in Mississippi."

Rosaleen's words jerked Jacob from his musings to the new home of railroad baron and financier, J. F. D. Lanier. She'd stopped their trek along High Street to admire the west side of the mansion with its brick facade painted light ocher brown.

"Yes, it's quite spectacular." He turned his attention to the grandiose example of Greek Revival architecture. Two white pillars supported a rather modest northern entrance, while at the south side four gigantic white pillars graced an expansive portico. Beyond that, a manicured lawn and garden swept down to the banks of the Ohio River.

"I'm sure I'll have to wait until I get to heaven for my mansion." His chuckle died at her somber demeanor. "Rosaleen, why do you avoid Sunday services? You should pay no attention to Opal's critiques of my sermons, you know." His attempt to inject levity failed to bring a smile to her face.

"I just don't think. . .I don't think it would do me any good."

"Why do you keep saying that? Have you read the scriptures at all?" An urgency to reach her caused frustration to rise within him.

"A little."

"But you don't think they pertain to you in any way?"

"No."

"How could you think that? The scriptures are for everyone."

"Reverend Hale!" Roscoe Stinnett's booming voice shoved its way into their conversation. "How are you on this fine May afternoon?"

Groaning inwardly, Jacob pasted a smile across his face. He preferred to believe that the quality of his sermons was the reason the president of Riverfront Porkpacking chose to attend his fledgling congregation. However, he suspected that was not the case.

In the midst of Madison's burgeoning industrialization, the forty-five-year-old Stinnett seemed determined to position himself as one of the town's fathers. Being a charter member of a new congregation could only elevate his standing in the community.

"I am quite well, Mr. Stinnett, thank you very much. Mrs. Archer and I were just admiring Mr. Lanier's new home."

A prickle of irritation marched up Jacob's neck when Stinnett afforded Rosaleen only a cursory nod. Jacob knew the man considered her an underling because she worked as a housemaid.

"Nice piece of architecture I suppose, though far too pretentious for my taste." Roscoe placed one hand over the other on the gold knob of his white walking cane and gave the financier's opulent abode little more than a glance. His haughty tone and dismissive attitude did nothing to hide the envy on the man's face. Jacob didn't doubt for a minute that Roscoe Stinnett would have a home twice the size of Lanier's if he could afford it.

Roscoe's tone and countenance brightened. "It is very fortuitous that we should have met this afternoon, Reverend Hale. My good wife and I have, only today, decided to make a considerable donation to the new church."

"That's very generous of you. I have opened an account at the bank, so you could simply—"

"No, no, my dear boy!" Stinnett's laugh shot through Jacob, causing his teeth to grind as his jaws tightened. "The donation is a piano. A Chickering square from Boston. Full cast-iron frame, new overstring design, all the rage, don't you know. Should arrive within the month."

Jacob felt Rosaleen's fingers grip his arm. His heart soared. A piano might be just the enticement needed to get her to services.

No one else will be able to play as well as. . .

"That is but part of our donation. Myrtle has graciously agreed to be pianist."

"I—I don't know what to say." Truer words could not have come out of Jacob's mouth.

"Just doing our part, Reverend. Of course there will be a modest plaque affixed to the instrument, denoting Myrtle and I as the donors." Stinnett puffed out his chest, causing Jacob to fear the brass buttons might pop off the man's robin's egg blue broadcloth coat.

"Thank you, Mr. Stinnett, and thank your good wife." Jacob watched Roscoe Stinnett saunter away, and the hope that had sprung briefly in his chest withered. He was glad for the new piano. Not only for the congregation, but so Rosaleen would have daily access to the instrument she loved. Yet what a perfect opportunity it would have been if she could have played for services and thus heard the Word proclaimed.

I trust You, Lord. I thank You for this and pray that in some way You will use this to bring Rosaleen to You.

Chapter 6

Never saw a man so eager to work that he plumb forgets to eat." Mrs. Buchanan smiled and shook her head.

Rosaleen watched Opal nestle a bottle of sweet tea and two tin cups into a basket, alongside freshly baked bread, fried chicken, and apple pie. Her large hands worked deftly, carefully tucking linen towels around the food.

Rosaleen chucked two pieces of wood into the Resor cookstove and chose not to be drawn into a conversation about Jacob Hale. After their afternoon outing the week before, she'd had enough trouble keeping the minister off her mind.

And Jacob Hale did unsettling things to her heart. His smile, his laugh, the sweet tenor of his voice, all set her heart dancing. She remembered the way his blue eyes had sparkled with appreciation at her piano playing. . . .

No, I must not allow myself to get too close.

"Rosaleen, would you please take this basket down to Jacob and Andrew?" Opal straightened to her full height of nearly six feet and pushed back a strand of graying blond hair that had escaped from the bun at the back of her head. "With four new boarders, I have a million things to do, and Patsey will not be coming until this afternoon."

Feeling the familiar clash of emotions, Rosaleen closed the stove door with a *clang* and turned toward the kitchen table. "Of course."

Jacob Hale was a boarder, and her job as hired girl was to tend to the boarders. She brushed her hands on her calico apron and wished she could stifle the gladness bubbling up inside her at the thought of seeing him.

"You tell the fine young reverend that if he doesn't get himself back here in time for supper, he'll get a right smart sermon from me."

Rosaleen only grinned at Opal's poor attempt at a stern face.

Outside, she inhaled deeply. The delicious smells of the bread, chicken, and apple pie blended with the pungent herbs growing in Opal's garden. Hollyhocks reclined against the white picket fence. Their bright pink flowers alive with the constant buzz of honeybees added to the cornucopia of fragrances.

As she headed up Mulberry toward Main-Cross Street, Rosaleen experienced a stab of sadness. She almost wished she could stay in Madison. On such a beautiful early June day, it was easy to believe she might actually blend into the population of the little river town.

As she walked the three blocks west on Main-Cross, she noticed fewer curious glances from the townspeople. It seemed most folks had become aware that she was Mrs. Buchanan's new hired girl.

Cool river breezes caressed her face when she turned south on Broadway Street. There, the downward grade of the street became steeper. She slowed her steps the final block to the building site of the church at the corner of Broadway and Second.

If only I could stay. If only I could have a future here with. . .

Rosaleen blinked away tears, unable to finish the thought. She looked down toward the Ohio, teeming with a flotilla of all shapes and sizes. Barges, ferries, and flatboats dotted the busy waterway.

The deep, breathy whistle of a steamboat wafted up from the river, sending a chill through her body. It reminded her of why she couldn't stay. Bill McGurty might be out there, lurking, ready to pounce like the predatory animal he was.

No, she couldn't stay. The moment she'd set aside enough money, she must leave for New York.

The ring of a hammer calmed her fears. Jacob was close by. The thought sent her heart skipping.

There is no future for me here in Madison, especially with a preacher, she scolded her errant heart. It paid no heed, quickening even more when the smell of freshly cut lumber reached her nostrils and the building site came into view.

Jacob rose from pounding a wooden peg into a floorboard. "Hallo," he called with a wave of his hand, a smile stretching his handsome mouth.

She thought he looked a bit disconcerted as he walked toward her, brushing sawdust from his white linen work shirt and black trousers. Returning his smile, she raised the basket. "Opal sent me with your lunch."

"Mrs. Buchanan is of the opinion that if left to my own devices, I'd starve to death." Lifting the cloth for a peek inside the basket, he sniffed its contents. "Mmm. I'm not so sure she's wrong," he said with a chuckle, taking the basket from her hand.

A thoughtful look knitted his blond brows together. "Andrew and the three other men who've been helping me today have gone home for dinner. As Mrs. Buchanan seems to have sent enough for about three people, I'd be more than happy if you'd stay and share the repast with me. It could be a picnic."

A pang of guilt caused her to glance up Broadway. She really should be getting back. Her guilt evaporated in the warmth of his hopeful smile. "Yes, I'd like that." Disregarding her sternest admonition, Rosaleen's heart leaped when he took her hand in his.

He led her toward a white-washed bench in the shade of a willow tree. Settling the basket on the bench between them, he handed her one of the two linen napkins then said a short prayer of thanks over the basket of food.

Rosaleen spent the uncomfortable moment watching men unload barrels from a flatboat. Prayers were for people like Jacob—people of whom God approved.

"I hope dining in the proximity of my friend's resting place does not offend you." A look of unease flitted across his face as he glanced at the nearby gravestone.

"No, not at all." She followed his gaze to the granite slab beneath the willow. Noticing the date on the marker, Rosaleen realized the grave was not an old one. "You were close to Mr. Whitaker, then?" She handed him a piece of buttered bread.

"Yes." He smiled down at the gravestone. "He was the circuit preacher who ministered to my home village. I'm afraid I was a bit of a scamp as a boy—got into a scrape or two." He grinned around a bite of the bread. "Along with my parents, Orville never gave up on me. One Sunday when I was nineteen, he preached a sermon from the book of Acts, the account of Peter preaching on the Day of Pentecost."

He paused to uncork the bottle of tea and pour them each a cup of the amber liquid. "I'd read that scripture many times. But somehow, that day, it spoke to my heart. I knew I'd come to a fork in the road and must either turn away from God's Word altogether or embrace it completely." Again, his face turned toward Reverend Whitaker's grave marker. "Thanks to Orville and my good Christian parents, I chose the latter."

Rosaleen had no knowledge of the scripture Jacob cited. What few sermons she'd heard her guardian preach had been thunderous admonitions from the Old Testament. She'd found no comfort in Wilfred Maguire's sermons.

"Was it then that you became a minister?"

"Yes. I began riding the circuit with Orville while he patiently taught me the deeper truths of the scriptures. Passages I'd read but never fully comprehended." His voice lowered. "Orville opened my heart to Christ's message of love." A pensive frown cleft his forehead, and he looked down at his dusty boot tops crossed at his ankles. "I only pray I might approach his deep understanding of the scriptures as well as his persuasive oratory."

His gaze shifted to the foundation and open floor of what would be the church. The distant look in his eyes suggested that he saw far beyond the bare beginnings to the finished building. "It will be beautiful, a fitting legacy to Orville. Especially after Andrew bricks it and we hang the bell."

He gave a quick wave of his hand, his voice sounding almost apologetic. "Oh, I know it sounds a bit boastful. Not all churches in Madison have bells. But I've been saving money for a five-hundred-pounder. According to the Verdin Bell Company of Cincinnati, it will cost a hundred dollars, but I'm determined to have it. At present, I've saved almost half the amount." His fists clenched, flexing his arm muscles. "I can almost feel the bell's glorious weight tugging against the rope in my hands as I ring it for the first time, inviting all within earshot to come and worship Christ."

Suddenly, he turned to face her, his blue gaze searching hers. "You were not taught the scriptures from childhood, were you?"

"No," Rosaleen murmured, glancing down at the cup of tea in her hands. She'd been content to sit and eat quietly as Jacob imparted bits of his past and future plans for the church. Now, she took a sip of sweet tea, wishing his quiet deduction hadn't felt so much like an accusation.

"I know nothing about you except that you worked at a young ladies' academy and play the piano like an angel. I'd like to know more, if you don't mind my asking. I'm afraid I'm a curious sort." With a disarming smile, he leaned back on the bench and began munching on a chicken leg.

Rosaleen felt her inhibitions melt at Jacob's caring tone. He might as well learn of her shameful heritage. Surely, then, he'd stop pestering her to attend his church services.

She looked down at the napkin in her lap, unwilling to watch disgust replace the kind expression on his face. The story began to tumble out like apples from a torn sack.

"I was raised until the age of twelve by my adoptive father, Rory Maguire. He was a gambler and the fourth son of an Irish earl. He met my mother, Rosie, a commoner, on the ship to New York from Ireland."

Rosaleen fidgeted, unfolding and refolding her napkin. This was the part she most dreaded telling. "My mother was alone, single. . .and two months away from my arrival." She cast a wary glance toward Jacob. Finding no look of disgust or condemnation on his face encouraged her to continue.

A smile tugged at her lips. "Papa said he fell in love with my mother almost immediately. That she was sweet, full of life, and the most beautiful woman he'd ever seen."

"Then you must resemble her."

Rosaleen's heart hammered at Jacob's quiet comment. Disconcerted, she fixed her gaze on her hands twisting the piece of linen in her lap. "When they reached New York, Papa got my mother a decent apartment and asked her to be his wife. As a token of his intentions, he bought her the brooch you've seen me wear."

Jacob nodded. "Yes, I've noticed it. It's beautiful. He must have loved your mother very much."

Jacob's gentle tone caused a knot of tears to gather in her throat.

"They married, then?" Jacob asked before taking a big bite of chicken.

"No. One evening Papa came to my mother's place to let her know he'd found a domestic position for her as soon as she delivered her baby. He found her alone and in labor. Unable to find a midwife, Papa helped to bring me into the world. An hour later, my mother died." Rosaleen's voice drooped. Tears stung her eyes, and she wondered why she still wept over a mother she'd never known.

"Rosaleen, I'm so sorry—"

She waved off his condolences. "Before she died, my mother begged Papa to take me and raise me as his own. And so he did." Her voice lifted with her spirit at the memory.

"We traveled the steamboats up and down the Mississippi, Missouri, and Ohio rivers—wherever the next card game presented itself. Papa provided me a happy and interesting childhood, although many times we barely had enough money to get by. I'm afraid my father, though a persistent gambler, was not a very successful one."

"Then you've never had a real home?" For the first time, she caught a glimpse of concern flit across his face.

She shook her head and took a sip of sweet tea. "No, but never having had one, I didn't miss it."

"Is that why your father sent you to the young ladies' academy—so you'd have a home?" He pitched the chicken bone to the grassy slope where a pair of blackbirds set upon it, noisily feuding over the prize.

"No. My father became ill." She fought new tears and somehow managed the hateful word, "Consumption. I was but twelve and he didn't want to leave me alone. His older brother and wife, from whom he'd been estranged for many years, live in Natchez, Mississippi. They reluctantly agreed to take me but found my illegitimacy unacceptable. Within a month, they sent me to Jackson, Mississippi, and into Mrs. Griswold's employ as a housemaid."

Her voice lowered, and she winced at the recollection. "Six months later, I learned of my father's death."

"Rosaleen, I'm sorry. I never meant to resurrect such painful memories."

The sweetness of Jacob's voice and his hand covering hers sent more tears sketching down her cheeks.

"Sooo," Jacob stretched out the word, "where does Mr. Archer come in?"

She drew in a shaky breath and continued. "August of last year, Mrs. Griswold's academy closed, and I returned to my guardian's home." Her lips twitched with a tiny, forced smile. "The moment I arrived, I was informed I'd be marrying Mr. Donovan Archer, a riverboat pilot thirteen years my senior." Rosaleen turned the thin gold band on the third finger of her left hand. Thoughts of her late husband always brought a rush of fond memories, and she smiled. "Donovan was looking for a wife familiar with life on the river."

"Then you and Mr. Archer weren't—I mean there hadn't been a courtship—I mean. . ."

Rosaleen hurried to Jacob's rescue when he stumbled for an appropriate description of her unexpected union. "It was a marriage of convenience. Mr. Archer was a widower of some years and a kind and honorable man." She met Jacob's intent gaze and hoped he could discern from her look the sentiment of love lacking in her brief marriage. She also hoped to convey the mutual respect and caring that had defined it.

"I'm sure he was," Jacob replied. "I'm so sorry to learn of the grief you've experienced but glad God sent you a season of joy, however brief."

While they finished the two pieces of apple pie in silence, Rosaleen found it impossible to read the thoughts behind his eyes.

Suddenly, he leaned toward her and took her hands into his, causing her to emit a soft gasp of surprise. The comfort of his strong, warm grasp filled Rosaleen with longing. She could only imagine how wonderful it might feel to be enveloped in the sanctuary of his arms, to rest her head against his chest.

"Rosaleen, you are young. God has so many wonderful things waiting for you, if you will only allow Him to guide you."

Her gaze followed his to the building under construction.

"I realize it doesn't look like much now, but God willing, by winter, I will be the pastor of a fine church and growing congregation. A congregation that could be the family you've been denied. I pray that you might allow me to be a part—"

"Jacob!" The man's shouted greeting and the mule-drawn wagon rattling to a stop on Broadway broke into Jacob's entreaty. "We got that load of two-by-eights from the lumber yard."

Heart pounding, Rosaleen stood and hastily covered the remnants of their lunch with the linen cloths. What had he been about to suggest? She told herself that she was thankful their conversation had been brought to an abrupt close. She attempted a light tone but couldn't keep the tremor from her voice. "Mrs. Buchanan will be wondering what's keeping me."

Jacob sent a quick glance of dismay toward the three men unloading the lumber from the wagon. As he caught her arm in a gentle grasp, his gaze searched hers. "Please, just consider the possibility of my suggestion."

Rosaleen nodded, amazed that he'd still want anything to do with her after what he'd learned. She hurried toward Broadway, the graveled street blurring through her tears. What must he think of her? She'd told too much. She was glad she'd stopped short of confessing the horrors she'd experienced at the hands of Bill McGurty.

He meant nothing more than wanting me to attend his church, that's all.

Whether she believed that made little difference. She knew it was best if she did believe it.

Three blasts of a steamboat's whistle shot fear through her, and she quick-ened her steps. She must leave Madison at the earliest possible moment.

As difficult as it might be to accomplish that task, it would be simple com-pared to the impossibility of expunging Jacob Hale from her heart.

Chapter 7

Jacob sat in a horsehair-upholstered wing chair, his face aching from the smile he'd pasted across it. He found only marginal consolation in the fact that the faces of every other person in the parlor mirrored his own.

Broken only by the occasional wince, the stiff features of his congregation expressed their mutual suffering.

Seeming oblivious to the torture she was inflicting, Myrtle Stinnett sat before the keyboard of the new piano, butchering "Rock of Ages."

Before the final note of the hymn had mercifully faded away, Jacob jumped to his feet. "Thank you so very much, Mrs. Stinnett, for that moving rendition."

He hurried to help her up from the piano bench, fearing she might be inspired to deliver an encore. After leading the congregation in the benediction, he wrestled with the thorny problem as he mingled with his flock.

The new piano, which had arrived earlier in the week, had indeed proved a mixed blessing. His heart sang remembering the joy that lit Rosaleen's face as workers uncrated it in the parlor. A near twin to Becky and Ephraim's instrument, it now graced the front left quadrant of the room.

Later that day, he'd caught Rosaleen walking around the piano. Watching her fingers stroking the beautiful rosewood finish of the cabinet, he'd begged her to play something from the complimentary sheet music the manufacturer had sent along with the instrument.

For the next half hour, he and Mrs. Buchanan, along with Andrew and Patsey Chapman, sat enthralled, listening to a hauntingly beautiful rendition of Beethoven's "Moonlight Sonata."

Frustration gripped Jacob as he left the parlor to bid his parishioners good day at the front door. Shaking hands absently, he prayed for God's intervention. *Lord, somehow You must help me find a way to replace Myrtle Stinnett with Rosaleen as pianist for worship services.* Psalm 27:14 sprang to his mind. "*Wait on the Lord: be of good courage, and he shall strengthen thine heart: wait, I say, on the Lord.*"

"Well, Reverend Hale, do you not agree that the new piano is a wonderful addition to services, especially with Myrtle at the keyboard?"

Roscoe Stinnett's question jerked Jacob from his reverie. Except for his sister, Becky, and her family, the Stinnetts were the last in the line of parishioners filing out of the boardinghouse.

Praying for guidance, Jacob chose his words carefully. "I do believe it shall prove to be a true blessing. Again, I thank you and Mrs. Stinnett for your generosity."

He turned his attention to Myrtle Stinnett's slight, retiring figure, half hidden behind her husband's robust bulk. Her reticent demeanor beside her overbearing husband always evoked a feeling of sympathy from Jacob. "As for your contribution as pianist, Mrs. Stinnett, I'm speechless."

"My playing would have been better if my rheumatism wasn't acting up," she murmured, her eyes not quite meeting his. Grimacing, she wrung her lace-gloved hands then lowered her pinched features until they disappeared behind her gray bonnet.

Loath to injure the shy woman's feelings, Jacob said, "I can honestly say, I found it unequalled by anything I've heard before."

A satisfied smile settled across Roscoe Stinnett's broad face. He made their farewells and guided his wife outside to join others of the congregation visiting on the lawn.

"Jacob."

Jacob turned at his sister's urgent whisper.

"Is there nothing you can do?"

"I only wish there were, Becky." He gave a wistful sigh and reached out and touched the soft, rosy cheek of his infant niece cooing in her mother's arms. "The sad thing is, I feel sure it was not Myrtle's idea to act as pianist but Roscoe's."

"Yes," Becky agreed, repositioning the ivory crocheted wrap the baby had kicked off. "I'm afraid the man bullies her. But you know Myrtle, she'd never say boo to a goose. If only—"

"I know," he finished her thought, "if only Rosaleen could play for services."

"Perhaps I can help." Ephraim, with Daniel in hand, joined his wife. "I confess I was tempted to accompany Daniel on his last trip to the outhouse."

"But what could you do, dear?" Becky asked.

Jacob, too, wondered what his brother-in-law had in mind.

"I'm not altogether sure, but a few prayers concerning the subject would not be misplaced this week," Ephraim told them, grinning.

As Jacob watched his sister and her family walk away, he prayed that God had given Ephraim a solution to their prickly problem. Now, if only he could convince Rosaleen to attend services.

Jacob stood at the front door shaking hands, eager to see the last parishioner from the boardinghouse. He continually cast glances down the hallway toward the kitchen where he'd last glimpsed Rosaleen.

Since the day last week when she'd disclosed her history, he'd found his course set and his heart determined. Somehow he must bring her to the knowledge of Christ's love and salvation.

The moment he bid the last straggler good day, Jacob noticed Rosaleen heading toward the stairway with an armful of linens.

He bolted toward her. "Rosaleen"—touching her arm, he halted her ascent at the bottom step—"I saw you listening during the services. . .out in the hallway."

"I—"

"Don't deny it." He couldn't help giving her a little grin. "I was wondering if you'd consider playing for Sunday services."

"But you have a pianist. I heard—"

"Then you realize just how desperately we require your assistance." Jacob widened his grin.

"But, I'm not—I mean I don't belong. . ."

The way her gaze dropped to the linens ripped at his heart. How could she not realize how talented, beautiful, and wonderful she was?

"But you do belong. You are exactly who belongs there." Lifting her chin with the crook of his finger, Jacob forced her to meet his intent gaze. "Rosaleen, you have an amazing talent. If you heard some of my sermon today, you know it dealt with the parable of the talents from the book of Matthew. God gave you this talent. Could you not give just a little of it back?"

He watched her delicate brows slant into a V. "Jacob, I wouldn't want to cause problems between you and your congregation."

Though her concern touched him deeply, his heart lifted, detecting a tiny crack in her resistance. He rushed to take advantage of the opportunity, however slight. "Would you take the position if it were open?"

She caught her bottom lip with her teeth, and then after a moment's hesitation, murmured, "Yes."

Jacob felt himself exhale a breath he hadn't realized he'd been holding. "Don't be concerned about injuring Myrtle Stinnett's feelings," he told her. "I am quite sure she would like to relinquish the position as much as the congregation would like for her to. I'm also confident that the good lady has other talents far more obvious than those musical."

꒰꒱

The following Wednesday afternoon, Jacob sat at the desk in the parlor, immersed in preparation for the next Sunday's sermon.

Suddenly, Rosaleen's soft voice pulled his attention toward the doorway. "Jacob."

As always, Jacob's heart quickened at her presence.

"Mrs. Stinnett is waiting in the front hallway and wonders if she could have a few minutes of your time."

"Yes, of course, Rosaleen. Please show her in."

Jacob's mind raced, trying to imagine what the woman might want. He found himself unprepared for the sight of Myrtle Stinnett dabbing at her eyes with a lace kerchief.

Hurrying to the distraught woman's side, he gently ushered her to the green velvet upholstered settee. "My dear lady, whatever could be the problem?"

After situating Mrs. Stinnett, he turned to Rosaleen. "Rosaleen, would you please bring Mrs. Stinnett a cup of tea and some of Patsey's little seed cakes?"

"Yes, of course," Rosaleen said, hurrying toward the kitchen.

"Please tell me, Mrs. Stinnett, what has so distressed you?" Jacob pulled the white and yellow silk-upholstered armchair nearer to the settee.

Seeming to have collected herself to some degree, Myrtle Stinnett winced as she twisted the lace kerchief in her lap. "I am sorry to have to inform you, Reverend, but I can no longer act as pianist for the congregation."

"And why would that be, Mrs. Stinnett?" Inwardly rejoicing, Jacob knew he must walk a very fine line. Surely no one would have been so discourteous as to have commented on her lack of musical ability. Careful not to suggest any such thing, he simply waited for her response.

"I had an appointment this morning with your kinsman, Dr. Morgan." She glanced down at her gloved hands folded in her lap. "It's my hands, you see."

"Your hands?"

"Yes. As I mentioned to you after services last Sunday, I suffer from rheumatism. My hands have been hurting worse than ever, and Dr. Morgan suggested that playing the piano for services may further aggravate the inflammation." With her left hand, she rubbed the knuckles of her right.

"I know this leaves you without a pianist, and I know Roscoe, too, will be so disappointed. . . ." Her words broke on a soft sob. She dabbed again at her eyes. "But it seems to be either that or my sewing, and I simply will *not* abandon my needlework."

"No, no, of course you mustn't." Jacob reached over to pat her hand, his heart going out to the woman. "I'm sure someone will step forward and fill the void."

Suddenly she sat straight up, a flash of inspiration registering on her face. "I nearly forgot. My niece, Sophie, will be arriving next week from Miss Ely's Young Ladies' Academy in Cincinnati. She has undoubtedly mastered the piano. Why, you must know her—Sophie Schuler? She hails from your home village up in Hamilton County."

"Sophie Schuler is your niece?" Stunned by the revelation, Jacob barely noticed Rosaleen enter with the tea and cakes.

"Why, yes. When Sophie was born, I promised my sister, Gertie, Sophie's mother, that Roscoe and I would see to her formal schooling." Murmuring a thank-you to Rosaleen, Myrtle accepted the offered tea. After pausing to take a sip, she chatted on about how she planned to bring Sophie into Madison's social circle and hoped to persuade her niece to make Madison her permanent home.

Allowing the woman to prattle on uninterrupted, Jacob found his mind flashing back to his earlier acquaintance with the young Miss Schuler. He'd known Sophie since she was a child. Two years ago, while spending a summer with his brother's family, he'd briefly courted the then seventeen-year-old Sophie. However, at that time, he'd felt the seven-year age difference too great, and they'd gone their separate ways—him to Madison and her to. . .*her to a young ladies' academy*.

"Oh Reverend, I feel so much better." Brightening, Myrtle Stinnett nibbled on a seed cake, her attitude much revived. "Of course Sophie can play the piano!"

Jacob's heart slumped with his shoulders.

Oh Lord, help me. What am I to do now?

Chapter 8

"Wonder what the reverend thinks 'bout his ole flame comin' to spend the summer in Madison?" Patsey asked as she cut out biscuits at the kitchen table.

At Patsey's giggled question, Rosaleen's gaze jerked up from the strips of bacon sizzling in the frying pan. She wondered whom Patsey could mean.

The housemaid's next words supplied the answer. "Yes sirree, wish I could'a been in the parlor when Mrs. Stinnett told him who her niece is! I can jist imagine the look on his face."

A sharp glance from Opal shushed Patsey, drying up her chuckle.

Patsey's inadvertent disclosure only added to Rosaleen's discomfort when an hour later, sitting beside the piano among a parlor full of worshipers, she found herself in the last place she'd wanted to be.

Rosaleen had been prepared to dislike Sophie Schuler, but she couldn't. Throughout the service, she'd found her attention drawn to the girl.

Her heart wilting, Rosaleen was forced to admit that the young woman would be a perfect match for Jacob. Her honey blond hair peeking from beneath her rose-studded bonnet matched his almost exactly. Her pale blue eyes were but a few shades lighter than his.

Squished between her aunt and uncle on the black horsehair sofa, the quiet, petite young woman seemed the picture of demure grace. Sophie's carefully fashioned side curls framed her face in gold ringlets. With the slightest movement, they brushed against her alabaster cheek that bloomed the pale pink of wild roses. Mostly, the Stinnetts' niece kept her gaze fixed on her white-gloved hands, clasped in the lap of her rose taffeta skirt. Occasionally, however, she'd cast a shy glance up toward Jacob, who stood preaching from the open Bible draped across his outstretched arm.

From her vantage point beside the piano, Rosaleen squirmed on the gold velvet-upholstered hassock. She wondered if anyone was actually listening to Jacob's sermon, as all eyes seemed trained on either Sophie Schuler or herself.

Lacing her fingers together, she pressed her balled fists into the lap of her blue chintz dress. Self-conscious, she felt sure everyone would recognize it as one of Becky Morgan's castoffs.

After the initial butterflies in her stomach settled down, she'd actually enjoyed playing for the service. Jacob's introduction had been mercifully brief and simple, describing her as "Mrs. Archer, an accomplished pianist in Mrs.

Buchanan's employ, who'll be filling in at the piano for a time."

Also, she'd been surprised to find herself enjoying watching him preach. What she heard bore scarce resemblance to the fire-and-brimstone sermons her former guardian had leveled at his congregation. Jacob's voice, tender and moving, spoke of God's enduring love and His calling of all to repentance.

All!

Jacob's impassioned but gentle voice reading the words of Jesus brought tears to her eyes. Could it actually mean what it said? Could it mean her?

She found the picture Jacob painted of Christ as the Good Shepherd a compelling one. One she longed to grasp. Yet she could still hear Wilfred Maguire's contradicting words ringing in her ears.

"You are a harlot's spawn—wicked and irredeemable."

It was all so confusing. Which was right? Which was wrong? Rosaleen didn't think she could bear opening her heart, hoping to find inclusion, only to learn that Jesus' invitation did not apply to her and that her former guardian had been right.

She looked at Jacob then at Sophie Schuler. One way or another, her heart seemed destined to be broken in Madison, Indiana.

At the conclusion of Jacob's sermon, Rosaleen watched for his nod. Taking her place at the piano, she accompanied the congregation in their singing of "Blest Be the Tie That Binds."

During the benediction, she sat quietly, feeling very apart from the others in the room. Did God actually hear Jacob's heartfelt words? Would he hear hers? The last time she remembered expressing anything that resembled a prayer had been that night in the river when she'd feared drowning. Had God heard her? Had it been His hand that saved her?

"Rosaleen."

Jacob's voice startled her from her musings, and she whirled around on the piano seat. Rosaleen hated the jealousy gripping her as Jacob approached arm in arm with Sophie Schuler.

"Rosaleen, there is someone I'd like you to meet." He smiled, glancing affectionately at the diminutive blond girl beside him. "This is Sophie Schuler, an old friend from my home village."

Standing, Rosaleen smiled, surprised at how easy and genuine the response came.

"Sophie, this is Mrs. Rosaleen Archer. She has graciously agreed to act as pianist for our congregation until such a time as you might feel prepared to accept that duty."

"I—I don't know. Oh Jacob, must I?" Sophie murmured through her fingertips she pressed against her lips.

Rosaleen saw stark fear glisten in Sophie's pale blue eyes.

"Why, no. Of course you don't have to if you'd rather not."

As Jacob patted Sophie's hand, Rosaleen felt a pain in the vicinity of her heart.

"Mrs. Archer is such a wonderful pianist. I'm afraid the piano was not one of the studies at which I excelled during my education at Miss Ely's Academy for Girls. Would you mind terribly continuing your music ministry, Mrs. Archer?" Hope shone from the girl's eyes.

At once, Rosaleen felt both ashamed of her own jealousy and compelled to relieve the girl's anxiety. "No, of course not."

Glancing at Jacob, Rosaleen experienced a flash of irritation when she saw him fight a grin. She realized he was reacting to Sophie's suggestion that her piano playing was some sort of "ministry."

"Like my aunt Myrtle, I'd much rather do needlework," Sophie admitted. "But I do dread telling Uncle Roscoe. He's already out of sorts because I spend so much time with Edith Applegate." She raised her chin in a defiant pose. "But Edith was my very best friend at Miss Ely's, and I can't help it if Uncle Roscoe is angry with her papa."

Rosaleen remembered Opal mentioning the falling out between Roscoe Stinnett and Edward Applegate. According to Opal, when Edward Applegate left Riverfront Porkpacking to start his own pork-packing business, the two men became bitter rivals, undercutting one another at every turn.

"Why don't you leave your uncle to me," Jacob offered, to which Sophie responded with a grateful smile.

"Oh, thank you, Jacob." Sophie bounced like a giddy child. She glanced across the room where her aunt and uncle stood conversing with another couple. "Now, while Uncle Roscoe's attention is diverted, I must catch up with Edith and her brother, Edwin." Sophie murmured a quick good-bye, and with a rustling of her taffeta skirts, went to join a young lady with strawberry blond curls, standing beside a tall young man of the same coloring.

"She's a very sweet girl." Rosaleen meant every word as she followed Jacob's gaze across the room.

"Yes. Yes, she is." His soft voice held a thoughtful tone. As he turned his full attention to Rosaleen, his tone and countenance brightened. "I want to commend you on the wonderful job you did today. I'm sure my heart was not the only one touched by your playing." His mouth quirked in a mischievous grin. "Sophie was right. It is a ministry, you know."

Rosaleen stiffened. "I play the piano, that's all." Suggesting that someone God refused to recognize could perform any kind of ministry seemed beyond absurd. She wouldn't be forced to be something she wasn't—not ever again.

"Rosaleen"—her heart pranced when he gazed into her eyes and took her hands in his—"I know this was not the first sermon you've heard me preach. For the last couple of weeks, I've noticed you in the hallway outside the parlor door during worship services. You're searching for something, and you don't know what it is. But I do."

Reveling in the touch of his hands on hers, Rosaleen made no comment, unable to speak over the knot in her throat. She wished he'd never let go.

When his fingers slipped away, she felt bereft. She watched him walk to the mahogany desk near the parlor window and retrieve a small brown paper package.

"Please take this. It is in appreciation of your agreeing to play for services." He pressed the package into her hands, and his gaze melted into hers. "Please promise me you'll read it. If you have any questions, any at all, please ask me and I'll endeavor to help answer them."

Rosaleen managed a smile and a nod.

That night she sat cross-legged on her straw mattress, the Bible Jacob had given her in her lap. In the flickering light of the lantern hanging from the wall sconce, she read the words of Jesus. Her eyes misted as she read from Matthew 11:28–29: "Come unto me, all ye that labour and are heavy laden, and I will give you rest. Take my yoke upon you, and learn of me; for I am meek and lowly in heart: and ye shall find rest unto your souls."

Could Jesus give her peace? Could He accept a soul that had been a mistake?

All afternoon her heart had warred. Jacob had spent the day at the Stinnetts', visiting Sophie. Rosaleen knew she should be happy for him if he were to renew his relationship with the sweet Sophie. He deserved a pure, unblemished wife.

Tears seeped through her lashes as she shut her eyes tight against the awful scenes flashing behind them: Bill McGurty's whiskey-laced breath hot on her face. Her useless struggles. Then there were the others—those Bill had sent to her in order to curry their favor. And those times he had forced her to steal what he hadn't taken from them at the gambling table.

Shame that no amount of tears could extinguish burned her face and twisted through her like a hot poker. Her heart crumbled beneath the weight of the disgusting memories, and she gave way to sobs.

Why had she ever allowed the thought to flit across her mind that Jacob Hale might ever care for her? She felt like a dirty rag beside Sophie Schuler's spotless purity.

Collapsing to the straw mattress, she pressed the Bible against her broken heart.

Oh Jesus, help me.

Chapter 9

The surprising aroma of baking bread met Rosaleen as she descended the stairs. Her curiosity growing, she glanced at the transom window above the front door. The first faint rays of dawn stained the glass pink. This was Tuesday. They always baked on Wednesday, but even then, they never began this early.

Since her arrival at the boardinghouse, one of Rosaleen's jobs had been to start the cookstove each morning. Confused, she quickened her steps, worried that Mrs. Buchanan might consider her negligent in her duties.

Just outside the kitchen door, she stopped short, her bewilderment compounding when she saw Patsey Chapman, who never came before seven in the morning.

"Patsey, what are you doing here so early?" Rosaleen snatched her apron off the peg behind the door, deciding Opal must have forgotten to mention to her they'd be baking early this morning.

At Rosaleen's exclamation, Patsey turned from the open oven door and pressed her finger to her lips. "Shh. Don't want to wake up the whole house yet."

Rosaleen lowered her voice to just above a whisper. "Why are we making bread on Tuesday, and so early? Opal never said anything to me about it."

Hampered by her expanded middle, Patsey groaned as she bent over and pulled another loaf of freshly baked bread from the oven. "Gonna have more mouths to feed in a day or two—lots more."

Still confused, Rosaleen shook her head. "Mrs. Buchanan never mentioned anything about more boarders."

Patsey lowered her voice, her bright eyes darting about as if concerned that someone else might be listening. "Not for here. For Georgetown." She shoved another loaf of bread dough into the oven. "Andrew jis got word yesterday. There's a train a-comin'."

"Runaways?" Rosaleen blurted, forgetting to whisper.

"Shh!" Patsey's brow furrowed, and she shot a nervous glance through the kitchen window into the half-lit, dewy garden. Even the mention of the word aloud infused her face with fear. She supplied further information in a quick, staccato whisper. "Andrew got word. Don't know when. Jis got to be ready."

"Good morning, Patsey. Rosaleen." Smiling, Opal walked into the kitchen, tying on her apron. Her demeanor gave no indication that she found anything at all odd about baking bread at the crack of dawn on a Tuesday. She dipped water from the bucket by the door into the teakettle and set it on top of the stove.

"Patsey, you know that big ham hanging near the door of the smokehouse?" At Patsey's nod, Opal continued in a conversational tone. "Well, I'm afraid it might go bad in this heat, so if you know people who could use it, have Andrew take it to your place this evening, would you?"

"Yes'm."

Rosaleen listened to Patsey's muted reply and scooped flour into a large crockery bowl from a muslin sack. Suddenly, she realized Opal, too, knew about the expected arrival of the runaways. Feeling a kinship with those running from oppression, Rosaleen turned to Mrs. Buchanan. "Is there anything I can do to help, Opal?"

Opal pinned her with a knowing stare, but her tone remained light and unconcerned. "Why, of course, Rosaleen. This is a boardinghouse," she said with a little chuckle. "There's always something to do."

Nodding, Rosaleen understood. She must make no mention of the Underground Railroad.

Opal turned her attention to cutting thick slices of bacon that she then laid in the sizzling-hot cast-iron frying pan. "Reverend Hale left before dawn to work on that church building again. That man's gonna keel over if he keeps workin' hours on end without eatin'. Rosaleen, I'd like for you to take him this bacon with some of Patsey's good bread and a little jug of milk."

Rosaleen jerked her head up from the bread dough she'd begun kneading at the kitchen table. Her mind raced with her heart. Feeling sure he'd renewed his relationship with Sophie Schuler, Rosaleen had vowed to spend as little time in Jacob's presence as possible. "But shouldn't I help Patsey—"

"Patsey has things well in hand, and any assistance she might need, I can give her." Opal packed the bacon, bread, and jug of milk into a linen-lined basket.

A few minutes later, Rosaleen headed out the back door toward Main-Cross Street. She slowed her steps when she reached Broadway. The morning sun shining through the trees dappled the street with gold. Its warmth on her shoulders did nothing to brighten her heart. Perhaps she could simply hand him the basket and leave.

I'll tell him I have work to do at the boardinghouse, I'll say—

Her musings broke off as she neared the building site. The mule team hitched to a wagon of lumber stood tied and unattended, but she heard no ringing of a hammer or *whoosh* of a saw. Fear grabbed at her heart. Had he been hurt? Was he lying somewhere injured or. . . "Jacob! Jacob, where are you?"

"Rosaleen?"

A relieved sigh puffed from Rosaleen's lips when Jacob's blond head popped up from the far side of the building.

"Mmm, breakfast." Smiling, he hurried to her side and took the basket from her hand. He lifted the cloth, releasing the delicious smells of fresh-baked bread and fried bacon. Rosaleen's heart bucked when he set the basket on the ground and took her hand in his.

"I was hoping you'd come this morning." He gave her a mischievous grin. "I can always depend on Mrs. Buchanan's insistence that I eat breakfast."

Happiness bubbled up inside Rosaleen at knowing he'd expected her, had been waiting for her.

"Come, I want to show you something."

They rounded the church, now framed by skeletal walls of vertical two-by-fours. "There will be stone steps later," he said, helping her up the makeshift wooden steps into what would be the sanctuary.

She grasped his hand and her heart ached at his nearness. *If only—if only. . .*

Never in her life had she wanted to feel a man's arms around her more than at this moment.

"Here." Oblivious to her thoughts, he towed her to a sunny spot near the front of the church. Stepping behind her, he gently grasped her shoulders and turned her toward an opening in the wall at the east side of the sanctuary. "This is the spot where we'll put the piano—here by the window, where the morning sun will shine through."

The angle presented a nearly uncluttered view of the Ohio River, shimmering in the morning sunlight.

"This is what I want you to see each Sunday morning." His soft breath caressed her face as he bent his head over her shoulder.

Though she found the scene beautiful, it was the nearness of his face that took her breath away.

How easy it would be to lean my head against his neck, to turn my face ever so slightly. . . No! I mustn't do this, I mustn't!

Pulling away from his grasp, she turned and stepped backward. When her left foot found only air, she gasped, her right foot teetering on the edge of the floor.

Fear constricted her chest when she glanced down at a pile of bricks below. Suddenly, she felt Jacob's arms around her, pulling her back into the building and hard against him.

Wrapped in his strong arms, she surrendered to temptation, pressing her head against his chest. Her heart hammering, she clung to him. This was what she'd wanted. The moment she'd dreamed of for so long—to melt in the embrace of her angel's arms.

"Rosaleen," he murmured, sounding as breathless as she felt. The stubble of his unshaven chin prickled against her cheek as he nudged her face back. For a moment, their gaze held. Then, as his eyes closed and his face lowered, their lips met.

Feeling as limp as a rag doll, Rosaleen luxuriated in the kiss, glad that Jacob's strong arms supported her, holding her tight.

The sudden realization of what was happening jolted her from the beautiful trance. She pushed away from him, tears of regret stinging her eyes.

Rosaleen felt wretched. How could she do this to Sophie? Sweet, naive little Sophie. Jacob deserved better. He deserved someone like Sophie. "We—we mustn't." Filled with panic and disgust, she stumbled away from him toward the front steps.

"Rosaleen, I—I never meant. . ."

Disregarding the look of bewildered pain in his blue eyes, Rosaleen fled down the steps and ran sobbing across town until she reached the boardinghouse.

Trembling at the backyard pump, she washed the tears from her face. How could she have allowed such a thing to happen? Her heart sank at the awful truth.

Reverend Maguire was right. I am evil.

Her resolve stiffened. She must leave Madison as soon as possible.

Glad to find Opal and Patsey gone from the kitchen, Rosaleen headed for the stairs. Still shaking, she sought the solitude of her little attic room.

Just as her foot touched the first step, she heard a sharp rap at the front door. With a sigh, she trudged across the front hallway in no mood to greet new boarders with a cheerful smile.

She swung the door open and stood, stunned.

Chapter 10

Alistair?" The name burst from Rosaleen's lips as she stood staring wide eyed at Alistair "The Earl" Ralston.

She'd known the accomplished young thimblerigger and three-card-monte sharp most of her life. Continually moving from one riverboat to another, she and her father had crossed paths with Alistair many times.

The puzzled look on the man's face changed to joyful surprise as recognition flickered in his eyes. "Rosaleen? Rosaleen Maguire, is it really you?"

Rosaleen managed to nod.

He grinned, showing off his gold front tooth. "Well, as I live and breathe! If it ain't our own little Rosaleen, all growed up. Ain't ya gonna invite me in? That is, if you have a room to rent."

"Yes—yes, we do." Still reeling from the surprise, Rosaleen stepped aside to allow Alistair into the front hallway.

His gaze seemed to sweep the little hallway, taking in its gold and white patterned wallpaper, mahogany table with a pair of Aragon lamps, and floral ingrained carpet. "Not bad." He gave her a wink. "Nice as any of old Vanderbilt's steamboats." His grin faded, and he pulled his black beaver hat from his wavy auburn hair. His gray eyes held a look of genuine sympathy. "Heard about your dad sometime back. Real sorry. Heard you went to live with relations or somethin'."

"Something like that." She questioned the wisdom of telling Alistair too much. Had he learned of her time with Bill McGurty? If he had, he'd chosen to pretend otherwise. Alistair would know as well as anyone that few crossed Black Jack Bill McGurty and lived.

"Little Rosaleen." Smiling, he shook his head in disbelief. "You've grown into a beauty, and that's a fact." Though his gaze roved over her, it caused her no unease. His benign assessment of her seemed to convey only a brotherly pride.

Rosaleen had to admit that the six-foot-tall Alistair cut a handsome figure in his dark green broadcloth coat and black tapered trousers. He held out his arms. "How about a kiss for an old friend?"

Before she could protest, Alistair caught her up in a bay-rum-scented bear hug. Lifting her feet off the floor, he planted a wet kiss on her mouth.

"Rosaleen, I came as soon as I got the chance. We need to talk—" Jacob's voice coming from the hall doorway that led to the kitchen sounded winded.

As Alistair set her down, Rosaleen whirled in time to see Jacob's face go ashen then bright scarlet. Without another word, he turned on his heel and strode back toward the kitchen.

Alistair gave a nervous-sounding cough and cleared his throat. "Well, I don't want to keep you from your work, so if you'll just show me to my room. . ."

Humiliated, Rosaleen paid only vague attention to Alistair's words, her helpless gaze fixed on the spot where Jacob had stood.

What must Jacob think?

She'd allowed him to kiss her earlier, and now Jacob had witnessed Alistair stealing a kiss from her. With her heart feeling as leaden as her feet, she mounted the stairs with Ralston in tow. At the landing, she glanced down at the open parlor door and felt torn. She desperately wanted to explain to Jacob Alistair's meaningless kiss. But that would undoubtedly lead to a discussion of the kiss she and Jacob had shared—a far more troublesome topic.

That evening as everyone sat around the supper table, Jacob was uncharacteristically quiet. It struck Rosaleen that he seemed to go out of his way to avoid looking at her. However, he shot continual scrutinizing glances toward Alistair.

Rosaleen was almost glad for Alistair's constant banter. The man had the gift of gab, but she made a mental note to count the silverware after supper.

"Never expected to find you working at a boardinghouse," Alistair said, smiling across the table at Rosaleen.

"Mrs. Archer is a wonderful help," Opal injected. "I'm truly blessed to have her."

"Archer?" Alistair's brows shot up then slipped down into a thoughtful V. "Ah yes, now that I think on it, I did hear something about Rory Maguire's girl marrying Donovan Archer."

Then turning quiet, he focused his attention on the large slice of ham on his plate. His sudden change of attitude made Rosaleen wonder if he'd also heard about Bill McGurty shooting Donovan to death.

Opal clucked her tongue and shook her head sadly. "Such an awful thing, Mr. Archer perishing in that steamboat explosion. We just thank the Lord Rosaleen was spared."

A look of surprise flashed across Alistair's face. "Real sorry to hear about Archer, Rosaleen. Good man from what I recall."

Rosaleen murmured her thanks. Although Alistair's surprise seemed genuine, she couldn't tell if it was from just now learning of her husband's death or because Opal's comment contradicted what Alistair might have heard about Donovan's murder.

She studied the gambler's features, but his face had gone poker plain, unreadable. If he did know the truth about how Donovan died and about her time with Bill McGurty, he didn't seem inclined to divulge that knowledge. And at the moment, that suited Rosaleen. As much as she would like to know if Alistair had seen Bill since the explosion, she would rather Opal and Jacob—especially Jacob—not learn of her time with Bill. So she was relieved when Opal steered the supper conversation in a different direction.

"I have to admit, Mr. Ralston," Opal said as she passed Alistair a plate of corn bread, "this is the first time I've had the privilege of entertaining an English earl at my dining table."

Alistair's gold tooth glinted in the candlelight. "Well, ma'am," he said slowly as if choosing his words carefully, "I don't reckon I'm a real earl. Not properlike on paper 'n such. But according to my mum, I can trace my heritage back to the gentry."

Rosaleen smiled at the wink Alistair shot in her direction. But her smile quickly faded when she turned it toward Jacob. The frown lines dragging down his mouth held no trace of the young minister's usual good humor.

She had no doubt it was Alistair's presence that had soured Jacob's mood. Did Jacob simply find the gambler unsavory? Or was he brooding over the kiss he'd seen Alistair give her that morning? She couldn't help hoping it was the latter.

The scowling face staring back at Jacob from the bureau mirror seemed foreign. He didn't like the way he looked these days, and he certainly didn't like the way he felt. He wiped off the remnants of the shaving soap with a quick swipe of the towel and then threw it hard onto the washstand.

Buttoning his dress shirt, he gazed out his upstairs window at Mulberry Street below. Madison was just beginning to stir to life this Fourth of July. Though the morning sun slanting through his window promised a beautiful Independence Day, worry over Rosaleen had robbed his heart of all celebratory feelings.

He'd been glad to notice that the gambler, Alistair Ralston, spent most of his time away from the boardinghouse. Gambling and running his ruses down in one or another of the taverns along the riverfront, Jacob guessed.

He didn't like the familiar way the man acted around Rosaleen. To be honest, he didn't like the familiarity Rosaleen showed Ralston, either.

The prayer he'd been praying in the week since Ralston's appearance rose again from his heart. *Oh God, please guide her. Just guide her.*

His fingers moved automatically as he tied his black silk cravat. Sighing, he licked his lips, remembering the one sweet kiss he and Rosaleen had shared. Recalling how she'd clung to him—her eager response to his kiss—he couldn't believe she didn't care for him.

When Sophie Schuler appeared unexpectedly in Madison, he'd steeled his resolve to renew a relationship with the girl he'd courted two years ago. With all good intentions, he'd tried to ignore his feelings for Rosaleen and lash his errant heart to the hitching post of practicality.

The touch of Rosaleen's lips against his had shattered that resolve. To encourage Sophie when his heart was bound to Rosaleen would be dishonest and potentially hurtful.

Thankfully, Sophie Schuler had become one of Madison's social butterflies and showed little interest in renewing their relationship. The previous Sunday, she'd casually mentioned that she'd be celebrating the holiday by joining a group of Madison's youthful elite on a railroad excursion to Columbus.

Ironically, it wasn't Sophie who seemed to be impeding the deeper relationship Jacob would like to grow between himself and Rosaleen, but Rosaleen herself. He felt heat spread from his neck to his scalp remembering her troubling reaction to his kiss. He still stung from the way she'd fled the church, as if he might do her harm.

She was, after all, a new widow. A decent amount of time needed to pass before he could, in all decorum, attempt to court her. Yet he'd seen no sign of decorum on her part when he watched her happily kiss Alistair Ralston.

And then there was the fact that she'd not yet given her heart to Christ. However, hope had been growing in Jacob that she might be nearing a decision about that. Sunday after Sunday, he watched her lovely eyes glisten with tears while she listened with what seemed rapt attention as he preached of Christ's love and salvation. He'd even noticed her following along in the Bible he'd given her.

Jacob shrugged on his dress coat, glad that he and Rosaleen would be spending most of the day with Becky, Ephraim, and their children. He silently blessed his sister for inviting Rosaleen to the Independence Day picnic at their home. Besides affording him an opportunity to make amends for his rash behavior at the church last week, it gave Rosaleen a reason to not spend time with Alistair Ralston.

As he entered the parlor, his heart did its usual little flip-flop when his gaze found Rosaleen. Looking stunning in the green sprigged muslin dress Becky had given her, she sat on the sofa beside Alistair Ralston. Her lighthearted laughter, directed at the gambler, sent a surge of jealousy through Jacob.

"No, Alistair, I know better than to play that shell game with you. And I certainly wouldn't bet my brooch." Her hand went to the ever-present brooch at the center of her bodice. When her gaze drifted to the doorway, she popped up from the sofa, the laugh dying on her lips. "Oh, Jacob," she said breathlessly, her demeanor resembling that of a guilty child.

"Are you ready, Rosaleen?" The forced smile hurt Jacob's face.

"The offer stands, Rosaleen." Alistair gave her a wink that ignited a flame of anger in Jacob.

Rosaleen accepted Jacob's proffered arm. "Then I should expect it will grow tired standing," she shot back at Alistair with a nervous-sounding giggle.

As they walked up Mulberry Street toward Main-Cross, Jacob fought to keep his voice light. Surely the man had not offered Rosaleen marriage. "What was Mr. Ralston's offer, if I might be so bold as to ask?"

"Oh, my brooch," she said with a light laugh. "Alistair knows good and well I'll not part with it, yet he can't seem to help himself from trying."

"Just how well do you know Mr. Ralston?"

"It seems I've known him forever. Like me, he's been moving from riverboat to riverboat most of his life. I think of him almost as an older brother."

"Do you miss it—life on the riverboats?" Jacob needed to learn the answers to the concerns pressing against his heart. In Ralston's vernacular, he might as well "go for broke."

"No."

He felt immense relief at the definitive tone of her voice. "You don't plan on going back to it then?"

She gave a little shake of her head. "No, not to the riverboats."

"But you do plan on leaving Madison. . . ." Jacob sent up a quick prayer that she would dispel his suspicions. It went unanswered.

"Yes," she murmured, sending his heart plummeting and confirming what he realized he'd known all along but had not allowed himself to admit.

"Where do you plan to go? You said you had no other family." *Maybe if she has nowhere else to go, I can convince her—*

"New York. When I was at Mrs. Griswold's Academy, a concert pianist, Maestro Levitsky, visited the academy and heard me play. He told me I had great talent, and if I could get to New York, he would help me become a concert pianist." Her voice deflated. "Donovan had promised to take me, but now. . ."

Learning of her plans to travel to New York jarred Jacob. Hope of her staying in Madison shriveled. He had no right to ask her to abandon her dream.

He forced his lips into a smile. "You'd be the toast of the New York concert halls."

They walked the next two blocks in silence until he realized he'd never apologized for frightening her at the church. He decided this might be as good a time as any. Perhaps then, the stiff formality that had grown between them would relax a bit.

"Rosaleen, I—I wanted to let you know, I'm sorry about what happened last week. . .in the church." His conscience chafed against the lie. He indeed regretted having frightened her, but he could not make his heart sorry for the kiss.

"It's all right, Jacob. I've thought no more of it, and neither should you."

Her quiet words were like a dagger through his heart, but he noticed her gaze remained fixed on the gravel at their feet.

At last, they reached the church on Main-Cross Street where the children of Madison's Sunday schools had gathered for a parade. The boys held patriotic-colored banners while the girls trailed red, white, and blue ribbons.

Grinning, Jacob returned Daniel's sharp salute. But he found little joy in the procession or the day's celebrations. Rosaleen's plans to leave Madison weighted his heart like a stone. How long did he have to win her heart to Christ—and to him?

Later, they followed the procession down to Ohio Street on the riverfront where local dignitaries gave addresses. But Jacob barely noticed the different speakers and their talk of imminent war with Mexico. With Rosaleen beside him, filling his senses, all other stimuli faded.

Following the addresses, the gunnery sergeant of the militia presided over a cannon salute. A burst of laughter and cheers trailed the gun's loud report. When Rosaleen jumped back at the *boom*, Jacob caught her around the waist, saving her from tumbling backward into the crowd behind them. Giggling, they clung to one another for one sweet, beautiful moment amid the acrid smell of gunpowder floating over the crowd.

Oh God, if I could only hold her like this forever. If I could only convince her never to leave Madison.

"Tell 'em to fire the cannon again, Papa." Daniel's innocent appeal to Ephraim shattered the spell, and they dissolved into laughter.

At the conclusion of the town's festivities, Jacob and Rosaleen joined his sister and her family at their home on Main-Cross Street. There, Rosaleen, Jacob, and Ephraim settled themselves on quilts spread beneath a large maple tree in the front yard, while Becky slipped into the house to feed baby Lucy.

Young Daniel marched up to Jacob and Rosaleen, offering glasses of lemonade.

"Thank you, Daniel." Jacob grinned at his nephew's hands, wet with the sticky beverage sloshing over the glasses' rims.

"Better than the Fourth of July refreshment you tried ten years ago, wouldn't you say, Jacob?" Ephraim asked with a sly, mischievous grin.

Jacob took a sip of the sweetened, tart drink and groaned at his brother-in-law's teasing reference to his one and only sampling of home brew at the age of sixteen.

"What Fourth of July refreshment?" Rosaleen perked, turning an interested smile toward him.

"When I was sixteen, I stupidly took a dare to drink half a keg of home brew." Forced to recount the embarrassing episode to Rosaleen, Jacob shot Ephraim a glare that set his brother-in-law to chuckling.

"You? But you're a preacher." She blinked, and then her eyes widened to puzzled, blue green pools.

Her obvious bewilderment concerned more than amused Jacob. "I wasn't then and hadn't yet given my heart and life to Christ."

"But I thought preachers were—I mean, never did. . ." A rosy blush prettily stained the confused look on her face.

"You thought preachers were perfect?" Jacob couldn't help smiling as he rushed to her rescue, but the depth of her misunderstanding troubled him. What other misconceptions might she have about preachers or Christians in general?

"Romans 3:23 says, 'For all have sinned, and come short of the glory of God.' No one is perfect; only Christ is. We are all saved by His grace, Rosaleen."

"You really believe that?"

Astounded, Jacob met her skeptical look. "Of course. The apostle Paul tells us in chapter one, verse sixteen of his letter to the Romans, 'For I am not ashamed of the gospel of Christ: for it is the power of God unto salvation to every one that believeth.' "

Becky poked her head out the front door. "Lucy's asleep, so Rosaleen, if you'll help me in the kitchen, we'll have the fried chicken, potato salad, and apple pie out here in two shakes."

His heart in conflict, Jacob watched Rosaleen follow his sister into the house. He prayed that their previous exchange indicated Rosaleen might be considering giving her heart to Christ. If not, how could he love a nonbeliever? Yet he could more easily empty the Ohio River than stop loving Rosaleen Archer.

After lunch, they gathered in the parlor where Rosaleen entertained them at the piano with renditions of patriotic songs. They all sang along to the stirring "Ode to George Washington" and "The Grand Constitution." Daniel especially enjoyed "Yankee Doodle," marching around the parlor as he sang.

When Rosaleen played a popular tune called "The Girl I Left Behind Me," its haunting melody permeated Jacob's heart like a melancholy fog. He had to wonder if it might be *he* who'd be left behind, knowing she planned to leave for New York as soon as possible. He found it even more worrisome to think that she might not be leaving alone. He felt his brows slide together in a frown as the image of Alistair Ralston muscled into his thoughts.

Chapter 11

One evening several days after the Fourth of July celebrations, Rosaleen sat on her little straw tick in her attic room. Rubbing her eyes in the sputtering light of the tallow candle, she read the words from Romans 1:16 that Jacob had quoted. "For I am not ashamed of the gospel of Christ: for it is the power of God unto salvation to every one that believeth."

Every one that believeth.

Rosaleen wanted to believe it meant her. She wanted to believe it more than she'd ever wanted to believe anything.

"For it is the power of God unto salvation to every one that believeth." Her whispered breath caressed each word. Perhaps there was hope. Perhaps the promise in that scripture *did* include her.

A quiet rap at her door yanked her attention from the scriptures, and she dropped the Bible to her mattress. "Yes, who is it?"

When no one answered, her heart began to pound. She crossed the little room, her bare feet padding softly on the floorboards.

"Who is it?" She managed the three breathless words, her face pressed against the door and her heart beating like a kettledrum in her chest.

"It's Andrew. Open the door."

At the rasped whisper, relief drained the strength from her limbs. With unsteady fingers, she unlocked the door. What on earth could Andrew want?

Panic gripped Rosaleen. *Patsey.* Was Patsey ill? Was the baby coming too early? If so, why hadn't Andrew simply gone to fetch Dr. Morgan?

When she opened the door, bewilderment replaced fear. A young black woman and two small children dressed in near rags stood trembling beside Andrew.

Suddenly Rosaleen remembered a conversation she had last week with Patsey. When Patsey asked her if she would be willing to hide runaway slaves, Rosaleen had agreed to help. Patsey went on to explain that Mrs. Buchanan had used the attic room from time to time to hide runaways when other accommodations could not be found. Although eager to help slaves on their road to freedom, Rosaleen hadn't expected such an opportunity to occur so soon.

"They jis crossed the Jordan and need a place to stay. Maybe a day. Maybe two," Andrew whispered. He darted anxious glances down the stairway then ushered the three into Rosaleen's room and pulled the door shut behind them. "Mrs. Buchanan knows. Cain't tell Rev'rend. If asked, he'd be obliged not to lie.

Cain't risk it. Can you act like nothin's different? Nothin' at all?"

Still a bit stunned, Rosaleen nodded. These were passengers on the Underground Railroad. She surmised the "Jordan" referred to the Ohio River.

"This is Sally, Lizzie, and Elijah," Andrew informed her.

Rosaleen's heart went out to the frail woman and the little boy and girl. Both children, who looked about Daniel Morgan's age, seemed to struggle just to keep their eyes open.

"But there's only one mattress." Rosaleen's mind raced. How would they all manage, even for a couple of days? The little attic room was barely large enough for one.

"They don't need no mattress. This floor's better'n what they're used to. Don't tell nobody. Not even Patsey. She don't know. Jis go on like nothin's different. Don't let on. Their lives depend on it." With those whispered instructions, Andrew left, quietly closing the door behind him.

Rosaleen hurried to lock the door, then without saying a word, guided the two children to the mattress and covered them with the quilt. The poor, exhausted little things fell asleep the moment their heads touched the mattress.

As she lay down beside Sally on the hard floorboards, Rosaleen shifted from side to side, unable to find a comfortable position. Yet the unexpected situation had left her heart and mind in far more unease than her body.

She'd been reading the words of Jesus, trying to learn how she could most please God. If scant chance existed that she might find salvation, she felt it depended upon being careful not to displease Him.

Jacob had said, "All have sinned," yet her guardian had called her "irredeemable." Her only hope, she reasoned, was to be perfect from now on. That chance, she realized with dismay, might just have been snatched from her. The memory of Wilfred Maguire's voice booming from his pulpit in Natchez sank her hope.

" '*All liars, shall have their part in the lake which burneth with fire and brimstone.*' "

Opal knew about the presence of the runaways, and whatever suspicions Patsey might have, Rosaleen knew she'd never ask. Jacob, however, seemed to have been watching her comings and goings more closely since Alistair's arrival. Now, she might very well be forced to lie to Jacob in order to protect him as well as the runaways.

For the next two days, with Mrs. Buchanan's help, Rosaleen managed to keep her three "guests" supplied with food and fresh water. The tiny attic space was stifling in the July heat, yet she dare not open the little casement window even a crack.

None of the three runaways had spoken a word to her during the time they'd been cloistered in her room.

Rosaleen made sure no one was around as she headed up the stairs to the attic, carrying a pitcher of fresh water and a towel-draped washbowl filled with bread and ham. Setting the pitcher down, she slowly opened the door and poked her head into the room.

Sally's and her children's eyes grew large with looks of fear, followed quickly by ones of stark relief. Yet all remained mute, grateful smiles stretching their sweat-drenched faces.

Retrieving the pitcher and bowl, Rosaleen choked back tears. She wished she could offer them assurances of safety as well as sustenance, but all she could do was pour them fresh cups of well water and offer them the food.

Later, as she walked into Jacob's vacant room to gather the bed linens for the weekly laundry, the fugitive mother and children clung to her mind. She found it amazing that anyone, especially children, could remain so silent for such a long time.

She found even more astounding the fact that Patsey seemed entirely oblivious to Sally's, Lizzie's, and Elijah's presence. Andrew had said she didn't know, and her demeanor bore out his claim. Though Rosaleen understood Andrew's intention to protect Patsey as well as the runaways, she couldn't imagine not disclosing such knowledge to a mate.

Rosaleen recalled happy talks she'd shared with Donovan. How they'd laughed over silly things like a lady's outrageous hat or an unusual landmark along the river.

She brushed a tear from her cheek, spread a fresh sheet over Jacob's bed, and tucked the ends under the feather mattress. When she gazed about the neat little room, her heart ached. His well-worn Bible on the bureau, his razor lying on the washstand, and the blue and white striped calico work shirt hanging from the bedpost all reminded her of the man who owned her heart.

She lifted the shirt from the bedpost to add it to the bundle of laundry. Closing her eyes, she laid it against her cheek, inhaling his familiar scent. Once again, she could feel his lips, soft and tender, caressing hers.

Visions of what life might be like as Jacob's wife played before her mind's eye. She imagined herself giggling in his arms as they shared humorous anecdotes. She could see his blue eyes laughing into hers and her reaching a finger up to trace the thin scar that ran the length of his cheek. His eyes would close, his mouth seeking hers. She could almost taste the sweetness of his kisses and feel the comfort of his arms.

More tears slipped down her face. She had no hope of such dreams ever coming true. No right to even dream. That future did not belong to her. It belonged to Sophie Schuler.

The best she could hope for would be to keep Jacob's respect. Now that, too, had been put in jeopardy. So far, she'd managed to avoid lying to him. But Elijah had developed a cough, causing the boy to press his little face into a pillow to muffle the sound. Sooner or later, Rosaleen feared she'd need to fabricate a story to explain the sounds.

She gathered the pile of linens in her arms and started down the stairs.

"Whoa there!"

At the bottom of the stairs, Rosaleen gasped. She'd walked straight into Alistair Ralston.

"Hey, come with me down to the Billiard Saloon tonight. We'll have some fun fleecing salesmen and farmers." He wrapped his long arms around her, sheets and all.

"I have work to do, and then I have to get up early in the morning, Alistair." She wriggled out of his grasp and attempted to walk around him.

He caught her around the waist, his muscular arm clamping her hard against him. Until now, she'd never felt afraid of Alistair. His friendly smile and chuckle did not match the roguish glint in his eyes. "You could send me signals like you used to do for your dad. With your looks and my skill, we could clean up, Rosaleen. You know we could."

"That's not my life anymore, Alistair. That's not who I am now." During her time here in Madison she'd begun to feel decent, and she liked that feeling. She wouldn't let Alistair—or anyone for that matter—suck her back into the unscrupulous gambling life. Besides, at the moment she had Sally, Lizzie, and Elijah to see to.

"Think on it, love." With a wicked wink, he pressed a quick kiss on her cheek. "You can find me at the Billiard."

As Alistair strode out the front door, her head pivoted toward a sound near the parlor doorway. Her face grew hot at Jacob's incredulous gaze. How much had he heard?

Her heart deflated when he said nothing. He simply turned and walked back into the parlor.

Rosaleen wanted to march into the parlor and tell Jacob she had no intention of joining Alistair at the Billiard Saloon. It took all her willpower to walk past the parlor and toward the backyard washtub. A conversation with Jacob would simply be too dangerous.

Chapter 12

Jacob snapped the Bible shut and pushed away from his desk. Heaving a deep sigh, he rubbed his hand over his face. He'd searched the Proverbs for God's wisdom yet found no answers to the troubles plaguing his heart.

Rosaleen was driving him crazy.

After giving her the Bible, he'd hoped she might begin asking questions about the scriptures. He'd been encouraged by the glimmer of interest she showed at Becky's Fourth of July picnic.

Lately, however, she'd shown little interest in speaking with him about the scriptures, or any other subject for that matter. Clenching his jaw, Jacob glanced toward the parlor doorway. He felt sure he knew who had caused the change in her.

Alistair Ralston.

Three nights ago, he'd heard the muffled but unmistakable sound of a man's boots on the stairway leading to her attic room. He and Alistair Ralston were the only two men presently living in the boardinghouse. Jacob hated the images forming in his mind but could find no logic to explain them away.

Only an hour ago, he'd caught her, once again, in Ralston's arms. What was worse, the man had kissed her and invited her to the infamous Billiard Saloon.

Jacob rose and gave the chair a resolute shove against the desk. It was useless to try to work on his sermon with his mind insisting on steering toward dark thoughts. He might as well go work on the church. At least there, he could see the results of an hour's endeavors.

At the intersection of Mulberry and Main-Cross, he was surprised to see Rosaleen leaving Maynard's Apothecary. A sudden fear seized him. Perhaps she'd been feeling unwell. That could explain her reticent mood of late.

"Rosaleen, are you all right?" He glanced at the basket on her arm.

"Oh, yes." Her face flushed a deep pink, and she scooted an amber bottle beneath a green and white gingham cloth. "Just—just an errand." Her face looked as if it might crack with the force of her smile.

"Are you sure, because if you're unwell. . ."

"No. I'm quite all right. Quite." She looked down Mulberry as if eager to be away and transferred the basket to her arm farthest from him.

What was she hiding? He wished he'd gotten a better look at that bottle. He'd thought it looked suspiciously like a whiskey bottle the instant before she'd hidden it. Maynard's sold spirits as well as medicines. Could it be for Ralston? But then, wouldn't the man simply get his liquor at the Billiard Saloon?

"I was just on my way to the church but would be glad to carry your basket and accompany you back to the boardinghouse first." Perhaps God had given him this opportunity to speak with her.

"No, thank you just the same, but I wouldn't want to detain you from your work on the church." Her rushed answer tumbled out while her glance darted about as if looking for escape.

"I don't mind, really. . . ," Jacob began.

"Reverend Hale. Ma'am." Constable Rafe Arbuckle's voice intruded as he stepped toward them, dragging his hat off his shock of salt-and-pepper hair. "The sheriff got wind of a bunch of runaway slaves. Just wonderin' if you'd seen any different faces, you bein' situated near Georgetown an' all."

Jacob stiffened. "No. No, I haven't." He knew the sheriff was a hot pro-slavery man. In the two years he'd been in Madison, Jacob would have liked to help the Chapmans and Opal in their work with the Underground Railroad. However, being a minister, he knew he'd be questioned often. He'd learned from Orville that he could best help the organization by being oblivious to its movements.

"I—I need to get back to the boardinghouse and help with the washing," Rosaleen murmured. Before he could stop her, she hurried down Mulberry Street.

"Don't mean to be a bother. Just supposed to ask, that's all," Rafe said, his voice apologetic as he shifted from foot to foot.

Jacob's heart sank at his lost opportunity to talk with Rosaleen. He dragged his gaze from her fleeting figure back to Rafe. He couldn't help feeling sympathy for the constable. Rafe Arbuckle was a good man who'd been sent on a distasteful errand. He gave Arbuckle an understanding smile and clapped his hand on the man's shoulder. "That's all right, Rafe. You're just doing your duty."

As he walked to the church, Jacob realized that instead of learning any answers to his questions about Rosaleen, he'd been presented with even more questions.

"Be ye not unequally yoked together with unbelievers."

The words from Second Corinthians screamed through his mind. But he *was* yoked. His heart was inextricably bound to hers.

The sight of the new church building no longer brought him the joy it once had. Each soul won to Christ in this building would be precious. Yet if he failed with Rosaleen, he feared he'd be forever haunted by the one soul his heart most longed to claim for Christ.

Oh God, help me to win her for You, or disentangle my heart from hers and emancipate me from this misery.

❧

Rosaleen jerked up from her bedroom floor with a start. She'd slept in her day dress expecting the knock, yet the soft rap set her heart pounding.

"Rosaleen." Andrew Chapman's voice slowed her heart to a canter. Without a word, she unlocked the door and let him in.

"Train's a'comin'."

"Already?"

Andrew nodded.

The encounter this afternoon with constable Arbuckle had been unnerving. She remembered how her heart had pounded and her knees had gone weak, fearing she would be directly questioned about the runaway slaves.

She knew the sooner they could move on, the better for all involved. Yet in the last two days, she'd become accustomed to the presence of Sally and the children. The sadness she felt at the thought of parting with them surprised her.

Sniffing back tears, she gently woke Lizzie and Elijah. It tugged at her heart to see the way they accepted the intrusion. She, too, had known what it was to be treated as less than human. Like these slaves, she'd lived with terror, accepting it as a matter of course. The cruelty she'd experienced in her own life caused her heart to bond with these innocent unfortunates who simply longed to breathe free. With tears streaming down her face, Rosaleen hugged the little ones in turn.

"God bless you, Miss Rosaleen."

Stunned at the first words Sally had uttered to her, Rosaleen hugged the frail woman. She pressed into Sally's hands the bottle of tonic that had done wonders for Elijah's cough. "Just stay well. All of you."

"Need you to come, too."

Startled, Rosaleen raised her face to Andrew's. "Why?"

Whispering, he kept his words pared to the essentials. " 'Case we're stopped an' somebody asks questions. Patsey ain't been feelin' none too good. Jis fetchin' you to see about Patsey, that's all."

A still, small voice spoke to Rosaleen's heart, nudging her to the straw mattress. She'd been reading the words of Jesus. With each new day, the longing in her heart grew stronger to obey His words. This evening she'd been reading from the nineteenth chapter of Matthew. Hungering for Christ's acceptance, she'd fixed her attention on Jesus' response to a young man who'd asked how he might attain eternal life. She'd read verse twenty-one over and over until she'd committed it to memory.

"Jesus said unto him, If thou wilt be perfect, go and sell that thou hast, and give to the poor, and thou shalt have treasure in heaven: and come and follow me."

Without hesitation or regret, she reached into the mattress slit and grasped the little calico bag then turned to Andrew. "I want them to have this. It's only six dollars, but maybe it will help."

"Bless you, Miss Rosaleen." The look of gratitude on Andrew's face as he tucked the bag inside his shirt was all the reward she needed.

Praying had now become a habit with Rosaleen. Though she remained unsure if Jesus actually heard the prayers, they simply made her feel better. She prayed hard as their little ragamuffin band stole down the stairs and out to Andrew's waiting wagon.

In the darkness, Rosaleen could just make out the farm wagon piled high with straw. While she wondered if Sally and the children would have to burrow deep inside, she watched Andrew reach beneath the wagon bed and unlatch a little door. To her amazement, the three runaways crawled up into the false wagon bottom, and Andrew fastened the door behind them.

Her heart hammering, Rosaleen bounced on the buckboard seat beside Andrew. They wended their way through the moonless night, northeast out of Madison. Andrew had told her the next station was at a place he'd called Eagle Hollow. He said the distance would be about a mile, but the crooked, elevated path made it seem twice as long.

At last, they stopped at a little stone house, and Andrew rapped softly at the door.

The door creaked open, revealing no light within the home's dark interior.

"I have the cargo you ordered." Andrew's whispered words carried through the still night air to the wagon.

No one answered, but a moment later he was at the back of the wagon helping the three runaways from their cramped hiding place.

Rosaleen's eyes strained in the darkness to catch one last glimpse of the three who'd shared her attic room for the past two days and three nights. A prayer rent from her anxious heart. *Jesus, be with them. You healed the sick, raised the dead, and stilled the tempest. Please, please just keep them safe.*

"Will they make it?" Rosaleen couldn't help asking the question as she and Andrew jostled over the rut-pocked road toward Madison.

"Good chance. Conductors from here on are pretty reliable."

"Is Patsey really sick?" Sudden concern for her friend tightened Rosaleen's voice. She hated the thought of Patsey sick at home alone without her husband beside her.

"She'll be all right." His teeth flashed a smile in the darkness. "'Jis took a hankerin' for some fried mush then couldn't abide the grease. She be sleepin' now." Rosaleen heard love and longing in his soft voice. "I can walk back to the boardinghouse from here," she said as they neared the Georgetown area of Madison.

Andrew shook his head. "Ain't fittin'. . .or safe. Like I said, Patsey be sleepin'. 'Nother few minutes won't make no difference to her."

Only moments after Andrew dropped Rosaleen off near the boardinghouse and headed back to Georgetown, she understood his concerns about her walking home. Her heart jumped to her throat when she saw a large shadowy figure looming in the dark street ahead less than a half block from where she stood. As the figure neared, weaving its way toward her from the south, she heaved a sigh of relief. It was only Alistair, making his way back to the boardinghouse from a night of gambling down at the Billiard Saloon on Ohio Street's riverfront. A good deal worse for the wear, it would seem.

"Rose'leen, m'little Rose'leen," Alistair slurred as he grasped her around the waist. "Too late, too late," he lamented, wagging an unsteady finger in her face. "Gamblin' done, drinkin' done. Time to go t'bed."

He stumbled and nearly fell when she pushed away from his whiskey-soaked breath. "I'd say *bed* is exactly where you belong, Alistair." She turned her face south toward the fresh breezes blowing off the river.

Wrapping her arm as far around him as it would go, Rosaleen prayed she'd be able to maneuver Alistair up to his room on the second floor without waking Jacob or Opal. She cringed at his every hiccup, laugh, and slurred verse of "Old Dan Tucker" until they reached the door of his room.

When she pushed open the door, he stumbled in, carrying her with him. Alistair fell back onto the bed with a *crash*, and she found herself pulled on top of him, his arms clamped around her. Pushing hard against his chest, she extricated herself from his grasp, but fell backward, landing on the floor with a *boom*. She could hear him snoring, already dead to the world.

Gasping for breath, she struggled to her feet. Her hair pulled loose from its pins and tumbled to her shoulders. It was in this disheveled state that she met Jacob's shocked gaze as she exited Alistair's room.

The lit candle in his hand illuminated his stunned features. He stood in his nightshirt, his blond head poking out from his bedroom door. "Everything all right?" he asked in a frosty voice.

"Yes—yes." Mortified, Rosaleen pushed the straggling hair from her face, realizing how stupid and ineffectual the motion must look. Racing past him, she hurried to the end of the hall and the stairway that led to her attic room. Behind her, the sound of his door snapping shut felt like a lance through her heart.

Chapter 13

Rosaleen fidgeted on her seat beside the piano. For the first time since she'd begun playing for Sunday services, she felt eager for the benediction.

She hadn't been able to look Jacob in the eye after her humiliating encounter with him outside Alistair's room. His demeanor toward her had not thawed one degree, and her heart screamed to give him a true accounting of last night's events. But even if she could tell him about her involvement in helping the runaway slaves, would he believe her if she tried to explain?

This morning, his sermon, taken from the second chapter of Proverbs, dealt with wisdom. She wondered if he'd chosen the theme especially for her benefit, though his gaze seemed to diligently avoid hers.

" 'To deliver thee from the strange woman, even from the stranger which flattereth with her words,' " Jacob read from verse sixteen.

She remembered the look on Jacob's face when he'd watched her stumble from Alistair's room. What emotions had she seen playing across his features in the vacillating light and shadows of the flickering candle? Astonishment? Of course. Anger? Disgust? Had he, like Wilfred Maguire, decided that she was beyond redemption?

The next passage of scripture that boomed from Jacob's voice seemed directed at her. " 'But the wicked shall be cut off from the earth, and the transgressors shall be rooted out of it.' "

Wicked.

There it was again—the word Reverend Maguire had consistently attached to her. And now she'd heard it from Jacob's own mouth. It reverberated through her stricken heart as if the very ax of the Almighty had fallen, severing her from any prospect of salvation. The hope she'd nurtured during hours of searching the Gospels for Christ's acceptance had all at once been consumed to ashes and blown away. Reverend Maguire had been right. She was wicked—wicked and irredeemable.

Struggling for breath, Rosaleen knew she had to get away. Gathering her skirts in her fists, she leaped from her seat and ran from the room, through the boardinghouse, and out the kitchen door. Her vision obscured by tears, she ran on trembling legs as if to escape the wrath of God. She hadn't even realized how far she'd gone until several minutes after she sank to the bench beside Jacob's new church.

Lifting her head, she gazed two blocks south where the sunlight danced over the Ohio River like silver sprites. A strong southwest breeze carried the dank, fishy scent of the river that blended with the fresh smell of new lumber. Cool river breezes dried her tears and brushed the leaves of Orville Whitaker's willow tree against her shoulder.

She'd so wanted to believe the promises of Christ were meant for her. But after the things Bill McGurty had forced her to do, how could she expect Jesus to look upon her with anything but disgust?

"Blessed are the pure in heart: for they shall see God." Jesus' words from the fifth chapter of Matthew seemed to seal her doom. Convinced she'd been sullied beyond repair, she pressed her face in her hands and sobbed.

Frantic to learn what had caused Rosaleen to flee the parlor, Jacob brought the sermon to an abrupt close. After offering a quick benediction, he began searching the house.

He raced from room to room. Panic rose inside him when he failed to find her. If she'd felt sick, surely she would have gone to her room. Yet he found the little attic room unoccupied. He forced himself to knock at Ralston's door. Receiving no answer, he opened it and found it vacant as well. He shoved his fingers through his hair in an attempt to calm his mind. Surely she hadn't gone off with the man.

Think, Jacob, think! Oh God, You know where she is. Please show me.

The second the idea entered his mind, he flew down the stairs, out the kitchen door, and across town.

His heart fluctuated between relief and concern when he found her crying beneath Orville's willow. Her agonized sobs ripped at his heart. Was she ashamed of what she'd done last night? Had the man forced her against her will? Or had last night not been the first time?

He remembered what he'd heard two nights ago. Footsteps and whispers in the wee hours of the morning on the floor above his. He'd heard the sound of a man's boots on the stairs leading up to Rosaleen's room. When these facts assembled themselves in Jacob's mind, the picture they painted sickened him. Yet what other conclusion could there be?

Oh God, help me to show her love, not condemnation.

"Rosaleen"—he knelt at her feet and tenderly took her hands into his—"please tell me what has distressed you so. Is it Mr. Ralston and what happened between the two of you last night?"

"No!" She raised her face to his, a combination of anger, pain, and frustration brimming in her eyes. "Nothing happened between Alistair and me last night. Nothing!" Pulling her hands from his, she balled her fists in her lap. "He was drunk. I was just helping him back to his room. If you don't want to believe me. . ." She turned her tear-streaked face toward the river.

"I believe you, Rosaleen." Even as he said the words, there was a part of him that still wondered. "Then what is wrong?"

She swung her hurt-filled face back to his. "I wanted to belong. I've been reading the Gospels. I thought maybe Jesus would accept me, but I was only fooling myself." Her voice broke over another sob. "Your sermon today—I'm the strange woman you need to be delivered from. I'm part of the wicked that shall be cut off from the earth."

Jacob groaned. It pained him to think that his own sermon had contributed to her agony. "When the scriptures speak of the 'wicked,' they are referring to those who turn away from the Lord. You just said you've been searching for Jesus' acceptance." His voice softened with his melting heart. "My dear Rosaleen, He's already accepted you."

"I'm not sure that's possible."

"Why on earth would you think such a thing?" Had nothing he'd tried to teach her taken root?

"Because I'm dirty. Dirty, wicked, and irredeemable. You don't really know who I am. You don't know all that's happened to me."

"What, Rosaleen? What happened that makes you think Jesus wouldn't accept you?" Jacob attempted to put his arms around her, to comfort her, but she pulled away. His heart ached to bring her peace. "Jesus loves you, Rosaleen, and there is no sin too great for Him to forgive."

"You don't know! You don't know what's happened to me. . .or what I've done. Donovan didn't die the night of the accident," she blurted, gasping between sobs. "Black Jack Bill McGurty, a gambler and murderer, shot him. Then he took me, and for six months. . .for six months. . ." She couldn't seem to bring herself to finish the sentence. "An hour before the boiler exploded on the *Cortland Belle*, I'd considered taking my own life." Her body shook with her crying.

Stunned by the revelations, Jacob could only wonder what other dark facts she might have kept from him. Yet his heart broke at her anguish. This time she allowed him to gather her into his arms, hold her, caress her. Now he understood her night terrors. The unspeakable horrors she must have endured. He rocked her in his arms, pressing his lips against her hair. A feeling of protectiveness flooded Jacob. He knew without a doubt, for the rest of his life, he wanted to love this woman and make her feel safe.

Oh God, just help me make her feel safe.

"It's all right, my sweet," he murmured. "I won't let anyone hurt you ever again. Jesus loves you, and I love you. I love you, Rosaleen."

"Don't say that! You're wrong!" Tears streamed down her face. She jumped up from the bench and stepped away as if fearing her nearness might contaminate him. "Didn't you hear me? I was born wicked and shall always be wicked. I'm irredeemable!"

"Rosaleen, no one is irredeemable. Where did you ever get such an idea?"

Frustration set a sharp edge to Jacob's rising voice.

"The Reverend Wilfred Maguire, my former guardian. He is the minister of a church three times the size of yours." It hurt when she cast a look of disdain toward the new church of which he felt so proud.

"He's wrong, Rosaleen." Furious at the man for what he'd told her, Jacob couldn't keep the anger from his voice. "Why would a minister, of all people, say such a thing?"

She drew a deep, ragged breath. "He said he'd seen women like me and my mother all his life. He said we were just like the loose, common women who'd lured his father away from his mother and broke her heart. When I refused to denounce my mother as a harlot, he declared me wicked and irredeemable. He quoted scripture that says something about God not having mercy upon me because I was conceived in shame." She looked at him with sad, vacant eyes. "God hates me."

Jacob groaned. How could a minister of the gospel, because of a hurt from his past, so grotesquely twist the scriptures?

"Of course God doesn't hate you. That is just ridiculous! I believe the scripture you cited is from the book of Hosea and refers to the children of Israel who had strayed from God." He took a deep breath. She did not need his reproach. It was not her fault that she'd been told such a cruel thing. Guiding her back to the bench, he sat down beside her and folded her hands in his.

Oh God, give me the right words that will bring her peace and lead her at last to You.

"Rosaleen, God loves all souls, no matter how they came into this world. Psalm 139 talks about how God knows us and loves us even before we are born. 'For thou hast possessed my reins: thou hast covered me in my mother's womb.'"

He searched the blue green depths of her eyes glistening with tears. "Have you read any in the Gospel of John?"

She shook her head. "No."

"John 3:16–17, says, 'For God so loved the world, that he gave his only begotten Son, that whosoever believeth in him should not perish, but have everlasting life. For God sent not his Son into the world to condemn the world; but that the world through him might be saved.' The *world*, Rosaleen. You are part of the world. Christ doesn't reject anyone. People reject *Him*. You can be lost only by rejecting Christ."

"But Jesus talks about being pure. 'Blessed are the pure in heart: for they shall see God.'"

Jacob couldn't help grinning in spite of himself. "You *have* been reading the Gospels."

"I'm not pure, Jacob." She closed her eyes.

Watching tears slide from beneath her lashes to streak down her face rent Jacob's heart. He could only imagine the terror-filled scenes playing behind her closed eyelids. "Rosaleen, what happened to you was not your fault, not your sin. Remember what I told you on the Fourth of July? 'For all have sinned, and come short of the glory of God.' The prophet Isaiah, speaking of Christ, said, 'Though your sins be as scarlet, they shall be as white as snow; though they be red like crimson, they shall be as wool.' There is no sin too great for Christ to forgive. He paid the price for everyone's sins and left them on the cross. All that is required of you is to accept His gift of salvation. Do you believe that?"

"I—I want to."

Jacob felt a flash of frustration at her hesitation. How much plainer could he make it? She either wanted to accept Christ or she didn't. Perhaps she wasn't as eager as she pretended to leave behind the sinful life.

Even if nothing had happened between her and Ralston last night, she'd come in with him so had obviously been out with him. Jacob had heard Ralston invite her to the Billiard Saloon. That, coupled with the suspicious sounds he'd heard coming from the third floor several nights ago, caused him to question her sincerity and lash out at her.

"Do you?" His dry tone reflected his doubts as the old insecurities crept back into his heart. Was he so unpersuasive a preacher that he couldn't even bring the woman he loved to the Lord? "Rosaleen, Luke 16:13 says, 'No servant can serve two masters: for either he will hate the one, and love the other; or else he will hold to the one, and despise the other.' You must decide whether you want to cling to God or to the evils of this world."

He saw her back stiffen. "You *do* think I'm evil!"

"No, of course not. I never said that. . .Rosaleen!" Jacob hated the pride that caused him to remain on the bench and watch her stride up Broadway. He scrubbed his face with his hands then looked down at the stone beneath the willow. "Well, Orville, I really botched that, didn't I?" Because of his own pride he'd pushed her, causing her to turn from making a decision to accept Christ.

Oh God, just give me another chance.

Chapter 14

I love that hymn."

At Jacob's quiet voice, Rosaleen's hands stilled on the piano keys in midchorus of "There Is a Fountain." Her heart thumping, she turned to face him.

He stood in the parlor doorway, his shoulder leaning against the doorjamb. The tenderness in his eyes took her breath away. "Rosaleen, I'm so sorry I pressured you Sunday." He stepped into the room, his gaze glancing downward, his voice contrite. "I had no right to push you. Accepting Christ into your heart is a very personal thing. I—I only wanted. . ."

"Jacob, I'm sorry, too. I shouldn't have walked away like that." Rising, she hurried to him and touched his arm. How could he imagine he needed to apologize after the gift he'd given her? He'd led her to the verses of scripture that opened her eyes to Christ's love and acceptance. Reading those verses by candlelight on her mattress, she'd run weeping into the open arms of Jesus, inviting His love and salvation into her heart. "Oh Jacob, I have. You made me understand that Jesus does love me. He does accept me, and I've accepted Him."

The tears glistening in Jacob's eyes touched a sweet, deep place in her heart. "Rosaleen, you've made me so happy." His voice thick with emotion, he pulled her into his arms. "The angels in heaven are rejoicing with me. Jesus is rejoicing, too," he murmured against her hair.

Standing in the circle of his arms, she found it easy to imagine staying in Madison. Knowing that Christ had forgiven her sins, she no longer felt dirty, unworthy of Jacob. For the first time, she'd allowed her heart to harbor a tiny glimmer of hope that a future with him might be possible.

His blue eyes seemed to search hers as he pushed gently away. "I know you have your heart set on going to New York, but I'd like you to reconsider—"

Three quick raps at the front door broke off his sentence.

Reluctantly, Rosaleen wrenched herself away from his embrace. As she left the parlor, Jacob followed her to the front door.

When Rosaleen opened the door, Roscoe Stinnett looked past her shoulder as if she weren't there. "Reverend Hale, I wondered if I might have a few moments of your time."

"Yes, of course, Mr. Stinnett," Jacob replied in a less-than-enthusiastic voice.

Rosaleen answered Jacob's glance of regret with a weak smile. She, too, wished he could have finished his thought a few moments earlier in the parlor. Had he been about to ask her to stay. . .or something more?

After parking Roscoe's gray beaver hat on the hat tree near the front door, Rosaleen went to the dining room and informed Opal of Stinnett's arrival.

Opal walked to the sideboard. "I suppose you'd better offer him some tea and cookies." She began arranging a tea set of her best china on a silver tray. "Personally, I can scarcely abide the man, but he's the wealthiest man in Jacob's congregation, so he must be appeased," she said, placing several ginger cookies on two dessert plates.

Rosaleen picked up the tray and turned toward the kitchen to brew the tea.

"Oh, and Rosaleen," Opal added, halting her at the doorway, "after you attend to Jacob and Mr. Stinnett, would you please make up the beds in the two empty rooms? I hear the *Kentucky Queen* has docked, so we'd better be ready for more boarders."

Rosaleen nodded. The arrival of a steamboat usually meant a full house for the Buchanan Boardinghouse.

A few minutes later, the tray of refreshments in hand, Rosaleen neared the parlor. Roscoe Stinnett's deep voice from inside the room brought her to a sudden stop, causing the china pieces to clink together.

"I'm as eager as you are to get the church built, Reverend," he said. "Why, just the other day, our little Sophie mentioned what a beautiful setting it would be for a fall wedding—the finished brick church with a fine, grand bell tolling the happy event. I'm sure you can appreciate and share that vision."

Jacob's voice stumbled slightly. "Yes, yes of course."

The smile left Stinnett's voice, which hardened to a no-nonsense business tone. "I realize our congregation is small, and the building funds, shall we say, insufficient to expedite the task. I'm prepared to make Sophie's vision of a finished church by September a reality if you are prepared to make the wedding a reality."

Rosaleen's heart stood still then broke at Jacob's quiet response.

"I'd say that would be for the lady to decide."

A numb emptiness filled Rosaleen. How could she have believed, even for one moment, Jacob would prefer her over sweet, pure Sophie? And even if he did, how could she stand in the way of all the dreams he held so dear? If she stayed and Jacob chose her, Stinnett might very well cause a rift in the congregation, jeopardizing Jacob's dream.

"You look like death warmed over!"

Rosaleen jerked at Patsey's voice.

Patsey shook her head and reached for the tray. "Better give me that 'fore you drop it an' smash Mrs. Buchanan's good dishes. Imagine you best go lay down. 'Spect you've got a touch of the ague."

Feeling the strength drain from her limbs, Rosaleen didn't argue with Patsey. Mumbling her thanks, she allowed her friend to take the tray from her limp hands.

Rosaleen knew she should feel happy for Jacob. He'd be getting his church before winter, the bell he had his heart set on, and sweet Sophie for a bride. A host of feelings surged through her, but happiness wasn't one of them.

At the staircase, she swiped at a tear coursing down her cheek, grasped the balustrade, and started up the steps. One thought formed in her mind as a prayer. *I have to leave Madison. God, help me find a way to leave Madison.*

On the second-story landing, she collided with something solid. Emitting a soft gasp, she found herself engulfed in Alistair's arms.

"You keep runnin' into me like this, and I'll start thinkin' it's on purpose," he said in a teasing tone that sounded superficial.

Pushing away from his grasp, Rosaleen rubbed at the place beneath her throat where Alistair's embrace had caused her brooch to bite into the skin. Like the summer heat lightning that lit the window at the top of the stairway, a sudden thought flashed into her mind. She fingered her mother's brooch and said the words she'd vowed never to say. "Alistair, how much would you pay for my brooch?"

His eyes narrowed. "You'd never sell it before. Why now?"

"I want to leave Madison. I want to go to New York."

"Ah, New York. I haven't been to that city for years." Interest flickered in his gray eyes. "A town ripe for the picking, if memory serves. How 'bout we go together? What do you say?" He reached for her again, but she evaded his grasp. "How much will you give me?" She needed to keep this on a business footing.

"Fifteen dollars."

"No, fifty." He must think she'd learned nothing during her years on the riverboats.

A slow grin crept across his mouth. "You drive a hard bargain, and that's a fact. Your dad would be proud." He cocked his head toward the south wall. "There's a couple fellers on the *Kentucky Queen* who owe me. That's where I'm headed. Let me call in some markers, and I'll get your money."

A blinding flash of lightning and near simultaneous crack of deafening thunder caused her heart to lurch with her body.

"Scared of thunder?" Chuckling softly, he cast a quick glance at the summer storm brewing outside the little second-story window and clamped one arm around her. With his other hand he touched the jeweled brooch at her bodice, his breath warm against her face. "I can turn this little bauble into enough money to keep us in high style for weeks in New York," he told her in a husky whisper. Slipping both arms around her, he wrapped her in an iron-hard grip. "I like to feel you tremble in my arms."

Panic rose inside Rosaleen when he lowered his head and pressed his lips against the hollow of her throat. He'd abandoned his earlier casual friendliness. Alistair left no doubt as to his intentions.

She knew she was playing a dangerous game, but the brooch was the only thing of value she owned. Shaken, she twisted from his grip. "Just get the money."

"Eight o'clock next Sunday morning, we can take the *Swiftsure* packet to Cincinnati." He caught her arm, his gaze softening with his voice. "Rosaleen, I wouldn't pay so much if it were anyone else."

Rosaleen watched Alistair descend the stairs. She hated the fact that she'd allowed him to think she would be leaving with him. According to the *Madison Courier*, the packet *Swiftsure* left at eight a.m. every Tuesday, Thursday, and Sunday. Alistair had said Sunday, so she would simply leave the Thursday before—that was, if he got the money to her in time.

Several minutes later, she finished making up the beds as Opal had requested, and still shaky from her exchange with Alistair, Rosaleen went back downstairs. She'd need to find Opal and inform her that the rooms had been prepared. Hearing Opal's voice in the parlor, she walked into the room and studiously ignored Jacob's presence.

Opal stood beside the long front window that rattled from the latest thunderclap. "Fixin' to blow up a real dandy," she said, pulling back the lace curtain to peer at the darkening sky studded with barbs of sharp lightning.

Jacob rose from his desk chair. "Good thing Roscoe left when he did."

Rosaleen stood in the doorway, planning to head for the kitchen as soon as she'd given Opal the information. "The rooms are ready, Opal," she murmured, refusing to look in Jacob's direction. For the next several days she would need to perform a delicate dance, evading both Jacob's questions and Alistair's advances.

Opal let the curtain fall across the window, a look of concern wrinkling her broad brow. "Are you all right, Rosaleen? Patsey said—"

"I'm all right," Rosaleen blurted, eager to get away. The last thing she wanted at the moment was sympathy in any fashion.

Leaving the parlor, Opal said nothing as she passed her in the doorway, but her quizzical look questioned Rosaleen's claim.

Rosaleen turned to follow Opal, but the serious tone in Jacob's voice halted her.

"Rosaleen, I'd like to talk to you."

"The kitchen windows will need to be shut." She mumbled the excuse to leave, poised for a hasty retreat.

Jacob shook his head. "Andrew and Patsey are both in the kitchen, so I'm sure they've already taken care of that."

"I—I. . ." Unable to think of another reason not to stay, she simply turned and started toward the kitchen. Her heart felt unready to hear from Jacob's own lips the news of his engagement to Sophie Schuler.

A banging at the front door turned her around, and she hurried to answer it.

"Is Reverend Hale home?" The wind whipped the black slouch hat Charley Keller twisted in his hands. The worried look drawing hard lines on his face struck Rosaleen's heart with fear. She knew that Charley, a member of Jacob's congregation, belonged to the Fair Play Volunteer Fire Company.

"What is it, Charley?" From behind her, the fear tightening Jacob's voice echoed her own.

"It's the church, Reverend. Lightning struck it. We have a bucket brigade goin' from the river, but. . ." The helpless look in his eyes conveyed his grim prediction.

Chapter 15

Opal gasped and Jacob's face went paper white.

Bolting out the open door, he leaped from the porch and raced up Mulberry Street toward Main-Cross, Charley Keller at his heels.

Dread squeezed Rosaleen's throat as she and Opal watched from the porch until Jacob disappeared at the junction of Main-Cross and Mulberry. "I think we need to pray, Opal." She slipped a trembling arm around Mrs. Buchanan. Together, they walked inside to join the Chapmans in the kitchen.

Outside, the winds wailed, and leaves from the bowing ash and oak trees blew past the kitchen window.

Opal arranged four chairs in a crude circle and asked Andrew to lead them in prayer.

Rosaleen slumped to the seat of a kitchen chair, her tears mimicking the rain sheeting down the windowpane. The image of Jacob's church—his dream—consumed by flames gouged at her heart. *Why, God? Why?* How could God do this to such a good man? A man who'd worked so hard for Him. The man who never gave up on her but helped bring her to the salvation of Christ. The man she loved. Her heart ached, remembering the pride in his face as he'd gazed at the unfinished church.

Andrew sat with his head bowed, his arms resting on the tops of his legs and his fingers laced together. "We don't know Yer mind, Lord. But we 'cept Yer will and rest in Yer promises."

As Andrew prayed, Rosaleen remembered a scripture from the Gospel of John she'd read the night before. *"Jesus answered, Neither hath this man sinned, nor his parents: but that the works of God should be made manifest in him."*

How could this tragedy glorify God? Perhaps the rain had put out the fire, saving the church.

Hours later, Rosaleen realized there'd been no such miracle. Long after the Chapmans had left for home and Opal had gone to bed, Rosaleen could not bring herself to climb up to her attic room while still unsure of Jacob's safety. Regardless of her earlier resolve to avoid him, she could not abandon him tonight.

She sat at the piano, softly playing "Rock of Ages" by the flickering light of a single lamp. The jingle of the front doorbell halted her fingers.

Jacob trudged slump shouldered into the parlor, bringing with him the smell of wood smoke. The despair on his soot-streaked face confirmed her fears.

"It's gone." With those two words, he walked to his desk, pulled out the chair, and sank to the seat, a vacant look in his blue eyes.

"Oh Jacob, I'm so sorry." Choking back tears, she rushed to him, knelt at his feet, and took his sooty hands into her own.

"Was it my pride, Rosaleen? Was I too prideful about the church? Or is God just trying to tell me I'm not called to preach?"

Though her heart wept for his loss, Rosaleen's love for Jacob wouldn't allow her to sit mutely by as he turned his back on his dream of preaching in a church he'd helped to build.

"Not called? Jacob, it's because of your preaching, your guidance, that I sought Jesus. How can you believe God hasn't called you?"

"I just can't believe it's happened again." As she'd seen him do many times, he absently touched the scar on his left cheek. She'd wondered about the scar but had never asked.

"Is that how you got that. . .in a fire?"

"My family's barn burned when I was sixteen. When I went into the barn to chase out the livestock, I was burned by a piece of hot metal on a harness.

Smiling, she reached up and traced the raised scar on his cheek with her fingertip. "I've always found it attractive." Love bubbled up inside Rosaleen as she imagined the young Jacob's bravery during his family's tragedy. "Did God restore your barn?"

Even in the dim light and beneath all the soot, she saw Jacob's face flush at her touch. "Yes, the community raised us a new one." His mouth lifted in a wry smile. "But that was just a barn, Rosaleen, not a church."

Rosaleen gave Jacob's fingers a little squeeze and willed him to look into her eyes. "Jacob, that night when the *Cortland Belle* caught fire, before I knew God loved me, I'd considered drowning myself. But when the fire forced me into the river, something inside me wouldn't let me die. I know now that it was God, saving me so you could bring me to His Son. You told me Christ doesn't reject anyone. It is people who reject Him." She cupped the side of his face in her hand. "I'm a perfect example that God doesn't give up on us. So we shouldn't give up on Him, right? If God restored your barn, I'm sure He will restore your church."

His eyes shimmered with tears in the dim lamplight. Rising, he gripped her hands and helped her to her feet. "You are amazing," he murmured.

Her heart pounding, she stood immobile, held captive as his gaze melted into hers and he drew her into his arms. Melding into his smoke-scented embrace, she welcomed his kiss with a fervor that matched his. Half believing it was all a beautiful dream, Rosaleen prayed it would never end. She wanted to stay here forever in the arms of her beloved "angel."

In one swift movement, he knelt before her on one knee. "Rosaleen, I love you with all my heart, and I'll need you for the rest of my life. I don't think I can manage without you. Will you please do me the honor of becoming my wife?"

Her heart full to bursting with joy, she gazed down into his dear face through a mist of tears. At first she could only nod, emotion choking her voice. "Yes," she finally managed to squeeze through a sob. "Yes, yes, yes—" She couldn't stop saying the word until he stood, pulled her into his arms, and pressed his lips against hers once more.

A troubling thought intruded into her beautiful dream, and she pulled away from him. "But what about Sophie? I thought you and Sophie. . . I overheard Mr. Stinnett this afternoon. He said he'd pay for your church, even the bell, if you and Sophie. . ." She couldn't bring herself to finish the sentence.

"Darling"—smiling, he cradled her in his arms—"what Roscoe proposed would not be fair to either Sophie or me. Sophie deserves a man who loves her. I don't love her—not that way. I love you. You are the woman I want to be my wife." He grinned. "Besides, from what I understand, Sophie has a constant bevy of suitors. Roscoe Stinnett has no right to choose a husband for his niece."

Rosaleen could not so easily dismiss the concerns dulling her joy. She pulled away again. "But, Jacob, you need Mr. Stinnett's offer more now than before. What if he becomes angry and causes you trouble?"

"Sweet Rosaleen." Jacob drew her back into his arms. "You just reminded me not to limit God. If my church is to be, God will find a way."

Even as Rosaleen snuggled against Jacob, unease gripped her heart, choking her happiness. What if God had provided Roscoe Stinnett's offer as an antidote to the church fire? What if her selfish desire to marry Jacob denied him the church and congregation he had his heart set on?

Oh God, why can't things be simple? Please don't let this cause Jacob trouble.

⁓

"What you grinnin' like a 'possum about?" Patsey asked the next morning as she walked through the kitchen door, a basket of freshly picked okra on her arm.

Smiling, Rosaleen glanced up from rolling piecrust on the floured table. She'd decided to make Jacob's favorite, blackberry pie, for supper to celebrate their engagement.

Enveloped in the sweet euphoria of her beautiful dream, Rosaleen could scarcely believe the events of the night before. Though still worried about potential repercussions of her engagement to Jacob, she'd decided to trust God and bask in her happiness.

Patsey narrowed suspicious eyes at Rosaleen, her brow scrunched. Her words slowed to a thoughtful crawl. "Come to think on it, the rev'rend seemed unusual happy this mornin', considerin' the church burnin' an' all."

"Jacob asked me to marry him last night," Rosaleen blurted. She'd planned to keep it a secret for a while and hadn't even told Opal yet, but she felt her heart might burst with the news if she didn't free it.

Dropping the basket of okra onto the washstand, a wide-eyed Patsey screeched. Waddling around the table, she hurried to her. "I knowed it, I knowed it, I knowed it!" She hugged Rosaleen as tightly as her extended belly would allow. "When?"

"We haven't set a date yet."

"This time next year, yer li'ble to be in the same shape as me." Patsey patted her belly.

"Patsey!" Though heat flooded her face, Rosaleen couldn't help grinning at her friend's excitement.

"I can jis see our young'uns playin' on the floor together." Patsey seemed compelled to give her another hug. As she embraced her, she whispered, "Another train's comin' tonight. Crossin' the river 'bout midnight. Need every willin' hand to help. Can you meet me and Andrew behind the boardinghouse after dark?"

Rosaleen nodded. It would be harder now to keep such things from Jacob. She knew he would approve of her work with the Underground Railroad, yet she felt the need to protect him from such knowledge just as Andrew and Patsey protected one another. Rafe Arbuckle, or worse, the sheriff, might come to question him again.

~

Later that afternoon in the parlor, Rosaleen had to think what Alistair meant when he said, "I have your money."

Remembering their deal, she fingered her brooch. There was no need for her to sell it now, or was there? This morning, it had pained her to see Jacob's glum face when he returned from the bank. He'd been unsuccessful in procuring a loan for more lumber, and a look of dejection had clouded his eyes as he left the boardinghouse to help clear away the charred remains of the church.

Alistair pulled five ten-dollar notes from his vest pocket. "C'mon, love. A deal's a deal." At her hesitation, he held out his hand. With impatient movements, he curled his fingers toward his palm.

Blinking back tears, she removed the brooch, placed it in his hand, and accepted the money.

Oh God, please let this buy lots of lumber for the church.

Rosaleen planned to surprise Jacob with the money at supper. But long after the supper table had been cleared, he dragged himself into the boardinghouse kitchen. The exhaustion and defeat in his face as he collapsed to a caned chair at the little kitchen table ripped at her heart. He seemed almost too tired to eat the cold chicken, fried okra, and blackberry pie she placed before him.

He looked up at her, his eyes full of regret, his weary face and blond hair streaked with the soot of yesterday's fire. "I'm sorry, darling. Opal told me you made the pie to celebrate our engagement. But we're halfway through July, and there's not a minute to lose. I'd sure like for us to be married in that church before the snow flies."

"What about your bell money?" The money from her brooch wouldn't come close to what he needed, but it would double the money he'd saved.

He gave her a sad smile. "I know it sounds irrational. What use is a bell if there's no church, right? Yet I can't seem to bring myself to spend it on lumber."

"God will provide, Jacob. In fact, He has." She dipped her hand into her pocket, her fingers curling around what now represented her mother's brooch.

Standing, he yawned and rubbed his hand over his drawn features. "Please, Rosaleen, let's talk about it in the morning. I'm just too tired right now." He brushed a kiss across her lips then plodded from the kitchen.

Rosaleen drew her hand from her pocket. Perhaps it was best this way. Maybe after a good night's rest, Jacob would be more apt to view her offering as a blessing rather than a pitiful fraction of what he required.

That night, she tucked the money deep amid her mattress's straw stuffing then stole quietly out to meet the Chapmans.

Pink streaks of dawn stained the eastern horizon by the time Rosaleen parted with Patsey and Andrew and slipped quietly into the kitchen door of the boardinghouse. She'd spent the past several hours near the river's edge assisting the Chapmans and others connected with the Underground Railroad. Mostly, she'd helped dispense food, water, and dry blankets to a dozen or so brave souls who'd managed to cross the river at a shallow point under cover of darkness. Although exhausted, Rosaleen felt good about her nocturnal endeavors. She'd even assisted Andrew in bandaging the wound of a young man who'd been shot while fleeing slave hunters.

In her dark room, she changed into her nightdress and collapsed to her mattress.

Her next conscious sensation was warmth bathing her face. She opened her eyes, blinking against the bright morning sun flooding through the little window above her. Jumping up from her mattress, Rosaleen realized she'd overslept.

Her fingers flew as she threw on and buttoned up the dress she'd worn the night before. She stuffed the fifty dollars Alistair had paid her for the brooch into the pocket of her skirt. After breakfast, she would walk to the church site and surprise Jacob with the money.

Downstairs, she glanced through the parlor doorway and caught a glimpse of Jacob's blond head bent over the mahogany desk. She was glad to see he hadn't yet left for the church and prayed that her surprise would help cheer him up. "Jacob," she whispered, reluctant to disturb his prayer time. She took a tentative step into the parlor.

He raised his head but didn't look at her. Something in his demeanor caused her heart to quake.

"Jacob?"

He sat motionless, an unspeakable anguish veiling his blue eyes.

Assuming his attitude was caused by his despondency over the ruined church, she pulled the bank notes from her pocket. "I want you to have this—to buy lumber for the church."

He sprang from the chair, knocking it backward, sending Rosaleen's blood sluicing to her toes. The muscles worked in his jaw as if straining to hold in check the anger smoldering in his eyes.

When at last he spoke, the words he ground through his clenched jaw shredded her heart. "How can you imagine I'd want your dirty money?"

Chapter 16

Jacob's heart throbbed with exquisite agony as Rosaleen smiled and thrust a fistful of ten-dollar notes toward him. Then anger—blessed, blessed anger—surged through him, anesthetizing the pain. "Where's your brooch?"

"I—I sold it."

His eyes closed against the lie. Her offering confirmed the truth his mind and heart had rebelled against since Constable Rafe Arbuckle's visit just after dawn. What the constable told him when he handed him Rosaleen's brooch had frozen Jacob's heart to his ribs.

A knife fight had broken out during a card game at the Billiard Saloon. A man had been stabbed, but no one either could or would identify him. The participants of the game had skedaddled just before the lawmen arrived.

Rafe said he'd found Rosaleen's brooch among the money abandoned on the gambling table. Having remembered seeing her wear it, Rafe had brought it by, figuring it had either been lost or stolen.

Somehow Jacob forced his gaze to meet Rosaleen's. "Where were you last night, and how did you get that blood on your dress?" Though he realized it was useless to interrogate her, he couldn't seem to help himself.

"What?" She glanced down at her stained skirt and gasped. Obviously she hadn't realized her clothes bore the evidence of last night's escapades.

Her wide eyes held the look of a trapped animal. "I—I—"

"No, don't lie." He held his palm out toward her as she opened her mouth. Jacob couldn't help wondering if she'd truly experienced a conversion. He should have realized her life on the riverboats would equip her with the skills of an actress. Could he even trust anything she'd told him? There was no way to discern the lies from the truth.

"There is evidence that you were gambling at the Billiard Saloon last night. A man was stabbed, but then you know that." His gaze settled on her incriminating bloodstained skirt.

"You'd believe that about me?"

He steeled himself against the tears streaming down her face. *She's acting*, he admonished his melting heart. "The evidence is before my eyes!"

"If you can think such a thing of me, then I can never be your wife." She choked the words through realistic sobs.

"That, Mrs. Archer—if that indeed is your name, may be the most truthful statement you've made to me thus far."

As she fled the room in tears, he reached down and righted his chair then sank to its seat. Opening the desk drawer, he gazed for a moment at the gold and rose quartz cameo framed by tiny pearls and rubies—the brooch Rosaleen had pretended she cared so much about.

Had her conversion—the event that had made him believe again in his calling—been nothing but a farce, a sham? How could he now ignore God's voice telling him he was not fit for the ministry? He slammed the drawer shut, feeling as if his heart had been hollowed out.

Sitting numbly, Jacob stirred at the sound of the front doorbell.

Quiet murmurings and sniffling sounds emanated from the front hallway before Opal ushered Sophie Schuler into the parlor.

"Oh Jacob, you must help me. I—I don't know what to do." Sophie's little face crumpled, and her words dissolved into sobs. She rustled toward him in a dress of pale yellow silk that nearly matched the curls dangling at the sides of her face. Always struck by her small stature, he thought she'd never looked more doll-like.

"Sophie, dear, whatever is wrong?" He gathered his friend into his arms. *This must be the day for broken hearts.*

"It's Uncle Roscoe."

"Is your uncle ill?" Jacob guided her to the settee. Pulling a calico work kerchief from his back pocket, he offered it to the distraught girl.

"No, he is in fine health. He's just stubborn." She stamped her little foot on the carpeted floor. "It concerns Edwin, Edwin Applegate." She dabbed at her reddened eyes with the piece of calico. "Edwin and I have come to love each other very much," she managed between sniffs. "He has declared his devotion to me but is afraid to ask Uncle Roscoe for my hand."

Sophie's revelation caught Jacob off guard. He knew she'd become very friendly with the Applegate twins and that her uncle was less than pleased with that fact. However, embroiled in his own concerns of the heart, he'd had no idea she and Edwin Applegate had developed a romantic relationship. He had to assume Roscoe suspected such an alliance. Her uncle's attempt to coerce him into asking for Sophie's hand began to make sense.

Learning that Sophie had situated her heart upon Edwin Applegate brought Jacob a measure of relief. Though heartbroken and disappointed by Rosaleen, he had no intention of marrying a girl he did not love.

Feeling an affinity with his childhood friend's heartache, he strove to comfort her. "Your uncle's dispute is with Edwin's father, not Edwin. Perhaps you might ease him into the idea gradually. Have Edwin come to court you."

"That's just it. . ." A new wave of sobs shook her. Then, with a ragged breath, she seemed to compose herself. "Uncle Roscoe won't allow anyone by the name of Applegate anywhere near the house. Aunt Myrtle sympathizes and likes Edwin, but she loathes discord above all else and will not bring up the subject. Neither Papa nor my brother, Will, is here to help me, and I simply did not know where else to turn."

"Couldn't you write to your family for support?"

"Of course. But not knowing Edwin, they'd defer to Uncle Roscoe. You know they would." This admission brought with it a fresh gush of tears. "Oh, Jacob, you must intercede. Uncle Roscoe will listen to you. He will. He must." She daintily blew her nose on the kerchief.

"Yes, of course, Sophie." He took her lace-gloved hands into his. "You know I will do all that is in my power to see to your happiness." Meeting her shaky smile with his steady one, Jacob wondered if God had allowed his heartache so that he might better understand Sophie's.

"Oh, thank you, Jacob!" She wrapped her arms around his neck and kissed his cheek.

Jacob prayed for a happier conclusion to Sophie's romance than he'd experienced with his own.

⬿

After changing her bloody skirt for a clean one, Rosaleen started down the stairs. She'd fled the parlor, hurt by the fact that Jacob had been so quick to believe she'd patronized the seedy Billiard Saloon. After several minutes of cool reflection, however, she realized that her past, the bloodstains on her skirt, and her lack of another explanation might cause him to wonder.

Yet he had said there was *evidence* she'd been there. What evidence? Had Alistair claimed she'd been there with him? But then, she could not imagine Jacob believing Alistair or that Alistair would even make such a claim.

Only two nights ago, Jacob had asked her to be his wife. Surely he would believe her if she explained. Since Rafe Arbuckle had already questioned Jacob about the runaways, he'd most likely not question him again.

Unwilling to allow her and Jacob's love—their future together—to be unraveled by a misunderstanding, Rosaleen headed back to the parlor, anxious to mend the rift in their relationship.

What she saw when she reached the parlor doorway drained her blood to her toes. Jacob and Sophie Schuler stood entwined in each other's arms. She heard Jacob promising in tender tones to see to Sophie's happiness.

Stunned to numbness, Rosaleen turned and walked back to the stairway.

At the second-story hallway, she gazed out the window. Tears filled her eyes, obscuring the image of the couple in the open landau below her. She watched Jacob and Sophie drive away, and her beautiful dream evaporated, distilled into bitter tears that slid down her face.

Jacob had wasted no time accepting Roscoe Stinnett's offer, it would seem.

Anger replaced the numbness, salving Rosaleen's wounded heart. She fingered the bills in her skirt pocket. At least she still had the money from the brooch. Tomorrow was Thursday, so she could leave for Cincinnati on the packet *Swiftsure*. If she exercised some care, the fifty dollars might even get her all the way to New York.

As she headed for the stairs that led to her attic room, she heard what sounded like a low moan. It came from Alistair's room. Curious, she stopped. "Alistair, are you all right?"

"Go away." A fit of coughing followed his strained reply.

"Alistair, if you're ill. . ." When she heard another moan in response, Rosaleen opened the door.

Alistair lay drenched with sweat, still in the clothes he'd worn the day before. A deep maroon stain covered the left side of his chest.

Jacob's words slammed to the front of Rosaleen's mind. "Alistair, did this happen at the Billiard Saloon?"

"Yeah, little weasel accused me of cheating."

"Were you cheating?"

"Maybe." His grin twisted into a grimace. " 'Fraid I lost your brooch," he said, squeezing the words between groans as Rosaleen worked to gently remove his jacket and shirt.

"You didn't tell Reverend Hale that I was with you, did you?"

He swore beneath his breath as she extricated his arms from his bloody sleeves. "Course not. Ain't seen the good rev'rend."

She gasped at the ugly red wound just below his left collarbone. His assailant had obviously been aiming for Alistair's heart. She sent a silent prayer of thanks heavenward that the man's aim had been poor. The fact that Alistair had managed to walk the distance from the riverfront to the boardinghouse in this condition testified to his considerable constitution. He'd need it all if he were to ultimately survive the assault, she realized.

She examined the inflamed area around his wound. It felt hot to her touch. "I need to get Dr. Morgan."

"No." He clutched her hand, his gray eyes wild with fear and fever. "No doctor. But if you'd see to me I'd be obliged." A fresh spate of coughing followed his labored words. "Please. I helped your dad once, remember, Rosaleen? Could you help me, for old times' sake?" With each coughing fit, more blood trickled from the wound on his chest.

Her heart softened at the memory of Alistair standing between her consumptive father and the man who'd intended to thrash him after a card game went sour. "Of course I'll help you, Alistair. But you're very ill. You need a doctor."

"Doctors ask questions," he said with a painful-sounding gasp. "Can't take the chance. Don't think I'll be in any shape to leave Sunday, either."

"Just lie still. I'll take care of you." Although unscrupulous and flawed, Alistair was an old friend. Looking down at his features reconfigured with pain as he lay wounded—perhaps mortally—she knew she could not desert him.

Rosaleen's heart fell. She wouldn't be taking the packet to Cincinnati anytime soon.

Chapter 17

S ure wish you were here, old friend." Jacob shoved his fingers through his hair and dropped to the bench beside Orville's grave.

His meeting with Roscoe Stinnett had been, at least in part, successful. Roscoe had grudgingly agreed to allow young Edwin Applegate to court Sophie on the condition that she would not promise herself to him immediately.

Though not entirely happy with the compromise, Sophie had grasped her uncle's proffered olive branch. Later, she intimated to Jacob that she felt confident she'd soon persuade her uncle to bless her and Edwin's engagement.

Walking back from the Stinnetts', Jacob's conscience chafed. Perhaps he'd been too hasty in his judgment of Rosaleen. Needing to sort out his jumbled feelings concerning the woman he loved, he'd gone to the place where he communed most closely with the Lord.

Oh God, show me what You'd have me do. If it is impossible for our lives to merge, then why has my heart twined so tightly around hers?

He gazed up at the charred debris that would have been the new church. As he remembered her sweet encouragements, regret smote his heart. As a new Christian, she couldn't be expected to cast away her old life so easily. Her heart had been in the right place; she'd simply gone about it all wrong. She knew he needed money. And he could see how, having learned to gamble at her father's knee, she might turn to the gaming table as a way to procure quick cash.

He also realized his initial anger had been caused by the vision of Rosaleen spending an evening gambling in the company of Alistair Ralston. Somewhere in a deep, ugly little corner of his heart, suspicions concerning her relationship with the gambler still festered. But if she loved Alistair, and not him, why would she have offered the money for the church instead of simply leaving with the man?

Jacob scrubbed his face with his hand. He gazed out over the river dotted with barges and flatboats—many arriving with merchandise from all corners of the world. Rosaleen, too, had come from the river. And just like the items on these boats, she'd come from a place—a life—far different from his.

Remembering the pain in Rosaleen's eyes at his hateful rejection of her offered money, Jacob winced. Shame bowed his head. *I even questioned her sincerity in accepting Christ!*

He'd failed her. As a minister, it was his place to guide her, to help her grow in her new Christian life. Instead, he'd flung accusations at her, giving her no chance to explain. Whether or not they should ever marry did not change the fact that he loved her. He would always love her, and now he'd shirked his duty in ministering to her.

The scripture he'd quoted earlier to Roscoe Stinnett from Luke 6:37 echoed through his anguished mind, convicting him of his own shortcomings: "*Judge not, and ye shall not be judged: condemn not, and ye shall not be condemned: forgive, and ye shall be forgiven.*"

For weeks he'd been teaching her of Christ's message of forgiveness, but when tested, he'd failed to forgive her.

At the sound of a steamboat's whistle, he turned toward the Ohio. Gazing at the white riverboat with its huge scarlet paddle wheel at the stern, his eyes misted.

God, is that why You allowed me to fall in love with someone who came from a life so different from my own? Are You testing my willingness to forgive?

His heart and mind in turmoil, he walked down to Ohio Street then east toward Mulberry. As he passed the Billiard Saloon, he fought anger and pain. He could imagine the woman he loved—the woman he'd asked to be his wife—gambling beside Alistair Ralston.

By the time he'd reached the Newell Carriage Company at the junction of Mulberry and Second Street, Jacob knew he needed to talk to Becky and Ephraim. Perhaps they'd be better able to help him put it all in perspective.

When he came to the intersection of Mulberry and Main-Cross, he turned west and walked to the home of his sister and brother-in-law.

"Oh Jacob, come in. I am so sorry about the church." Becky gave him a warm hug as she ushered him inside.

What a comfort to feel his sister's arms around him. "Thanks, sis, but that's not why I'm here."

"What's the matter?" Becky's blue eyes, which so mirrored his own, filled with concern. She guided him toward the parlor.

Daniel bounded into the room, hope lighting his little face. "Uncle Jacob, will you take me fishing down at the river?"

Jacob gave his nephew a weak smile. He hated disappointing Daniel, but right now he needed Becky's counsel. "Sorry, Daniel. Next week, I promise."

"Daniel, go get that basket by the back door and pick a nice big mess of green beans from the garden for supper, please." Becky smiled at her son's sour expression. "And don't pick them too small," she added as he headed toward the kitchen.

When the back door slammed shut, she turned again to Jacob. "Is it Rosaleen?"

Sinking uninvited to the seat of a wing chair, Jacob felt a wry grin pull at his mouth. "How do you always know these things?"

Becky sat opposite him on the sofa. "I know the look of heartbreak when I see it. What's happened?"

He blew out a long sigh. "I thought I knew her, Becky. I was so sure she cared for me. So sure she'd given her heart to Christ. How could I have been so wrong—as a man and as a minister?" He raised his shoulders in a defeated shrug. "I'm seriously doubting that I'm fit for the ministry. . .or if I should even rebuild the church."

"Jacob, if you don't tell me this minute what's happened, I'm going to shake you!"

"She gambled down at the Billiard Saloon with that Ralston character then had the gall to offer me the money she'd won to help rebuild the church." Hurt and anger hardened his words.

Ephraim entered the parlor, a frown wrinkling his brow. "Excuse me for intruding, but I overheard some of what you were telling Becky. When do you believe Rosaleen was at the saloon?"

Jacob turned to face his brother-in-law. "Last night. Rafe Arbuckle brought her brooch by this morning. There was some kind of ruckus down at the Billiard Saloon last night. A gambler was supposedly stabbed during a card game, but all the players took off before Rafe got there. He found Rosaleen's brooch on the table where the fight took place."

Jacob hated the tears that sprang to his eyes when he recounted how Rosaleen had offered him fifty dollars this morning to help rebuild the church. He swallowed past the painful knot in his throat and fixed his brother-in-law with a hard stare. "Ephraim, I saw blood on the front of her skirt. What am I supposed to think?"

"I don't know how her brooch came to be at the Billiard Saloon, but she wasn't there. Not last night, anyway." Ephraim's voice slowed as he joined Becky on the settee, sliding his arm around his wife.

Jacob prayed Ephraim was right. "How do you know?"

Becky and Ephraim exchanged a long, knowing look, and Becky gave her husband a little nod.

Ephraim turned back to face Jacob. "Because she was down at the river with Andrew and Patsey, helping people come across."

"The Underground?" It had never crossed Jacob's mind that Rosaleen might have become involved in that work.

Ephraim nodded. "Andrew sent word this morning, asking me to stop by their house. I assumed it was to check on Patsey."

He went on to explain that when he arrived at the Chapmans', he found a young runaway slave who'd been shot in the shoulder. The doctor's lips tipped in a reassuring smile. "Andrew told me how Rosaleen helped him bandage the fellow when he came out of the river bleeding."

"She's been doing this, helping with the Underground?" Stunned, Jacob sat straight up.

"Yes." His brother-in-law hesitated before continuing. "I'm not at liberty to divulge any particulars, but I know she's been involved in several instances."

As much as he wanted to believe Rosaleen innocent of the happenings at the saloon, Jacob had to know for sure. "Maybe she was at the Billiard before she went to Georgetown?"

"Did Rafe say what time the altercation occurred?" Ephraim asked.

"About midnight."

Ephraim shook his head. "According to Andrew, Rosaleen was with them from about nine thirty last night until nearly dawn this morning."

Relief washed over Jacob.

Ephraim's smile broadened. "She obviously got the blood on her dress while helping to bandage that young man's wound."

Jacob groaned. A smothering wave of regret doused his joy at Rosaleen's exoneration. "You say she's helped with the Underground before?" That could explain the nocturnal sounds of comings and goings emanating from her third-floor attic room.

Ephraim nodded. "According to Andrew, yes."

"Jacob"—Becky's eyes were kind, her voice gentle as she took his hand— "talk to her. Get it all aired out. Don't let your pride get in God's way. And whatever you do, don't jump to any more conclusions."

Riddled with remorse, Jacob hurried back to the boardinghouse. He prayed that somehow Rosaleen could find it in her heart to forgive him.

When he arrived, he poked his head into the kitchen. "Opal, have you seen Rosaleen?"

His landlady turned from stirring a pot of beans on the stove. "I think she's upstairs." She gave him a questioning look. "Have you two had a spat? I thought I saw her crying earlier."

"Something like that, yes." Jacob forced a weak smile. He knew Mrs. Buchanan meant well, but he was in no mood to share the particulars of his and Rosaleen's difficulties.

While he passed Alistair Ralston's room, the sound of Rosaleen's voice stopped Jacob.

"Shh, Alistair. I promise I won't leave you." Her tender words, followed by deep moans and the creaking of a mattress moving, froze Jacob's blood.

The image forming in Jacob's mind cleaved his heart. With Herculean effort, he restrained himself from flinging open the door, revealing their shame.

What a fool he'd been. His desire for reconciliation with Rosaleen disintegrated as he flew down the steps.

Chapter 18

A listair, you must allow me to call Dr. Morgan." Rosaleen supported the back of his head and held a glass of water to his parched lips.

"No. I'll live or I'll die here, but I won't die on the floor of some jailhouse," he said, pushing the glass away.

Gently lifting the cotton bandage from his chest, she gasped at the putrid-smelling wound oozing pus. "Dr. Morgan won't turn you over to the sheriff, I promise you."

He grasped her wrist, his feverish gray eyes glistening with tears. "Rosaleen, the only promise I ask is that you, alone, will tend to me."

Rosaleen hesitated. She would do what she could to help Alistair, but she wouldn't lie for him. "All right, but I don't know how much longer I can keep your condition from Mrs. Buchanan, Patsey, . . .or Jacob." Her voice caught at the thought of the man she loved. In the two days since their confrontation in the parlor, she'd seen very little of Jacob.

Opal's and Patsey's subdued attitudes suggested they sensed the rift in Rosaleen and Jacob's relationship. But respecting the couple's privacy, the two women had said nothing.

Rosaleen simply told them she needed to attend to her friend, Alistair, who was under the weather—an expression they'd translate as having drunk too much.

As discreetly as possible, she'd carried bandages and fresh water to his room, but she had nothing to combat the deadly fever.

"At least allow me to get a bottle of that Smith's Tonic Syrup fever remedy Maynard's Apothecary has been advertising in the *Madison Courier*."

"All right." He seemed too weak to argue. "Look in my vest pocket. There's some money." As usual, too many words precipitated a coughing fit.

"Don't talk. I'll get it." She dipped a piece of cloth into the washbowl, wrung it out, and gently dabbed his mouth.

God, don't let him die. I've seen enough death. And maybe—just maybe—I can bring him to You.

She peeled a dollar from the folded bills in his vest pocket and could not help shaking her head. *Such a little bit of money couldn't have been worth risking your life for, Alistair.*

Assured that Alistair was again resting easy, Rosaleen left to purchase the medicine.

"Rosaleen."

As she closed Alistair's door behind her, Rosaleen jerked at Jacob's soft voice.

"I need to talk to you." There was a cool formality to his tone.

"I—I have to get something for Alistair." She couldn't bear another scathing diatribe from Jacob.

"This will only take a moment." His demeanor seemed more contrite than condemning. "I owe you an apology." His gaze avoided hers. "I was wrong to accuse you the other day. I've since learned from Ephraim that you were not at the Billiard Saloon the other night." He reached into his pocket. What he produced caused her eyes to widen.

"My brooch! Where did you get it?"

"Constable Arbuckle found it at the Billiard Saloon. I should have given it to you days ago." His penitent words seemed at odds with his stiff tone. "I'm sorry. I have no excuse for my actions."

Rosaleen paused, waiting for him to ask her to reinstate their engagement. When he didn't, disappointment surged through her. She shook her head. "It's no longer mine. I sold it to Alistair. . .for money to go to New York." Her voice faltered as she remembered Jacob's angry rejection of that money.

To his credit, a look of surprise registered on his face, followed by something akin to shame. "You're still going, then?" His voice tightening, he looked everywhere but in her eyes.

"Yes." Her voice caught on the word. She could see no reason to stay. Jacob would soon be marrying Sophie. As fond as Rosaleen was of Sophie, she couldn't bear to stay and watch it happen.

"Guess I should give this to Mr. Ralston, then," he said.

Tears sprang to her eyes as she watched Jacob hold in his open palm the piece of jewelry she'd treasured all her life.

"He's—he's not been feeling well for the past couple of days." She stumbled, not wanting to lie, yet at the same time, trying to keep Alistair's injury secret. "Would you please keep it until he's better?"

"Of course." A hint of a smile?

Brushing past him, she fled down the stairs. Alistair needed the fever medicine, and Jacob Hale's nearness inflicted far more torture on her heart than Rosaleen cared to endure.

❧

Jacob started toward his room but stopped at the door. He gazed at the jeweled pin in his hand. It reminded him of his love for Rosaleen. No matter what her relationship with Alistair Ralston, Jacob knew he would always love her. Why should he keep this reminder of his loss a minute longer than necessary? If Ralston had a throbbing head from drinking whiskey down at the Billiard Saloon, that was just too bad.

"Mr. Ralston? Mr. Ralston?" He rapped twice on the man's door. Getting no reply, he pushed it open. What he saw set him back on his heels.

"Go away! She said she wouldn't tell." Ralston reared up then fell heavily back onto the pillow, coughing.

Like a lightning bolt, the larger reality shot through Jacob. Ralston must have been the man knifed down at the Billiard. "You're in a bad way, man."

Jacob walked to the bed where Ralston lay shirtless, a bloodstained bandage covering his chest. He realized, too, that what he'd imagined happening between Rosaleen and Alistair two days ago could not have been possible. Jacob's groans echoed those of the wounded man on the bed. "Rosaleen never told me. She only said you weren't feeling well. I supposed you'd just had too much to drink."

"You won't tell anybody about my. . .accident, will you, Rev'rend?" Fear flickered in the big gambler's eyes.

Jacob glanced at the bloody bandage covering the man's chest. "I won't tell if you don't want me to, but if a doctor doesn't attend you soon it won't matter. You'll be dead."

"There was a bit of a misunderstandin' down at the Billiard a couple nights ago. I don't want to go to jail—" A wheezing cough swallowed Ralston's words.

Jacob lifted the bandage. "My brother-in-law is a doctor. Ephraim won't tell the sheriff. He'll simply tend to you." The look of relief on the man's face sparked sympathy in Jacob.

Tension seeped out of the man's ashen features. "All right, but would you promise me something, Rev'rend?"

"Sure."

"I—I don't have much, but if I die, would you see to it that Rosaleen gets everything?"

"Yes, of course." Jacob gave the man a small smile. "I've seen men in worse shape make it." He hoped his voice carried more conviction than he felt. "Would you like me to pray for you?"

Alistair's soft chuckle turned to a series of coughs. "Sure, Rev'rend. Rosaleen's been prayin' over me for two days. Maybe somethin' will get through, huh?"

"It all gets through, my friend," Jacob said, patting the man's shoulder. After offering up a prayer for Alistair, Jacob added a silent prayer, asking God's forgiveness for misjudging Rosaleen.

"I believe I have something of yours, Mr. Ralston." Jacob fished in the pocket of his trousers and pulled out the brooch. "Rosaleen tells me she sold this to you some days ago."

"Yes." Alistair's eyes grew wide, and, with a deep groan, he pushed up to a sitting position.

"Was this still in your possession when you left the gambling table?" If he'd lost it in the game, Jacob would hand it back to Rafe Arbuckle to put in the sheriff's sale.

"Yes. I'd just thrown it into the pot, but it was still mine. I never got the chance to finish the hand."

"You swear that's the truth?"

"That's the truth, Rev'rend."

"Then I'd like to buy it from you." Jacob didn't blame Rosaleen for hating him. He'd accused her without allowing her an opportunity to explain. He didn't deserve her love or her forgiveness, nor did he expect them. The thought skewered his heart. He could never make up for how he'd treated her, but he *could* do this for her. "How much did you pay her for it?"

Alistair glanced down at the patchwork quilt. "Seventy-five dollars."

A quick anger replaced the sympathy Jacob had felt for the man. Rosaleen had offered him fifty, and his heart told him she would have offered all she had. "This is no time for a ruse, Ralston," he growled. "I'll give you fifty."

"Fifty will do."

Jacob walked to his room and reached under his bed for the tattered cigar box. A feeling of gratitude washed over him. Perhaps this was why he'd resisted spending his bell money even after the church burned.

Thank You, Jesus, for whispering to me not to spend this on new lumber.

Back in Alistair's room, Jacob counted out the money. "Fifty dollars."

"Put it in my vest pocket." Ralston rammed a thumb toward his gold brocade vest draped across the back of a wing chair.

Jacob stuffed the bills into the showy piece of apparel then turned back to the man. "Mr. Ralston, I made a promise to you, and now I ask you to make a promise to me. Don't tell Rosaleen that I bought the brooch."

"I won't. You love her that much, don't you?" His soft tone sounded distant.

"Yes." Jacob watched the expression on the man's face closely, but Alistair gave little away. The wince could very well have been from the pain of his wound.

"She's in love with you, too, you know." An odd grin pulled up the corners of Ralston's lips. "In my line of work, you learn to read people. Listen,"—a frown puckered his forehead—"beware of a gent by the name of McGurty. He'll have designs on Rosaleen."

"She told me about him." A sudden fear twisted inside Jacob. What if he were in Madison? "The man survived the sinking of the *Cortland Belle*?"

"Can't rightly say."

"You haven't seen him?"

Ralston shook his head. "No. Heard it both ways, but then—" Several more wracking coughs took him. "You can't take as gospel what fellers deep in their cups say over a blackjack table."

Jacob studied Ralston's face. The best he could discern, the man's answer seemed candid. "What does McGurty look like?" Madison teemed with strangers from the steamboats. A description of the man would be helpful.

The gambler's features took on a thoughtful look. " 'Bout your height. In his forties, I'd reckon. Black Irish. Black hair, thinnin' some and streaked with gray. Little black eyes, dead cold as polished onyx—stares right through a body. Chills ya to your soul. Got a bit of a paunch. Likes good food, drink, and women, not especially in that order." A wheezing cough that troubled Jacob interrupted Alistair's description of McGurty.

"Here, take a drink of water." Jacob filled a glass from the pitcher Rosaleen had left on the table by the bed.

"A real dandy dresser," Alistair continued after a sip of the water had eased his cough. "Always carries a silver-headed, ebony walking stick."

"Thanks." Jacob offered the man his hand and was surprised at the strength of his grip, even in his weakened state. "I'll fetch Dr. Morgan."

Later, Jacob placed the brooch in the cigar box where he'd kept his bell money. In a few days, Rosaleen would be leaving for New York. He'd like to think that Ralston's perception of her feelings about him were correct. Maybe they had been once. But he felt certain he'd destroyed any hope of rekindling her love.

His heart twisted as he gazed at the jeweled pin. Maybe when he presented it to her as a farewell present, she'd at least remember him with some measure of kindness.

Chapter 19

After Dr. Morgan treated Alistair Ralston, Rosaleen followed him and Jacob to the hallway outside Alistair's room.

Ephraim Morgan turned a stern look toward Rosaleen. "Jacob was right to fetch me, Rosaleen. I know you were trying to protect Mr. Ralston, but by not calling me sooner, you allowed your friend to become dangerously ill."

Rosaleen gave him a penitent nod. She sent up a prayer of thanks that God found a way to get the doctor here without her having to break her promise to Alistair.

The doctor's features relaxed to a reassuring smile. "He should heal fine as long as the fever doesn't return and the wound doesn't become infected again."

Brightening, Dr. Morgan turned his attention to Jacob. "Becky tells me Roscoe Stinnett has offered to put up the collateral in order to procure a loan for the church. That's great news."

"Yes, it is." Jacob fidgeted, seeming uninterested in elaborating on the subject.

An awkward moment of silence ensued while Rosaleen and Jacob watched the doctor descend the stairs.

Rosaleen broke the silence. "I'm glad you're going to get your church rebuilt, Jacob. That is wonderful." She meant it, too, but at the same time wondered if he'd taken Roscoe up on his offer concerning Sophie after all. If so, why had Jacob not told her? Was he too embarrassed to admit he'd made such a deal?

"Thank you." His gaze skittered away from hers.

She managed to push her trembling lips into a smile. "I'm glad you didn't listen to me and went in to see about Alistair."

"Me, too." He grinned. "He's not such a bad fellow for a gambler and a rogue. He'll soon be off running his thimblerig again with the best of them."

"I'd like to think I could convince him to reform, but I'm afraid it is unlikely, even with all my prayers."

"I'm sure you've planted the good seeds, Rosaleen. In the end, praying is the best thing we can do." His smile faded. "You'll be leaving with him, then?"

"No." Rosaleen's heart felt as wounded as Alistair's chest. If only she could have stayed. If only things had turned out differently. "Alistair will be going places I don't care to go now and doing things I know Jesus would not want me to be a party to."

"I'm glad to hear that. Then you'll be leaving on your own for New York?"

His voice sounded strained. Did he want her to stay?

She fought the tears stinging behind her eyelids.

Please, Jacob, beg me to stay. Take me in your arms and tell me you want me to stay here with you forever.

She struggled to inject lightness into her answer. "Yes, I promised Alistair I'd take care of him until he's well. Then I'll begin my journey to New York."

The corner of Jacob's mouth lifted. "I'd very much like it if you'd continue to play for services while you remain in Madison. Would you do that for us and save the congregation a little while longer from Myrtle Stinnett's charity?"

Her heart galloped when he took her hands into his. Both their gazes focused on their clasped hands.

"Yes, Jacob, I'd like that very much." Hope withered. If he still loved her and hadn't given his promise to Sophie, now was the time he should beg her to stay—to entreat her never to leave him. Tears she couldn't allow him to see stung Rosaleen's eyes. Pulling her hands away from his strong, warm fingers, she fled down the stairs.

～∞～

During the next couple of weeks, Rosaleen used the excuse of caring for Alistair to avoid Jacob. Though she'd relinquished the hope of ever becoming Jacob's wife, she held tight to her newfound faith. She'd always love Jacob. How could she not? He'd led her to the knowledge that God did indeed love her and would one day welcome her into heaven.

She longed to share this promise with others. Perhaps she could find a way to use her musical talents for the Lord. At present, she'd content herself with sharing the gospel with Alistair. Though an admitted challenge, he presented a captive audience.

"Never thought you'd become a church lady." Grinning, he shook his head, interrupting her daily scripture reading.

"I'm not a church lady. I'm a Christian." Rosaleen closed the Bible on her lap. "Alistair, you could have died. Aren't you concerned about what lies beyond?"

"Don't reckon I like to give it much thought." He grimaced, shifting to a more comfortable sitting position on the bed.

"Well, you need to think about it." She set the Bible on the table by the bed and bent over to adjust the pillows behind his head.

"You'll make a right pretty angel someday, Rosaleen." His gray gaze looked a little sad as he ran the back of his curled fingers across her cheek. Then his demeanor perked up with his voice. "I do like the music, though. I never knew you played the piano." He leaned his head back on the pillow and closed his eyes.

"I didn't before I went to the finishing school. I suppose I can thank my guardian for that, even if he did send me for selfish reasons. Funny how the Lord can take a bad situation and turn it into a blessing."

She'd been astounded at how much lighter her heart had become after she obeyed Christ's command and forgave Wilfred and Irene Maguire. With repeated reading, she'd etched into her heart Jesus' words from Matthew 5:44: *"But I say unto you, Love your enemies, bless them that curse you, do good to them that hate you, and pray for them which despitefully use you, and persecute you."*

Black Jack Bill McGurty? He'd be far harder to forgive, but Rosaleen would try.

Alistair rolled his head on the pillow, his gray eyes peering at her from beneath half-open lids. "Would you sing me that song again? The one about the rock."

Rosaleen smiled. Perhaps she could get through to Alistair with her music. She softly sang "Rock of Ages" until his deep, even breathing told her he'd fallen asleep.

A recurrence of infection along with another bout of fever had kept Alistair bedridden. But under the watchful care of Dr. Morgan, he was now showing steady improvement, causing the doctor to predict Alistair would be back on his feet within the week. Rosaleen would soon be free to leave for New York. A pang of sadness accompanied the thought as she slipped quietly from Alistair's room and climbed to her own room in the attic.

Knowing she would need to prepare for that day, Rosaleen stuck her hand into the mattress slit and felt for her calico sack. Finding it, she separated one of the ten-dollar notes from the fold of bills, shoved it into her apron pocket, and headed downstairs.

Exiting through the kitchen door, she paused on the path between the boardinghouse and the garden to glance back at the gray brick building. It hurt to think of leaving Madison and all the people who'd become dear to her. Yet if Jacob had wanted her to stay, he could have asked. Her heart still stung from the fact that he hadn't.

Squaring her shoulders, she raised her chin. She must concentrate on practicalities. She'd need a small steamer trunk or portmanteau to transport her few but precious possessions to New York. She could probably procure what she needed at King and Brother Merchants on Second Street.

"Rosaleen!" Patsey's cry sounded tight with pain.

Whirling toward the garden patch, Rosaleen caught sight of Patsey's red head kerchief, just visible above the browning leaves of the potato plants.

"I—I think the baby's comin'." Sitting in the dirt amid the drying vegetation, Patsey glanced down at her drenched calico skirt.

"But it's too soon! It's almost a month too soon." Rosaleen fought mounting fear.

"Reckon you'd best tell that to this young'un." Groaning, Patsey doubled over.

Rosaleen's mind raced with her heart. Andrew was down at the building site of the church with Jacob. She didn't know whether it would be better to help Patsey up or have her sit until she could get Andrew.

Oh God, just help me know what to do.

Drawing a deep breath, she forced her mind to rational thought. *Mrs. Buchanan will know what to do.*

"Just sit still, Patsey. I'll find Opal."

Patsey's answering groan warned there might not be a moment to spare.

Racing through the kitchen, Rosaleen began calling for Opal.

"Rosaleen, what on earth—" Opal began as she emerged from the dining room.

Rosaleen caught her hand. "Patsey's in the garden. I think she's in labor."

Opal paled and bolted for the kitchen door.

Rosaleen ran to catch up with the older woman's long-legged strides, directing her to the spot where she'd left Patsey.

"Come on, Patsey, you can't have this baby in the tater patch." Opal grasped Patsey under the arms and carefully but firmly lifted her straight up.

Together, Opal and Rosaleen helped Patsey into the house.

"I know it won't be easy, Patsey, but we must get you upstairs to a bed," Opal urged in a no-nonsense tone as she and Rosaleen practically carried Patsey between them.

"I can make it," Patsey gasped. "Ain't gonna' have this chil' on the floor or the dining room table, neither!"

Rosaleen breathed a relieved sigh when they reached the second floor.

They maneuvered the mother-to-be into a room Rosaleen had readied for prospective boarders. Opal yanked the covers down on the bed, sat Patsey on the edge of the mattress, and then turned to Rosaleen. "I'll get her into a nightdress. You hurry and fetch Andrew and Jacob."

Rosaleen flew down the stairs, out the boardinghouse, and up Mulberry Street. She raced down Main-Cross Street and just missed being hit by a passing carriage.

Oh God, give me strength and speed.

By the time she reached the church, her burning lungs felt as if they might burst.

"Rosaleen!" Jacob caught sight of her and threw his hammer to the ground with a thud. "What's happened?" Running to her, he drew her into his arms and held her while she gasped for breath to speak.

"It's Patsey." She gulped a lungful of air. "The baby's coming."

At his wife's name, Andrew dropped the wheelbarrow of bricks he'd been pushing, paying it no heed as it toppled and spilled its contents onto the ground. His dusky face blanched to only a few shades darker than Jacob's, and he raced for the wagon.

Her legs spent, Rosaleen sagged against Jacob. She allowed his tightened arm around her waist to propel her to the wagon. He helped her up then climbed to the seat beside her.

Andrew hollered and smacked the reins down hard against the mules' backs. The animals bolted, causing the wagon to lurch to a dizzying speed.

The wagon bed full of lumber bounced and clattered as they careened along. Rosaleen clung to Jacob, fearing they might overturn at the junction of Main-Cross and Mulberry. There, they narrowly missed a wagonload of pork barrels.

Ignoring the frightened neighs of the rearing horses and the angry protests of their driver, Andrew urged the mule team around the corner, stopping only when they reached Opal Buchanan's boardinghouse.

In a blur, Patsey's husband leaped from the wagon, bounded to the porch, and shot through the front door.

Jacob helped Rosaleen down then climbed back to the wagon seat. "I'll go get Ephraim," he called over his shoulder as he turned the wagon around.

Rosaleen nodded and headed inside. Upstairs, she informed Opal and the expectant parents that Jacob had gone to fetch Dr. Morgan.

Andrew nodded but kept his eyes fastened on Patsey's face, scrunched with pain. Kneeling beside his wife's bed, he gently took her hand in his. In soothing tones, he whispered words of love and encouragement.

"First babies always take awhile," Opal said lightly, bathing Patsey's face with a wet cloth. But the lines around the older woman's mouth looked tight.

When Dr. Morgan arrived with Jacob, the concern on his face struck fear in Rosaleen's heart. He immediately banished her and Jacob from the second story. He allowed Opal, and on Patsey's insistence, Andrew, to remain in the room.

Guilt-ridden, Rosaleen sank forlorn to the settee in the parlor. She'd spent too much time the past couple of weeks with Alistair, shifting a larger portion of the household work to Patsey. Now Patsey and her baby might have to pay with their lives. The thought was more than Rosaleen could bear. Slumping forward, she sobbed into her hands.

"Ephraim has delivered lots of babies. I'm sure everything will be all right," Jacob's quiet voice comforted.

"It's my fault," she choked through the sobs. "I spent too much time attending to Alistair and not helping Patsey."

His soft voice murmured consolation. "No, my dear Rosaleen. No." Sitting down beside her, he gathered her into his arms and rocked her against him. "You know Opal would never allow Patsey to do more than she should. You felt an obligation to Mr. Ralston. You are not to blame—not in any way."

Rosaleen wondered how she could have been so selfish. Why had she not once thought of Patsey's condition during the past two weeks? "If anything should happen to Patsey or the baby, I don't know if I could bear it." Devastated, she clung to Jacob, weeping against his neck.

"Shh, my sweet, don't do this to yourself. It is not your fault. Ephraim says many times babies come early and only God knows why." He pushed away enough to wipe the tears from her cheeks with his thumbs. "I think we should go to God right now, don't you?"

She nodded, reluctant to leave the haven of his embrace.

Holding her hands in his, he pressed the side of his face against hers. His breath felt soft, warm, and comforting against her ear as he whispered a prayer for Patsey and her baby's safety.

~

The sound of an infant's lusty cries caused them to spring apart. Jumping up, they ran to the bottom of the stairs.

After a few breathless moments, Dr. Morgan came to the second-story landing at the top of the stairway, his shirtsleeves rolled up to his elbows. "It's a boy," he announced, grinning. "He's a bit small, but by the sound of him, there's nothing wrong with his lungs. Patsey's exhausted but doing well," the doctor said before returning to Patsey's room.

"Thank You, Jesus!" Jacob shouted his prayer of thanks.

"Yes, Jesus, thank You! Thank You!" Rosaleen echoed, wiping the tears from her face. She felt weak as the tension drained away from her body.

Jacob and Rosaleen fell into each other's arms, their mutual relief gushing out in joyful laughter. When Rosaleen pushed away, Jacob gazed into her eyes. His smile faded as he whispered her name. Suddenly his eyes closed and his arms tightened around her, his mouth capturing hers.

Returning his caresses, Rosaleen floated for a glorious moment in the fantasy of her beautiful dream before reality gripped her. *No! I mustn't do this. Not until Jacob makes his intentions clear. Not until he asks me to stay.*

Shaken, she pulled away from him and fled upstairs.

After Dr. Morgan left, Rosaleen tidied up Patsey's room, glad to have something to take her mind off the kiss she'd shared with Jacob.

Opal washed the newborn infant then swaddled him in a soft cotton towel.

"He is the most beautiful thing I've ever seen," Rosaleen said, tensing as Opal placed the tiny, squirming infant in her arms. "I've never held a baby, let alone a newborn baby."

"You're doin' fine. Just support his head," Opal instructed with a smile.

"We've decided to call him Adam, since he's our first," Patsey said, grinning from her bed. "Andrew couldn't wait to git over to Georgetown to crow about him."

"I should think so, with a fine son like little Adam here." Rosaleen carefully deposited the mewling baby in the crook of his mother's arm.

Offering to start supper while Opal tended to the new mother and baby, Rosaleen descended the stairs. Jacob was nowhere in sight, and she was glad. Her heart still quaked from their impulsive kiss.

As she neared the bottom step, three quick raps sounded at the front door. She answered the door and blinked in surprise to find Sophie Schuler's beaming countenance.

"I'm afraid Jacob is not here," Rosaleen said, managing a weak smile.

"It's not Jacob I want to talk to. It's you."

"Me?" What business could Sophie have with her? The answer came as swiftly and unexpectedly as a stiletto through the heart.

"Oh, Rosaleen," she said with an excited squeal, "I so have the hypo, I can scarcely contain myself!"

Rosaleen knew from her time at the finishing school that "hypo" was a term young ladies used to express extreme excitement.

"I've just become engaged to be married, and I want you to play for my engagement party as well as for my wedding."

Staring at Sophie's face crinkling with excitement, Rosaleen felt the blood drain from her own. So Jacob had gone directly from kissing her to proposing marriage to Sophie.

Chapter 20

On the front porch, Sophie bobbed back and forth, her hoop skirt swaying like a tolling bell. "Could I speak with you in the parlor, please?"

"Yes, of course. Please come in." Reeling from the shock of Sophie's announcement, Rosaleen tried to remember her manners. She stepped aside, allowing Sophie to swish past her into the front hallway. As she led the girl to the parlor, Rosaleen knew she must not forget that Sophie was an innocent in all this. "Would you like some tea, Miss Schuler?"

"No, please don't trouble yourself." Sophie carefully arranged her skirts as she lowered herself to the settee. "I am most anxious to discuss the particulars with you."

"Well, Miss Schuler"—Rosaleen hesitated as she took a seat opposite Sophie—"I'm not at all sure my participation will be possible." With sheer force of will, she battled the tempest raging inside her. It took all her strength to stay seated in the armchair, wearing what she hoped was a pleasant expression on her face. "Actually, I'm not planning to stay in Madison much longer."

In truth, Rosaleen longed to race to her room, grab her fifty dollars, and leave Madison with the clothes on her back by whatever means available.

"Oh." Sophie's delicate features wilted. "Edwin will be so disappointed."

"Edwin?" Rosaleen blinked in confusion.

"Yes, my fiancé, Edwin Applegate."

Astonishment, relief, and confusion swirled through Rosaleen. "You're—you're not marrying Jacob?"

"Jacob? Good heavens, no!" Sophie cackled. "I must confess I considered it once or twice when I was a child. But now that I'm grown, I find my affection for Jacob more closely resembles that for my brother, Will." As she exhaled a soulful sigh, a dreamy look came into her pale blue eyes, and she pressed her hand against her heart. "Only Edwin, my darling Edwin, causes my heart to take flight, then lighting, it indulges itself in hours of happy contemplation of our coming union."

Rosaleen couldn't help smiling at Sophie's poetic effusion, so representative of young ladies of the social elite.

"My engagement ball is only two weeks away. Surely you can stay that long." Her eyes hopeful, Sophie bit her bottom lip.

"Yes, I suppose I could." Still attempting to adjust to this new revelation, Rosaleen found the smile came much easier to her lips.

"Oh, that is wonderful!" Clapping her gloved hands together, Sophie actually bounced on the settee. "Of course, you must have a new gown for the occasion. I will send Aunt Myrtle's seamstress to take your measurements."

"I—I really can't afford a gown. . . ." Every precious dollar Rosaleen had gotten for her brooch would be needed for her trip to New York, not to mention accommodations.

"Oh, fiddle-dee-dee!" With a flip of her hand, Sophie dismissed the concern. "Uncle Roscoe and Aunt Myrtle are paying for everything. The weather has stayed warm, so Swiss muslins and linen lawns would be permissible, but this being an evening affair, we simply must be in silks and taffetas. Don't you agree?"

"I—I suppose."

Sophie is not marrying Jacob. The thought drowned out the girl's prattle about the newest fabrics that had just arrived at the dry goods store.

Rosaleen mentally wrestled with the puzzling turn of events. *If Jacob isn't planning to marry Sophie, why hasn't he asked me to stay in Madison?* He'd once asked her to marry him—begged her to marry him. He confessed that he'd wrongly accused her of gambling at the Billiard Saloon, even asking her forgiveness for his hasty judgment. Had he since thought better of it and decided to leave well enough alone after she'd called off their engagement?

"Rose. Yes, rose for Rosaleen," Sophie said with a giggle.

"What?"

"Rosaleen, you *must* keep up!" Sophie gave an exasperated sigh. "I said, with your coloring, that rose silk I saw at Fitch & Williams would be just perfect for you, don't you think?"

Rosaleen smiled. "That sounds wonderful. I can't wait to see it." There would be plenty of time to assimilate the heart-jarring news. Just now, Sophie deserved her full attention.

After a half hour of discussing quadrilles, ballads, and serenades, Sophie rose, smoothing wrinkles from her apricot lawn skirt. "Well, I have a million things to do and little time to accomplish them all."

Rosaleen hugged Sophie, realizing she hadn't even offered the girl her best wishes. "Please allow me to extend my most sincere felicitations."

"Thank you, Rosaleen." Sophie gave her a quick peck on the cheek. "I can scarcely wait to tell Edwin you've agreed to play for our engagement ball." Her eyes grew round while her little pink lips drew into a dainty pout, reminding Rosaleen of a child begging for a treat. "Won't you please consider staying until after the wedding in October? It would mean so much to us if you were to play for our wedding."

"I will consider it," Rosaleen said as she walked Sophie to the front door.

Returning to the parlor, Rosaleen stood at the front window and watched Sophie's carriage drive away. Her heart sagged with her shoulders. Jacob had said he wasn't in love with Sophie. Now she must assume, despite the kiss they'd shared earlier, he must have decided he wasn't in love with Rosaleen, either.

⟞∾⟝

Jacob stood in the Madison Branch Bank beside Roscoe Stinnett. "I want to thank you for this loan, Roscoe," he said, dipping a pen into an inkwell and scratching his signature onto the document. "I reiterate the fact that it is a *loan*. You will be paid back with interest."

"I'm a businessman, Reverend. Loans are part of what I do." Stinnett cleared his throat. "Besides, Myrtle and Sophie have their hearts set on that wedding taking place in your new church. If I don't make that happen, there'll be no living with them."

Their business concluded, they exited the bank together.

Jacob couldn't help a little grin. "Still, I thank you. The church will provide more room for a larger number of worshipers at services, and I pray many more souls won to Christ. You've done a good thing this day, Roscoe."

Roscoe only nodded, but Jacob noticed a softening of his hard-shelled, all-business facade. Never having had children of his own, the man seemed to have been blindsided by the wiles of his niece.

As Sophie had predicted, soon after her uncle allowed Edwin Applegate to court her, Roscoe grudgingly agreed to the match. Jacob hoped the young couple's relationship would help repair the rift between Roscoe and the elder Applegate.

With a handshake, the two men parted company.

Jacob touched his vest pocket where the copy of the loan crinkled beneath his fingers. He felt glad but not joyful. This was what he'd wanted for two years—plenty of money for material and labor to build the church. He was glad, too, that he'd be able to pay Andrew in a timely fashion for his masonry work on the church. With the arrival of baby Adam, Andrew and Patsey could well use the money. So why, Jacob wondered, wasn't he shouting his thanksgiving to the heavens? What had dulled the joy in his heart?

"Rosaleen."

Her name floated from his lips on a soft sigh of regret. He hadn't realized how long he'd imagined standing before his congregation in the new church and seeing her lovely face beaming up at him from beside the piano. He swallowed hard, blinking quickly as Mulberry Street dimmed before him.

Two days ago, when Alistair Ralston left Madison, Jacob had breathed a sigh of relief to find that Rosaleen had indeed stayed behind at the boardinghouse. He'd thanked God when he learned that Sophie had managed to persuade Rosaleen to stay and play for her and Edwin's engagement party. He prayed that Sophie might convince her to play for the couple's wedding in October as well.

Entering the boardinghouse, Jacob reminded himself of Christ's promise: "And all things, whatsoever ye shall ask in prayer, believing, ye shall receive."

Believing. That was the thing. Did he truly believe he could win her love again, convince her to stay and be his wife? The larger question remained: *Do I even deserve her love?*

He felt a sardonic grin pull up his mouth at the absurd question. Of course he didn't deserve her love. He'd made a grand mess of everything. He'd wrongly accused her of gambling and impropriety and even questioned her conversion and honesty.

Jacob winced at the excruciating memory. How *could* she love him? How could she even think of marrying a man who'd accused her of such things?

"Did you get the loan?" Rosaleen asked, stepping from the dining room into the hallway.

"Yes." Jacob touched his chest where his heart raced beneath the folded document in his vest pocket. Lately, he found himself studying Rosaleen with a sense of urgency. Every curve of her face. The way the afternoon sun revealed glints of copper in her wavy auburn hair. It seemed imperative that he commit each detail to memory.

"I'm glad." Her gaze dropped to the carpet when his lingered on her face.

"It's a blessing that Sophie was so adamant about getting married in the new church," he said in an attempt to prolong their conversation. The afternoon sun shafting down through the second-story window wreathed her in a golden glow. If he could keep her here at the foot of the stairs for a few moments longer, he might burn the image indelibly into his mind.

"This time I'm taking no chances." He reached into his pocket and pulled out the insurance papers he'd had drawn up. "Roscoe insisted that the church be insured." Rosaleen smiled and nodded, but the fact that she wouldn't meet his gaze hurt.

Jacob wished Mr. Blackmore down at the Delaware Mutual Insurance Company issued policies insuring against broken hearts.

Maybe if he could convince her to stay in Madison a little longer... "Sophie mentioned to me last Sunday how happy she is that you've agreed to play for her engagement ball. She confessed that she hopes to entice you to remain for the wedding." Jacob's hope faded when Rosaleen glanced away.

"I—I don't know. Sophie's wedding is set for mid-October, and I'd like to travel while the weather is still warm."

"On the whole, the weather should remain very clement through October." She'd loved him once. If she allowed him time to show her he was completely repentant, perhaps she could love him again. "Please consider it, Rosaleen. It would mean so much—to Sophie."

His heart nearly stopped when she raised her face. Her beautiful blue green eyes glistened as her gaze seemed to search his. "If it means that much—to Sophie—then I will consider it. I will give her a definite answer at her engagement ball."

As he watched her ascend the stairs, Jacob's heart crawled to the mercy seat of his Lord. He, too, had been invited to Sophie and Edwin's engagement ball next week. Something he'd seen in Rosaleen's eyes rekindled within him a tiny spark of hope, and his heart refused to concede defeat.

I know I don't deserve her, Lord, but I may have one last chance—just one. Please guide me. Don't let me mess this one up as well.

Chapter 21

Patsey tugged at the back of Rosaleen's silk gown. "If you don't stand still, I'll never get this buttoned up!"

Rosaleen stopped fidgeting and gazed out the second-story window down onto Mulberry Street. The view did little to calm her nerves. Through the deepening dusk, she could see the shiny black landau with its beaver-hatted driver waiting in front of the boardinghouse. The Stinnetts had sent the open carriage to transport her and Jacob to Sophie and Edwin's engagement party. Rosaleen tried to forget that in a few minutes she'd be riding through the summer evening opposite Jacob. "Are you sure you should be doing this? I could get Opal to help me."

An impatience-laden puff of breath sounded. "It's been two weeks since I had Adam, and if you and Mrs. Buchanan don't quit babyin' me, I'm gonna scream," Patsey said. "Now turn around and let's take a look at you."

Raising her face to the bureau mirror, Rosaleen had to admit she was pleased with the fabric Sophie had chosen for her. The rose silk gown showed off her hair and complexion to their greatest advantage.

Patsey tucked tiny rambling rose blossoms above the ringlets she'd fashioned at Rosaleen's temples. "Well, I don't know what Miss Schuler's gonna wear, but you're the woman every man'll be eyein' tonight."

"No one is going to pay much attention to the piano player, Patsey."

" 'Cept Rev'rend Hale."

"Patsey!" Rosaleen strove to keep her voice light but saw her smile fade in the mirror.

Patsey slipped another pin into Rosaleen's hair to secure the blossoms. "Don't know what's come between you two, and it ain't none of my business, but I'm prayin' God'll use this evenin' to help mend it. All right," she said with a smile and a hug, "I'm done makin' you nervous."

Rosaleen adjusted the lace shawl over her bare shoulders, her heart quickening. She ignored Patsey's veiled attempt to garner information. As much as she'd love to unburden her heart to her friend, the wound still felt too raw to touch with words.

"Thanks, Patsey, I can use all of your prayers." Swallowing salty tears, Rosaleen gave Patsey a warm hug.

A sense of bereavement gripped Rosaleen at the thought of leaving her best friend behind when she left Madison. The only way she could stay would be if

Jacob asked her to. Her hope of that happening diminished with each passing day. He'd had every opportunity to ask her again to marry him, yet he hadn't.

Rosaleen believed with all her heart that Jesus had wiped away her sins. Yet deep down, she wondered if Jacob could ever see her as pure. He'd once questioned her sincerity.

When he looks at me, does he still see a smudge on my soul? The thought pierced her when she met Jacob's formal countenance and rather stiff smile at the bottom of the stairs.

Other than his complimenting her appearance and their mutual agreement that it was, indeed, a fine evening, they accomplished the ride to the Stinnett home in virtual silence.

He looked as ill at ease as she felt. She thought his attitude seemed extra quiet, pensive even. Seeming to avoid her gaze, he fixed his attention on the passing scenery beyond the carriage.

Had he been disappointed that Sophie had chosen Edwin Applegate? Though curious about his thoughts at this moment, she wondered if God might have blessed her by sparing her the pain of that disclosure.

Resting against the black velvet upholstery of the carriage, Rosaleen felt like a grand lady. Yet a sadness wrapped around her heart as the matched pair of dappled grays clopped along Mulberry Street, transporting them through the summer evening.

Glancing at her handsome companion caused an ache deep within her. How painful to be given a glimpse of what her life might have been like here in Madison with Jacob, yet to know it would never be.

They turned onto High Street, and she looked to her left. A block away, the red and gold August sunset spilled across the surface of the Ohio River, painting the water with its vivid hues.

What a hauntingly beautiful place.

Her heart clenched. She'd come to love the town almost as much as she loved the man sitting opposite her in the carriage. When she left, she'd be leaving a very large part of her heart in Madison, Indiana.

When they reached the front of the Stinnett house, the driver let down the steps of the carriage with a rattle. Jacob climbed from the carriage first then helped her down.

At the front door, a young housemaid with an Irish accent took her shawl and Jacob's white beaver hat. She ushered them into a large double parlor. There, a crystal chandelier tinkled above them with the movement of the milling guests. It cast a golden glow over the expanse of the bare wood floor, polished to a high gloss. The room had been emptied of all furniture except for some seating around the walls and the piano in the corner.

Rosaleen searched the room for familiar faces. Besides the Stinnetts, she recognized the Applegates and Dr. and Mrs. Morgan. Jacob's sister, clinging to the arm of her tall, handsome husband, looked stunning in a lilac taffeta gown.

Sophie's azure silk skirt whispered as she fairly skipped toward them, a tall, bespectacled young man in tow. "Oh Rosaleen," she squealed, "you look lovely! I just knew that color would be perfect for you."

"Thank you again for the dress—"

"Oh, fiddle-dee-dee!" Sophie swept aside her expression of gratitude with a giggle and a shake of her blond curls. "I don't believe you've been formally introduced to my fiancé, Edwin Applegate." She lifted an adoring smile to the shy visage of the young man beside her.

"Mr. Applegate, I do remember seeing you with your sister at worship services," Rosaleen said, offering him her hand.

"Mrs. Archer," Edwin murmured, dipping a quick nod of his reddish blond head over her hand. He brushed his lips across the tops of her fingers, and then his chocolate brown gaze drifted back to his diminutive fiancée.

Sophie grinned at Jacob. "Everything is perfect. Edith is prepared, just as planned."

Before Rosaleen could ponder the girl's cryptic comment to Jacob, Sophie whisked her toward the piano with instructions concerning the order in which the tunes were to be played.

"I hope this evening will be as wonderful for you as it is for me." Sophie gave her a quick squeeze then skipped away to join Edwin and Jacob.

Unable to guess what Sophie had meant by her statement, Rosaleen dismissed it as a manifestation of the girl simply being "hypo" about her engagement ball.

She'd played only two quadrilles when Jacob appeared beside the piano with Edwin's sister, Edith.

"I'd like very much to speak with you."

The seriousness of his expression both puzzled and troubled Rosaleen.

"I—I need to begin the serenades. Sophie expects—"

"Edith will take over." He clasped Rosaleen's hand in his, urging her up.

Edwin's twin sister settled herself in front of the piano, her sage green silk skirt rustling as she arranged it around the stool.

"Are you sure?" Rosaleen asked, bewildered as he led her across the parlor. She glanced back at the piano where Edith had begun playing the serenade "Come, the Moon Plays on the Roses." She didn't like thinking she was shirking her duty.

"I'm sure." He slipped his arm around her waist, guiding her toward the French doors that opened to the back veranda.

The boughs of the giant ash tree swayed in the gentle evening breeze, caressing the veranda with soft shadows. The fragrance of honeysuckle and roses hung heavily on the night air. "Rosaleen," he whispered as he took her hands into his.

Rosaleen's hammering heart glowed like the pale moonbeams shimmering across the dusky ribbon of the Ohio River.

His lips lifted in that familiar quirk of a smile so dear to her. "As lovely as that gown is, it lacks something." He reached into his vest pocket.

Flabbergasted, she gazed with widening eyes at the object in his open palm. "My brooch!" she blurted. "But I thought Alistair—"

"I bought it from him."

"But how?" Her mind spun. Alistair had wanted that brooch for a long time. He wouldn't have sold it cheaply. Had Jacob taken out a separate loan with Mr. Stinnett?

Suddenly, Rosaleen remembered Jacob's savings, and she emitted a soft gasp. His face blurred through her tears. "Oh, Jacob, no—not your bell money."

"This means more to me. You mean more to me than any bell, any building, anything else on the face of this earth."

Accepting the brooch, she stared at him mutely then caught her breath as he slowly sank to one knee before her.

"I know I don't deserve you." He lifted his tear-streaked face to hers. "I'm a wretched, sinful man, who has no right to ask for the love of a heart as pure as yours. Yet I do—I must. I cannot bear to contemplate a life devoid of your presence. I pray you can find it in your sweet heart to forgive my grievous trespasses against you."

His blue eyes brimmed with remorse, and his voice palpitated with agony. "Nor do I have the right to ask you to give up your dream of traveling to New York. But if you can love me even a little, please say you'll stay in Madison and be my wife."

Rosaleen's heart pulsed with joy. Now she understood Sophie's peculiar comments. She must have been aware of Jacob's plans. Happy tears slid down her cheeks.

Oh, thank You, God! Thank You for answering Patsey's prayers. Prayers she realized she'd been too afraid to pray for herself. *Oh God, You are so wonderfully good, so loving and merciful.*

"I shall kneel here before you in petition until you give me an answer one way or another, or until Roscoe Stinnett throws me off his veranda."

Rosaleen felt a little laugh shake through a happy sob. Stunned by the unexpected events, she realized she'd left her darling still on his knees, his question unanswered. "Yes, oh yes, Jacob. I've never stopped loving you. Never."

Rising, he pulled her into his arms, smothering her tear-drenched words with his kisses.

The ball passed in a blurred whirl for Rosaleen. Jacob followed Sophie and Edwin's engagement announcement with his and Rosaleen's.

He kept Rosaleen from the piano for the remainder of the evening. They danced to quadrilles and serenades between congratulatory handshakes, hugs, and kisses by all present. To Rosaleen's amazement, even Roscoe Stinnett wished her well and offered her a kiss on the cheek and a belated welcome to Madison.

"Rosaleen, I'm so thrilled to be getting you for a sister." Becky Morgan gave her an excited hug. "We must make a date to go shopping for material for your wedding dress. Jacob is determined that your wedding be the first in the new church, so time is short."

Even as her heart soared on the winds of her beautiful dream come true, Rosaleen beat back an intangible fear. No, this time her future was secure. No evil could snatch it away.

❧

It had been the better part of a week since the engagement ball, and Rosaleen still felt as if her feet had not touched ground.

Roscoe Stinnett hired a crew of carpenters to complete the church. However, Jacob, insisting that everything be perfect for their special day, spent every spare moment at the church, adding finishing touches of his own.

They'd agreed to a wedding date three weeks away. Rosaleen, also feeling the pressure of limited time, was thankful for Becky Morgan's offer of help.

In the boardinghouse's front hallway, Rosaleen hesitated at the front door. "Are you sure it's all right for me to leave this morning, Opal?" Feeling a little guilty, Rosaleen tied the ribbons of her gray silk bonnet beneath her chin. "I hate to leave you shorthanded on washday with two new boarders."

Opal snorted. "The day Patsey and I can't handle a washing and two salesmen is the day I shut down the boardinghouse! You run along now and let Mrs. Morgan help you pick out something special for your wedding dress."

As she neared the Fitch & Williams dry goods store, Rosaleen fingered her brooch pinned at the bodice of the green-sprigged muslin frock. Remembering Jacob's sacrifice, she felt warmth suffuse her heart. She smiled. Thanks to Edwin Applegate's persuasion, his father had offered to buy the bell for the church. It was just one more blessing in a bountiful harvest of God's blessings.

She gazed down Main-Cross Street. Becky Morgan had said she would need to get a widowed neighbor lady to sit with the children and might be a few minutes late.

"Well, well, it seems I've found you at last."

Rosaleen's heart lurched at the quiet voice behind her. An icy chill shot through her, and she whirled to face her nightmare.

Chapter 22

Willing her voice to steadiness, Rosaleen tried not to focus on Bill McGurty's beady black eyes. "This is my home now. I'm never going back to the riverboats."

"Is that so?" His slow grin looked terrifyingly self-assured. "Well, we'll see about that."

She shivered as he tapped the silver tip of his ever-present ebony cane on the boardwalk. Many times she'd felt the sting of it against her flesh.

Hitching up her courage, she realized he could not hurt her here. He wouldn't dare try to abduct her in broad daylight on Main-Cross Street. "Yes, that is so. I'm engaged to be married and will be staying here in Madison."

"I heard." The quiet, congenial tone of his voice made it all the more frightening. "A young reverend, I understand." The sarcastic snort that followed this disclosure infuriated her. "My, my! What would he think if he knew—"

"Jacob knows everything!" *Oh Jesus, help me. Give me courage.* Rosaleen raised her chin in defiance. "You cannot intimidate me or drag me back to the riverboats!"

At his laughter, fear and anger mingled within her.

"My dear Rosaleen, who said anything about dragging you back? No, no, my dear"—he reached out and with a crooked finger, caught a strand of her hair that had escaped her bonnet—"I'm sure I can persuade you to come of your own accord."

Instinctively, she turned her head away and shrank from his touch. But then, swinging back to face him squarely, she glared at his confident smirk. Shaking with fury, she nearly spat her reply. "Nothing you could say or do would ever convince me to leave Jacob!"

"Jacob? Oh, you mean that nice-looking, blond young man I saw working alone on that church building on the corner of Broadway and Second Streets?"

"How do you know that?" she asked in a raspy whisper, panic robbing her of breath.

"Ask the right questions, and folk are always eager to help." His demeanor switched to a far more malicious posture. "It would be a real shame if anything bad were to happen to that young man," he said with a sneer. "I've looked too long and hard to simply turn on my heel and go back to the *James Seymour* without you!" His manicured fingers bit into her wrist. "Without a groom, you'll not be a bride. I killed your first husband in order to have you. Don't think for a second I wouldn't do it again and not twitch an eyelid!"

A sick feeling settled in the pit of her stomach at his revelation. She'd had no idea Bill had planned to kill Donovan before he ever sat down at that gambling table.

The sun glinted off the silver pocket watch he pulled from his scarlet brocade vest. "The *James Seymour* leaves Madison at five o'clock this evening. Be in front of the Madison Hotel in a half hour's time, or Jacob Hale will meet the same fate as Donovan Archer."

She didn't doubt it for an instant. In dismay, she heard the defeat-laden words drop from her lips. "I'll be there."

All thoughts of Becky Morgan and their morning of shopping were swept away in a tempest of mind-numbing terror.

Rosaleen hurried down Mulberry Street toward the boardinghouse, cold fingers of fear tingling down her spine. Alarm consumed her. Bill knew exactly where Jacob was, and that he was alone.

Her mind raced. Patsey had said Andrew would be working on a masonry job near Hanover for the next several days. Even if she could get word to him, she'd only be putting him in danger as well. If she attempted to alert the sheriff, Bill might very well see her, kill Jacob, and slip away onto any number of steamboats or ferries leaving the Madison shore.

No. Jacob's only hope was for her to obey Bill.

Nearing the boardinghouse, she prayed she could get what she needed and leave without being noticed. She glanced behind the garden where newly washed sheets flapped and billowed in the breeze. The sound of Opal and Patsey's laughing chatter gave her a measure of hope.

She entered the front as quietly as possible, grimacing when the front doorbell emitted a tiny jingle. Hiking her skirt to her knees, she took the stairs two steps at a time.

Panting, she stumbled into her little attic room. Her hands shook as she rolled up the few frocks she owned and stuffed them into the leather portmanteau she'd bought at King and Brothers before the engagement ball. Reaching into the mattress, she grasped the remainder of her money and tucked it into the folds of her rose ball gown. She picked up the little Bible Jacob had given her and pressed it for a second to her heart before dropping it into the portmanteau.

Rosaleen paused at the doorway, allowing her gaze to sweep the little room that had been her haven for the better part of four months. Bereft, she quietly closed the door and headed downstairs.

In the parlor, she went to Jacob's desk and took a sheet of paper from the stack he used to pen his sermons. Drawing a deep, ragged breath, she dipped the pen's nib into the inkwell and forced her trembling hand to stillness.

Oh God, forgive me for the lie and let him believe this. Please, just let him believe this.

The scribbled words of her good-bye note blurred, and she sniffed back tears. She started to sign it "Love, Rosaleen," then scratched out the word "Love," and simply signed it "Rosaleen."

Out on Mulberry Street, she turned for one last, fond look at the boarding-house. *Oh God, just let me get away unseen, and please, please protect Jacob!*

Numb, she clutched the portmanteau and hurried up Mulberry, praying she could reach the Madison Hotel without running into Becky Morgan.

She fought to push from her mind images of what awaited her. There'd be plenty of time later to deal with the grief of her loss and the terror of Bill McGurty. Keeping Jacob safe was all that mattered now.

⟶

The bottom of the oilcan popped beneath Jacob's thumb as he lubricated the last of the church doors' hinges. Assuring himself that the two oak doors worked perfectly, he opened and shut them several times.

He descended the four stone steps. His heart skipped with his feet as his hand slid along the wrought-iron railing. A few paces from the building, he turned to gaze at his dream, now a reality.

The redbrick church stood like a stalwart sentry looking down on the Ohio. The gleaming white cross atop the belfry would be visible to those passing on the river as well as from the Kentucky side. Thanks to the Applegates' generous hundred-dollar donation, the five-hundred-pound bell should be arriving next week from Cincinnati's Verdin Bell Company.

"Well, there it is, Orville." He glanced down at his friend's gravestone. "I hope it is everything you dreamed of."

A stiff river breeze brushed the gold-tinged willow branches against the headstone as if in nodding agreement.

"With God's help, I will work tirelessly to fill it, Orville. I promise." The smile spreading over his face reached all the way to the center of his heart. "I won't be alone in my work. I will soon have a wife to help me. I only wish you could have been here for my wedding." A sweet sadness tempered his joy. "You'd have loved Rosaleen," he whispered. "Her heart is as beautiful as her face, and she loves the Lord." He grinned down at Orville's marker. "The true miracle is that she says she loves me, too."

Walking down Mulberry Street, Jacob could not stop smiling. He knew Rosaleen had planned a day of shopping with Becky. His pace quickened, eager to learn of her day and share with her all he'd accomplished at the church.

When he entered the boardinghouse parlor, the look of sadness on Opal Buchanan's face wiped the smile off his.

"Opal, what is it?" Fear tightened around his chest like an iron band. Had something happened to baby Adam, Andrew, or Patsey? Just then, he heard the baby's normal cry. Through the parlor doorway, he caught a glimpse of Patsey carrying Adam. Whispering soothing hushes, she headed upstairs with the infant.

"Oh Jacob, I'm so sorry." Opal held out a page of his letter paper that trembled in her hand.

"Rosaleen? Has something happened to Rosaleen?" Frantic, he rushed to the woman's side and snatched the paper from her hand, terror twisting his insides.

"I didn't want you to find it alone." Opal sank limply to the sofa.

Jacob had to read the terse missive three times over before his mind would assimilate its meaning. Numb, he dropped to the settee. Yet he could not budge his gaze from the unbelievable words that continued to rip at his shredded heart.

Jacob,

I've come to realize that I cannot marry you after all but must follow my dream and journey on to New York. Please forgive me, and do not try to find me.

Rosaleen

His voice cracking, he raised his face to Opal's tear-streaked one. "Did she say anything to you—tell you why?"

"No, not a hint." Opal's befuddled voice shook. "She left this morning to go shopping with your sister, and I never saw her again. Patsey and I spent the entire morning behind the garden doing the laundry. When Rosaleen didn't return by noon, I began to wonder but figured they'd gone on to Becky's house."

"Becky must know something." With unsteady fingers, he folded the note and tucked it inside his shirt next to his heart. Though these few words had shattered his life, they were all he had left of Rosaleen. So in that, they were precious.

In a daze, he walked the distance from the boardinghouse to Becky's home.

Could everything have been an act? The thought was indescribably excruciating. His mind would not accept it. His heart would not accept it. *God help me. Show me what to do. She wouldn't have done this. Something is wrong! Something is terribly wrong!*

He pounded at his sister's front door with both fists.

The door eased open, revealing his sister's perturbed face. "Jacob, please! You don't have to knock down the door. Lucy is sleeping."

"What happened with you and Rosaleen today?" Ignoring Becky's admonishment, he strode past her into the front hall.

"Nothing." His sister's face held a bewildered blankness. "She never showed up. I was late arriving at Fitch & Williams. Mrs. Pearson wasn't feeling well and couldn't watch Daniel and Lucy, so I had to take them with me."

"She's gone." Somehow he managed to squeeze the painful words from his throat.

"You can't mean *gone*. Surely there's been a misunderstanding."

"Does this look like a misunderstanding?" He pulled Rosaleen's note from his shirt and handed it to his sister.

"Oh, Jacob, I can't believe she'd do this." Becky raised a baffled gaze from the paper in her hand. "She seemed so exited about your wedding—about staying here."

"I don't think she wanted to go." Daniel's small voice intruded from the bottom of the stairway.

Jacob and Becky turned to the boy, who stood looking down at his dusty shoes.

Rushing to his nephew, Jacob grasped the boy's shoulders. "Daniel, what do you mean? Did you see Rosaleen today?" He tried to calm his racing heart. The child might only want attention. It could mean nothing. It could mean everything.

"I—I. . ." Daniel stammered, his dark eyes large with fear.

"Daniel!" Jacob nearly shouted in frustration.

"Jacob, you're scaring him." Becky's quiet voice and hand on his arm flooded Jacob with remorse.

"I'm sorry, Daniel." Kneeling beside his nephew, Jacob brushed the tears from the child's face. "Please, Daniel, I need to find Rosaleen. If you know anything, please tell me. Have you seen her today?"

Daniel nodded.

"Where?" It took all Jacob's strength to keep his voice calm.

"In front of the Madison Hotel," Daniel mumbled, dropping his gaze to his shoes again. "I saw her when me and Nate Ross went to the confectionary down by the carriage company."

"Daniel, it's 'Nate and I,' " Becky corrected her son's grammar, "and you know your father and I don't want you near that hotel alone!"

Ignoring his sister, Jacob turned back to his nephew, hope and fear tangling together inside him. "What did you mean when you said you didn't think she wanted to go?"

"An angry-looking man pushed her into a carriage, and she was crying."

"You're sure it was Rosaleen?"

"Yes. She was wearing that green and white dress that used to be Mama's."

In spite of his anxiety, Jacob felt a grin tug at his lips. It faded quickly. "Was it a tall man? A man as tall as your Papa, with reddish hair?" Could Alistair have returned after all and forced Rosaleen to go with him?

"No." Daniel shook his head. "He was kind of fat around his belly like Mr. Stinnett, but shorter. He had a black walking stick with silver at both ends."

Alistair Ralston's description of Bill McGurty slammed to the front of Jacob's mind, filling him with fury and terror. *"Always carries a silver-headed, ebony walking stick."*

"McGurty. Which way did the carriage go?"

"Down toward the river."

"Who's McGurty?" Becky asked.

"The man Rosaleen was running from when the *Cortland Belle* caught fire—the man who killed her husband."

Becky's hand flew to her mouth, stifling a gasp.

Jacob felt a rage he'd never known. *How dare he?* How dare the man come to Madison and pluck Rosaleen from his life? Had he been lying in wait at the hotel? Had McGurty threatened her? Jacob's mind spun with unanswered questions. Disappointment pierced his heart at the realization that Rosaleen hadn't trusted him to protect her from McGurty. Surely she knew he'd lay down his life for her without a second thought.

"Am I in trouble?"

Jacob's heart melted at Daniel's shaky question. "No, Daniel." He brushed the boy's dark hair from his face and placed a heartfelt kiss on his little nephew's head. "You may have just saved Rosaleen's life. I pray you have."

"Jacob, you can't go down to the riverfront alone. You don't know what that man might do." Becky gripped his arm, fear shining in her blue eyes. "Please wait until Ephraim returns from his call and can go with you."

"Becky, I can't wait. I can't risk that man's leaving Madison with Rosaleen. When Ephraim returns, have him fetch Sheriff Rea down to the docks." He forced a smile and gave his sister a quick hug and kiss on the cheek. "Just pray for us, Becky, and try not to worry."

Racing down Main-Cross Street, Jacob prayed with all his heart that he might rescue Rosaleen safely. But if his last act on earth before facing his Lord was an attempt to wrench her from McGurty's grasp, then so be it.

Chapter 23

Breathing hard, Jacob stopped at the junction of Mulberry and Ohio Streets. He darted desperate glances up and down the docks. He'd run the full distance from his sister's home on Main-Cross then down Broadway past the church. But here at the riverfront, he paused, unsure which way to go.

It was Monday afternoon, so the steam packet *Wm. R. McKee* had left for Cincinnati hours ago, and the *Swiftsure* wouldn't be docking again until tomorrow morning. Several flatboats were loading barrels of pork from the numerous pork-packing plants, but he saw no signs of a ferry.

Suddenly, the blast of a steamboat whistle drew his attention several blocks east where East and Ohio Streets intersected. He raced to where the steamboat was docked. There, ladies in full skirts of satins and lawns, shaded by parasols, made a moving ribbon of color on the arms of broadcloth-clad, beaver-hatted gentlemen.

Battling panic, Jacob scanned the passengers embarking and disembarking the stern-wheeler *James Seymour*. Out of the corner of his eye, he caught a glimpse of green and white on the top deck near the stern. Fear quickly swamped his initial feeling of relief.

"Rosaleen! Rosaleen!" The bustle of the busy riverfront drowned his calls. She would never hear him from this distance amid the off-loading of freight and the happy, loud chatter of passengers.

His heart leaped at the sight of her. She stood bareheaded, grasping the rail. Her light-colored frock stood out in stark contrast against the green and gold wooded hills of Kentucky behind her. Even at this distance, he could see the sun revealing coppery lights in her hair as the river breezes played with curling wisps of her dark auburn tresses.

Watching her turn and gaze upriver toward the church, he could only wonder what might be going through her mind and heart. He blinked away tears, remembering that morning last April when his heart first stirred at her beauty. The memory solidified his determination.

I won't let him have her. I won't!

Ignoring the protests of embarking passengers, Jacob elbowed his way up the boat ramp. She seemed to be alone. Perhaps if McGurty were otherwise occupied, Jacob just might be able to convince her to leave with him.

Oh God, just help me convince her to leave this boat!

❧

The white cross atop the belfry of Jacob's church blurred. Rosaleen closed her damp eyes, and the image of her beloved's face appeared behind her eyelids. It seemed so real she might reach out and touch the scar on Jacob's cheek. She opened her eyes, unable to bear the agony of the vision any longer. She drew in a lungful of fresh air then exhaled a ragged breath, hoping Bill would not learn she'd disobeyed him.

Upon embarking, he'd shoved her into the tiny cabin with orders that she stay there until he finished a card game. Unwilling to leave Madison without another look, she'd dared to make her way to the outside deck. For a better look at the town, she'd climbed the stairs to the top deck. She'd deal with Bill and the consequences of her actions later. In truth, any punishment Bill might mete out paled in comparison to his having ripped her from the man she loved and the only place that had ever felt like home.

Gripping the railing, she fought the panic that urged her to flee this steamboat and run back to Opal's boardinghouse and into Jacob's sweet embrace. Yet to do so would be to seal her darling's fate. She had no doubt that Bill meant every word of his threat.

Dear Lord, help me. Give me the courage to save Jacob and leave it all behind.

From the top deck of the *James Seymour*, her gaze drifted along the shoreline of Madison, Indiana, and she stifled a sob. The place had entangled itself in her heartstrings. Dear faces she might never again see in this life swam before her eyes through a mist of tears. Yet one visage overshadowed them all, saturating her whole heart.

"Jacob." His name snagged on the ragged edges of her sobs.

"I'm here, my darling."

Catching her breath, she swung around, sure she'd imagined his voice. Unbelievably, his blond head emerged from the stairwell connecting the upper and middle decks.

Her heart seized as joy, love, and fear collided. She stepped toward him then felt her body jerk back as fingers bit into her arm.

"I told you to stay below. Now see what you've done? You've complicated things and put this nice young man in jeopardy." Bill McGurty's warm, whiskey-laced breath sent shivers through her.

"Let her go, McGurty." Jacob's voice was calm as he took a step toward them.

"Ah, I see my reputation precedes me." Bill slipped his left arm around her waist, holding her against him in a vice-tight grip. With his free hand, he pulled a walnut-handled derringer from his vest. Flicking his wrist, he motioned toward the stairwell with the little pistol. "Young reverend, I suggest you turn around and go back down those steps and off this boat if you want to preach another sermon."

Fear twisted through Rosaleen when Jacob continued to advance. "Go away, Jacob! Go back to the boardinghouse. I don't love you." *God, please let him believe it.*

A sweet smile lifted the corners of Jacob's mouth, and her hopes plummeted. "You're a terrible liar, Rosaleen."

"I suggest you listen to the little lady, Reverend." A tiny *click* told Rosaleen Bill had pulled the hammer back on the derringer.

"I won't go without Rosaleen," Jacob replied, his voice steady, his blue eyes as calm as the placid Ohio on a windless day.

To Rosaleen's horror, she saw him take another step toward her. The awful scenes of Donovan's death played before her eyes. She couldn't let that happen to Jacob. She wouldn't!

Please, God, give me the strength and courage to do this.

The words of one of the scriptures she'd committed to memory flashed to her mind: "*I can do all things through Christ which strengtheneth me.*"

The next few seconds passed as if in a nightmare. She leaned back and as far away from Bill as his grasp allowed. The low railing edging the steamboat's top deck bit into her lower back. With all her strength, she brought her arm closest to Bill forward then reared back, sinking her elbow into his ribs.

"Uhh!" His exclamation seemed more of surprise than pain, yet it caused him to double over and lower his hand that held the derringer. The shot pinged harmlessly into the deck.

The instant Bill's grip loosened, Rosaleen pulled free of him. Clinging to the rail, she watched, terrified, as Jacob plowed into Bill. The impact brought both men down and sent the spent, one-shot derringer clanging to the deck.

Rosaleen was relieved when Jacob managed to extricate himself from Bill's grasp and push up into a kneeling position. But when he glanced to his side as if looking for Rosaleen, Bill, who'd also righted himself, reached over and snatched his walking stick from the deck and swung it in an arc toward Jacob's head. The stick made contact with an ugly *smack*. A scream caught in Rosaleen's throat when another blow landed solidly against Jacob's jaw, sending him sprawling.

Bill scrambled to his feet and lunged at Rosaleen. "Come here, you little—" He slipped on the derringer, cutting his sentence short.

In shock, Rosaleen watched his feet go out from under him, the momentum of his lunge propelling his body over the short railing. For a moment, she sat motionless, stunned by what had just transpired.

Then her gaze fell upon Jacob, who'd righted himself and was rubbing his jaw. "Jacob, are you all right?" Weeping, she rushed to throw her arms around him.

"I thought I'd come to save *you*," he told her with a grin, holding her tight against him.

Two deafening blasts of the steamboat's whistle and the *shug, shug, shug* of the paddlewheel announced the *James Seymour*'s departure.

"Help me up, man! In the name of all that's holy."

In disbelief, Rosaleen's face swung with Jacob's toward the sound of Bill's voice. Somehow, he'd miraculously caught hold of the railing with one hand, saving himself from the deadly drop.

Pressing a quick kiss on her cheek, Jacob extricated himself from her embrace and went to assist his nemesis.

He almost had Bill up, when in horror, Rosaleen saw the sun glint on the barrel of a second derringer in McGurty's free hand. Jacob must have seen it at the last moment and jerked back, letting go of Bill's arm.

The instant the bullet whizzed past Jacob's ear, Bill fell backward to the churning water below. His head hit the iron rim of the giant paddlewheel with a sickening *crack*! An instant later, his body disappeared beneath the surface of the Ohio.

Trembling, Rosaleen stared down at the water.

"Don't look, darling. Don't look." Jacob pulled her away from the railing, stifling her sobs against his chest. Rocking her in his arms, he murmured sweet hushes while he kissed her hair.

Dimly aware of excited voices and a flurry of activity around them, Rosaleen noticed that the *James Seymour* had reversed, returning to the Madison shore. "Thank You, Jesus. Thank You, thank You." A bevy of thankful prayers winged their way heavenward from her grateful heart as she clung to Jacob, burying her face in his chest. Then a flash of quick anger blazed inside her and she pulled away from him. "Jacob, I told you not to follow me. You could have been killed!"

"But I wasn't." He gave her that crooked grin of his that had won her heart her first day in Madison. "Hebrews 13:6 says, 'The Lord is my helper, and I will not fear what man shall do unto me.' Rosaleen, I was not going to let that man take you away from me."

She felt sure he knew, yet she couldn't let it go. She had to say it. "Jacob, when I told you I didn't love you, I didn't mean it. I do love you. I love you so much. I will love you every day for the rest of my life."

"I know, my darling." His beautiful blue gaze melted into hers. Smiling, he brushed the tears from her cheeks with his calloused thumb. "And I'll love you as long as God gives me breath." With his whispered confession, he pulled her into his arms and pressed his lips tenderly against hers.

Epilogue

Boang! Boang! Boang!
The sound of the new church bell rang out, announcing to the town of Madison that God had just joined together the hearts and lives of two of His own.

Rosaleen Hale clung tightly to her husband's arm as they descended the stone steps of the church that had been his dream. Careful to hold the voluminous folds of her yellow silk skirt away from her feet, she scarcely noticed the congregation behind them calling out a potpourri of congratulations and good wishes.

Over her shoulder, she sent the crowd a smile and a wave before turning her gaze toward the Ohio River framed by the boughs of trees dressed in the deep reds, oranges, and golds of autumn. The undiluted joy in Rosaleen's heart matched the pristine clarity of the cloudless October sky.

"Happy, darling?" Jacob asked as he settled her on the maroon velvet seat of the phaeton.

Her husband's quiet question caressed her heart. "Superbly," she managed before a knot of emotion gathering in her throat rendered her mute. How could she articulate to her dear husband her wonder over all God had wrought in her life these past six months? Changes she'd never have imagined the night she fled the burning deck of the *Cortland Belle*.

Jacob flicked the reins against the sorrel mare's back, and they rolled down Broadway toward Ohio Street and the river.

Rosaleen gazed at the broad waterway that held so many memories, both sweet and awful. She marveled at how God had turned grief to joy, tragedy to triumph, and despair to hope. Since her father's death, she had ached to belong to a real family. Breathing a soft sigh of contentment, she snuggled in the circle of Jacob's arm. Now, thanks to her darling "angel," she belonged to the family of God and could look forward to a sweet life, as well as a sweet forever.

EVERLASTING
PROMISE

Dedication

Special thanks to: The Canal Society of Indiana and historians Bob and Carolyn Schmidt; Historic Metamora and historian Paul Baudendistel; Cambridge City Library, Cambridge City, Indiana, and historian Patty Hersberger; Kim Sawyer for her invaluable critique work; and my husband, Jim, and daughters, Jennifer and Kelly, whose love, encouragement, and support for what I do never falters.

Chapter 1

Wayne County, Indiana
April 1851

The sharp, clear notes of a bugle yanked Susannah Killion's attention from the pot of beans. She turned from the stove to the inn's kitchen window. A quick glance confirmed the unexpected announcement.

A canal boat, its hull emblazoned with a gold eagle in full wingspread, neared the canal basin wharf.

The Flying Eagle? Hadn't Garrett Heywood said that his boat would be undergoing repairs in Cincinnati and wouldn't be making the trip to Promise this week?

The happy chatter of the boat passengers wafted up from the canal basin a few yards from the inn's back door.

Susannah smoothed back an errant strand of hair straggling across her forehead and tucked it behind her ear. A coach was due off the National Road in less than an hour, and she hadn't planned nearly enough supper to accommodate guests from both the stagecoach and the canal boat.

The prayer for strength budding in her breast withered. Let Naomi pray. Susannah had stopped expecting answers to her prayers long ago.

Watching the line of people making their way toward the inn, she blew out a resigned sigh. She had neither the time nor the energy for futile prayers or self-pity.

"Susannah, the beans!" The alarm in her mother-in-law's voice whirled her around.

A *hiss* sent Susannah bounding to the stove. She grabbed a towel from a wall hook and snatched the hot lid off the cast-iron pot, letting it fall to the stovetop with a clatter.

The acrid smell of burned beans filled the inn's little kitchen.

Susannah's heart drooped. *Perfect!* In another moment, hungry guests would be filing into the building, and the unappealing aroma would definitely not enhance their first impressions of the Killion House Inn.

A mixture of sympathy and dismay played across Naomi Killion's face before she turned to greet the packet passengers at the inn's side door.

Susannah transferred the salvageable portion of beans and ham to another pot, almost wishing she still believed in prayer. But prayer wouldn't feed her guests. A heaping bowl of mashed potatoes and a platter of fried ham would. Mentally brushing aside the urge to reach out for divine assistance, she headed for the pantry. Hadn't the past four years taught her to depend on no one but herself?

⁓

Thad Sutton's stomach knotted as he disembarked from Captain Heywood's canal packet. Gripped by trepidation, he gazed at the rear of the three-story brick building before him. He wondered how the conflicting feelings of relief and dread could, at once, dwell together in a man's breast.

The journey from Cincinnati had taxed his patience, the trip alternating between mind-numbing boredom and physical exhaustion. Each of the half dozen times they ran aground, the captain had commandeered him, along with the other able-bodied male passengers, to help pole the boat into a floatable depth of water—twice during a chilly April shower. What little sleep he had acquired the past couple nights aboard Captain Heywood's packet had been fitful, disturbed incessantly by a group of young rowdies on their way to the California goldfields.

The young ruffians, their minds filled with dreams of riches and their bellies filled with whiskey, had kept all aboard awake with riotous conversation, singing, and discharging of their firearms—two rounds of which had barely missed Thad's bunk last night.

With each passing hour on the canal boat, Thad came to agree with his father's assessment—the Whitewater Canal was an ill-begotten folly, best replaced by a railroad with all possible expedience. With that precise goal in mind, his father had convinced his fellow board members of the Union Railway Company to hire Thad as engineer and surveyor.

The corner of Thad's mouth tugged into a sardonic grin. Nothing he'd done before had bought him an iota of respect in his father's eyes. Not his two years of service as captain of a U.S. Army regiment in Texas or his decorations for valor at the Battle of Buena Vista. But at the moment of his appointment to this post, he had seen the esteem he'd longed to earn shining in his father's eyes. Because he had found favor with Josiah Sutton's beloved Union Railway Company, Thad had at last basked in the admiration of his usually cool and distant parent.

However, he realized his father's rare display of approval came with a caveat. Thad was expected to deliver a short, direct, and cost-effective railroad route from Cincinnati to Indianapolis.

He'd pleased the board by quickly accomplishing the work up to forty miles southwestward of Indianapolis. And now, having accumulated the mathematical calculations needed from the Cincinnati end of the project, he was ready to do the work on this stretch along the Whitewater Canal. Situated in the approximate center of the forty-mile area he'd be surveying, the town of Promise, Indiana, seemed the ideal base from which to work. It also gave him an opportunity to repair an oversight in his duty to the widow of one of his fallen Army subordinates.

Though glad to have ended the tedious trip from Cincinnati, he did not especially relish the meeting awaiting him within the walls of this unpretentious inn. He pressed his fingers against his navy blue broadcloth coat. The crinkle of paper he felt against his chest reminded him—as if he needed any reminding—that he'd been derelict in his duty four years ago. Somehow, instead of sending George Killion's last letter on to his widow, Susannah, Thad recently discovered he'd accidentally filed it away among letters he'd received from his own family during the war. No, he did not look forward to admitting his error to George Killion's widow.

Susannah Killion. He would have no trouble recognizing the woman. Her pleasant, comely features seemed burned into his brain. He could close his eyes and see her smiling at him from the daguerreotype George had placed in his keeping.

What reaction was he to expect from her in response to his grievous negligence? Tears? Anger? He'd marched unflinchingly into battle dozens of times on the dusty Texas plains. And right now, he would much prefer facing a full regiment of Santa Anna's best rather than the Widow Killion.

Stepping from the boat, Thad's stomach growled, and the knot in his gut cinched tighter. The food aboard the *Flying Eagle* had been a bit too heavy on the grease for his taste. Hopefully, Susannah Killion's table offered better fare.

That hope withered when a slight, middle-aged woman ushered him, along with the other travelers, into the Killion House Inn. The unappetizing smell of burned beans assaulted his nostrils and caused his spirit to groan with his stomach.

At the massive desk in the lobby, he signed in and accepted the little brass room key from the woman who'd introduced herself as Naomi Killion. If George Killion's mother recognized his name, she showed no sign of it, turning to focus on the couple behind him who were demanding a room with an easterly view.

Thad started up the staircase, lugging his carpetbag and case of surveyor's instruments. He would introduce himself formally to George's mother later. Glancing down at the lobby, he hitched up his courage for his impending meeting with the man's widow.

⤳

After putting a large pot of potatoes on to boil and slicing down a quarter of a smoked ham, Susannah crossed the kitchen and headed to the hallway linen closet. By now, Naomi would have all the passengers from the packet signed in and shown to their rooms.

She snatched the feather duster from the closet's top shelf. While she waited for the potatoes to cook, she'd give the lobby a quick go-over. As she scanned the walnut-paneled sitting area, she couldn't help the pride welling up inside her.

No other inn within fifty miles had as elegant a lobby. Her late father-in-law had gone into debt to make it so.

She crossed the rose-patterned carpet, maneuvering between the horse-hair sofa and green velvet settee. At the fireplace, she swiped the duster across the stone mantel and repositioned one of the gold silk wing chairs flanking the hearth.

After flicking the feather duster over the two marble-topped tables on either side of the sofa, she breathed a contented sigh. Despite the hard work and demanding life, Susannah loved this inn with all her heart. And now, with the canal navigable again, the inn was actually beginning to prosper. For three months in a row, she'd been able to put a little extra money aside.

Though harried, Susannah realized this was one of the better days. Most of the rooms would be filled tonight. The canal had been operational again for several months, and spring had brought an increase in stagecoach travelers. Even the worrisome rumors of a railroad that would threaten the existence of the entire town of Promise, as well as the Killion House Inn, seemed to have subsided.

She redeposited the duster in the closet and started for the stairs. Thankfully, Naomi had put Georgiana down for a nap a half hour ago. But Susannah decided she'd best check on her four-year-old before returning to the kitchen.

"Mrs. Killion?"

Susannah paused at the bottom of the staircase and turned to discover who possessed the quiet male voice.

"Mrs. George Killion?" With a few quick strides, a man closed the distance between the sitting area and stairway. There was nothing alarming in the elegant dress or quiet demeanor of the handsome young gentleman, yet something about him made Susannah's heart quake.

"Yes." Susannah turned to face the traveler. He stood about six feet in height, she guessed. His brown hair curled slightly over his ears. He had a strong-looking face with a square jaw that tapered to a cleft chin. The only remarkable feature about him was the intense look in his gray eyes.

"I'm sorry, sir. I thought my mother-in-law had registered all the new guests." Susannah took a step toward the main desk.

His hurried words stopped her. "I have acquired my room. Thank you, ma'am." He dipped a low bow. "Thaddeus Sutton—Captain Thaddeus Sutton—at your service, Mrs. Killion. If I may beg a moment of your time?"

Captain Sutton. . . Susannah's mind raced, trying to think why that name sounded familiar.

The man drew a yellowed envelope from a pocket inside his coat. "I'm afraid I've been tardy in delivering this missive."

As Susannah reached for the proffered letter, his next words sent her blood sluicing to her toes.

"It's from your husband, George."

Susannah's legs went weak, and she swayed with the room that seemed to swirl around her. A swarm of questions crowded her stunned mind as she slumped against the stranger who reached out strong arms to support her.

Chapter 2

I t was a girl." Thad voiced his thoughts as his gaze followed the towheaded moppet scampering past him through the inn's dining room doorway.

"I beg your pardon?" Susannah Killion placed a bowl of mashed potatoes in the center of the long table and glanced up at him. Her placid expression suggested she'd sufficiently recovered from the shock he caused her an hour earlier when he handed her George's letter.

Once again, remorse smote Thad's heart at the memory of her delicate features blanching paper-white. He hadn't once thought that receiving such a letter might disturb her. Expecting her to be angry that he had not sent the letter to her years earlier, he never considered she might misconstrue its existence, thinking George had not died in Buena Vista after all. Shifting his gaze to the child sitting on the dining room floor, playing with her doll and munching on a biscuit, he wished with all his heart that were true.

He nodded toward Susannah Killion's little girl. "The child. I remember how George crowed for days after he received your letter telling him he was to be a father. It was the only thing that brought him consolation, learning at the same time about the death of his father."

"Did you know my husband well, Captain Sutton? He always spoke highly of you in his letters." She didn't look at him as she transferred a platter of ham to the table from a buffet against the south wall. He noticed a subtle stiffening of her demeanor, as if she were steeling herself against the painful subject.

"Yes—well, I suppose as well as any captain can know a sergeant under his command." Thad marveled at her disciplined composure. He'd witnessed the same starch in her earlier when he handed her George's letter. For a moment, he'd feared she might faint dead away. Instead, his admiration for Susannah Killion had grown as he watched her battle her emotions while he explained that George had written the missive just prior to his death.

Thad moved toward the end of the table, hoping to change the subject. The conversation had taken a turn down a road he didn't care to travel. "Should I be seated, or do you have a seating order?"

"First come, first served." Her well-shaped lips lifted in the first true smile she'd given him. It sent warmth radiating through him, causing him to hope for many more of Susannah Killion's smiles.

As if mesmerized, his gaze followed her graceful movements around the long dining table. He'd always thought her picture attractive, but he now realized it was but a poor representation of the real woman. With a more than pleasing figure, hair the color of clover honey, and green eyes flecked with amber, Susannah Killion was heart-joltingly beautiful.

"Will you be returning to Cincinnati then, Captain Sutton?"

Several other patrons had filed into the dining room. Thad gripped the back of a chair near the end of the table and awaited the seating of the ladies. "No. Actually, I plan to use Killion House Inn as my residence for the next several months. In civilian life, I'm an engineer and surveyor and have come to do work along this stretch of the canal."

He'd taken a quick jaunt along the canal towpath and had made some preliminary notes. From what he had seen, the towpath seemed solid. Beyond that, he estimated it would be a challenge to find land solid enough on the marshy landscape to support tracks.

Surprise lit her hazel green eyes, and this time her smile lingered on him for a long, sweet moment. "Then we shall be glad to have you, Captain Sutton. Perhaps with your expertise, you can figure a way to keep floods from plaguing our canal."

Thad opened his mouth to correct her misunderstanding. But before he could, she hurried from the dining room just as a minister in the group pronounced a blessing over the supper.

❧

Susannah opened the top drawer of her cherrywood dresser to retrieve one of her Sunday-best embroidered handkerchiefs. Her gaze drifted to the envelope she'd tucked in the drawer's lower right-hand corner. It had been over a week since Captain Sutton handed her George's last letter, but she hadn't yet found the courage to open it.

She allowed her fingertips to glide across the yellowed paper. George's left-slanted handwriting brought a smile to her lips and a lump to her throat. He'd been left-handed all his life, to the consternation of every teacher who'd tried to set him right.

She remembered the autumn when they were eight years old and Mr. Greathouse first came to teach. George's poor little left hand had stayed swollen and red from constant raps of the new teacher's rod. Susannah had felt every whack dealt to her playmate's hand. Once, she'd tried to warn George to move his chalk to his right hand before the teacher noticed. They both were caught, spanked, and made to stand in opposite corners of the schoolhouse. From that day on, they'd been nearly inseparable.

The jumble of uncomfortable feelings that always accompanied thoughts of her late husband balled up in Susannah's chest. Their last day together had been filled with angry words. Sometimes at night, when she closed her eyes, she could still see George standing on the deck of the retreating canal boat, a gentle breeze ruffling the tangle of blond curls framing his boyish face. Susannah remembered how she'd stood on the bank watching him wave until the boat became a speck in the distance and she could no longer see the red bandanna tied about his neck. Because of her anger at his leaving, she'd refused to wave back.

It was the last time she saw him. Seven months later, he died at the Battle of Buena Vista.

She scrunched her eyes tight against the tears stinging the backs of her eyelids and tried to conjure up George's likeness. Fear gripped her when a clear picture of him would not develop. Instead, another visage shoved its way before her mind's eye.

Captain Sutton.

He had no right to intrude—to replace George's image with his own.

Her conscience pricked at her uncharitable thoughts of George's former commanding officer. In every one of his letters, George had nothing but the highest praise for Captain Sutton.

She picked up the envelope. Captain Sutton had cared enough to deliver George's last letter in person, albeit four years late. And he was here to work on the canal—the canal that brought patrons to the inn.

She turned the letter over and slipped a thumbnail beneath an edge near the sealing wax. Her hand froze. She couldn't bring herself to read the last words George had written to her. Somehow, to read this letter was to close the door on their marriage forever. She wasn't ready to do that. Maybe tomorrow. Maybe never. Susannah dropped the letter into the drawer and pushed it shut.

"Mamma, look what Tad taught me."

Wiping tears from her face, Susannah forced a smile as she turned at her daughter's excited voice.

"See?" Georgiana pulled herself up to her full height, stiffened, flattened her hand, and brought the edge of her index finger to her brow. "Tad taught me to salute."

Susannah couldn't help a tiny smile. "That's a fine salute, Georgiana, but girls don't join the army, so I don't think saluting is something you'll need to know how to do."

Immediately smitten with Captain Sutton, Georgiana had spent the week since his arrival following him around the inn like a puppy. He, in turn, seemed to delight in her attention, often surprising her with penny candy from the general store when he returned from his daily forays along the canal.

Susannah appreciated the kindness Thaddeus Sutton showed her daughter. But she worried that Georgiana's attachment to the man might cause the child grief when he concluded his business here.

She bent to redo her daughter's crookedly buttoned dress. "You should really call him Captain Sutton instead of his given name. It's more respectful, don't you think?"

"But he told me to call him Tad," Georgiana argued as Susannah covered her daughter's blond curls with a little yellow bonnet and fashioned its ribbons into a bow beneath the child's chin.

"Captain Sutton's given name is Thad, not Tad. We need to work on your *th* sound."

As they descended the stairs, Susannah wrestled with her own confused feelings about Thaddeus Sutton while Georgiana practiced the correct pronunciation of his name.

"Th–Th–Thad. Th–Th–Thad. Tad!" Georgiana squealed with delight. Pulling away from Susannah's grasp, she scurried down the last few steps into the lobby. Susannah hurried to catch up with her daughter and felt her heart quicken. It was a response she'd come to expect whenever in the company of the handsome surveyor.

Clutching his dark beaver hat by the brim, Thaddeus Sutton swept a deep bow. "Would you lovely ladies do me the honor of allowing me to escort you to worship services?"

"Pease, Mamma, peaaase!" Georgiana bounced up and down in her yellow calico dress like a daffodil in a stiff spring breeze.

"That's very gracious of you, Captain, but. . ." Susannah grappled for a reason to decline his offer. The effect the man had on Susannah unsettled her, and she'd found herself rebelling against it. She looked down at her silk skirt, smoothing an imaginary wrinkle from its pewter-colored folds. "Naomi's not quite ready yet, and I wouldn't want to keep you—"

"I'm here." Naomi bustled into the lobby, her slight figure swathed in black bombazine. "How gallant of you, Captain Sutton. We would be more than pleased to have your company, wouldn't we, Susannah?"

Outnumbered, Susannah surrendered. "Yes, thank you, Captain."

Taking his proffered right arm while Naomi accepted his left, Susannah scolded her unruly heart, which bounced and giggled along with Georgiana.

As they walked to the carriage house, he turned a devastating smile toward Susannah and she caught a faint wisp of bay rum and the clean smell of shaving soap. "Although it is a fine day and the church is only a few blocks away, I took the liberty of asking young Ruben to hitch that fine black gelding of yours to the phaeton. I hope you don't mind."

Her return smile came as easily to Susannah's lips as her honest answer. "Not at all, Captain Sutton." Under other circumstances, she might have thought his action impertinent. But instead, she felt both appreciation and relief for having a responsibility, however small, lifted from her shoulders.

As they neared the carriage house where her sixteen-year-old nephew, Ruben, waited with the horse and buggy, Thad again inclined his head toward her. "I was hoping after church I might prevail upon you to give me a proper tour of the town. I've seen little of it beyond the shops and houses that border the canal."

Thad paused to press several coins into Ruben's palm, winning Susannah's admiration with the show of kindness to her young kin. The captain helped Naomi into the back of the two-seat phaeton. Then he swung a giggling Georgiana in a wide arc before depositing her on the black leather seat beside her grandmother.

When he turned his full attention to Susannah, his twinkling gray eyes sent her heart into a canter. "Well, Mrs. Killion, will you show me Promise?" His strong hands grasped her waist, lifting her easily to the front seat.

During the preceding interlude, Susannah had tried and failed to think of a graceful way to decline his request. So the words that popped from her mouth surprised her. "Yes, of course." She wished her voice didn't sound so breathless.

As he settled beside her and took the reins, she found herself looking forward to the sightseeing excursion, and she turned a good-natured grin toward him. "Although your business is to improve the Whitewater Canal, you should know there is more to Promise than our glorious ditch."

He gave her a bemused look. "Forgive me, but I'm afraid you've misunderstood my work here. I have not come to improve the canal itself, but to survey for a railroad that would replace it."

Chapter 3

Susannah reached into her pocket for another handful of hard, dry seed peas. Bending over the furrow Ruben had earlier gouged into the newly plowed and harrowed garden plot behind the inn, she dropped the seeds onto the earth with such force they bounced. Rising, she drew back her shoulders and stretched her spine. She closed her eyes, lifted her face, and allowed the April sun to bathe it in warmth. Perhaps the soothing rays would help calm her troubled mind.

Since Thaddeus Sutton's jarring revelation yesterday, she hadn't enjoyed a moment of peace. A battle raged inside her. Anger and fear warred for the upper hand. She had no doubt that anger would win out, for she could not abide the fear.

Another emotion clung to her heart like a dank mist. Disappointment.

The handsome surveyor with his gallant ways and winning smile had stridden into her heart, awakening feelings she thought she'd never experience again. Then, in a matter-of-fact tone, he'd uttered the devastating statement that unleashed the conflict still clashing inside her.

Susannah had enjoyed the cordiality that marked their acquaintance, promising a burgeoning friendship. It still pained her to discover they were destined to be adversaries.

And how could she explain to Georgiana that her beloved "Tad," who gave her penny candy and piggyback rides, represented the industry that would snatch away their home and livelihood?

Susannah pressed her fingers to her throbbing temples.

"Are you pwaying, Mamma?"

At Georgiana's voice, Susannah's eyes flew open. "No, honey, Mamma just has a little headache." She managed a tiny smile as guilt rippled through her. It had been a long time since she'd made a conscious effort to pray—even in church.

"Gwamma closes her eyes when she pways."

"Prays, Georgiana. You can pronounce your *r*'s if you try. I've heard you do it."

"Well, she does when she pr–r–ays."

"Good girl. See, I knew you could do it." Susannah hoped to steer her daughter toward a less troublesome topic.

"Look, Mamma, I planted lots of peas." Georgiana beamed as she pointed to the crooked trail of seeds she'd scattered along the furrow ahead of them.

"Tad said he likes peas and we should plant a bunch."

"Georgiana. . ." Susannah grappled for the right words as she bent to pick up the hoe from between two rows of planted seeds. "Georgiana, it is good that you want to please our guests," she said as she began raking dirt over the peas then gently tamping it down with the flat of the hoe blade. "That means you are a good innkeeper. But as I've told you before, you must not become too attached to any of the guests because they are not here to stay."

"Tad is not a guest. He is my friend. He's going to let me look through his spyglass. He pwomised—pr–r–omised!" Scowling, Georgiana firmly planted dirty fists on her little hips.

Susannah ignored her daughter's indignant tone and stance. "Very good, Georgiana. See, you can pronounce your r's." Then, feeling her smile fade, she hunched down next to her child. She brushed away a smudge of soil from the apple of Georgiana's soft, pink cheek. "Georgiana, I'd rather you didn't bother Captain Sutton or his surveying instruments."

Georgiana, her face sullen, never answered as Susannah poked a stick into the soft earth to mark the end of the planted row.

"Four rows should be plenty." Hefting the hoe in her left hand, Susannah took Georgiana's hand in her right and led her daughter back to the inn. Knowing the child's attention flitted from one thing to another like the robins hopping about the garden plot, she figured if she dropped the subject of Thad Sutton, Georgiana would, too.

But the moment they stepped into the kitchen, she learned she was wrong.

Georgiana raced to her grandmother, who stood at the washstand. "Grr-amma, me and Mamma planted lots of peas 'cause Tad likes 'em. Won't he be happy?"

Drying her hands on a towel, Naomi Killion turned and gave her grand-daughter a fond smile. "I should think Captain Sutton will be very pleased, indeed."

"I planted almost as many seeds as Mamma did, but she had to stop. Not to pw–pr–r–ay, but 'cause her head hurts," Georgiana told her grandmother as Naomi wet a cloth in a pan of water and began washing dirt from the child's hands.

Naomi sent Susannah a quick glance that promised a sermon the moment they were alone then turned back to Georgiana. "Now, I think it is time for you and Dolly to have tea in the lobby, don't you? You know how particular Dolly is about her tea time."

Georgiana gave a somber nod and headed toward the doorway that led to the lobby. "Dolly gets very cwoss when she misses her tea."

Susannah didn't look forward to time alone with her mother-in-law. Though she loved Naomi as if she were her own blood, their relationship had been strained for the past several months. An uncomfortable stiffness had replaced the easiness with which they'd shared their lives since they became mother and daughter. And Susannah knew she bore a large portion of blame for the change.

Naomi seemed to have sensed the erosion of Susannah's faith. Susannah knew her mother-in-law couldn't understand why the tragedies of the past several years had diluted her faith when they'd strengthened Naomi's.

"A little prayer from time to time would not go amiss, daughter," Naomi said quietly as she passed Susannah, carrying the pan of dirty water toward the back door.

The faint hint of reproach in her mother-in-law's voice sent a prickle of irritation up Susannah's back. "You pray enough for all of us, Naomi."

Naomi opened the back door and pitched the water outside. "I'm concerned that you are pulling away from the Lord," she said as she shut the door and headed back to the washstand with the empty pan. "Even Georgiana has begun to notice. It's not a good example for the child." She poured hot water into the pan from a kettle on the stove then tempered it with cold water from a bucket beside the washstand.

"And I'm concerned that you continue to encourage Georgiana's friendship with that. . .that man!" Susannah reached up and snatched a large crockery bowl from the shelf beside the stove. She plunked it down onto the table so hard she wondered that it hadn't cracked.

"Captain Sutton? Why, that young man is pure Christian kindness. I can see why George spoke so well of him." Naomi gave a little chuckle that sent another trail of annoyance rasping along Susannah's spine.

Susannah pointed toward the window that framed the canal basin. "At this very moment, that man is out designing a railroad route that would ruin our inn—this inn Papa Emil and George left to our keeping!"

"Captain Sutton is simply doing the job he was sent here to do, nothing more. What happens as a result of his work is in God's hands." With infuriating calmness, Naomi went back to washing the stack of stoneware dishes and cups.

The quiet clinking of dishes filled the uneasy silence between the two women.

Susannah breathed a deep sigh and headed for the lobby to check on Georgiana. She didn't like quarreling with Naomi, but sometimes Susannah felt as if she was the only one willing to fight for their home.

And fight she would, even if her enemy was the charming Captain Sutton.

⋘

At the rumbling sound of a farm wagon passing on the National Road, Thad paused in recording the measurements he'd just taken. Transferring the pencil and record book to one hand, he waved and hailed a friendly greeting across the canal to the farmer.

When the man glanced toward him, his smile turned to a dark glower. The farmer's hand, which he'd raised momentarily in return salutation, shot back down to grasp the reins draped across the draft horse's rump.

The farmer turned his attention back to the road, and an uncomfortable feeling twisted through Thad's chest. He lifted the transit from the tripod and placed it in its leather case. Then, for a long moment, he stood watching the farmer's slump-shouldered back, now obscured by the road dust kicked up by the wagon wheels.

It seemed increasingly clear to Thad that the majority of Promise had little use for him or his business.

While most communities welcomed the prospect of a railroad, Promise was not among them. Many here had helped to build the Whitewater Canal. For years they'd fought for it, enduring floods that washed out locks and culverts. Thad was aware that some residents had even donated money to the Whitewater Canal Company to fund repairs on the waterway when the state refused to throw good money after bad.

The citizens of Promise had poured both emotional and financial capital into the sorry ditch. They seemed to look upon it as a long-ill kinsman, only now gaining a measure of vigor. Thad knew they viewed him as someone who'd come to deal the canal a deathblow just as it rose from its sickbed.

In truth, he understood why the people of Promise held him in distain. But the reality was that a railroad would be coming. Maybe not next year, or even in five years, but eventually one *would* come. He might as well be the one to chart its path. Besides, his father had left little doubt that failure to do so was not an option.

Only the regard of one person shook his resolve.

Susannah Killion.

The look in her eyes yesterday when he'd explained his business here still haunted him. His insides had twisted painfully when the soft lines of her sweet face hardened in contempt. But it was the stark fear he'd seen flicker in her green eyes that had kept him awake last night.

He wished he could assure her that the Union Railway Company would situate a passenger depot in Promise, but he knew that possibility was remote.

Thad blew out a long breath as he lashed the tripod to the back of Chieftain, the roan stallion he'd purchased for his longer treks along the canal. He might as well accept the fact that he'd killed any possibility of winning the favor of the lovely Susannah Killion.

As he rode toward Promise, he realized the only residents who ever offered him a greeting or ready smile were Naomi Killion and her granddaughter, Georgiana.

Thoughts of the blond cherub lifted his spirits along with the corners of his mouth. The child had quickly entangled her chubby fingers in his heartstrings. What joy to watch her little face beam as he handed her a piece of penny candy, a spinning top, or a length of colored ribbon for her hair.

As he neared the inn's back door, Susannah Killion emerged from the building, holding a basket against her trim waist.

The sight set his heart prancing. Dismounting, Thad smiled and dipped a quick bow. "Mrs. Killion."

"Captain Sutton." With an unsmiling but pleasant voice, she murmured the quiet acknowledgment and settled herself on the top step with the little basket beside her. She reached into the basket, lifted out a square cloth he recognized as a table napkin, and began working a needle around the edge of the material.

Trying to think of something to say, Thad looked behind the inn where he could see a dark brown patch of tilled ground. "Georgiana told me yesterday that the two of you were planning to plant peas this morning." He tethered Chieftain to a low branch of a large, old pin oak. Tender young leaves had begun emerging from the buds that tipped the tree's branches. When fully grown, the leaves would shade the entire east quadrant of the backyard.

While the horse munched on grass, Thad settled himself on the bench beneath the tree. He prayed that a congenial chat might help to restore the friendliness he and Susannah Killion seemed to have lost. "Fine day for making a garden. Extra warm for the middle of April."

"Yes, I suppose it is." A hint of a smile touched her lips, raising his hopes, but she didn't elaborate.

For several moments, Thad sat still, content to soak in the lovely picture of the late morning sun lacing golden threads through her honey-colored hair. The honking of a gaggle of geese near the canal basin punctuated the lengthening silence. As he contemplated what sufficiently intelligent comment he might offer in way of further conversation, she spoke first.

"I trust your work has been going well, Captain."

He started at her unexpected comment, feeling heat rise from his neck to his face. The subject of his work would not have been his choice of conversation, so he attempted to change it. "Yes—that is, on such a beautiful day, it's a blessing to have an opportunity to work outside." His gaze swept from the azure sky decorated with cotton clouds to the lush meadow separating the canal and a strip of woods. "My aunt Edith would have called this an extra-glad day."

"Extra-glad?" Now her pink Cupid's bow lips stretched to a full smile, showing straight white teeth. Her smile elicited the same feeling in Thad as when the clouds parted, allowing the sunshine to pour over him.

"Yes, as in Psalm 118. 'This is the day which the Lord hath made; we will rejoice and be glad in it.'" Even to his own ears, he sounded as breathless as if he'd run a quarter-mile foot race.

She only nodded, and her smile faded as she returned her attention to the work in her lap.

Thad wondered at her change in demeanor but, determined to keep their conversation going, he allowed his gaze to travel from the fertile fields left of the canal basin to the bustling infant town on its right.

"Promise. This place must be peopled with folk full of faith in the divine Word."

Susannah didn't look up from her busy fingers continuing to deftly work the needle around the piece of cloth. "Some more, some less, I reckon."

"And in which camp do you consider yourself?" Thad regretted the question the moment it left his lips.

Her fingers stilled. She lifted her face, and he read her answer in the empty look in her hazel green eyes. "Reckon I quit believin' in promises, divine or otherwise, when I got your letter four years ago informing me of George's death."

Sadness and guilt twined together around Thad's heart, cinching tight until he winced inwardly. "But you continue to attend worship services. . . ." He turned his gaze toward the town's little church. He could see the white steeple three blocks away. Like a resolute arm, it thrust the symbol of the cross from the midst of surrounding sycamores into the clear blue sky.

Her lips lifted in a wry grin. "That's mainly to pacify Naomi." She dropped her gaze to the work in her hands and started moving the needle in and out of the cloth again.

At her reply, Thad felt irritation skitter through him, setting a sharp edge to his voice. "George was Naomi's son, and she hasn't lost her faith."

Susannah stood. In a slow, deliberate motion, she bent and retrieved the sewing basket then turned toward him. Her back stiffening, she fixed him with an icy glare. "Captain Sutton, I've come to learn that promises are as fragile as blown glass. George promised to return from Texas. He didn't. The canal builders promised the canal would bring prosperity. It hasn't. And now you have come with your plans for a railroad that will, in all probability, put my inn out of business."

Her tone had softened, but the bitterness remained. "Where was God's help and mercy when George's father died suddenly a month after George left for the army? Where was God when George fell in Texas or the floods washed out the canal for the better part of a year? No, Captain, I don't put much stock in promises."

Thad's heart ached as he watched her walk back into the inn. He longed to help her understand that only faith in God brings peace in times of trouble. But how could he, when his own doing had contributed to at least a portion of her problems?

Chapter 4

*P*irouette.

Yes, that was the word—*pirouette*. Last fall, a woman traveling on the stagecoach to Indianapolis had shown Susannah a playbill from a ballet she'd attended in New York. The playbill depicted lady dancers in filmy pink dresses. They stood on tiptoe with their arms arced above their heads. The woman said they would actually twirl on their toes. She called it "doing a pirouette."

That's how Susannah felt each time she looked at Thad Sutton. Her heart did a pirouette.

From the back door of the inn, she gazed across the meadow at the surveyor striding through knee-high grass, his tripod resting on his shoulder.

Her heart spun like a ballerina.

Something in his purposeful gait and the strong, chiseled lines of the man took her breath away. A freshened breeze ruffled his wavy brown hair. His shirtsleeves, rolled above his elbows, revealed strong, tanned forearms. She caught faint snatches of a happy whistled tune wafting from his striding figure. Though too far away to see, Susannah could imagine a twinkle in his gray eyes.

Unable to make her heart dislike the man, she had grudgingly come to agree with Naomi's rationalization—Captain Sutton was just doing his job.

In no way did her decision alter her fear and dislike of the railroad or diminish her fervent hope that his work here would prove unsuccessful. Each morning she awoke with half her heart wishing he would leave and the other half fearing he might.

A tug at her skirt wrenched her attention from the troublesome Captain Sutton.

"I got a sack for the gweens, Mamma."

"Good, Georgiana. That's good," she answered absently, not bothering to correct her daughter's mispronounced word. Her gaze drifted back to the man walking toward them.

"Tad!" Georgiana caught sight of her hero and bounded toward Thad Sutton, trailing the yellow calico sack behind her like a pennant.

"Georgiana!" Susannah called after her.

The mother's admonishing tone ignored, she sprinted to catch up with her daughter, allowing the basket on her arm to bounce against her side.

"Well, Miss Georgiana! Where are you off to this fine day?" With a wide grin, Thad Sutton dropped his surveyor's tools to the ground and snatched up the giggling Georgiana, swinging her in a wide arc against the blue sky.

Georgiana's breathless answer tumbled out as he set her feet back on the ground. "Mamma and I are going to hunt mushwooms and gweens. See, here's my sack. It's for the gweens." She held up the calico sack.

"Well, that should hold a nice mess of greens." His broad smile swung from Georgiana to Susannah, setting her heart twirling on its toes again.

"May I look thwough your spyglass now, Tad? Will you go mushwoom hunting with us?"

"Georgiana, you shouldn't bother the captain." Susannah took Georgiana's hand and drew her to her side, causing her daughter's hopeful face to droop. "And you should not address Captain Sutton by his given name." Susannah's face heated as much from the twinkle in Thad Sutton's gray eyes as her daughter's lack of etiquette. "I apologize, Captain Sutton. I really have taught her better manners."

He shook his head at her apology. "Georgiana and I are friends, and friends should address one another by their first names." His gaze seemed to melt into hers. "I would like to consider us friends as well and would be honored if you'd address me as Thad. May I be so bold as to call you Susannah?"

"Well, I. . ." The plea in his eyes dried up her intended refusal of his suggestion. "Certainly, Cap—Thad."

"May I? May I look thwough your spyglass?" Georgiana, her wilted expression revived, tugged at his pant leg.

"Sure," he said with a chuckle, "if it's all right with your mamma."

At Susannah's nod, he knelt beside Georgiana and unlatched the leather case. He took out what looked like a telescope mounted on a short tripod above a compass.

Susannah gave a little gasp when Thad allowed Georgiana to grasp the telescope. "Be very careful, Georgiana."

Thad shot her a grin as Georgiana leaned an eye against the telescope lens. "Nothing to be concerned about, Susannah. Old William J. Young made these things nearly indestructible."

"Ooh, the twees look so close!" Georgiana giggled as she alternately peered through the telescope at the little woods behind the inn then looked without the benefit of its magnification. She turned wide eyes toward Thad. "I saw a birdie in its nest!"

He chuckled, and Susannah wondered why she hadn't noticed before how the right corner of his mouth dimpled when he smiled.

"Now," he told Georgiana as he nestled the transit back into its case, "we'd better not use up any more of your mamma's morning."

"Will you. . . ," Georgiana heaved a sigh laden with frustration. "Will you come mushwoom hunting with us?"

"That sounds like great fun. I haven't gone mushroom hunting since I was a boy." His gray gaze lingered on Susannah's, causing her heart to flutter and her face to grow warm. "But we'd need to ask your mamma if I might accompany your hunt."

Georgiana grabbed a fistful of Susannah's skirt and tugged. "Peaase? Peaase, Mamma, may Tad come?"

"Yes, of course, if we are not keeping you from your work—Thad." Susannah stumbled over his name and scolded herself for feeling as giddy as Georgiana about the prospect of Thad Sutton's company.

"Work can wait. It's not every day I get an invitation to a mushroom hunt." He bent and retrieved the tripod poles and transit case. "If you ladies will indulge me for a few moments while I return my instruments to my room, I'll rejoin you directly."

While she and Georgiana waited beneath the oak tree, Susannah struggled with her conflicting feelings about Thad joining them. The man was too bothersome by half! She should have simply refused him. Surely she could have thought of something. But that would have meant disappointing Georgiana.

She glanced at her daughter, who was bouncing up and down while gleefully mispronouncing Captain Sutton's name. Susannah followed Georgiana's adoring gaze. Watching Thad emerge from the inn's back door, she knew it hadn't been the prospect of a whiny child that had caused her to agree to his company.

Striding toward them, he clapped his outstretched hands toward her daughter. "How about a piggyback ride, Georgiana?" At the child's enthusiastic nod, he laughed and swung her up to his shoulders.

They waded their way through the tall grass toward the woods, and Susannah couldn't help thinking what a perfect picture of domestic contentment the three of them must make. At the troubling thought, she accelerated her pace, marching ahead of Georgiana and the captain.

The refreshing coolness of the forest greeted her as she pushed aside the branches of an elderberry bush and stepped beneath the canopy of young leaves. The woodsy scents of bark, moss, decaying leaves, and wildflowers tickled her nose.

"Mamma, don't go so fast! Wait for me and Tad." Rustling leaves and snapping twigs accompanied Georgiana's complaint.

Susannah glanced over her shoulder at her daughter. Now back on the ground, Georgiana ran toward her, ahead of Captain Sutton.

"Tad and I already got some dandelion gweens." Georgiana held open her yellow sack.

"Greens, Georgiana. Remember your *r*'s."

Joining them, Thad tousled Georgiana's curls. "I hope we didn't delay you, Susannah, but we found a nice patch of dandelions near a big sycamore."

"No—no, not at all." Susannah busied herself picking an elderberry leaf from Georgiana's hair. It seemed odd to hear Captain Sutton address her by her given name. What was more disconcerting—she realized she liked it.

"I see some gwe–gr–eens!" Georgiana bounded toward a sun-dappled clearing.

"Don't go far," Susannah cautioned. "Don't step in mud puddles, and watch out for snakes."

"You're doing a wonderful job with her." Thad's voice pulled Susannah's attention from Georgiana, who crouched a few feet away, picking dandelion greens. "The inn and raising a daughter—I don't know how you do it all. As my aunt Edith would say, 'You're a caution and a wonder.'"

Susannah warmed beneath his praise. Keeping her gaze fixed on the forest floor, she maneuvered around several puddles. Recent rains had made the woods marshy, but Susannah knew the dampness along with the warm spring sun promised a bounty of mushrooms.

"I'm not sure I could do it without Naomi." Casting a quick, reassuring glance at Georgiana, Susannah headed toward a decaying elm stump.

Thad chuckled. "Yes, she's a caution and a wonder, too. I think Naomi and Aunt Edith would get on quite well."

"You must be very close to your aunt Edith." Susannah had wondered at his several references to his relative.

"Yes. After my mother died when I was about Georgiana's age, my father left me with his sister, Edith, and her husband while he pursued various business ventures. She and my uncle Joe nearly raised me in Vernon, down in Jennings County."

"You are not close to your father, then?" Susannah watched his face cloud and wished she had not voiced her thought.

"No." His terse reply increased her regret.

He focused his attention on the far side of a decaying tree stump, and his tone brightened. "Ah, here is what we are looking for," he announced, seeming as happy to change the subject as to find the mushrooms.

He knelt and brushed black humus from the rotting wood, revealing a large cluster of honeycomb mushrooms. Taking a small knife from his pocket, Thad sliced through the spongy beige stems and handed the grayish-brown fungus spears to Susannah.

"I can see you've had experience in mushroom hunting, Captain Sutton." Susannah chuckled as she carefully arranged the delicate mushrooms in her linen-lined basket.

"Thad, remember?" A hurt look flickered in his eyes for an instant before his smile vanquished it. "As a boy, I spent many a spring day hunting mushrooms with Uncle Joe in the woods along the Muscatatuck River." His gaze panned the immediate area. "You seem very familiar with this little wood. Were you raised in Promise?"

"No, George and I were both raised in Hamilton County."

They made their way toward Georgiana, who had abandoned her greens hunting to study a black and yellow butterfly flitting about a patch of bluebells a few yards away.

"Do you still have family there?" Thad took Susannah's hand and helped her over a fallen tree.

"Only my older brother, Frank, and his family."

"Ruben's father?"

Susannah's voice lowered. "Yes." Frank's displeasure with her for taking Ruben in and allowing him to work for her rather than sending him back home still chaffed. Though Thad seemed genuinely interested in her family history, Susannah did not feel comfortable divulging the rift that decision had caused between her and her brother.

"And your parents, do they still live there?"

"No, they died of cholera when I was twelve." A painful stab near Susannah's heart accompanied the memory of that awful summer day when she lost her parents. She remembered how she'd fought to enter the quarantined cabin when she learned of their deaths. And how Ephraim, her doctor brother-in-law, would not allow her inside but physically hauled her away to the home of Frank and his wife, Miranda.

"I'm sorry." The genuine compassion in Thad's soft voice brought tears to Susannah's eyes, blurring the brush and dead leaves covering the forest floor.

Not trusting her own voice, she only nodded and headed toward a nearby heap of rotting wood. In Thad's silence, she sensed he understood that the dozen years since her parents' deaths had not diminished the pain of her loss.

"Ruben's father is your only sibling, then?" He crouched to harvest another crop of mushrooms.

Susannah silently blessed him for not lingering on her sad memory. "No, my sister, Becky, and brother Jacob, and their families live in Madison. My brother-in-law, Ephraim, is a doctor there, and Jacob is a minister."

Thad's smiling, upturned face looked almost angelic caught in a sunbeam shafting through the forest canopy. "Ah, Madison is a lovely town. A couple of years ago while on railroad business, I had an occasion to visit Mr. Lanier's home there." His smile stretched wider. "I may have unknowingly passed your siblings on the broad thoroughfare of Main-Cross Street."

The fact that he seemed to seek even so tenuous a connection between them caused her heart to mimic the hammering *rat-a-tat* of a nearby woodpecker.

In their long-exchanged look, Susannah felt as if she might melt into his pewter gaze. The almost tangible attraction between them set off warning bells inside her. She wrenched her gaze away to break the spell.

I must be daft! How could I even imagine. . .

Thad cleared his throat. His casual tone could not disguise an uncharacteristic tightness in his voice. "Naomi reminded me of the church social on Sunday afternoon a week from tomorrow to welcome the new minister and his family. I thought maybe. . ."

Thad's voice faded from Susannah's consciousness as a sudden unease gripped her. Her senses became keenly acute. Her body tensed, and her gaze darted around the little woods.

Thad gripped her arm. "Susannah, what is it? What's wrong?"

"Georgiana," Susannah croaked through her fear-constricted throat. "I can't see her anywhere! Georgiana! Georgiana!"

No answer came except for the chirping of the birds.

Chapter 5

Susannah dropped the basket of mushrooms and raced toward the clump of bluebells where she'd last noticed Georgiana watching a butterfly. Only a few discarded bluebells and yellow dandelion blossoms evidenced her daughter's recent presence.

Guilt poured over Susannah. "I should have been watching her more closely. I should have—"

"She can't have gone far. We'll find her." Thad's confident tone as he came up beside her helped tame the panic raging in Susannah's belly.

As she searched his face for reassurance, Susannah felt her guilt reconfigure itself into resentment. How could she have allowed Thad Sutton to distract her from the most important thing in her life—her daughter?

She shrugged his hand from her shoulder and welcomed the anger replacing her mind-numbing dread. "I'm holding you to that, Captain Sutton," she said, fixing him with a glare.

Susannah felt a prick of remorse when he dropped his gaze to the ground. *Georgiana is my responsibility. I shouldn't be blaming anyone else. . . .*

Thad crouched down. With his finger, he traced an indention that looked like a tiny shoe print in the dark, sticky mud. Rising, he grasped her hand and with long, purposeful strides began hauling her through the woods. "She's gone this way."

Susannah ignored the brambles clutching at her skirt and the branches whipping near her face. As they emerged into the meadow, she frantically scanned the grassy expanse between the woods and the canal.

No Georgiana.

Thad paused. His intent gaze turned northwest toward the canal, and Susannah's heart jumped to her throat.

"Surely she hasn't—I've told her so many times. . ."

He answered by towing her across the meadow, his gaze fixed on what seemed to Susannah an indiscernible path through knee-high grass and wildflowers.

Susannah prayed Thad knew what he was doing as she struggled to keep up. Exertion and fear robbed her breath, rendering her unable to call out her daughter's name.

When they came upon two young boys baiting fishhooks near the canal's edge, Thad stopped. "Have you seen a little girl?"

"Georgiana," Susannah gasped, catching her breath. "Have you seen Georgiana?"

The boys, whom she recognized as Alex Milton and Davy McLeod, dropped their willow poles. Nodding, they turned wide eyes and guilty expressions toward her and Thad.

"Saw her up by the feeder dam." Alex pointed a grimy finger westward toward the dam that supplied the canal with water from a reservoir fed by the Whitewater River. "Hey, you won't tell our folks you saw us here, will ya? Cause we're s'posed to be. . ."

A distant *splash* jerked Susannah and Thad's attention from the boys and sent them sprinting toward the dam.

Oh, Lord, no! Please, no! The words tore from Susannah's terror-squeezed heart.

She stood shaking near the canal's edge, dimly aware that she'd just prayed her first heartfelt prayer in months.

The tranquil sound of the falling water sluicing over the dam into the canal only heightened her fear. Last summer she'd had Ruben teach Georgiana to swim in case she ever fell into the canal. But here, with the constant pouring of water into the canal, she feared her baby would be relentlessly pounded beneath the surface.

Without a word, Thad divested himself of his boots, socks, and shirt and slid down the muddy bank. The four-foot-deep water came only midchest.

Susannah held her breath along with Thad as he dipped his face beneath the churning surface near the dam. Soon, he completely disappeared beneath the swirling white water.

An eternity seemed to pass while he remained submerged. She couldn't imagine how he'd held his breath so long. At last, he came up gasping for air and shaking his head, sending water droplets flying. "She's not here."

His pronouncement set Susannah's frantic heart oscillating between relief and dread.

Thad scrambled up the slippery bank. For a moment he stood looking west, beyond the lock, then east, toward the inn. "Come on." He fit the words between deep breaths as he snatched his shirt, socks, and boots from the muddy towpath and turned toward the inn.

Susannah struggled to match his long-legged strides. What had he seen? Was it just a hunch? She fought hysteria and the urge to jump into the canal and slosh a mile of its length in search of her baby.

As they neared the basin and Garrett Heywood's packet, Susannah perked her ears, and her heart began to race. Had she truly heard Georgiana's musical giggles wafting from the *Flying Eagle*?

"Georgiana! Georgiana!" Susannah leaped to the deck of the canal boat as she called her daughter's name.

"Hey, Susannah! This what you're lookin' for?" Smiling, Garrett emerged from the interior of the boat, carrying Georgiana. His cinnamon brown eyes sparkled beneath his shock of russet hair. "When I saw Georgiana, I figured you must be close by." He gave her a flirtatious wink.

They'd been playing this little cat-and-mouse game for the better part of a year, and Susannah had long grown weary of it. Ten years or so her senior, she had to admit Garrett Heywood, in his midthirties, was still quite a looker. But her feelings for him had never grown beyond friendship, and she doubted they ever would—especially while he continued to live the rather rowdy life of a canaler.

She ignored his wink, turning her attention to her daughter. "Georgiana, you had us sick with worry! Whatever possessed you to take off like that?" Wilting with relief, Susannah sagged against the outside wall of the canal boat's cabin.

Perched on the crook of Garrett's arm, Georgiana blinked at the reprimand while she clung to his neck and munched a sugar cookie as big as a man's hand. "I couldn't find you and Tad. T'ought you went home," she explained around a bite of cookie, sending golden crumbs showering onto Garrett's green coat.

Sallie O'Donnell, Garrett's canal boat cook, appeared from inside the boat. She pushed her straggling brown hair from her concerned face. "I'm right sorry if we caused you to fret, Missus Killion. I reckon it's my fault yer young'un's here."

The woman wadded the hem of her apron in her hands, an apologetic tone edging her words. "The child smelled my sugar cookies and asked Captain Heywood if she could have one. He brought her onto the boat fearin' she'd fall into the canal." She shot a nervous glance toward Garrett. "The captain would have carried her back to the inn directly, but I couldn't find it in me to deny her a cookie. I hope you don't mind me givin' her the treat."

"No—no, of course not. Thank you for looking after her." Susannah shot Sallie an unsteady smile and reached out trembling arms to take Georgiana from Garrett. "We were just frightened when we lost track of her in the woods. . . mushroom hunting."

Surprise joined the relief flooding through Susannah. She'd never heard the reclusive Widow O'Donnell string more than three or four words together. Though still a young woman—in her early thirties, Susannah guessed—Sallie generally kept to herself when in Promise. The only exception being her faithful attendance at worship services as Garrett docked the *Flying Eagle* here in Promise from Saturday evening until he headed the boat back toward Cincinnati early each Monday morning. But even at church, the retiring woman rarely socialized. Because of her timid manner, many folks in Promise considered Sallie O'Donnell a bit odd.

"Little early in the season to go for a swim in the canal, ain't it, Captain Sutton?" Garrett narrowed his eyes toward Thad, who'd replaced his shirt and boots and stood dripping puddles of water onto the towpath from his drenched breeches.

An easy grin quirked Thad's mouth. "We feared Georgiana had fallen into the canal. Two boys sent us down to the dam when we inquired if they'd seen her."

Garrett gave a quick chuckle that turned into a snort. "Young Milton and McLeod. Their paps'll give 'em a good hidin' if they catch 'em skippin' school to go fishin'."

Switching subjects, he fixed Thad with a cold glare. "Mushroom huntin', huh? Find any? Don't see a sack."

"We left the sacks in the woods when we noticed Georgiana was missing." Susannah snapped the terse reply as indignation stiffened her back. Was Garrett suggesting anything improper between her and Thad? How dare he even imply such a thing!

"I'll tell you what I *did* find, Captain Heywood." All humor had evaporated from Thad's face and voice. "While in the canal down by the feeder dam, I noticed the thing is riddled with muskrat burrows. Worse, they've compromised the towpath bank."

Thad cocked his head in the direction of the dam then pinned Garrett with a stare. "The ground is near saturation." His voice lowered as concern etched his brow. "One good rainy spell and both the dam and much of the canal bank will likely crumble and half of Promise will be flooded. I suggest the entire stretch from the dam to the basin be shut down immediately for repairs."

A concerned look flitted briefly across Garrett's face before his expression hardened again. "Maybe. And maybe you just want another reason to put this canal out of business. . .Captain Sutton." Thad's name dripped with scorn from Garrett Heywood's lips.

Even if Thad's appraisal of the canal's condition gave Garrett pause, Susannah knew Garrett would never accept a railroad man's word without checking for himself.

Thad's posture stiffened, and the muscles worked in his jaw. "Now listen here, Heywood, are you calling me a liar? Maybe you don't care about this town, but a lot of other people do."

Concerned by the escalating tension, Susannah turned to the canal boat cook. Perhaps by injecting a new topic, she could break up the men's verbal sparring match before it turned to fisticuffs. "Sallie—that is your name, isn't it?" she asked in a bright voice.

Looking as uneasy as Susannah felt, the O'Donnell woman gave her a shy nod.

"Are you planning to attend the church social a week from tomorrow, Sallie? My mother-in-law, Naomi, is on the organization committee." Susannah fully expected a negative response from the woman, but at least Thad and Garrett had stopped arguing.

"I'd thought I might." Sallie murmured the startling reply and swiped a strand of hair from her brow.

"Actually," Garrett barged into the conversation, "I was thinkin' I might go, too. Sounds like some good eats, and Sallie is always pesterin' me to go to church." He dipped a quick bow toward Susannah. "But I'll only go if you'll allow me to squire you to the event, Susannah."

Stunned, Susannah almost dropped Georgiana. She'd never known Garrett to darken the door of a church, at least not in Promise.

"Well. . .I. . ." Susannah tried to think of a way out of this uncomfortable position. She certainly didn't want to encourage Garrett's attentions. But although her own faith had waned, it bothered her to discourage an unsaved soul from being exposed to the scriptures. "Yes—yes, of course, Captain Heywood. I'll be happy to accompany you."

She didn't dare look at Thad as her attention shifted from Garrett's self-satisfied grin back to Sallie. "And I look forward to seeing you there, too, Sallie." If Sallie did attend, her presence could provide a buffer between her and Garrett. But Susannah's hope of that happening dwindled when the woman gave a non-committal shrug and ducked back into the boat.

During their walk back to the inn, Georgiana's happy chatter filled the uneasy silence stretching between Susannah and Thad. Susannah suspected Thad had been about to ask her to the social before they realized Georgiana was missing.

"We forgot the mushwooms and gweens. Tad, you're not listening!" Nestled securely in Thad's arms, Georgiana tugged on his sleeve.

The frown that had cleft his brow dissolved, and his lips lifted in a smile. "Don't worry, moppet. I'll go back to the woods and fetch them."

When they reached the oak tree behind the inn, Thad lowered Georgiana to the ground then glanced at the sun riding high in the eastern sky. "It must be nearly ten o'clock," he said, giving Georgiana a serious look. "Didn't you tell me your dolly takes her tea at ten o'clock sharp, moppet?"

"Ohh!" Georgiana's eyes widened and she pressed her fingers to her lips. "Dolly will be cwoss," she muttered before whirling around and scampering off toward the inn's kitchen door.

When her daughter disappeared inside the building, Susannah turned to Thad. "You're very good with her."

His lips tipped up. "She's a sweet child. I like her a lot."

Suddenly, Susannah blurted the question that had scratched at her mind since Thad's argument with Garrett. "Do you really think the canal is in danger of collapsing?" The memory of past floods made her want to believe Garrett was right and Thad simply aimed to impugn the canal. But if that were true, it meant Thad was less than honest—a notion she found more than a little disheartening.

"Yes, I do." His answer came without hesitation, and his gaze never flinched from hers.

Susannah nodded somberly. She believed him. And that made her glad, despite learning of the canal's instability. But worrying about the canal would have to wait. She'd had enough worry for one day.

Taking in Thad's bedraggled condition, a new wave of gratitude rolled through her. "Thank you for helping me find Georgiana. I'm glad you were with us. I don't know what I would have done if I'd been alone and lost track of her. . . ."

"You would have managed very well, I have no doubt."

The respect shining in his gray eyes set Susannah's heart singing ridiculously.

"I want you to know I enjoyed this morning very much—except, of course, for the scare with Georgiana," he added, the corner of his mouth dimpling with his grin.

Warmth flooded Susannah's cheeks. She turned her face askance in an attempt to hide her blush. "Thank you, too, for offering to fetch the sacks of greens and mushrooms. You may leave them on the worktable in the kitchen," she murmured and stepped toward the inn.

"Susannah. . ." His quiet voice stopped her, turning her around and sending her pulse racing again. "I was going to ask you. . .you know, to the church social."

"I know." She gave him a weak smile. "I hope you will still come—for Naomi's sake."

"Wouldn't miss it." He cast the parting comment brightly over his shoulder then headed for the meadow.

Disappointment skittered through Susannah as she walked back to the inn. There was nothing more to say. Garrett had beat Thad to the invitation, and she had accepted. Perhaps it was better this way. Though potentially aggravating, a Sunday afternoon spent in the company of Garrett Heywood would not be as unsettling as one spent in the company of Captain Thad Sutton. Yes, perhaps it was better this way.

At the kitchen door, she turned and gazed across the meadow at Thad's stalwart figure striding toward the woods through the knee-deep expanse of grass and wildflowers. Leaning against the doorjamb, she heaved a soft sigh.

So why doesn't it feel better?

Chapter 6

The horse neighed and jerked its head in protest as Thad yanked the harness belly cinch tight.

"Sorry about that, boy." He patted the glossy black side of the animal's head. It wasn't this poor creature's fault that Thad had allowed Garrett Heywood to beat him out of enjoying Susannah's company at the church social.

Thad remembered how Heywood had shown up early in a rented buggy to escort Susannah and Georgiana to church, and a streak of jealousy shot through him.

As consolation, Thad had offered to escort Naomi to Sunday services as well as the social immediately following. Although shorter and slighter built than his aunt Edith, Naomi Killion's personality reminded him of his beloved relative.

A wry grin twisted his mouth. He could use some of Aunt Edith's comforting hugs and homespun wisdom about now.

Grasping the leather bridle strap, he led the horse with its attached buggy to the inn's side door. The dull sound of the horse's plodding clops on the dirt path echoed Thad's drab mood.

A moment after he brought the rig to a halt, Naomi appeared at the inn's open door with a baking pan swathed in linen. "Captain Sutton, it's so nice of you to drive me to church."

"Here, let me take that for you." He relieved her lace-gloved hands of the pan.

"You are a true blessing, Captain." Heaving a sigh, she gave him a grateful look. "Besides this pan of corn bread, Susannah and I have prepared two pies and a basketful of fried chicken for the social. Garrett Heywood had no room to transport any of it in that little rented shay, and Ruben left on horseback to fetch that Macklin girl he's sweet on."

Thad deposited the pan of corn bread in the storage box at the rear of the buggy then followed Naomi into the inn.

The spry little woman hurried to the kitchen, her silky black skirt whispering as she walked. "I don't reckon this is quite the way you'd envisioned your Sunday morning, is it?" She grinned, her quick hands deftly wrapping linen towels around apple and rhubarb pies.

Thad couldn't help inhaling the delicious aromas that greeted him at the

157

kitchen door. "Actually, I've been looking forward to the social since last Sunday when you first invited me—"

"You know that's not what I meant, Captain Sutton." Naomi gave him a knowing grin, thrusting a little hamper that smelled of fried chicken toward him.

Thad accepted the hamper, unsure how to answer. Surely she didn't expect him to admit his disappointment at missing Susannah's company.

"Well, I. . ." He searched for something evasive to say but failed to form any intelligent thought.

Naomi swished past him, a pie in each hand. "It's not exactly the day she'd planned either, you know." She tossed the statement over her shoulder as they exited the inn.

Thad nestled the pies and chicken beside the corn bread then helped Naomi into the buggy. He'd have to watch himself. Like Aunt Edith, the woman seemed adept at reading his mind.

They rolled along Sycamore Street in congenial silence. Above them, the trees for which the street had been named reached out a canopy of graceful branches beginning to fill out with young green leaves. A warm spring breeze carried the fragrance of lilacs to Thad's nostrils and fluttered the ends of his carefully tied cravat. A red-winged blackbird called out a salutation as they passed its fence post perch.

Thad wished he felt as tranquil as the spring morning. Although thoughts of Susannah dominated his mind, he was reluctant to voice those private musings to her mother-in-law. However, mindful of his extended reticence, Thad gave the lady beside him a sidelong glance. He felt compelled to inject some subject of conversation.

Suddenly, he realized he'd never personally offered Naomi his sympathy concerning George's death. "I fear I have never sufficiently extended my condolences in regard to your son's passing. I'd like to rectify that now, however belated." A tiny ball of anxiety wound in his belly as he wondered how she would respond to both the subject and the oversight.

Naomi's pleasant expression softened to a kind smile. She touched his arm. "Captain Sutton, your eloquent letter four years ago was more than sufficient."

Thad's fingers tightened on the reins. "George was a brave and loyal soldier."

Naomi's blue eyes glistened, but her smile never wavered. "He would have been."

Thad marveled at her serenity. "How have you been able to accept it when. . ."

"When Susannah can't?" She fixed him with that look that seemed to see more than he'd like and made him want to squirm. "I know my boy's in the arms of Jesus. 'And we know that all things work together for good to them that love God, to them who are the called according to his purpose,'" she quoted.

"Susannah doesn't believe that?" Thad guided the horse left, down Laurel Street, toward the churchyard.

"Oh, she believes it. . .deep down." Weary regret tinged Naomi's tone. "Susannah's and George's lives were twisted together since they were little. I think it's just easier for her to be angry with God than to open her heart and look for His greater purpose in her life."

Naomi shook her head sadly. "I'm not sure she's ever really faced George's death. I think she shoved it all back into a dark cubbyhole in her heart and threw herself into running the inn and raising Georgiana." She shot him a grin. "I'm afraid I have no head for business. I must confess Susannah is the reason we have managed to keep the inn open."

Thad pulled on the reins, bringing the buggy to a stop beside the little stone and clapboard church. Contemplating Naomi's words, he jumped to the ground and tied the horse to the hitching post. Had Susannah's heart died with George, or might it be possible for someone else to rekindle a new purpose in it?

When he helped Naomi from the buggy, Thad's gaze wandered to the church's side yard. Susannah and Heywood, with Georgiana at their heels, giggled together while they worked with several others to set up the food tables. He frowned, almost hoping Naomi was right and Susannah's heart remained closed to the notion of a new love.

"If she'd wanted Heywood for a husband, she could have had him six times over this past year."

At Naomi's words, Thad felt heat march up his neck. The woman did see more than he would like. Not trusting his voice, he offered her his arm.

As they mounted the church steps, his face turned unbidden toward the side yard. He saw Susannah playfully smack Heywood's hand when he snatched a tablecloth from her.

A weight like a cannonball seemed to lodge in Thad's chest, and he felt Naomi give his arm two soft pats.

Yes, the woman sees far too much.

At this moment, however, that realization was somehow comforting.

~

In the churchyard, Susannah smoothed a bunched corner of the quilt she'd spread on the shady grass beneath a flowering tulip poplar tree. She'd staked out the spot earlier while helping to set up the trestle tables for the food. If the picnic's location was ideal, her companion for the occasion certainly wasn't.

Garrett Heywood had seemed uncomfortable during the church service. He'd sat across the aisle from her on the men's side of the church, and his constant fidgeting had raked down her nerves like a flax carder. She'd found his deportment a stark contrast to Thad Sutton's attentive reverence.

Thad Sutton.

Susannah looked toward the hitching posts near the front of the church and watched Thad hand Naomi a linen-swathed pie. The ever-present war of emotions raged inside her. If Thad Sutton's railroad replaced the canal, it spelled the end of the Killion House Inn. Yet that knowledge didn't prevent her from wishing she'd be sharing this picnic spot with Thad instead of with Garrett. So her heart fluttered when she saw Naomi and Thad making their way toward her after depositing the food on the tables.

Georgiana, who'd been bouncing beside Thad like a happy puppy, skipped to her. "Mamma, I told Tad and Gwamma to bwing their quilt over here by you," she said, plopping down on the quilt, a pink puddle of calico skirt splaying around her.

Naomi bustled up, a crazy quilt draped across her arm. "What a perfect patch of shady yard, Susannah. Do you mind if Captain Sutton and I share it with you?"

"No, of course not." Silently blessing her mother-in-law, Susannah hurried to help Naomi spread out her quilt. Since Sallie O'Donnell had refused her invitation to sit with her and Garrett, Susannah welcomed the extra company.

"Georgiana insisted we all eat together," Thad explained with a grin that sent Susannah's heart into silly somersaults.

"I think that is a wonderful idea," Susannah said in a rush. But when she cast a glance at Garrett, who was striding toward them, a new concern bloomed. His frown suggested he didn't share her sentiment. She worried that unfriendly sparks would fly again between the two men.

"Mrs. Killion." Unsmiling, Garrett dipped a stiff bow in Naomi's direction then turned to Thad. "Captain Sutton." His voice hardening, he spared Thad a quick nod but didn't offer his hand.

Susannah's stomach knotted as she watched the two men's glares cross rapiers for an instant. News of Thad's business in Promise had spread like a grass fire in August. She'd heard the angry grumbles around town. Even before the Whitewater Canal had been dug, the town had sprung up on the promise of its coming—giving birth to the town's name. So the presence of someone who threatened to take away its reason to exist raised the community's collective hackles.

She also understood Garrett's personal concern. He'd built up a fairly profitable packet business that ran weekly between Cincinnati and Promise. If a railroad turned the canal into a useless ditch, he stood to lose as much as she, or anyone else in Promise.

When the preacher gave the invocation from his spot in the center of the churchyard, Susannah struggled to keep her mind off her worries and on Pastor Ezekiel Murdoch's words.

She actually liked the new minister, finding him exceedingly personable. A robust man of some fifty-odd years, he possessed a hearty laugh, a jolly disposition, and an eloquent oratory fueled by a fiery zeal.

But his message today from the first chapter of Second Corinthians extolling God's promises to comfort the suffering had echoed hollowly in her ears. God had promised to answer her prayers, yet so many times His answer had been "No."

She glanced at Thad, handing Georgiana a tin plate. Now, in a seemingly cruel twist of circumstance, the man who would snatch away her livelihood also made her heart misbehave.

Folks filled their plates from the vast array of dishes covering several trestle tables.

Carrying both her and Georgiana's plates of food, Susannah joined the others around the quilts. There, Naomi took charge of Georgiana, leaving Susannah stuck between Thad and Garrett.

Thad hurried to assist Susannah with her plate, and Garrett held her glass of tea while she situated herself on the quilt. Taking extra time to carefully adjust her ivory-colored cotton skirt around her, Susannah hoped to extend the uneasy truce between Thad and Garrett. But the moment she'd settled her plate on her lap and had her glass of tea in hand, the men began their verbal sparring.

"Really, Sutton, I don't see any need for a railroad now that the canal is operational again." Sitting cross-legged beside her, Garrett poked a fork at his potato salad with a ferocity that suggested he'd rather poke the utensil into Thaddeus Sutton's ribs.

"But for how long?" Thad picked up the chicken leg from his tin plate and jabbed it in the general direction of the canal. "As you've experienced, one good flood renders the thing unusable."

Although it irked her to do so, Susannah felt compelled to come to Garrett's assistance. "But they fixed the canal," she said and was rewarded by an appreciative smile from Garrett.

Thad shook his head and frowned. "Not from what I've witnessed. I've already told you about the muskrat damage I noticed near the feeder dam. Hard telling how many other places along the bank have been compromised."

Garrett snorted in reply.

For the next several minutes, a strained silence reigned while they ate. At length, Naomi rose. "If you'll excuse me, I think I'll go have a word with Pastor Murdoch and his wife."

Susannah knew Naomi avoided discord whenever possible, but she couldn't help wondering if Naomi, too, was bothered by Thad's opinion of the canal's instability. Whatever the case, Susannah envied Naomi's opportunity to walk away from the unsettling conversation.

"I'm all done," Georgiana declared, wiping the back of her hand across her mouth. Making her way over to Susannah, she crawled into her mother's lap and snuggled.

Susannah rocked her daughter in her arms, reveling in her child's baby softness. Tears stung her eyelids as she nuzzled her face against Georgiana's blond curls. At four years old, Georgiana was fast approaching an age when she would no longer care to cuddle.

Garrett mumbled something about rhubarb pie and headed for the food tables.

Thad sat still, a tender expression softening the angles of his face. His gentle smile as he watched her hold her child touched a deep, warm place inside Susannah.

"Pastor Murdoch seems to have been very well received here," Susannah said, trying to find a subject of conversation that had nothing to do with the Whitewater Canal or Thad's business in Promise.

Thad followed her gaze to the church's front yard enclosed in white pickets. There, Pastor Murdoch and his plump wife stood visiting with several parishioners, including Naomi. "Yes, Promise is lucky to have him. I can't remember when I've heard such an inspiring sermon."

Susannah couldn't think of an appropriate, yet honest, response. Dismayed, she realized she'd unwittingly steered the conversation to another uncomfortable topic.

As she grappled for a reply, a boy of about six, whom she recognized as the miller's youngest son, stepped toward them. He glanced shyly from his dusty shoe tops to their faces and back again.

"We're playing "Ring Around the Rosie." May Georgiana play, too?"

"Where?" Susannah darted a quick look about the churchyard. She wouldn't want to send Georgiana out of her field of vision or among children too much older than her daughter.

"Over there." The boy pointed to a group of children of varying ages gathered in a grassy meadow several yards beyond the food tables. "I'll take care of her and see she doesn't get hurt or dirty."

"Good man," Thad said, the corner of his mouth twitching.

"Pease, Mamma, pease!" Georgiana pushed away from Susannah and jumped up from her lap.

"I suppose." These were all children with whom Georgiana regularly attended Sunday school. Susannah eyed the children playing in the distance and started to get up. "It's quite a ways away. Maybe I should go. . . ."

Thad stood. "You stay. I'll handle this reconnaissance." He turned a serious face to Georgiana. "What do you think, moppet? Shall we go join the maneuvers?" At Georgiana's affirming nod, he swung the giggling child to his shoulders and gave the boy a smart salute. "Lead on, soldier." The quick wink he cast over his shoulder to Susannah sent her heart tumbling.

Garrett called her name twice before Susannah wrenched her attention from the sight of Thad striding across the churchyard with Georgiana perched atop his shoulders.

"I took the liberty of bringin' you a piece of cherry pie for dessert. I remember you mentionin' once that it was your favorite."

"Thank you, Garrett." Susannah accepted the dessert dish and gave him a wobbly smile.

He lowered himself beside her on the quilt. "Now that we're alone, I've been meanin' to ask you somethin' real important." He seemed to study the piece of rhubarb pie on his dessert dish. "I know it can't be easy, bein' a widow woman and all. . . ."

Panic grabbed at Susannah's chest. She should have known he'd eventually get around to this, yet she found herself unprepared. "Garrett, don't. I mean. . . Naomi and I are managing very well, and we have Ruben. . . ."

Garrett shook his head. "Your nephew's a fine boy. But it ain't like havin' a man of your own."

Susannah gave his arm a gentle squeeze. "You're a dear friend, and I appreciate your concern. I really do. But I'm not sure I'll ever marry again."

The sound of children's laughter turned her face toward the meadow, and her gaze lit upon the figure of Thad Sutton.

Garrett's look followed hers, and his voice hardened, taking on a sharp edge. "Maybe you will, and maybe you won't. But just remember who cares about what's important to you—your inn and the Whitewater Canal!"

Leaving his piece of pie untouched, Garrett sprang up and strode away, disappearing behind the church.

Susannah rose and heaved a frustrated sigh. Garrett was a good friend, and she hated to hurt him. She noticed Sallie O'Donnell scowling from across the churchyard where she sat with several older widows. Susannah wondered if Garrett had mentioned to his cook that he intended to propose and Sallie surmised by his actions that he'd been refused.

Deciding she should at least try to soothe Garrett's wounded feelings, she headed behind the church. But as she neared the back corner of the building, the sound of Ruben's distraught voice stopped her cold.

"I'm sorry, Lilly. I know it's all my fault. I—I could marry you."

Lilly drew an audibly ragged breath. "I'm not sure I'm ready to marry. I'm only fifteen. But my dad. . .my dad. . ." Her words faded to muffled sobs. Although the couple remained out of her line of vision, Susannah imagined Ruben muffling Lilly's sobs against his chest.

Susannah knew she shouldn't continue listening but found herself rooted to the ground, anger and concern twisting through her like a hot poker. For the first time, she began to regret having taken in her brother's son when he appeared at the inn two years ago.

The eldest of Frank's children, Ruben had no interest in or aptitude for his father's blacksmith trade, which had caused constant friction between the two and prompted the boy to run away from home. And because Susannah provided

Ruben sanctuary rather than sending him back to his parents in Hamilton County, she'd angered her brother. Although she'd had no further communication with Frank, she had received a letter from Ruben's mother, Miranda, thanking her for taking Ruben in and asking her to look after him. And so she had—or had at least tried to.

Frank and Miranda had trusted her with their son, and she'd let them down. Hugging her arms around her trembling body, Susannah's pulse pounded in her head. She felt sick.

Chapter 7

Dawn stained the inn's kitchen with a rosy hue. Susannah yawned as she pitched another piece of kindling into the flaming belly of the cookstove and clanged the door shut. Sleep had been fitful.

She hadn't confronted Ruben with what she'd heard or mentioned it to Naomi. If what she suspected was true, it would come to light soon enough.

When she'd first walked into the kitchen, she'd glanced out the window and barely made out the white form of the *Flying Eagle* gliding away from the inn, down the canal's dark trough.

Usually Garrett stayed long enough on Monday mornings to take his breakfast at the inn before heading back to Cincinnati. This morning, she supposed she couldn't blame him for choosing Sallie's canal boat fare instead.

She had no regrets about turning down Garrett's proposal or, more accurately, stopping him before he finished proposing. Yet, his words had played through her mind all night. *"Remember who cares about what's important to you—your inn and the Whitewater Canal."*

Susannah snatched a bag of flour from the pantry. She slammed it down hard on the kitchen worktable, sending up a plume of white dust. Garrett was right. If the man who made her heart dance cared one jot about her, Naomi, or Georgiana, why didn't he pack up his surveyor's gear and leave the Whitewater Canal alone?

He *didn't* care.

She mixed the biscuit dough with ferocious hands, squeezing until the sticky stuff oozed through her fingers. If only she could squeeze Thad Sutton from her mind—and her heart.

The sound of Thad's bright whistle sent a flame of anger spiraling through her, puckering her forehead in a scowl.

He strode through the kitchen doorway and glanced toward her, and the happy tune fell silent. "Sorry, I didn't mean to disturb anyone. I was wondering if Master Ruben might be up and about. I could really use a pole man today."

Susannah frowned at the lump of dough she patted on the table's floured surface. "I haven't seen him. But as he seems careless about how his actions affect others, he'll probably be willing to help you." She punctuated her ambiguous comment with jabs to the innocent biscuit dough.

Thad's left eyebrow shot up. Then, blowing out a long breath, he set his transit case on the floor and stepped closer. "Look, Susannah, what I'm doing here is not personal, nor do I have any sort of feud with the canal. But change is coming. And if you, Heywood, and the rest of the people in Promise don't prepare for the change, it could be a jolt."

"A jolt?" Susannah shoved flour-covered hands against her hips. "Garrett could probably take his boat to the Erie or Wabash Canals, and the farmers and mill owners could transport their products to the nearest train depot." She tapped her chest. "But what am I to do? If the railroad decides to bypass Promise by placing a passenger depot at Connersville or Metamora, the Killion House Inn is done."

He had the decency to look embarrassed. "There's always the National Road traffic, and you have my promise I'll do all in my power to encourage the railroad to place a depot here."

Susannah rammed a tin cup down on the dough, twisted it, and cut out a biscuit. She plopped it in a baking pan then pinned him with a glare.

"Each time the canal has been down and we've had to depend on only the National Road traffic, we've barely made ends meet. A railroad will cut into the stagecoach traffic, too, drawing away travelers who are foolhardy, curious about train travel, or just plain impatient." She fought the fear that crawled up her chest and clutched at her throat. "And like I told you before, I don't put much store in promises."

The amber rays of the morning sun highlighted the muscles working in his angular jaw. He strode stiffly out the kitchen door and didn't return to the inn for breakfast or dinner.

Her contentious exchange with Thad Sutton hung heavily on Susannah's conscience throughout the day. Even now, as the afternoon shadows stretched across the inn's backyard and she took down Monday's washing from the clothesline, she couldn't divest herself of the guilt prickling at the back of her mind. She knew everything he'd told her made sense. But every day he worked to map a way for the hated rails marked a day closer to the demise of the Killion House Inn.

If he'd just go away. . . .

If he went away. . .what? She would feel better?

No.

Susannah grasped the corner of a billowing sheet, freeing it from the wooden pins that anchored it to the line. If only she could get Thad Sutton and his railroad off her mind. The next moment, her wish was granted in the most unexpected way.

"Aunt Susannah?"

Susannah whirled at Ruben's quiet voice. She felt heat rush to her face. Had Ruben noticed her in the churchyard yesterday? Did he suspect that she'd heard his conversation with Lilly Macklin?

"Ruben, what is it?" Her sorry attempt at a light tone came out a nervous squeak.

"I have something real important I need to ask you." Ruben crushed the brim of his black felt hat in hands larger than a sixteen-year-old boy should have. His stocky build, broad shoulders, and wavy auburn hair reminded Susannah of her brother Frank. But in his dark eyes glancing anxiously from her face to his boot tops, Susannah saw the shy, sensitive eyes of his mother, Miranda.

"Wha–what?" Her limbs going noodle-weak, she dropped the sheet and pins into the laundry basket. She walked to the oak tree and sank to the bench beneath it.

"I need to ask a favor." Ruben followed her and scuffed the toe of his boot in a bare patch of sandy loam. "Do you think maybe you could hire Lilly to help here at the inn?"

Susannah's mind raced. Was this Ruben's solution to his and Lilly's predicament? "Well, I don't know. . . ." Should she hire a girl in Lilly's condition? Beyond that, the inn had been doing financially better in the past few months but certainly not well enough to pay for extra help.

"Thing is"—anger clouded Ruben's handsome boyish features—"her pap's been beatin' her real reg'lar the last couple months. He don't like it none that we've been keepin' company." His dark, soulful eyes met hers. "She needs someplace else to live—someplace where she'll be safe."

Susannah rubbed her throbbing temple. She couldn't allow Lilly to continue being abused, especially if she was in the family way. Yet, it didn't change the fact that she really couldn't afford a hired girl. George's father had borrowed two-thirds of the money from the bank to buy and furnish the inn. Next month, another installment would be due on that loan. "I don't know, Ruben. We can't afford to pay a hired girl—"

"You don't have to pay her. Like me, she'll work for room and board. She'll be a lot of help. She can watch Georgiana when you and Naomi have other things to do." His brown eyes glistened, and the plea in his voice crumpled her resistance.

"All right." Susannah managed a weak smile.

Ruben's face split with a toothy grin, and he grabbed Susannah in a hug that snatched away her breath. "Thanks, Aunt Susannah!" He planted a quick kiss on her cheek. "You won't be sorry, I promise!"

Susannah watched her nephew sprint to the front of the inn and across the National Road in the general direction of Macklin's Sawmill. Her insides churned with trepidation. *Another promise.*

❧

Susannah started up the stairway with a load of clean bed linens. Two weeks had passed since Lilly's arrival at the inn, and Susannah was glad to admit that Ruben had been right. The slight, shy girl worked tirelessly each day from dawn until dusk, cheerfully doing whatever was asked of her without so much as a pout.

Susannah and Naomi had both stifled gasps when Ruben first escorted Lilly into the inn's kitchen, toting a brown calico sack filled with her few belongings. An ugly purple bruise darkened a quarter-moon shaped area beneath her left eye and puffed up her discolored cheek. She'd draped a broad swath of her strawberry blond hair across her face as if attempting to hide the injury. The sight made Susannah glad she'd given in to Ruben's plea.

It amazed Susannah how quickly and seamlessly Lilly fit into the routine of the inn. The girl seemed mature beyond her fifteen years, and Susannah enjoyed the daily company of another young woman. Their employer-to-employee relationship quickly evaporated, replaced by a warmer, almost sisterly friendship.

Susannah had been both thrilled and relieved by Lilly's discreetly whispered question one afternoon shortly after her arrival. The girl had sidled up to her in the kitchen's pantry closet and confided that she was on her monthly and needed to know the location of the clean rags used for such occasions.

A surge of guilt had quickly swamped Susannah's initial relief. Realizing she'd sadly misjudged Ruben and Lilly, Susannah vowed to try and put a little extra money aside to pay them each a small salary.

Georgiana, too, had taken to the girl immediately, and Lilly seemed to enjoy spending time with the child as well. Susannah noticed that her daughter's speech improved after Lilly began making a game of helping Georgiana with her pronunciations.

On her way to one of the guest rooms, Susannah stopped in the hallway when she caught sight of Georgiana helping Lilly make a bed.

Georgiana plunged her little fists into the ends of a pillow. "Just like the story you told me about the three bears, Lilly, this pillow will be just wite!"

Lilly grinned, her brows shooting up. "Just what?"

Georgiana shook her head. "I meant right."

Lilly gave Georgiana a quick hug. "That's six this afternoon! You pronounce your *th* sounds and *r*'s correctly four more times today, and I'll read you another fairy story."

Smiling, Susannah stepped into the room, amazed at the improvement in Georgiana's enunciations. "Lilly, you are a born teacher," she said, giving the girl a hug. "I wanted to let you know"—Susannah brightened—"I can't promise anything, but I hope to be able to pay you a little at the end of the month. You've been such a wonderful help."

The unabashed joy shining from Lilly's face caused Susannah to wonder how long it had been since the motherless girl had heard a word of appreciation.

"Oh." A look of recollection lit Lilly's eyes, and she dug into her apron pocket. "Captain Sutton gave me this for taking such good care of his room." She held a half-dollar piece toward Susannah. "I thought I should give it to you—for the inn."

Georgiana skipped to Susannah. "Thad gave me money, too." She dipped her hand into her own apron pocket and pulled out a shiny penny.

Susannah shook her head at Lilly. "Captain Sutton meant for you to have it—not the inn. The railroad pays quite handsomely for him to board here. Even though he's often gone surveying for days on end," she added, disliking the wistful tone she heard in her voice.

The mention of Thad Sutton churned up troubling emotions in Susannah. She shifted her gaze to the open window overlooking the canal. After their argument in the kitchen two weeks ago, she'd seen little of him. Although she knew his work was taking him farther afield, she couldn't help wondering if their disagreement had something to do with his extended absences. If he had ever entertained special feelings for her, surely their impasse over the canal had squelched them.

"Me, too, Mamma?"

Georgiana's voice jerked Susannah's head around to her daughter, who proudly held up her penny.

"Yes, Georgiana." Susannah smiled at her child's hopeful look. "In fact, I think you should put it in your piggy bank right now before you lose it."

"He asked after you," Lilly said quietly when Georgiana had scampered from the room.

Susannah's cheeks tingled as heat spread up from her neck. "Who?" she asked in a voice she hoped sounded casual.

Lilly lifted the load of linens from Susannah's arms. "You know very well 'who.' Captain Sutton, that's who."

"Is there something the captain requires?" Susannah ignored the teasing lilt in the girl's tone.

"By the way he looks at you since he returned to Promise, I'd say he requires your company, or at least, your good graces, if I might say so—"

"No, Lilly, you should not say so!" Susannah tried her hardest to sound stern. She realized she'd failed when Lilly answered her admonishment with a giggle.

"Anyway," Lilly said, her voice skipping over a chuckle, "I told him you are quite well but seemed a little sad and that maybe he should say a word or two to cheer you up."

Susannah's jaw went slack, aghast at the girl's audacity. "Lilly, surely you did not!" Susannah pressed her palm to her searing cheek. What if Thad thought she'd put Lilly up to making such a suggestion? It didn't bear thinking.

"I surely did"—Lilly lifted her chin—"and don't look so horrified. You know you're really glad."

"I am *not* glad!" The feeling bubbling inside Susannah disputed her claim. "And you must shoo such fanciful thoughts from your head and never do such a thing again, do you hear?"

"I hear." Seeming unfazed, Lilly cast a soft chuckle over her shoulder and headed for the next room.

Descending the stairs, Susannah's mind raced with her heart. She labored to recall a word or look she'd gotten recently from Thad Sutton that might support Lilly's claim. The harder she tried to shove the notion of Thad's affection from her mind, the more it possessed her thoughts. As she reached the bottom step, she was determined to pay particular attention to the man's demeanor the next time she saw him.

She turned the corner to head toward the kitchen and gasped when her face smacked against Thad's chest.

"Whoa, there!" His soft voice sounded breathless. His arms encircled her, steadying her from the jarring impact.

"I'm sorry," they said in unison then laughed.

Thad kept her captive in his arms far longer than necessary before letting her go and taking a jerky step backward.

"I *am* sorry, you know." The penitent look in his gray eyes suggested his comment was not confined to their silly collision.

"So am I," Susannah managed to mutter.

A sweet sadness gnarled around her heart as she headed for the kitchen. A bouquet of wishes sprang up in her breast, each wish-blossom fading quickly, like flowers picked in the heat of August. She wished Thad Sutton had never come to Promise. She wished she'd never heard of trains or railroads. But mostly she wished Lilly Macklin had been wrong.

Chapter 8

Thad stood at the window of his room, his mood as dark as the storm clouds assailing the glass with their relentless deluge. With a frustrated shove, he pushed the navy blue wool curtains away from the pane.

The rain had continued almost nonstop for nearly three days.

It wasn't his inability to do his surveying work that concerned him. In truth, he'd amassed close to half the data needed by the railroad. It was the sight of the swollen Whitewater Canal—now a raging torrent—that gripped him with a mounting unease.

Boats were still managing to navigate the bloated ditch. Two days ago, Garrett Heywood had deposited a boatful of sodden, ill-tempered passengers at the side door of the Killion House Inn. But Thad feared the *Flying Eagle* might be the last boat to make it to Promise for some time to come. Much more of this rain, and the muskrat-pocked canal walls would crumble for sure.

Thad let the curtain fall across the window, partially obscuring the depressing vista. He turned away from the glass as if ignoring the rain might make it stop.

Sinking to the blue and white patchwork quilt covering his featherbed, he rubbed his forehead. A regiment of worries rumbled through his mind like the jaw-jarring thunderclaps, making his head pound.

He wasn't the only one concerned. Yesterday afternoon he'd watched Susannah standing at the kitchen door, gazing at the burgeoning canal. The fear he'd seen flickering in her eyes left little doubt as to what thoughts had drawn her brow into a worried V. With the canal basin only feet from the inn's back door, an overflow could easily send floodwaters through the building's ground floor.

Thad couldn't remember when he'd felt so helpless. He'd wanted to take her in his arms and assure her he wouldn't allow anything bad to happen to her or her inn.

But he couldn't. He was but a mere man, and they were at the mercy of the Lord.

A flash of lightning lit the room, illuminating the blue-and-white-striped wallpaper and dark rag-rugs scattered across the bare floor.

He scanned the cozy little space that had been his home these past six weeks. Like its proprietors, this inn had become dear to him. Guilt drenched his heart as Susannah's words of two weeks ago echoed accusingly through his mind. *"If the railroad decides to bypass Promise by placing a passenger depot at Connersville or Metamora, the Killion House Inn is done."*

Thad knew it was far more likely that the railroad board would choose the larger town of Connersville over tiny Promise for a depot location. Now a flood threatened, and there was nothing he could do to stop it. Or was there?

His gaze drifted to his little black Bible on the bedside table. The Bible he'd carried with him to war on the Texas plains. The Bible he'd read from while standing over countless graves—including George Killion's.

Another wave of guilt rippled through him. He'd taken so much from Susannah Killion—even her will to ask for God's mercy. He reached over and grasped the little book with its frayed black cover. With his fingertip, he lovingly traced the words HOLY BIBLE, their gilt lettering nearly rubbed away. He could at least pray for Susannah's inn, something he felt sure she would not do herself.

Grasping the Bible in his hands, he slumped forward, his elbows on his knees, his forehead pressed against the book's grainy cover. "Dear heavenly Father, I ask that You stop the rain and spare this inn from floodwaters. And please, Lord, give me the right words that I might convince the board to situate a depot here."

Unsure if it were seemly to ask the Lord for Susannah's affection, Thad's prayer faltered. He felt his lips twist in a wry grin. God knew the deepest secrets of his heart. "Dear Father, whether or not she could ever feel any measure of affection for me, just allow my actions to be a blessing to Susannah's life, and never again a trespass against it."

Thad winced as the dagger of remorse jabbed at his heart. To love the widow of a man he sent to die seemed somehow repugnant and perhaps evil. He couldn't deny that he had admired Susannah's picture George had shown him weeks before he sent George on that fateful mission. Had the haunting image of the lovely Susannah played a part in his choosing George to lead that mission?

Thad shook his head. He didn't want to think that. In his heart, he knew Sergeant George Killion had been the best choice to lead the reconnaissance mission. But with his affection for Susannah Killion growing daily, he couldn't help drawing parallels with the story of King David, Bathsheba, and Uriah.

He shoved the troublesome thought back into the dark corner of his mind from where it had crept. "Dear Father, just help me to save Susannah's inn."

Thad raised his head and rested the Bible on his lap. He stuck his thumb into the pages and allowed the book to fall open randomly. His gaze lit on the last two verses of the eighty-fourth Psalm. *"For the Lord God is a sun and shield: the Lord will give grace and glory: no good thing will he withhold from them that walk uprightly. O Lord of hosts, blessed is the man that trusteth in thee."*

Thad read the scripture over twice. When he closed the Bible and set it back on the table, he noticed the thunder had ceased and the room had lightened. His gaze traveled to the floorboards in the center of the room. There, morning sunlight pooled from a bright shaft slanting between the dark curtains. The rain had stopped.

A soft rap at his door pulled him up from the bed. He opened the door to find Lilly holding a steaming pitcher of water.

"I'm sorry for being so tardy with your shaving water, Captain Sutton." She hurried past him into the room, clean towels draped over her arm. "The inn is full of travelers and every one of them out of sorts, it seems."

"It's quite all right, Lilly. The weather would have delayed me anyway." Smiling, he took the pitcher of hot water from her frail-looking hands. Despite her slight build, Thad had found young Lilly Macklin to be a bundle of energy when it came to keeping up the rooms. Georgiana had explained in her childish innocence that "Lilly has to live here now 'cause her papa was mean to her."

Not only was Thad glad that Lilly had a safer environment, but he was also happy that some of the workload had been shifted from Susannah's shoulders.

Lilly carefully laid the towels on the washstand. "Is there anything else you require, Captain Sutton?"

"I was wondering if you knew whether or not Ruben might have time today to help me with a project?"

She blushed prettily, causing Thad's smile to widen. He'd seen the two young people holding hands at the church social and determined they were sweethearts. "Captain Heywood's drivers see to his mules, and another stage is not due till Friday, so I don't see why he wouldn't."

After Lilly left the room, Thad quickly shaved, scraping off his stubble of beard with impatient strokes of his razor. He scooped handfuls of hot water from the washbowl and splashed his face, wincing when it stung the place on his chin he'd nicked in his hurry. He wiped the towel over his face. Glimpsing his reflection in the washstand mirror, he dabbed at the drops of blood oozing from the cleft of his chin.

No time to fuss with shaving cuts or linger over breakfast in the dining room. He might grab a cup of coffee and one of Susannah's biscuits, but he couldn't afford to waste one minute of daylight.

Thad glanced out the window. The pewter clouds had parted, showing widening patches of clear blue sky. A blue jay squawked and flew from the oak tree, sending a shower of rain droplets shimmering in the sunlight. God had answered his prayer, gifting him with a clear day. If he and Ruben could get a load of lumber down to the feeder dam, maybe—just maybe—they could shore up the canal walls enough to hold if the Whitewater River overflowed.

⌘

Susannah dropped dollops of dumpling dough into the large pot of bubbling chicken broth. Though it was the twenty-fourth of May, the past several evenings had been cool. After a day of working in chest-high canal water, Thad and Ruben would appreciate a hearty plate of chicken and dumplings.

She glanced through the open kitchen door. The sun sat like a red ball just above the little woods behind the inn. Soon it would slip behind the stand of trees. She hadn't seen Thad or her nephew since noon, when she'd hastily packed them a lunch basket.

For five days, they'd worked from dawn until dusk alongside a dozen or so of Promise's residents, reinforcing the canal walls. Each evening she'd watched Thad, covered in mud and sweat, lumber up to the inn's backyard pump.

Her admiration for Thad had grown daily. He had no vested interest in saving the canal—or the Killion House Inn. Yet he'd alerted the town council to the erosion he'd found in the canal walls. Too proud to admit they needed advice from a railroad man, the council had claimed they knew of the damage and had planned to address it—something Susannah doubted. Then, despite their contempt, Thad had worked shoulder to shoulder with the men of Promise to shore up the canal walls.

"Mmm, tell me that's chicken and dumplings."

Susannah whirled around at Thad's voice, feeling as if her thoughts had caused him to materialize. "Yes. Yes, it is." She wished she could rein in her galloping heart that sent heat surging to her face.

Thad stepped into the kitchen and inhaled deeply. His shirtsleeves were rolled above his elbows and droplets of well water sparkled on his dark curls. The late afternoon sun streaming through the open kitchen door wreathed his chiseled features in a golden aura.

The sight snatched Susannah's breath away.

Flustered, she turned her attention back to the dumplings, lifting the lid from the pot for a quick peek. Hopefully he'd attribute any extra color in her face to the steam spiraling from the bubbling pot. "Where's Ruben?"

"He's still washing up at the pump." Thad stepped nearer the stove to sniff the savory steam.

"Do you think the canal will hold?" Susannah kept her face averted from his, trying not to let her voice reveal her concern. Yesterday they'd gotten word that in the lowlands several miles north of Promise, the Whitewater River had breached its banks.

"It has a better chance of holding than before we began reinforcing the banks. But if it doesn't, Ruben and I have a wagon full of gunnysacks filled with sand to build a barrier between the basin and the inn."

He touched her shoulder, sending pleasant tingles through her body. "Susannah, you know I will do everything I can to protect this inn."

Susannah slid the pot of chicken and dumplings to the front corner of the cookstove farthest from the firebox. She reached up and gave the damper on the stovepipe a twist, half closing it, then turned toward Thad. The gratitude that had been simmering inside her all week bubbled to the surface, flooding her eyes. She gave his hand a quick squeeze while her lashes beat back the tears misting her features. "I want you to know that whatever happens, I—all of us here at the inn—appreciate your efforts."

A sweet smile tipped the corners of his mouth. He caught both her hands in his, giving her fingers a warm return squeeze.

The sound of multiple footsteps trouping down the stairs, accompanied by a jumble of muted, unintelligible voices, registered vaguely in Susannah's ears. At the moment, it didn't matter to her that the inn's guests were filing into the dining room. Thad's nearness filled all her senses, crowding out all other stimuli.

"I know you do," he replied barely above a whisper while his tender gaze embraced hers.

Gripped by a trancelike state, Susannah's eyelids closed and she leaned toward him. The next moment, she would be in his arms.

"Mamma, I can't find Dolly anywhere!" Georgiana's urgent whine yanked Susannah from the spell, and she jerked away from Thad, her face burning.

"Where is the last place you remember being with Dolly?" Thad had come around to kneel beside Georgiana. He brushed his thumb across her cheek, catching a tear.

Georgiana's little brow puckered. Thad's quiet voice seemed to have calmed her panicked tone. "We were having tea over by the mule stable with Captain Heywood's mules, Mac and Mol," she said with a sniff.

Susannah gasped. "Georgiana, that is much farther from the inn than you should go alone. And I've warned you about those mules. They could step on you!" Perhaps she'd depended too much lately on Lilly watching Georgiana.

"I wasn't alone, Mamma. Dolly was with me, and we stayed away from the mules' feet." Georgiana headed for the kitchen door. "I'm going to look for her."

Susannah started toward Georgiana. "No, you are not, young lady! It's nearly dark and we have a dining room full of guests waiting for supper." She glanced across the kitchen into the adjoining room. Through the doorway, she could see Lilly cutting bread at the sideboard while Naomi worked her way around the table pouring water into goblets.

Thad swung Georgiana up to his broad left shoulder. "Tell you what, moppet, I'll go look for Dolly first thing after supper, all right?"

Georgiana's head bobbed as Thad carried her to the dining room filling with guests.

A half hour after supper, Susannah absently lifted the last dripping plate from the dishpan and handed it to Naomi. She glanced toward the dark rectangle of the open kitchen door and felt her heart quiver.

Good to his word, Thad had left to look for Georgiana's doll the moment he'd finished eating. But he still hadn't returned, and Lilly had put Georgiana to bed still fussing for Dolly.

Susannah walked to the kitchen door and voiced the irrational concern squeezing her chest. "Captain Sutton's been gone a lot longer than it should take to walk to the mule stable and back."

It was unlike Thad to disappoint Georgiana. That thought filled Susannah with a warm glow. Yet she knew it wasn't just the kindness and affection he showed Georgiana or his daily toil to protect the inn that drew her heart to Thad Sutton like a sunflower following the sun's beam. That moment they'd shared just before Georgiana had walked into the kitchen this evening had wiped all doubt from Susannah's mind and heart. She cared for Thad Sutton like she'd never cared for any man since George.

Naomi dried a dish with a linen cloth and set it atop a stack of several others then cocked her head toward the kitchen door. "What on earth's got into those mules? They're just braying and carrying on like I've never heard! Maybe I should ask Ruben to go check." She deposited the plates in the cupboard, closed the doors, and twisted the wooden latch to fasten them.

"No, he's already gone to bed." Susannah smiled fondly. Earlier, she'd passed her nephew's bedroom, situated behind the dining room and between the storage room and linen closet. The poor boy was fast asleep. Susannah's heart swelled with pride for her brother's son. For days, he'd been working as hard as any grown man alongside Thad and the others repairing the canal walls.

"I expect Captain Sutton disturbed Mac and Mol's sleep looking for Georgiana's doll, but I'll go take a look." Susannah lifted the copper lantern from the iron hook beside the back door. She opened the lantern's glass door and lit the tallow candle from the sputtering flame of the lard-oil lamp on the kitchen table.

"Do you want me to go with you?" Stifling a yawn, Naomi removed her apron and hung it beside the washstand.

"No, just look in on Georgiana and go on to bed. I'm sure I won't get halfway to the stables before I meet Tha—Captain Sutton," Susannah amended, her cheeks tingling with warmth.

Naomi nodded and turned, but not quick enough to hide the knowing grin pushing up the corners of her mouth.

Outside, a chorus of chirping crickets and a honeysuckle-laced breeze welcomed Susannah to the late spring night. Naomi's smug look hadn't even bothered her. It would be useless to try to hide from her mother-in-law the fact that Thad Sutton lit her heart like the lantern in her hand lit the dew-laden grass at her feet.

As she neared the mule stable, she heard muffled voices and the sound of hurried footsteps retreating down the dirt towpath. Her heart sped with her feet. "Thad?"

Only a deep moan answered.

Lifting her lantern to direct its beam of light toward the sound, Susannah gasped, terror gripping her throat. Thad lay in a crumpled heap, his head resting in a pool of blood.

Chapter 9

Sure he'd heard his name being called, Thad tried to open his eyes. But when he managed to force his lids apart, a bright light sent shards of pain stabbing at his eyeballs. The unmistakable, sickly smell of blood assailed his nostrils.

Had he died? He thought he'd glimpsed the vision of an angel wreathed in a golden halo before the pain slammed his eyes shut. But there'd be no more pain in heaven. He'd read that in the Bible, hadn't he? *"There shall be no more death, neither sorrow, nor crying, neither shall there be any more pain."* Yet his head throbbed like a fourteen-pound shot had been dropped on it. And someone was crying—no, sobbing.

Thad opened his mouth but could only push a groan through his lips.

"Thad! Thad, what happened?"

"Su–Susannah?" The effort to say her sweet name taxed his strength. Though fractured memories of the last several minutes began to assemble themselves in his scrambled brain, Thad had no energy to attempt to articulate them. He didn't want to move. He wanted simply to lie there, his head cradled in Susannah's soft lap.

But that wasn't what she was demanding of him. "Thad, you have to help me get you up. I can't lift you by myself."

When she gently lowered his head back to the ground, the sense of loss hurt Thad as much as the bands of searing pain rippling through his head.

She tugged on his arm, gasping between sobs with the exertion. "Dear Lord, help me get him to the inn, please. . . ."

An unexpected joy penetrated the dense fog threatening to swallow Thad's consciousness. Susannah had just called upon the Lord for help. *Lord, help us both.* He struggled to get onto all fours, but his limbs refused to obey.

"Susannah, what's happened?" Garrett Heywood's unmistakable voice intruded into the scrap of night Thad had shared with Susannah.

"Garrett, you've got to help me get him inside—" Sobs choked off Susannah's voice.

Surprised and somewhat dismayed by the manner in which his prayer for help had been answered, Thad's body tensed as he bristled against accepting Heywood's help. Not only did he see the man as a rival for Susannah's affection, but Garrett Heywood could very well have been the assailant who'd bashed him in the head. He remembered a man's voice calling his name just before the night exploded in a shower of stars and the world went black.

"I heard Mac and Mol settin' up a commotion and thought I'd better see if a bobcat or some other critter was about." Heywood hoisted Thad to his feet and gave a low whistle. "Looks like somebody tried to take your head off, man."

Thad didn't even attempt to answer as Heywood, with Susannah's help, propelled him toward the inn. He fought for consciousness just so he could continue to feel Susannah's arm around him and her soft cheek against his.

Inside the inn, the lantern swinging in Heywood's hand set apparition-like shadows dancing around a little room. The earthy smells of wheat flour and coffee beans helped Thad recognize it as the inn's storeroom.

Susannah and Heywood lowered him to a rough pile of burlap sacks.

Thad struggled to stay awake. He wanted to find out who'd attacked him— and he didn't want to leave Susannah alone in the dark with Garrett Heywood. But as their faces blurred and the room dimmed, he had no choice but to surrender to the blackness closing over him.

⊷

A feeling of warmth was Thad's first conscious sensation. Peering through squinted eyelids, his little blue and white room came into focus. The warmth he'd felt was the morning sun streaming through the window.

Had he dreamed it all?

He pushed against the feather mattress and tried to sit up, but the intense throbbing in his head caused him to sink back onto the pillow. It felt as if a couple of burly steel drivers wielding ten-pound hammers were driving railroad spikes into his head.

He groaned and touched his forehead. His fingertips found a smooth, cool band of cloth that told him it had not all been a bad dream. Someone had tried to kill him.

The door to his room creaked, snapping him to attention. Puzzled, he saw no one until his gaze slid down the doorjamb. It lit on a tumble of blond curls.

Georgiana crept in with an uncharacteristically somber look on her cherubic face.

Thad managed to rise up on one elbow and force a smile. "Hi there, moppet." His mind raced, trying to think of a gentle way to tell her what he'd found just before he'd been whacked. The memory of her beloved Dolly lying in the dirt with its china head smashed made his stomach go queasy.

She wandered over to his bed, and her little fingers picked at the patchwork quilt draped down the side of the mattress. "I'm sorry your head got bwoke, Tad. Dolly's head got bwoke, too." Her blue eyes shimmered for a moment before sending large teardrops sliding down her cheeks. The trauma seemed to have set back the progress the child had been making in her enunciation.

Thad's heart rent. "I'm sorry about that, moppet. I truly am." He reached down and caressed her baby-soft curls. He couldn't love this child more if she were his own daughter.

"Does your head hurt?" Georgiana unceremoniously climbed onto the edge of the mattress and crawled over the quilt to gently touch his bandaged head.

"Yeah, some," he lied as the steel drivers continued to slam their hammers down.

"I'm glad you didn't die. Dolly died." She sat cross-legged beside him, fresh tears sketching down her little face.

"I know, moppet." Thad reached over and with his fingertips wiped the moisture from her petal-soft, baby-plump cheeks. Her next comment froze his fingers there for a long moment.

"My Papa died. Mamma said you were with him. Did his head get bwoke?"

At Georgiana's innocent question, the awful scenes from the Battle of Buena Vista came thundering across the forefront of Thad's mind. "No, Georgiana, your papa's head didn't get broke." How much did she know? How much should a four-year-old be told of such things? While he pondered these questions, Georgiana moved on to a new question.

"Did they put Papa in a box? Gwamma said when Gwampa died they buwied him in a box."

"Yes, they did." Thad decided the best way to respond to her simple questions was with simple answers.

"Why?"

"Why do they bury people in boxes?" Thad realized that Georgiana, having never known her father, was simply exercising her childish curiosity. "Well. . ." He rubbed his thumb across a day's worth of stubble on his chin as he contemplated how to answer in terms Georgiana could understand. "The box is called a casket, and burying people we love in them is a way of showing respect."

"Wespec?"

"Respect." Thad couldn't help grinning. He'd never thought of himself as a teacher—except maybe of raw recruits. "It means we think well of someone."

"Georgiana!" Susannah's sharp voice yanked both Thad's and Georgiana's attentions toward the doorway.

"I'm sorry, Captain Sutton. She knows better than to go into guests' rooms." Her face full of dismay, Susannah hurried to his bedside and set Georgiana on the floor.

Georgiana planted her little fists on her hips and wrinkled her brow in defiance. "He's not a guest. He's Tad!"

"Now, soldier, we can't have any insubordination," Thad chided. But Georgiana's puzzled look destroyed his stern demeanor, tugging his mouth into a grin. "You have to mind your mamma," he explained then turned to her mother. "Georgiana was just expressing her concern for my head, and I was extending my condolences—in regards to Dolly."

Susannah gave her daughter a sharp pat on the bottom. "You go on downstairs and help Lilly dust the lobby—and stay out of the guests' rooms."

Georgiana lingered in the doorway. "I hope your head gets better, Tad."

Thad smiled as his heart melted. "Thanks, moppet. I'll be up and giving you piggyback rides before you know it."

He watched the little girl scamper out and wished with all his heart he could stay in Promise. As his gaze slid to Georgiana's mother, the feeling intensified. But his spirit drooped. The reasons he could not stay were myriad.

Susannah's fingers worried the edges of her blue calico apron. "I'm sorry if Georgiana disturbed your rest." She seemed to study the pattern in the quilt covering him. "I'll see that she doesn't bother—"

"Please don't. Don't deny me the joy of her company—or yours." He reached over and clasped her hand in his. Thad had always found her hands compelling, lovelier in form than those of many debutantes he'd known. Though not as soft as the idle hands of wealthier ladies, Susannah's hands, roughened by honest labor, were hands to which a man could trust his life. And his love.

Their gazes both drifted to the third finger of her left hand resting in his— the finger still adorned with George Killion's gold wedding band.

Guilt jabbed at Thad's heart, and he released her hand.

She lifted her gaze to the bandage wrapped around his head. "How does your head feel?" Her voice sounded flustered, and her cheeks turned a deeper shade of rose.

"Like a crew is laying rail inside it." His chuckle, which made his head pound harder, was rewarded by Susannah's smile. "How'd I get up here, anyway? Last I remember I was on a pile of gunnysacks in the storeroom."

"After you fainted, I insisted Garrett help me get you to your room."

"Garrett, huh?" Thad heard his voice harden as a streak of jealousy slithered through him.

Her chin lifted a notch, and her voice sharpened. "Captain Heywood wasn't the one who attacked you, if that's what you're thinking." She glanced toward the window. "As you've well noticed, you're about as welcome in this town as a skunk at a picnic. The men who attacked you are cowards, but I'm sorry to say Promise has its share."

"Men?" Thad's interest piqued. He'd imagined his attacker had been a lone assailant. How could Susannah know it had been more than one man unless she'd seen the attack?

"When I went looking for you, I heard at least two men's voices and what sounded like more than one pair of boots running down the towpath. It was too dark to make out more than shapes. . .and when I saw you—" The catch in her voice sent Thad's repentant heart soaring.

Thad's sense of fairness convicted him. "I'm sorry I impugned Captain Heywood." The man *had* assisted him. The least he could do was to give Heywood the benefit of the doubt. An old worry crowded out thoughts of who might have cracked his head open. "Has the water level in the canal receded or is it rising?"

Susannah's face clouded. "It's at least six inches higher today than it was yesterday."

Thad pushed the quilt to his waist and tried to scoot to the edge of the bed. "Ruben and I need to sandbag the curve of the basin nearest the inn." He swung his bare leg over the edge of the bed, then realizing he was in his nightshirt, quickly pulled his leg back under the covers. Heat rushed from his neck to his bandaged hairline. He felt his eyes grow wide as he looked aghast at Susannah.

Her soft giggle did nothing to relieve his unease but her following comment helped. "Gar—Captain Heywood prepared you for bed."

He strove to restore some dignity to his voice. "I must ask you to leave so I can get dressed. We may have one more day before the floodwaters reach Promise."

She bent over him and gently grasped his shoulders, sending the pleasant scents of lye soap and rose water cascading to his nostrils as she eased him back against the pillows. "You are going nowhere until your head is healed."

Their faces were only inches apart when their gazes locked and a sweet understanding seemed to pass between them. Then Susannah jerked away, breaking the connection as if she'd suddenly realized she was in a man's bedchamber.

A series of looks Thad could not entirely define registered on her beet red features before she turned toward the door. "I–I'll send Lilly up with a breakfast tray," she mumbled over her shoulder before making a hasty retreat.

Thad heaved a deep sigh and fell back onto the two feather pillows. She cared for him—deeply—as he cared for her. He'd seen it in her eyes. But the knowledge that his feelings for Susannah Killion were reciprocated did not erase the mountain of obstacles blocking any hope of a relationship between them.

In that brief moment of understanding—of connection—what emotions had he seen flash across her face? Surprise? Of course. Fear? A touch. Longing? Without a doubt. But it was the look of immense sadness he'd seen in her hazel eyes that continued to slash at his heart. She, too, saw the hopelessness of such a relationship. And now, this attack on him made it clear to Thad that for Susannah to be tied to him could make her, at best, a pariah in Promise or, at worst, put her in danger.

He rubbed the temples of his throbbing head and sent a desperate prayer winging heavenward from his heart. *Oh, Lord, I love them so much. There must be a way for Susannah and I to make this work—find a future together. Please show me a way. Just give me some hope. . . .*

Chapter 10

Hope. That's what it was.

An hour before supper, Susannah stepped out of the kitchen door with a bucket full of potato peelings. For the past several days, she'd attempted to define the feeling that caused her heart to float like the gossamer-winged butterflies flitting around the honeysuckle bush beside the stone steps.

She flung the bucket of peelings toward the ever-present greedy gaggle of geese, knowing something important had changed inside her. And it had happened the morning after Thad's assault.

That moment in his room when their gazes locked, something was planted in her heart that had not grown there for a very long time.

Hope.

Hope that she might actually be able to love again—to contemplate a life beyond widowhood. She longed to wrap her fingers around this blossoming hope, hold it to her heart, and breathe in the sweet fragrance of its promise. But she couldn't.

Her shoulders sagged as her heart deflated. He couldn't stay. Someone had tried to kill him. Or at least strongly encourage him to leave Promise. He could no more fit into her world than she could fit into his.

She gazed at the canal water still a good foot below the bank. Despite her best attempts to convince him to take a few more days of bed rest, thirty-six hours after his injury, Thad had returned to helping Ruben reinforce the canal.

This morning at breakfast, Naomi offered a prayer of thanks that the waters had lowered a bit. Following the prayer, she'd read from the Gospel of Matthew. *"Ask, and it shall be given you; seek, and ye shall find; knock, and it shall be opened unto you: For every one that asketh receiveth; and he that seeketh findeth; and to him that knocketh it shall be opened."*

The words of the scripture had filled Susannah with bitter bile. In the past several years, it seemed God had delighted in slamming the door in her face while bellowing a resounding "No!"

And now He cruelly presented her with the hope of a new love, yet sent it in the person of a man whose very purpose here opposed her own.

⁓

Hours later Susannah tossed on her featherbed, her rolling mind keeping sleep at bay. Dim moonlight streaming into the room cast soft shadows on the papered walls. Undulating leaves on the maple tree outside her window stroked the room with shadowy fingers.

She pushed aside the quilt and swung her bare feet to the smooth, cool surface of the wood floor.

Rounding the trundle bed, she smiled at the small quilt-covered mound. Georgiana lay fast asleep, a peaceful look on her angelic features. The sight of her daughter's blond curls framing her face pinched Susannah's heart. The child looked as much like her father as a four-year-old girl possibly could.

At the dresser, Susannah touched the top drawer's round knob. She pulled the drawer open, and as she'd done countless times during the past weeks, she lifted out George's last letter. How could she feel free to give her heart to Thad—or to anyone—when in so many ways, it remained tied to George? Perhaps reading his final words might release her heart, allowing it to move on.

With a resolute sigh, she pushed her thumbnail against the sealing wax. But a series of quick raps on her bedroom door stilled her hand, and she dropped the envelope back into the drawer, unopened.

"Susannah!" The urgency in Thad's whispered voice propelled her to the door.

What on earth could be the matter?

"Shh, you'll wake Georgiana," she warned in a rasped whisper as she opened the door a crack.

"I'm sorry to wake you, but I thought you should know, the canal has breached its banks. The water's just a couple yards from the inn's back door."

Fear slithered through her. Last year when floodwaters had gotten into the inn, she'd had to beg the banker for an additional loan to make repairs. It was doubtful the bank would extend her further credit. Even if she did somehow manage to secure the necessary funds, she would not be able to repay.

Susannah hurriedly dressed, knocked on the door to the adjoining room shared by Naomi and Lilly, and alerted them to the threat. A drowsy Lilly agreed to sleep in Susannah's bed so she could attend to Georgiana. Naomi insisted on accompanying Susannah downstairs.

"Lord, help us." The whispered prayer puffed from Naomi's lips as the two stood at the open kitchen door.

Dread knotted inside Susannah. A few minutes ago, Thad had said the water was a couple yards from the inn. But in the circle of light cast by the lamp he held aloft, she could see that the floodwaters had crept even closer and now covered the bottom step beneath the kitchen door.

"I'll go get Ruben," Naomi said as she turned and disappeared into the dark kitchen.

A few minutes later, Susannah and Naomi huddled together in the kitchen doorway, watching Thad and Ruben wade into the knee-deep water.

Susannah turned to Naomi. "We're going to have to make a barricade with the sandbags Thad and Ruben stockpiled. You might as well go back to bed."

"You know I won't sleep, daughter, but I can do something. I can pray."

Naomi gave Susannah a quick hug. "It will be all right, daughter," she murmured before slipping back into the kitchen.

Susannah longed to possess Naomi's stubborn surety that everything would be all right. Hot tears prickled the back of her throat. At least, unlike Naomi, she could physically fight against the threat.

Soft, sandy mud squished between her bare toes as she stepped down into the floodwaters. It would just feel good to do something—anything.

"What do you think you're doing?" Thad's voice held a hard edge in the darkness.

She turned toward him, blinking against the light from his lantern. "This is my inn, and I'm going to help protect it from the flood, Captain Sutton."

His soft chuckle should have infuriated her, but it didn't. Instead, it sent ripples of joy surging ridiculously through her. He hung the lantern on one of the oak tree's lower limbs. His voice turned soft—concerned but not condescending. "I'm not sure you're strong enough to lug twenty-pound bags of sand."

"I've lugged around a fussy thirty-five-pound child on my hip while doing any number of chores at the same time," she told him in a dry tone.

"Excellent point!" His laugh blended with the summer night sounds of chirping crickets and croaking frogs, but the surrender in his voice was edged with admiration.

The rumbling of a wagon turned their attention to Ruben, who led their black gelding, Raven, hitched to the wagon full of sandbags.

"Don't come any closer, Ruben."

Thad's warning caused a new fear to spring up inside Susannah. In this darkness, it would be hard to tell flooded ground from the canal basin. If the horse or wagon fell into the canal, it could be disastrous.

Thad climbed to the back of the wagon and lifted down bags of sand to Ruben and Susannah. For the next three hours, they worked with little talk, only the occasional grunt as they passed the sandbags from one to the other.

At some point, Susannah realized it had started raining. Although she was used to physical work, her arms and back soon tired from the exertion. The rain plastered her hair to her face and her wet skirts clung to her legs until she could hardly move in the knee-deep water. She began to hope they would soon run out of sandbags.

Just when she thought she might collapse, Thad called out, "Well, reckon that will have to do."

Ruben went to unhitch the horse and wagon while Susannah and Thad gazed at the wall of sandbags about three feet tall and twenty feet long edging the canal basin in a crude semicircle.

Would it be enough? Susannah could only hope.

"Now all we can do is pray and see what the morning will bring." Thad's deep sigh held a weary resignation.

Susannah had no comment, allowing the croaking of the bullfrogs to fill the dark silence between them. Let Thad pray. Let Naomi pray. Susannah's prayers never seemed to reach beyond the treetops. Or if they did, God must turn a deaf ear to them. No, she would waste no more effort sending up prayers that would never be answered.

"Won't you pray with me, Susannah?" His soft entreaty gripped her with a sweet sadness.

The temptation to accept his invitation was strong, but she resisted it. If she didn't ask, she couldn't be rejected. "I—I don't think God listens to me."

Thad took her hand, sending tingles up her arm. "He listens, Susannah, and He answers. Sometimes He doesn't answer the way we want, but He always answers the way we need."

She pulled her fingers from his grasp. "Then tell Him I need my inn."

Afraid the lamplight might reveal the tears streaming down her face, Susannah turned away. Slogging through the water, she climbed the stone steps to the kitchen.

Up in her bedroom, she took off her drenched clothes, moving quietly in the darkness so as not to wake Georgiana or Lilly. She cleaned up the best she could at the washstand then wiped the linen towel over her wet skin and hair before slipping into her nightdress.

Every muscle in her body ached as she climbed into bed beside Lilly. In less than four hours, it would be dawn. Though she was exhausted, worries about whether they'd have a useable inn in the morning made sleep seem improbable. Like Thad had said, all they could do was to wait and see.

She rubbed her hands, stiff from the work with the sandbags. A vague sense that something wasn't right niggled in her tired brain.

Suddenly, she felt the naked third finger of her left hand and gasped as the realization struck. Her wedding ring was gone. The likelihood of finding it in the mud was remote. It might have even fallen into the canal. Perhaps when the water receded she could look for it. . . .

An acute sadness engulfed her, and hot tears streamed from her eyes to her ears. She closed her eyes and tried to focus on George's image. It flickered for an instant, but the smiling face she saw as she drifted off to sleep belonged to Thad Sutton.

Chapter 11

Susannah poured sugar over a bowl full of tart cherries and glanced out the kitchen door. The sandbag dike she'd helped Thad and Ruben construct had kept the floodwaters at bay. In the week since they'd built it, the barrier had instilled in her a measure of security.

For now, the water level remained stable. However, they'd heard an aqueduct and two locks had been damaged between Cincinnati and Promise. No canal boats had made it to Promise in a week. But at least the road hadn't been washed out, and a stage was due within the hour.

She ladled the cherries into waiting pans of dough, capped them with more dough, crimped the edges, and then used a paring knife to prick a wheat design in the top of each pie to vent. As she slid the pies in the oven, Susannah knew she wasn't making them for the stagecoach travelers. She'd planned the dessert with Thad Sutton in mind.

In fact, Captain Thad Sutton was never far from her mind. Each Sunday he was in Promise he squired her, Naomi, and Georgiana to church. He'd labored to protect the inn from a flood as if the place were his own. He obviously adored Georgiana, allowing her to follow him like a happy puppy. Since his arrival two months ago, Thad had become part of Promise, part of the Killion House Inn—part of Susannah's life.

But in recent days, he'd seemed withdrawn. She sensed his work here might be coming to a close. A melancholy wave rolled through her. She had warned Georgiana of becoming attached to the handsome captain, yet Susannah realized she, too, had succumbed to his charms.

"Have you seen young Ruben?"

The sound of Thad's voice from the threshold between the kitchen and hall set Susannah's heart bouncing. She turned from cleaning the worktable of flour and dough scraps. "No, come to think of it, I haven't seen him since breakfast. A stage is due in soon, so he's probably in the carriage house."

When Thad stepped into the kitchen, the frown on his face and the way his gaze avoided hers troubled Susannah.

"I—I'll be leaving for Indianapolis in a couple of days." Now, he looked directly into her eyes. "I want you to know that I'm going to do all in my power to convince my father and the other members of the railroad's board to situate a depot in Promise."

"I appreciate that—we all do." *Two days. In two days, he'll be gone.* The

186

realization that Thad Sutton would be leaving her life filled Susannah with a crushing sadness.

"Ruben shows a real aptitude for surveying. I wanted to ask him if he'd be interested in learning the trade. He could begin as soon as I return from Indianapolis."

"Return? Your work is not finished here?" She went back to scraping flour and dough into a pie tin, hoping the happiness exploding inside her didn't register on her face.

"Yes, the preliminary work is done, but if the board is satisfied with my findings, there will be more work to do." He walked closer. "Are you glad, Susannah?" His soft voice had grown husky.

"Of course. I mean, Georgiana will be happy to hear it." Why did he have to stand so near? In another moment, the rockets igniting giddily inside her would propel her into his arms.

He reached out and touched her temple, gently turning her face toward his. "I'm glad Georgiana will be happy. But how do *you* feel about it, Susannah?"

She tilted her face, allowing it to press against his palm. How could she explain how she felt? In the space of one minute, he'd sent her to the pit of sadness and then shot her to the mountaintop of joy. Dizzy, that's how she felt. Dizzy with gladness. "I—I—"

"Mamma, I made pies, too." Georgiana stepped through the back door, covered in sandy mud, a dripping, grass-embedded, brownish-gray blob of the stuff in each hand.

Susannah rushed to her mud-caked child while Thad roared with laughter.

"Have you been digging in the garden again?" Susannah gently grasped her daughter by the shoulders. It was the only part of the little girl that didn't seem covered in dirt.

Georgiana nodded. "Lilly got Dolly's pieces so we could have a funeral for her. But Lilly had to go, so I had the funeral by myself." She held up the mud pies. "You and Gwamma make pies to take to funerals, so I made pies."

At her daughter's words, regret assailed Susannah. She remembered having promised Georgiana that they would have a funeral for the broken doll. But with Thad's injury and the floodwaters threatening the inn, she'd completely forgotten about it.

Thad's cheek dimpled with his grin. "Georgiana, that was a very nice thing you did for Dolly. And you have a couple of the best-looking pies I've ever seen." He knelt beside the little girl and examined her handiwork.

"Yes, but they need to be outside, baking in the sun." Susannah guided her daughter out the kitchen door. After instructing her to place the "pies" on a flat stone near the back steps, she took Georgiana's mud-encrusted hand and led her to the pump.

Thad followed them from the kitchen and stopped at the pump to tousle

Georgiana's mess of curls. "You two keep up the fine baking; I think I'll go to the carriage house and have that talk with Ruben."

"He's not there," Georgiana said, clapping her wet hands together and watching the droplets fly.

"Ruben's not in the carriage house?" Susannah turned to her daughter, whose expression suggested she relished knowing something adults didn't know.

"Do you know where he is?" Irritation skittered through Susannah. The stage would be along soon, and she needed Ruben to help the driver with the team.

"He went with Lilly 'cause her papa is angry," Georgiana supplied.

Susannah crouched down to get on eye level with her daughter. "Did they go to Macklin's Sawmill?"

When Georgiana hunched her shoulders, dismay pushed a frustrated sigh from Susannah. She hated to ask Thad to help with the stage, but if Ruben didn't return in time, she'd have little choice. Susannah knew that one of the reasons stagecoach drivers were favorably disposed to stopping at Promise and the Killion House Inn instead of traveling on to the next town was because she provided them assistance with their teams.

"Don't concern yourself, Susannah. I'll see to the stagecoach if Ruben doesn't return in time," Thad offered as if he could read her thoughts.

Susannah rose. "Thank you." The words came out in a whoosh of relief.

"No trouble at all." He fixed her with a tender look that caused her pulse to quicken. "I'm glad I'm coming back, too," he intoned just above a whisper.

❧

After checking on her pies and putting Georgiana down for a nap, Susannah decided to see if she could find Ruben and Lilly. Whatever problems Lilly had with her father, they could have at least let her or Naomi know they were leaving the inn. And when she found them, she planned to tell them just that, in no uncertain terms.

She stepped to the stairs where Papa Emil had fashioned a secret compartment for the cash box beneath the third riser. If she had to leave the inn, she might as well stop by the gristmill and buy a bag of cornmeal.

But when she lifted the tread, her heart froze. The little space was empty. She lowered the board back in place and rushed to the desk. Maybe Naomi had moved the cash box for some reason. Praying that was the case, she peered into the dark interior of the desk's cubbyhole.

Nothing. All she could see was the extra supply of pens, ink, and register books. Frantically, she poked her hand into every pigeonhole shelf in the desk. No cash box.

Real fear shot through her. She needed that money to make the next note payment on the inn.

Hearing footsteps on the stairs, she stood and turned to see who it was.

Naomi, holding a piece of paper, her face as white as the sheet in her hand, stopped in her descent. She sank to the bottom step, allowing the paper to fall to the floor. Her narrow shoulders slumped as if all the strength had drained from her muscles. Her voice sounded hollow as she said, "They've gone—eloped it seems."

Ruben and Lilly must have taken the cash box. Fear, anger, and disappointment tangled in a painful wad in Susannah's belly. The bank had made it abundantly clear. Another late payment and Susannah must forfeit the inn.

Her mind raced, thinking of anyone who might be able and willing to loan her the money. There wasn't time to get word to her brother Frank in Hamilton County or her sister, Becky, or brother Jacob in Madison. Even if there were time, she hated to ask, especially since she'd been such a poor guardian to Ruben.

There was only one viable solution and everything in her rebelled against it. She'd have to ask Thad Sutton for a loan.

～

Thad carried the last two buckets of water to fill the horse trough beside the inn. His heart felt as if it sparkled like the water in the early afternoon sun. He'd seen gladness in Susannah's eyes when he told her he would be returning to Promise.

His next thought tempered his joy. Perhaps it had not been gladness but hope that the board would not approve the railroad project after all. No. It was the news that he'd be returning that had lit her eyes. He was sure of it.

Why, he wondered, was he so afraid to believe his affection for Susannah was reciprocated?

George. George and the order Thad had given that ultimately resulted in George's death. Even if Susannah could get beyond the fact that Thad worked for the railroad—a railroad that threatened her inn every bit as much as the floods—she would one day have to learn about his involvement in George's death.

Thad's heart deflated just as the sharp blast from the coach driver's trumpet jerked his head up.

In a cloud of dust, the four matched sorrels brought the coach to a rattling stop in front of the inn.

Thad grabbed the bridle of one of the lead horses.

"Where's young Hale?" The coach creaked and swayed as the robust driver jumped to the ground with a jarring thud.

"I'm just filling in." Thad glanced up at the driver, who dragged his slouch hat off to swipe a red bandanna across his bald pate.

"Got to be back on the road in twenty minutes, so if you'd jist see to it that the horses each get a good drink then harness 'em back up, I'd be obliged." The driver cast the request over his shoulder as he opened the stagecoach door.

"Sure thing." Thad went about his work, paying little heed to the several passengers disembarking.

"Thaddeus Sutton, is that you?"

The vaguely familiar-sounding female voice yanked Thad's attention from the two horses sucking noisily at the trough. Stunned, the reins slipped from his fingers.

He found himself staring into the incredulous gaze of Olivia Vanderpohl, daughter of Hirem Vanderpohl, vice president of the Union Railway Company. Her dark eyes twinkled with fun from the midst of her green bonnet as she smoothed her lace-gloved hand over the skirt of her traveling frock. The pale green-striped material reminded Thad of a gooseberry.

"Papa mentioned you were working in this area. But if the company is paying you so little you must do menial work to supplement your income, perhaps I should speak to him about giving you a raise."

Thad felt heat spread from his neck to his face. In the past year, he'd met the lovely debutante at several soirees. Something about her self-assured demeanor and the lift of her patrician nose always made him feel inferior. "I'm just doing a friend a favor," he managed.

One of the horses whinnied and shook his head, sending water droplets flying in all directions.

Thad grabbed the reins.

Olivia Vanderpohl took two steps backward. Giving an exasperated huff, she swiped at her skirt again. "I cannot wait for Papa to get the railroad built so I won't have to endure these barbaric stagecoach rides every time I visit Cincinnati!"

She turned to the middle-aged woman in black garb beside her. "Sadie, you go ahead and take the bags and sign us in. I'll be along directly."

Olivia's traveling companion gave a mute nod and headed to the inn's side door with two rather substantial-looking carpetbags.

Miss Vanderpohl's lips parted to show a glimpse of even, white teeth. "I'll have to tell Papa I found you hard at work, if somewhat unconventional work."

"I'll be traveling to Indianapolis myself in a couple of days to present my preliminary report to the board." Thad immediately regretted having divulged the information.

Olivia's face brightened. "How fortuitous! I'd planned to only stay overnight here, but perhaps I shall stay an extra day and we can travel on to Indianapolis together."

Thad's mind raced to find a reason not to share a stagecoach with Olivia Vanderpohl. "I had thought to travel by horseback."

Miss Vanderpohl's dark eyes sparked with apparent mischief as her voice affected a wounded tone. "Thaddeus Sutton, do you mean to tell me you'd prefer a sweaty old horse to me as a traveling companion?"

"No—no, of course not. . . ."

"Hey, man! I have four horses here that need water, not just two!" The driver's perturbed bellow as he unhitched the two remaining horses from the stagecoach saved Thad from any further explanation.

Olivia tapped Thad's forearm. "Wonderful! We'll travel together then. Well, I'll leave you to your. . .work," she said with a grin. "It's been ages since we last talked. The governor's ball, wasn't it?" She gave him a knowing look, her smile widening. "I look forward to catching up this evening at supper."

An uneasy feeling wriggled in the pit of Thad's stomach as he watched Olivia Vanderpohl walk through the inn's side door. He remembered well their conversations during the governor's ball last year. She'd flirted openly, leaving little doubt about her interest in him. Though she'd been one of the prettiest girls at the ball with her graceful, statuesque form, large dark eyes, and shiny chestnut hair, something about her had set his teeth on edge.

A worried frown dragged down the corners of Thad's mouth as he led the remaining two horses to the trough. A scorned Olivia Vanderpohl could be dangerous—not only to him, but to Promise and the Killion House Inn.

Chapter 12

"May I have a word with you, Captain Sutton?" Susannah approached the lobby sitting area, struggling to keep the tremor from her voice. The presence of Miss Vanderpohl sitting beside Thad on the sofa did nothing to improve the state of Susannah's nerves.

Since her arrival yesterday afternoon, the daughter of the Union Railway Company's vice president had insisted on being treated like royalty. She'd demanded that her breakfast be brought to her room and complained about everything from the food to the bed linens. But Susannah realized what bothered her most about Olivia Vanderpohl was the attention she paid Thad Sutton.

"Yes, Susannah, of course." Thad sprung from the sofa, mumbling a quick apology to his seatmate.

The expression on Miss Vanderpohl's face could have been chiseled from ice.

Susannah led Thad to the kitchen. She dreaded the next few minutes worse than the time Elmer Gorbett, the local barber, had pulled two of her wisdom teeth.

"Susannah, what is it?" The kindness in Thad's voice and the way he took her hands in his nearly snatched away her nerve.

For a moment, Susannah entertained the idea of pretending she simply wanted his opinion of the supper menu. But to lose her courage now would mean she'd lose the inn to the bank. Instead, she took a deep breath and forced her gaze to meet his. "My cash box is missing—has been since yesterday, after Ruben and Lilly left."

"You think they took it?" A look of anger hardened his features, and his gray eyes flashed like cold steel.

"What else can I think?" The tears she'd been determined to keep in check rolled unheeded down her face.

"Would you like for me to try to find them? Because I'd be glad to—"

"No." She shook her head. Ruben wasn't Thad's responsibility. "I—I need a loan—to make my note payment on the inn," she blurted, feeling her nerve slipping.

"Of course. How much do you need?"

"Forty dollars." Susannah cringed inside. It was a lot to ask, and she had no idea how she might repay it.

His sweet smile caressed her troubled heart, sending more tears sketching down her face. "The railroad has allowed me to set up an expense account at the bank here. I'm authorized to draw upon it for accommodations and other necessities." He gave her fingers a warm, comforting squeeze. "The Killion House Inn has simply requested an advance payment, that's all."

Susannah swallowed hard and looked down at the floor. If she kept gazing into his kind eyes, she'd fall into his arms and bawl like Georgiana. "I can't promise when I can repay you."

"No payment needed. Like I said, I'm simply making an advance payment against the time I plan to stay here. Now, don't fret another minute about it. I'll see to the business tomorrow." He bent and brushed a kiss across her forehead before striding back toward the lobby.

Touching her fingers to the skin still tingling from Thad's kiss, Susannah walked into the dark little pantry and pulled the door shut behind her. The emotional bubble that had grown inside her over the last twenty-four hours burst. She slid to the floor, hugged her knees against her chest, and sobbed.

The *click, click* of Naomi's quick, light steps on the kitchen floor filtered into Susannah's hiding place. The sound reminded Susannah that an inn full of patrons, including Thad and Miss Vanderpohl, would be expecting supper soon.

Rising, she sniffed, dried her eyes on her apron hem, and reached for a jar of pickled beets on the dusty shelf above her. She couldn't afford the luxury of unbridled emotions.

With a jar of beets in each hand and her gumption bolstered, Susannah emerged from the pantry. This month's inn payment would be met. Beyond that, she would do as she'd done for the past four years—she'd take each day and each problem as it arose.

❧

Four days later, Susannah lifted a newly washed pillowcase from the laundry basket. The roses embroidered on its hem told her it was from the room lately occupied by Olivia Vanderpohl.

Reminded of the woman who'd flirted so outrageously with Thad, Susannah snapped the fabric so hard it made a loud *crack*. She reached into her apron pocket for a wooden pin and rammed it down on the wet cloth she'd draped over the line.

If ever a woman had set her cap for a man, Olivia Vanderpohl had set hers for Thad Sutton! And the way he'd taken Olivia's elbow and assisted her into the stage then smiled as he followed her into the conveyance suggested he enjoyed her attentions.

Susannah welcomed the anger welling up inside her, flowing into her arms and exploding from her fingers. It helped to numb the hurt. Why had she been so silly to allow herself to become attached to Thad Sutton?

A match with Olivia Vanderpohl would secure Thad's position with the Union Railway Company and guarantee his advancement. And she'd gleaned from the conversations she'd overheard between him and Miss Vanderpohl that their fathers were the best of friends.

Jealousy gnawed at Susannah's belly. She flopped a wet sheet over the line and tugged out the wrinkles. Olivia Vanderpohl could offer Thad everything his heart might desire. All Susannah could offer beyond her ever-growing and abiding affection was a mortgaged inn—the very existence of which was threatened by the Union Railway Company.

Thad's departure seemed to have had as devastating an effect on Georgiana as it had on Susannah. The child had moped around since Thad left, even though he'd promised to bring her a surprise from Indianapolis.

A frown wrinkled Susannah's forehead when she glanced around the flapping sheet at her little girl. Georgiana sat listlessly on the bottom step beneath the kitchen door. The little rag doll Susannah had made for her to replace Dolly lay discarded at her feet.

Susannah's gaze drifted to the canal basin wharf from where Garrett Heywood's *Flying Eagle* had departed for Cincinnati a few hours earlier. A stab of guilt shot through her. Georgiana needed a father. Ever since the church social at the end of April, Garrett had faithfully attended Sunday worship services here in Promise. And she hadn't noticed so much as a hint of alcohol on his breath for months.

She pinned her spare day dress to the line, her heart sagging like the burdened twine. She shouldn't allow her own selfish feelings to deny Georgiana the benefit of a father figure in her life.

Besides, Thad could very well return from Indianapolis with news that he'd become affianced to Olivia Vanderpohl.

Thad.

There he was again. Always there. Always hovering—patrolling the boundaries of her consciousness. For years, she'd used the excuse of her undying love for George to cloister her heart away from any chance of further hurt.

She smiled, remembering the words of her brother Jacob when he officiated at her and George's wedding. *"The threefold cord of the husband, wife, and Lord is not easily broken."*

For years, she'd let her heart lay fallow, unwilling to allow the plowshare of a new relationship to crack its crusty surface. Yet Thad had slipped into her heart, planting something there she'd thought would never grow again. How could love. . . Yes, she'd call it what it was—love. How could love have bloomed in a heart kept so carefully uncultivated?

She looked over her shoulder at the meadow, and the answer nodded at her from myriad wildflowers. Her gaze flit like a butterfly over the expanse of yellow mustard plants, pinks, blue bachelor buttons, and snowy Queen Anne's lace. Only His hand that had planted this meadow could have planted the feeling growing inside her.

Another surge of anger shot through her, and she snapped a pillowcase against the faded blue of the summer sky. God had done this to her. Did He enjoy allowing her to touch the promise of love, just to snatch it away so He could watch her mourn the loss?

God had taken George. Her home and livelihood remained in constant jeopardy. A new love—a new dream—had been allowed to grow, only to be ripped away, leaving a fresh wound on her heart.

What next, God? What will You take from me next?

"Susannah? Susannah, do you hear me?"

Naomi's voice jerked Susannah from her reverie, drawing her attention to the bottom step beneath the kitchen door.

"I said this child is burning up!" Naomi stood, holding Georgiana and pressing her free hand against her granddaughter's rosy cheeks and forehead.

Susannah dropped a wet tablecloth back into the laundry basket and raced to her daughter. Fear shot through her as she touched Georgiana's frighteningly hot skin. She took her baby into her arms and headed inside.

The child had gone as limp as her rag doll, and her eyes looked glassy.

No, God, no! You can't have her, too!

Naomi followed them into the kitchen. "I'll brew some catnip tea." Her calm tone belied the concern in her eyes.

Upstairs, Susannah struggled to keep her voice light as she tucked Georgiana into her trundle bed. "Do you want your rag doll?"

Georgiana rolled her head back and forth on her pillow. "No. I want Tad."

Her daughter's reply squeezed Susannah's heart.

Out of the mouth of babes.

Susannah realized that Garrett Heywood—or any other man—would never be able to replace the man both she and her daughter wanted in their lives.

"I know, darling," Susannah murmured as she caressed her child's feverish face. "Me, too."

Chapter 13

Atop the jostling stagecoach, Thad inhaled a lungful of fresh country air as he watched the Indiana countryside bounce along. At the last stop, he'd opted to ride on the leather seat just behind the driver.

Inside the coach, his traveling companions had consisted of the Cheathams, a family of six on their way to Pennsylvania. Mr. Cheatham kept the coach's interior filled with cigar smoke, which blended nauseatingly with his wife's overpowering perfume. Their children, two boys and two girls, bickered constantly, making Thad's heart long for sweet-tempered Georgiana.

In truth, Thad's heart had never left Promise. Every time he closed his eyes, he could see Susannah standing in front of the inn, watching him climb into the coach bound for Indianapolis. She'd waved and smiled, but her hazel eyes had seemed extra bright. . .with unshed tears? He liked to think so.

The journey to Indianapolis had been no more pleasant than this return trip to Promise. But at least now he could escape the torments of his fellow travelers. There had been no escaping Olivia Vanderpohl's constant, maddeningly trivial chatter.

He couldn't help comparing Olivia's whining about difficulties in planning a soiree with the quiet grace Susannah displayed daily as she ran her inn. Or Olivia's tiresome chatter about the latest fashion and social gossip compared with the stimulating, if somewhat confrontational, conversations he'd had with Susannah.

In Indianapolis, he'd found himself caught up in Olivia's whirlwind of social events. With his jaw tightly locked, he'd grimaced through her birthday ball.

He'd carefully—and, to his mind, artfully—evaded Olivia's none-too-subtle hints that a marriage proposal from him would nicely crown her birthday soiree. Thad had to smile, remembering how he'd even managed to parry his father's hints that he should seriously consider the benefits of a Sutton–Vanderpohl alliance.

A frown immediately dragged down his smile. All his careful maneuvering around the matrimonial pitfalls seemed to have bought Thad little goodwill in the Union Railway Company boardroom. Although the members seemed pleased with his work, as well as his preliminary findings, they adamantly opposed the idea of situating a depot in Promise.

Hirem Vanderpohl insisted that the depot that would serve the Wayne County stretch of track be placed a few miles south, at Connersville. Vanderpohl also opposed Thad's alternative suggestion of placing a freight depot at Connersville and a passenger depot at Promise.

Remembering the pointed look the man gave him, Thad wondered again if Vanderpohl's opposition wasn't in retaliation for Thad disappointing Olivia. The frown deepened, and his jaw clenched. Olivia Vanderpohl is disappointed, so Susannah Killion must pay with her inn. The whole idea sickened him.

Anger sizzled inside him, and he closed his eyes, seeking out his Lord for peace. He dragged his wide-brimmed felt hat from his head, allowing the cool breeze to drift through his hair, imagining it as the touch of God's own calming fingers.

Heavenly Father, help me break the unhappy news to Susannah. Give her peace, show her Your love, and somehow, Father, find a way to save her inn.

Thad opened his eyes and realized they were nearing Promise. To his right, he could see the little woods that stretched down behind the Killion House Inn. A wagon full of lumber, undoubtedly from Macklin's Sawmill, rolled past them on the road.

Sadness and guilt twined around his heart, cinching tight. Along with the Killions, this little town had become an important part of his life. Thad swallowed the lump of remorse that gathered in his throat. He'd failed Promise. And he'd failed Susannah.

He braced himself as the driver lifted his brass horn to his mouth and loudly trumpeted their arrival.

When the coach rumbled to a stop in front of the inn, Thad climbed down, taking extra care with his leather satchel. A smile pulled at his mouth. Perhaps Georgiana would have something to smile about anyway.

He strode through the inn's front door, his heart hammering with anticipation of seeing Susannah again. Instead, he found a somber-faced Naomi registering the rowdy family that had been his coachmates.

When the last of the Cheathams headed up the stairs, Thad hurried to Naomi. For a moment, relieved surprise relaxed the tense lines in her face.

"Naomi, what is the matter? Where is Susannah?" The questions tumbled from his lips as a mounting sense of concern gripped him.

"Oh, Captain Sutton, I'm so glad you've returned. It's Georgiana. She's been suffering with an awful case of ague for days now."

The tears welling in Naomi's eyes sent fear spiraling through Thad. "It will be all right, Naomi." Thad patted the woman's hand and then bounded up the stairs, two steps at a time, praying that God would make his words come true.

❦

The sound of the bedroom door creaking open jerked Susannah's head up from her arm. Her muscles rebelled as she sat straight up and pushed her stiff shoulders back. She'd fallen asleep sitting on the floor beside Georgiana's trundle bed.

Blinking away the sleep, she touched Georgiana's face. Worry deepened and a weary sigh heaved Susannah's torso. Her child's skin still burned and her little chest barely rose with her shallow breaths.

The sound of footsteps crossing the threshold told her Naomi must be bringing fresh water to bathe Georgiana.

"Susannah."

At Thad's soft voice, Susannah scrambled to her feet, waves of emotion surging through her. "Thad, I—I. . ." The tears springing in her eyes breached her lids and slid unheeded down her face.

The next moment he had her in his arms, lifting her to her feet and whispering soothing hushes and comforting reassurances in her ear.

Susannah clung to him, savoring the blessed moment. Only now did she realize just how much she'd missed him, how much she needed his nearness.

"My dear, dearest, Susannah," he murmured then pressed a kiss on her forehead as if she were Georgiana. "How is she?"

With his strong, comforting arm around her waist, they walked together to Georgiana's low bed.

"She's still feverish, but the dreadful shivers have calmed."

She walked to the washstand and poured the last bit of water into the bowl. Taking the damp scrap of cloth draped over the bowl's rim, she rewet it in the tepid liquid. "Naomi should be bringing fresh water soon." Susannah glanced at her sleeping daughter and felt a strong maternal tug. She knelt and bathed Georgiana's face with the cloth.

"You think that is wise, bathing her face with the window open?" The concern in Thad's voice touched a deep place in Susannah's heart.

What a wonderful father he would be to Georgiana.

She hurriedly shooed the thought from her mind and focused again on her daughter. "You sound like Dr. Wiggins," she told him, her lips stretching into a smile. "But my brother-in-law is a fine physician in Madison, and he's successfully treated many fever patients with this method."

"You mentioned Dr. Wiggins. She's being attended by a physician, then?" Thad knelt beside Georgiana and brushed a golden ringlet from her forehead.

Georgiana's pale lashes curling against her rosy cheeks fluttered for a moment, and her rosebud mouth pursed. Her little face rolled against the palm of his hand.

Susannah marveled, struck with the notion that even in her child's sleep, she must sense Thad's presence. "Yes, Dr. Wiggins has been treating her with quinine. He promised to come by again tomorrow." A lump of fear gathered in her throat. She felt Thad's arm slide around her waist again to give her a quick, reassuring squeeze, and the gripping fear ebbed.

All through the afternoon and evening, Susannah, Naomi, and Thad took turns sitting with Georgiana. The inn still had to be run, meals had to be made, and guests needed to be tended. The loss of Lilly and Ruben's help had become even more acute. Thad's willingness to help with everything from attending to Georgiana to serving and helping clean up after supper made Susannah want to weep with relief.

Though Susannah had wanted to stay by her child's bedside through the night, Thad insisted that she and Naomi rest in Naomi's room while he kept watch over Georgiana.

But after a couple of hours of fitful sleep, Susannah woke in the middle of the night to the distant sound of hushed murmurings. Wondering if Georgiana had awakened, she quietly slid from Naomi's bed. Wrapping her voluminous dressing gown around her, she padded across the moon-drenched room to the door that opened to her and Georgiana's bedroom.

There, in the pale halo of a single taper, Thad knelt with his head bowed over Georgiana's bed, whispering prayers for her healing.

Susannah trod softly into his shadow that stretched across the floor, guilt smiting her conscience. Not once had she allowed her worried heart to prostrate itself before the throne of God on Georgiana's behalf.

"Tad. Mamma."

At the tiny voice, raspy with sleep, Susannah rushed to her daughter's bedside. Grabbing the low rail of the trundle bed, she sank to the floor beside Thad.

"We're here, darling. We're both here." She touched Georgiana's face, and relief surged through her. Though her child's skin still felt far warmer than Susannah would like, Georgiana's fever seemed to have cooled some.

Georgiana's hand went to her throat. "Mamma, my thwoat hurts." She scrunched up her face with a visibly painful swallow. "Gwamma and Tad pwayed for me," she rasped. "Why don't you pway for me? Don't you want my thwoat to get better?"

For so long, Susannah had allowed her anger at God to separate her from Him. Like a petulant child, she had turned her back and refused to speak to her Lord. Now God might take from her the most important thing in her life.

"Of course, my darling," she murmured through a broken sob. "Of course I will pray for you." And it was true. Suddenly, Susannah wanted to reconnect with her heavenly Father—to pray and beg the Almighty to spare her child—to find again the solace she had spurned for years.

A giant knot of panic balled up in her chest. She wasn't sure she even knew how to pray anymore. She turned helplessly to Thad and felt his arm tighten around her waist.

His gaze melted into hers as he pulled her against him, seeming to sense her silent plea for help. He turned a gentle smile toward her sick daughter. "Would it be all right if your Mamma and I pray together for you?"

Georgiana nodded.

Thad clasped Susannah's hand in his and prayed the words she couldn't say.

"Oh, Father, we ask that You cover our precious Georgiana with Your healing hand and restore her health. And please, Father, open our hearts to Your endless love and strengthen our faith."

Naomi's constant prayers hadn't managed to dent Susannah's stubborn resistance. But here in the darkened room on her knees, the words of Thad's prayer pried open the door to her heart, so long barred shut. For the first time in years, Susannah felt the blessed light of God's love shine its warmth all the way to her soul.

"Please, God, please heal my baby. Please. . ." Joyful sobs swallowed her words as a sense of peace overwhelmed her. God had heard her. She knew it. She felt it. Whatever else might happen in her life, she knew she would never again attempt to sever the blessed cord that connected her soul with the Almighty.

For a long while, as Georgiana slept peacefully, Susannah sat on the floor and wept in Thad's arms. How wonderful to be rocked in his comforting embrace as sweet, blessed moments stretched into the night like their linked shadows that reached across the room and up the walls.

Susannah knew she belonged here—belonged in Thad Sutton's arms. But at length, she wiped the remnants of her tears against the soft cotton of his shirt-front and pushed away. Thad had slept even less than she or Naomi. "You've hardly slept at all. Go on to your room now and I'll watch over Georgiana." Pushing against his shoulders, she forced her stiff legs to lift her body up.

"I've done without sleep many a night on watch while in the army," he whispered, his voice husky—with sleep, or something else?

He rose and stood beside her, his arms slipping around her waist. "Let me know immediately if there's any change."

Susannah nodded, afraid to trust her voice. Did he know what his nearness did to her? Did he feel it, too?

It happened so suddenly, she had no time to prepare, to think, or to respond. He bent his head and brushed a tender kiss on her lips. "Good night," he murmured in a breathless whisper and then slipped out the door into the hallway.

Susannah closed the door with a tiny *click* and trudged back to her daughter's bedside. Her heart sank with her body as she lowered herself again to the floor.

She licked her lips as a sweet ache burrowed deeper inside her. Did his kiss mean anything more than friendship? How could it? His life belonged in Indianapolis. She realized that since his return, Thad hadn't once mentioned what had transpired between him and the Union Railway Company's board of directors—or Olivia Vanderpohl.

Chapter 14

"Please Mamma, me and Miss Lacy want to go, too." Clutching the china doll Thad had brought her from Indianapolis, Georgiana followed Susannah to the kitchen door.

Torn, Susannah hesitated as she reached for her bonnet on the peg beside the door. Her daughter had been free of the fever for scarcely three days. Yet Susannah's heart was still so full of thanksgiving for Georgiana's recovery, she found it difficult to deny her daughter anything. She didn't even correct the child's grammar.

"I don't know, Georgiana. It's a long walk to the blackberry thicket, and you're just beginning to get your strength back. Besides, there are snakes and chiggers around those brambles."

"Actually, I think an outing might do Georgiana and Miss Lacy some good." As he entered the kitchen from the hallway, Thad's quiet voice caused Susannah's heart to do a somersault.

"I'm not afraid of snakes and chiggers and I'll bwi–br—ing my own basket." A hopeful look shone from Georgiana's uptilted face.

Susannah's resistance melted with her heart, and her lips emitted a sigh of surrender. "All right, but I'd better bring along an old quilt in case you and Miss Lacy need to rest."

"Come with us, Tad!" Bouncing with excitement, Georgiana tugged at his shirtsleeve.

The same longing exhibited in Georgiana's childish petition surged through Susannah. But she'd decided that both she and her daughter had become far too attached to Thad Sutton. One day soon, he would leave for good. Better now to begin pulling away from this man they'd come to love.

"Georgiana, I–I'm sure Thad has work to do," Susannah said weakly.

"Not at all. Free as a bird today."

His broad smile sent Susannah's heart tumbling again.

"I love blackberries." He bent down and lifted Georgiana to his shoulders. "Your mamma and I could pick from the middle canes while you pick from the ones higher up. And it would keep you away from the snakes and chiggers."

"I'll get that quilt," Susannah murmured amid Georgiana's gleeful giggles. She hurried from the kitchen, hoping her face didn't display the happiness pinging around inside her.

A few minutes later, the June sun beat down on them as the three traversed the meadow between the inn and the little woods. Susannah's berry basket on her right arm bounced against her hip while she carried the small quilt for Georgiana's pallet tucked beneath the crook of her left arm. She was glad she'd insisted Georgiana wear a bonnet, but she still worried the heat might cause a recurrence of the fever.

From atop her perch on Thad's shoulders, Georgiana pointed toward the east end of the little woods. "I can see it! The blackbewwies are over there."

Susannah marveled at the patience Thad showed with Georgiana. He never murmured a complaint as the little girl's berry basket, with the china doll nestled inside, bumped against his shoulder with each step. Instead, he kept a running conversation with his diminutive passenger about all the delectable desserts that could be made from blackberries.

A familiar pain raked at Susannah's heart. If only she could allow herself to believe there was a way for the three of them to make a family. *Oh, Lord, if there could just be some way for him to stay in Promise. . .*

She smiled at the ease with which the prayer flitted from her heart. She looked at Thad's profile with her laughing daughter on his shoulders, his hands securely wrapped around Georgiana's tanned bare feet. Susannah's thankful tears blurred the image. She knew her reconnection with God was one of the greater blessings Thad had brought into her life. Somehow he'd been able to revive her faith, something no preacher's sermon or even her devout mother-in-law had been able to accomplish.

"Blackbewwies!"

With Georgiana's triumphant announcement, Susannah's nostrils caught the sweet fragrance of the berries on the summer breeze. She realized they had indeed reached the northeast edge of the woods and the blackberry thickets.

The rough-leafed, sprawling canes shone with the glossy, dark fruit. Little specks of pinkish red dotted the brambles where berries had not yet ripened, and Susannah noticed several yellow-centered white blossoms that promised later berries.

She turned to Thad and grinned up at the perspiration beading on his forehead. "You may want to put Georgiana down now and rest your shoulders after that walk. Besides, you're likely to end up with blackberry juice matted in your hair."

He threw back his head and laughed as he swung Georgiana to the ground. "Believe me, during my two years in the army, my hair saw much worse than blackberry juice!"

As they shared a laugh, his gaze twinkled into hers, setting her heart dancing. Disconcerted, Susannah turned away and busied herself with spreading the quilt in a shaded patch of grass.

Georgiana set Miss Lacy, named for her snowy lace-over-rose taffeta dress, on one corner of the quilt.

"Be careful not to get blackberry stains on Miss Lacy's dress," Susannah cautioned her daughter. "You know how hard it is to get those stains out." The doll was one of the finer ones Susannah had ever seen, and she knew it must have cost dearly.

Thad's fond smile swung from Miss Lacy to Georgiana. "Miss Lacy seemed so lonely on that store shelf. I knew she needed a little girl to love her more than she needed a dress that never got mussed."

Susannah blinked quickly, swallowing the knot of tears that had gathered in her throat. Every time she thought her affection for the man could not deepen, he proved her wrong. She'd seen the pained regret on his face several weeks ago when he'd been unable to save Georgiana's beloved Dolly. Susannah was glad that her daughter had attached herself so quickly to the new doll. Miss Lacy seemed to have helped heal the unhappy incident with Dolly for both Thad and Georgiana.

For about an hour, they worked around the brambles, plucking the plump, dark berries.

"Be careful of the thorns, moppet," Thad warned Georgiana, who once again sat astride his shoulders.

Susannah noticed his careful movements so as to keep a safe distance between Georgiana's face and the briars. She glanced up to see a big juicy berry slip from Georgiana's hand and plop onto Thad's forehead.

Thad just grinned and swiped at a sticky, dark rivulet trickling down his forehead.

"Can't say I didn't warn you." Susannah laughed and sent him a sideways grin, earning her a barrage of berries against the back of her bonnet.

At length, Georgiana, who'd most likely eaten more berries than she dropped into her little basket, yawned. "I'm sleepy." She rubbed her eyes with blackberry-stained fists.

Thad reached above his shoulder and took her basket, handing it to Susannah. "I think it's time for you and Miss Lacy to take a nap, moppet."

In one smooth motion, he lifted Georgiana from his shoulders and cradled her in his arms. He tenderly laid her on the quilt pallet, tucking Miss Lacy beside her.

After he returned to the blackberry brambles, several minutes of silence stretched between him and Susannah. An indefinable tension charged the atmosphere around them.

Compelled to break the uneasy silence, Susannah spoke first. "Thank you for Georgiana's new doll." Did her voice sound too stilted? "I don't think I thanked you."

He sent her that devastating grin that had become so familiar to her. "The look in Georgiana's eyes when I handed it to her was plenty thanks for me."

"Did you have a pleasant trip to Indianapolis?" The harder she tried to sound casual, the more her voice tightened. She wasn't about to mention Olivia Vanderpohl but hoped in a roundabout way to glean some sense of his feelings for the woman.

"Pleasant enough, I suppose." His tone unreadable, he kept his gaze fixed on his hands, gingerly plucking berries from the thorny brambles.

Something in his evasive demeanor troubled Susannah. Did it have to do with the railroad, Miss Vanderpohl, or both?

After several more minutes of uneasy quiet, he set his basket down in the grass and then slowly straightened to face her. At last he sighed deeply and looked her directly in the eyes.

Susannah quaked inwardly as she watched serious lines draw his features taut.

"I'm sorry, Susannah. I wasn't able to convince the board to situate a passenger depot here."

The news should have hit her harder than it did. Instead, Susannah found herself wanting to relieve the look of remorse furrowing his brow.

"I know you did your best." She reached out and took his hand. "We still have the stagecoach traffic," she said, forcing a smile.

At a rustling of the grass near her feet, she glanced down in time to see a little green snake slither past the front hem of her skirt.

"Ahh!" she screeched. Startled more from the sudden movement than the harmless snake, she jumped in the opposite direction from which the reptile had headed.

The next instant, she found herself in Thad's embrace. Flustered and ready to push away, she lifted her face, and their gazes locked.

His arms gently pulled her closer. And this time, there was no doubt what emotion she saw in his eyes.

Her heart slamming in her ears, Susannah closed her eyes as his mouth captured hers. She eagerly welcomed his kiss. For one blissful moment, the coming railroad, Olivia Vanderpohl—all of Susannah's questions and concerns—drifted away.

Too soon, he lifted his head and released her lips, leaving her with a forlorn yearning for the tender moment now past.

In the harsh light of day, reality came rushing back. This kiss was no surprise. She had allowed it—perhaps even invited it. Heat leaped to Susannah's face. As badly as she would like to believe she and Thad could have a future together, a mountain of immovable obstacles still stood in the way.

She pushed hard against his chest, twisting out of his embrace.

A confused, stricken look dulled his gray eyes. "Susannah, I—"

"Mamma! I'm thirsty!" Georgiana's sleepy voice broke in, saving Susannah from any further exchange.

Susannah hurried to her daughter's side. Helping Georgiana up, she took ridiculous pains to smooth wrinkles from the child's patched and faded dress. "It's time to head back so you can get a drink at the pump. We have enough berries for several pies, and Grandma will soon need us to help with dinner."

Although every word was the truth, Susannah knew the real reason she wanted to get back to the inn. She couldn't bear another moment alone with Thad.

She folded the quilt and gathered the baskets as Thad hoisted Georgiana to his shoulders. The kiss had shaken her to her core. She couldn't look at him. The embarrassment smoldering inside her like hot coals flamed into a quick anger. How could he have allowed something like that to happen when he knew they had no hope of a future together?

Susannah carefully kept her steps a pace or two behind his, discouraging any conversation. She trudged through the knee-high weeds, clutching the berry basket so hard her fingers cramped.

She should never have allowed him to come with her and Georgiana. She'd vowed to distance herself from him, and that was exactly what she must do. But the longer he remained in Promise and at the Killion House Inn, the harder that task would be.

Oh, Lord, if he cannot stay, please hurry and send him back to Indianapolis.

As they waded through the weeds, Susannah gazed at Thad Sutton's broad back and felt her resolve wither with her prayer.

Chapter 15

Thad Sutton slammed his pen on the desktop. He picked up the paper before him, wadded it into a crumpled ball, and pitched it among several of its fellows littering his bedroom floor.

Leaning back in his chair, he stretched his cramped shoulder muscles and pressed his fingertips against his throbbing temples. At last, he surrendered to the realization that securing both the Killion House Inn and his position with the Union Railway Company was an impossible fool's errand. His every attempt to accomplish both goals in a respectful, yet persuasive, letter to his father seemed woefully inadequate.

"Drivel! Idiotic drivel!" Thad's brain echoed with the imagined sound of his father's irate voice.

He gazed through the window in front of his desk and blew out a tired breath. Since the floodwaters had receded, a constant flow of travelers had brought prosperity back to Susannah's inn. And now because of Josiah Sutton's stubborn insistence that he control his son and bend Thad to his will, Susannah, Naomi, and little Georgiana might well face homelessness.

Susannah.

Her image, her smile, *her touch*, never left him. Sweet thoughts of her continually strolled along the edges of his mind. Thad closed his eyes as his tongue crept out to taste, again, the remembered kiss on his lips.

Lord, help me, but I love her so.

In war, he'd led countless charges against the enemy. Yet here he sat, shrinking from the thought of igniting his father's ire.

He loved Susannah and Georgiana. He loved them with all his heart. And now they needed a champion.

Renewed anger straightened Thad in his chair, and he squared his shoulders, his resolve stiffening with his back. He would not cower like a frightened boy when the livelihood of the woman he loved hung in the balance.

Determined to not falter, he slipped another sheet of paper from the stack on his desk and dipped the nib of his pen into the inkwell.

Dear Lord, give me the words that will soften my father's heart and save this town and this inn.

Laying aside all concerns about his position with both the railroad board and his father, Thad penned his petition with forceful strokes. He shared with his father his feelings for Susannah and begged Josiah to use his influence with the board and join him in calling for reconsideration of a depot in Promise.

A few minutes later, Thad crossed the National Road, purposefully striding toward the post office. Not for the first time, he felt frustration at the lack of a telegraph office in Promise. Having become used to the service in Indianapolis, to be forced to wait for a reply to a letter seemed excruciatingly slow and primitive. He'd observed that it was generally the coming of rail service that brought the telegraph to a community. But paradoxically, it was that very rail service that threatened the existence of this town.

He wiped away the trickle of sweat meandering down his forehead. It wasn't so much the mid-June sun that caused the outcropping of perspiration as it was the missive tucked in his coat pocket. If his father viewed his request as insubordination, he could lose his position as engineer and surveyor for the railroad. But he'd never be able to live with himself if he sat by mutely and allowed the railroad to doom the Killion House Inn.

Lost in his reverie, Thad climbed the two steps to the post office's porch. He looked up just in time to prevent a collision with Susannah, who appeared lost in her own thoughts.

"Whoa there!" The words puffed breathlessly from his lips as he caught her about the waist. Finding her unexpectedly in his arms set his heart bucking like a skittish colt.

"Oh, I'm sorry!" Susannah jerked back, her face suffusing a deep pink. "I'm afraid I wasn't paying attention."

"Not at all. It was my fault entirely." He had to force his lips into a smile. It hurt that she always seemed repelled by his touch. To cover his disappointment, he glanced at the open letter in her hand. "Not bad news I hope."

"No." Her faint voice sounded evasive as she hurriedly shoved the paper into her skirt pocket.

At the sound of heavy-booted steps, Thad glanced over his shoulder to see Mick Macklin storming toward them.

Red-faced, the man fixed a narrowed glare on Susannah. "Susannah Killion, you'd better tell me right here and now where that whelp of a nephew of yours went off to with my Lilly!"

Thad stepped quickly between Macklin and Susannah. The sawmill owner already reeked of alcohol, and it was not yet midmorning. Thad wanted to thrash the man for the bruises he'd seen on Lilly's face. *If that reprobate so much as lays a hand on Susannah. . .*

Drawing himself up to his full height of six feet, he glared at Macklin. "Mrs. Killion has no idea where your daughter is."

"I wasn't talkin' to you, railroad man!" Macklin infused the last two words with scorn and then spat over the porch rail.

"Mr. Macklin, I have not seen Lilly or Ruben for over two weeks." Susannah stepped from behind Thad's shoulder. Her voice was calm and her face placid, but Thad caught a flicker of fear in her hazel eyes.

The man squinted, his bloodshot eyes nearly disappearing in his unshaven face. He stabbed the air in front of Susannah with a meaty finger. "But you know where they are, don't ya?"

Thad grasped the man's shoulder. Even if Susannah did know the couple's whereabouts, which he doubted, he knew she wouldn't be keen on sharing that information with Macklin. "I suggest you be on your way, Mr. Macklin. And any further business you might have with Mrs. Killion, you can bring to me."

Through mean slits, Mick Macklin's glower swung between Thad and Susannah. "So that's the way it is, is it?"

His sly grin and snort strained Thad's self-control. The impropriety suggested in the man's look sent waves of molten anger bubbling up inside Thad. Only consideration for Susannah kept Thad from pummeling the drunkard senseless right there in front of Promise's post office.

"As friend and commanding officer to the lady's late husband, it is my duty to protect her honor as well as her person," he ground through his clenched jaw. "Mrs. Killion has told you she's not seen your daughter, so unless you have other business with her, I must insist you be on your way." He took another step toward Macklin, who backed up, nearly falling down the porch steps.

"I'll go, but I ain't done with ya. Neither of ya!" Mick growled, grabbing the handrail to regain his balance. He shot them a parting glare over his shoulder before plopping another wad of spittle onto the dusty path.

Thad turned to Susannah, his protective instincts raging. "Perhaps I should walk you back to the inn. I wouldn't want Macklin to cause you any trouble."

She gave her head a dismissive shake, though her face looked pale and her smile a bit wobbly. "Thank you, Thad, but I've handled far worse than a drunken Mick Macklin."

"Are you sure?" Thad allowed his gaze to melt into her lovely green eyes. He didn't want to leave her alone. He didn't want to leave her at all. "If you wait just a few moments while I mail this letter—"

"No, I really need to be getting back." She gave an unconvincing little laugh. "I'm sure Mick is halfway to the mill by now and has probably forgotten the entire conversation."

Thad watched her cross the National Road and head toward the inn. Only when he felt confident that Macklin was nowhere in sight did he turn back to the post office.

He touched his coat breast and the letter crinkled beneath his fingers. Over the summer, his mission in Promise had changed. Thad couldn't help wondering if God's reason for sending him here had less to do with surveying for a railroad than providing Susannah with a champion. He liked the thought. *Oh, Lord, if You would just allow me to spend the rest of my life as Susannah's champion. . .*

Susannah sank to the bench beneath the pin oak tree in the inn's side yard. Her heart still raced from her near collision with Thad Sutton. Heat suffused her face as she remembered how the joy of feeling his arms around her had swamped her momentary embarrassment.

The familiar warm longing rose in her heart only to be drowned by a cold wave of reality. Thad was the enemy. However they might feel about each other made little difference. Almost certainly, his business at the post office had to do with communicating with the coldhearted company that seemed determined to starve Promise to death.

Another thought stabbed more sharply at her heart. Perhaps all his correspondence was not business related. Susannah's mind quickly fled painful imaginings of Thad exchanging letters of affection with Miss Olivia Vanderpohl.

Her gaze shifted to her brother's surprising letter in her lap. A renewed sense of relief and astonishment rolled through her as she eyed, for the third time, her sibling's firm script:

Dear Little Sister,

I hope this finds you, your kinswoman, Naomi, and precious little daughter, Georgiana, well. I write to inform you that our nephew, Ruben, and his sweetheart, Lilly, arrived safely at the parsonage here in Madison Tuesday last. They insisted upon being married, and although I harbored grave reservations, my dear wife, Rosaleen, persuaded me to agree, and I reluctantly consented to perform the nuptials. The newlyweds are living with us at the parsonage. Ruben has procured employment at Riverfront Porkpacking here in Madison. Lilly is proving to be a wonderful help with our three little girls. With another baby on the way, Rosaleen considers her a true blessing.

Both Ruben and Lilly regret deeply that they were not able to inform you of their leaving Promise prior to the event. It seems that threats made by Lilly's father, a truly unsavory character by all accounts, prompted their departure. They feared should they linger the man might bring his wrath to bear upon not only themselves but you and the Killion House Inn. Together, our young kin beg your forgiveness and pardon for any grief their actions might have caused. Lilly is eager to pen you a personal note of contrition but asked me to predicate it with this explanatory missive, desiring I assure you they are safe and legally united in marriage, sanctified by our Lord Jesus Christ.

The remainder of the letter held only news of their sister, Becky, and her family and recent happenings at their church in Madison.

Praying God will keep you and yours always in His tender care,
Your humble servant and beloved brother,
Jacob Hale

Irritation prickled as Susannah read the salutation. She'd found no mention of the money with which the young couple had absconded.

While she considered how she might broach the subject to her brother in an answering letter, a quiet shadow fell across the pages in her hand.

"Susannah." The unexpected voice sounded troubled.

Susannah's attention jerked up to Esther Murdoch's distraught face. A normally cheerful person, the preacher's wife's grim expression filled Susannah with alarm.

"Yes, Esther, is something the matter?" A sense of dread caused Susannah's fingers to tremble as she slipped Jacob's letter back into the envelope and shoved it into her skirt pocket.

"It's Mr. Sutton, the railroad man." She held up her hand and shook her head. "I don't abide any kind of gossip, and for my part, it won't go any further than this. But since the man is staying at your inn, Ezekiel thought you should know." Her gaze skittered across the canal, and she laced her plump fingers together as if in prayerful petition. Her next words came out in a rush, suggesting her eagerness to be done with the distasteful errand. "Sheriff Lykins has arrested him for vandalism."

Chapter 16

Vandalism?" Thad yanked his arm from Sheriff Lykins's grasp. "Are you mad, man?" His anger mounting, he turned on the boardwalk in front of the general store where he'd just bought penny candy for Georgiana and faced his accuser. He knew that the sheriff, like many people in Promise, did not hold him in high regard. But to trump up false charges against him was beyond the pale!

Lykins shook his head. "I'm sorry, Mr. Sutton, but charges have been made by two eyewitnesses. Said they watched you saw the wicket clean off the upstream gate at Connell's Lock."

"Who said they saw me do that?" Thad tried to keep his voice down and his temper in check. "I have a right to know who my accusers are." He'd always known the people here were not keen on him, but he would never have imagined anyone would stoop to such treachery.

Thad felt the pressure of Sheriff Lykins's hand against his back, urging him on toward the brick courthouse half a block from the post office.

"Mick Macklin and Art Granger claimed they saw you leavin' the lock with a saw in your hand," the sheriff told him as they walked.

Lykins showed no interest in Thad's protest or assertion that he had no access to a saw.

As they walked the narrow alley beside the courthouse, the situation became frighteningly clear. Thad remembered Macklin's thinly veiled threat less than an hour ago in front of the post office. He suspected Macklin had done the damage himself. Thad also knew that Art Granger was a generally drunken ne'er-do-well who worked for Macklin at the sawmill. A jug of whiskey would easily buy the man's allegiance.

Behind the courthouse, Lykins guided Thad toward the jail. The weathered gray clapboard building jutting out from the rear of the courthouse looked as cheerless as Thad felt. Fear tightened around his chest like an iron band. With Thad unable to protect her, Mick Macklin might very well attempt to do Susannah harm.

When they reached the jail's open door, Thad stopped and tried one last desperate time to retain his freedom. He turned to the sheriff. "Listen, Macklin threatened both me and Susannah Killion earlier today. He's upset that she allowed his daughter, Lilly, to stay at the inn after he'd beaten the girl. He's trumped this up to get me out of the way. I'm afraid he may harm Mrs. Killion or her inn."

"Tell it to the circuit judge next week." The increased pressure of the sheriff's hand on his back forced Thad through the doorway and into one of the two iron-barred cells. Lykins clanged the cell door shut and rammed a large iron key into the lock.

Thad heard the lock's tumblers click as he paced the spartan six-by-five-foot space. He shoved his fingers through his hair, fear and frustration raging through him. What if Mick Macklin was this very minute threatening Susannah?

"Please, Sheriff Lykins. . ." Thad grasped the cell bars, unashamed of the imploring tone tightening his voice. "Please check on Susannah Killion—"

"Thad!" Susannah burst through the jailhouse door, cutting off Thad's words. "I couldn't believe it when Esther Murdoch told me you'd been arrested."

The tears glistening in her lovely green eyes sent Thad's heart soaring. They confirmed what her sweet kiss had conveyed in the blackberry thicket—she cared for him.

Relief washed over Thad. At least, for the moment, she was safe. Even in the midst of his predicament, Thad couldn't help grinning as Susannah turned her indignation like a lioness on Sheriff Lykins.

"Tom Lykins, you let Captain Sutton out of that cell this instant!"

Lykins scratched the back of his neck and looked more than a little uncomfortable. "Wish I could, but I had two eyewitnesses swear they saw Captain Sutton here saw the wicket off the gate on Connell's Lock."

"That doesn't even make good common sense!" Susannah's passionate argument caused Thad to seriously consider having her represent him before the circuit judge. "Why on earth would he trouble himself to do such a silly thing? Why, Cy Pittman has probably already installed a new wicket by now. If Thad wanted to do real damage, wouldn't he have set fire to the lock. . .or blown it up. . .or something like that?" Her wild gesturing and raised voice set Lykins back on his heels. "Besides, only a month ago, Thad helped reinforce the canal walls to keep them from crumbling when the floodwaters came."

Tom Lykins scrubbed his hand across his weary-looking face and sighed. "Listen, Susannah, it's not my job to try and figure out why somebody might or might not do mischief. Shoot, it ain't even my job to figure out if he did it. That's the circuit judge's job. Mick Macklin and Art Granger said they saw him do it, so I'm obliged to hold him here until Judge Hendershot gets here next week and tries the case."

"Mick Macklin and Art Granger?" Susannah actually snorted. "You would take the word of two of Promise's most notorious drunks over a surveyor and engineer for the Union Railway Company?"

"I told ya, I don't have a choice." With outstretched hands, Lykins gestured his helplessness.

"Surely there is bail." The hopeful lilt in Susannah's voice clawed at Thad's heart.

"Well," Sheriff Lykins drawled, scratching the back of his neck again, "the judge'd have to set bail and the judge ain't here. Most likely, a forty-dollar fine for such mischief would prob'ly satisfy the court. If you can pay that and sign a voucher promising to be responsible in case he takes off 'fore the judge gets here. . ."

Thad could stand mute no longer. "I won't leave Promise, Sheriff Lykins. And if you will just let me out, I can get you the money for the fine. The Union Railway Company has set up an expense account for me at the bank." There was no way Thad was going to allow Susannah to use her own money for his fine.

The sheriff shook his head. "Sorry, I cain't let you out." He glanced at the clock on a shelf above his cluttered desk. "The missus oughta be gittin' dinner on the table about now, and I know better'n to keep her waitin'." He gave a little chuckle. "I'll bring you a plate of grub when I get back."

"That won't be necessary, Tom," Susannah said in a quiet voice. "I'll see to Captain Sutton's meals." The sweet look on her face as her gaze swung from the sheriff to Thad made his arms ache to hold her.

"Suit yourself." Tom Lykins hunched his shoulders, plucked the cell key from his desktop, and lumbered out the jailhouse door.

Susannah neared the cell bars, her eyes flashing green fire. "I'm so angry with this town I could just spit!"

"Probably better be careful." Thad couldn't help teasing. "Lykins might arrest you for that."

She sent him a withering glare, and for the first time, Thad was glad for the bars between them. "How can you make jokes when you're in this—this cage?" She pointed at his dreary little confines.

"I'm sorry." The words floated out on a small chortle he couldn't hold back. He wrapped his hands around her fingers gripping the black iron bars between them. An overwhelming urge to protect her swept through him. "Promise me you will be careful of Mick Macklin. If he comes anywhere near you or the inn, let the sheriff know."

"It's Mick Macklin who should be afraid of me," she snapped, making Thad almost believe her.

Grinning, Thad caressed her fingers, reveling in the feel of her soft hand against his. "Don't worry, this will all be sorted out soon. Just go to the bank and ask them to write up an authorization note to have forty dollars withdrawn from my expense account. Bring the note here and I'll sign it, and then the bank manager will give you the money for my fine."

Susannah nodded again, but her smile quivered slightly. "I'll bring your dinner along with the note from the bank," she promised, giving his fingers a quick, warm squeeze before she turned and hurried out through the jailhouse door.

Thad gazed at the retreating back of this beautiful, courageous woman and swallowed down the lump that had gathered in his throat. What an amazing helpmate she would be if only God would allow him to make her his forever.

Dear Lord, please protect her. Just protect her until I can get out of this place.

Her jaw clenched, Susannah wiped the tears streaming down her face as she stomped toward the bank. How petty and mean of Mick Macklin to have Thad arrested just to get back at her for helping Lilly. Although she was still disappointed at Ruben and Lilly for taking the inn's money, Susannah was thankful Ruben had taken Lilly away from that awful man.

Stopping before the three stone steps in front of the bank, Susannah took a deep breath. Though her relationship with Fergus McDougal, the bank manager, had been strained at times, she felt confident he would understand the situation and respect Thad's wishes.

Oh, Lord, please let Fergus allow me to do this on Thad's behalf.

With another deep breath, she mounted the steps and entered the brick building. In the large, high-ceilinged room, her footfalls echoed on the smooth wood floor. The smells of ink, paper, and leather assailed her nostrils. Three clerks wearing green eyeshades sat huddled together in one corner. They seemed oblivious to everything but the mounds of paper on their desks over which they bent, constantly scribbling.

Susannah always found the bank more than a little intimidating. Everything about it reminded her it was a man's domain. But this time, especially, she mustn't allow herself to be cowed by the place. Thad's freedom depended upon it.

She strode to a large mahogany table usually occupied by Mr. McDougal. Gleaming dust-free in the late morning sun spilling across its top, the desk displayed an exactly centered green felt blotter. Above the blotter, a half dozen inkwells holding black pens stood like military sentries. But the overstuffed brown leather chair behind the desk sat empty.

"Mrs. Killion, is there something I can do for you?"

Susannah jumped at Fergus McDougal's booming voice. Heat suffusing her face, she willed her heart to a slower canter.

"The payment on your note is not due for another two weeks." Sending her a congenial smile, he motioned for her to be seated in one of the two ladder-backed chairs flanking the desk.

After she'd situated herself on the chair's horsehair-upholstered seat, McDougal rounded the desk and lowered his rotund bulk to the giant padded desk chair. He lounged against the chair's cushy back, smoothed down his gray mustache, and emitted a long, contented sigh. Fergus McDougal always reminded Susannah of a plump Scottish terrier.

"It is not on my own behalf that I'm here today, Mr. McDougal." Straightening her back and squaring her shoulders, Susannah laced her fingers in her lap and strove to affect her most businesslike voice and demeanor. "I am here on behalf of one of the residents of the Killion House Inn. Captain

Thaddeus Sutton of the Union Railway Company—"

McDougal waved a beefy hand and shook his head, his bushy gray eyebrows knitting together in a grim scowl. "On my way back from dinner, I heard that Sheriff Lykins has the scoundrel in jail for vandalism. It seems he can't wait for the railroad to bring an end to our canal."

Irritation marched up Susannah's spine, stiffening her back. She knew McDougal had helped to finance the canal project and only grudgingly did business with the Union Railway Company. His eagerness to believe Thad guilty irked her. She swallowed down the retort that clawed at her throat for its freedom. The worst thing she could do would be to offend Fergus McDougal.

She clasped her hands in her lap until they were nearly numb and tempered her voice. "Captain Sutton maintains his innocence in the matter and has asked me to request a withdrawal of forty dollars from his expense account."

McDougal shook his head. "The man would have to come in and sign for it, and since he's not in a position to do that, there's really nothing I can do."

"I will take the note to him and bring it back to you signed." Susannah hurriedly blurted the offer, anxious to clear away all impediments to acquiring the money that would free Thad.

Fergus McDougal gave her a condescending, almost pitying smile. "I know you are not used to doing business beyond your little inn, but I would really need to witness the signature."

"You wouldn't trust me or Sheriff Lykins to witness the signing?" Susannah didn't even try to keep the contempt from her voice.

The banker's round face turned a deeper shade of pink, and he cleared his throat. He looked toward the trio of clerks and crooked his finger. "Boswell!"

A few spindly-legged strides brought the summoned clerk to McDougal's desk.

"Boswell, bring me Mr. Sutton's file, please."

The young clerk murmured his acquiescence and left for his cluttered corner. After a few tense moments of silence, he returned and placed several papers on the bank manager's desk.

McDougal perused the papers and, following a series of muted harrumphs, looked up at Susannah. "I'm afraid it is just as I recalled. Mr. Sutton has drawn within ten dollars of the account's limit until the Union Railway Company refreshes the account with a new infusion of capital." He looked at Susannah as if he were addressing a slow child. "There is not forty dollars in the account. Only ten."

Fear warred with fury inside Susannah. Was Fergus McDougal telling the truth, or did he want to keep Thad in jail for spite? She had no idea but wished she could slap the smug grin off the bank manager's fleshy face. Instead, she thanked him for his time and left the bank before she said something she might later regret.

Dear Lord, why does life have to be so unfair?

The late June breeze dried her tears as she headed for the inn. Hadn't she learned to not rail at God? Thad himself would tell her to only trust. Life was what it was.

But she had no time to ponder such weighty questions. Right now, she needed to fetch Thad his dinner—along with the bad news.

Chapter 17

The morning following Thad's incarceration, Susannah returned to the jail laden with creature comforts. If he had to be in this disgusting place, at least she could make his stay a little more tolerable.

Yesterday afternoon when she told him what the bank manager said, Thad confirmed Fergus McDougal's claim, admitting he had completely forgotten the nearly depleted condition of his expense account.

Unwilling to accept the ridiculous situation, Susannah had voiced the obvious. "Surely if you wrote to your father or the Union Railway Company they would send you more money. . . ."

But Thad shook his head, withering her hope. "Even if I sent a letter today, it would be at least a week—maybe two—before any money could arrive. With no way to get a telegraph to Indianapolis, I'll just have to wait it out," he'd told her.

His admission had filled her with guilt, knowing that if he hadn't given her the money for her inn payment, he could have used it for bail.

If Ruben and Lilly had just not taken that money. . . The useless thought caused Susannah's welcoming smile to quaver as she neared Thad's cell.

"Breakfast smells wonderful." Smiling broadly, he rose from a little three-legged stool, the only seat in the tiny cell.

As she stepped to the iron bars, Susannah set down the linen-covered basket filled with buttered bread, jam, sausage, scrambled eggs, and milk to better grip the clean bedding she carried in her other arm.

Sheriff Lykins murmured a polite greeting and opened the cell door, the hinges protesting with a loud *squeak*. Mutely, he transferred the basket of breakfast, clean sheets, and feather pillow to Thad's side of the bars.

From behind Sheriff Lykins, Susannah eyed the straw tick on the floor with disdain. "I'm sure accommodations here can't be comfortable, but maybe these will help."

"It's not the Killion House Inn by a long shot," Thad said with a little laugh, "but it's better than the bedroll I slept on many nights during my army days." His gaze held hers in a sweet embrace. "Thank you, Susannah. These will help considerably."

"I'm just so sorry this has happened to you." Susannah's anger and embarrassment about the false witness borne against Thad hadn't diminished. It hurt her to think of him caged like an animal for something he didn't do.

"Ezekiel Murdoch visited me yesterday after supper. He reminded me that all things work together for the good." Smiling, Thad lifted his Bible, which Susannah had brought yesterday at his request. "God has a reason for this, Susannah. We just don't know what it is yet."

Susannah marveled at his faith. Thad Sutton had helped her to see, acknowledge, and appreciate God's answered prayers. The flood that receded before damaging the inn, Georgiana's recovery, and Thad's advance on his rent providing her with last month's payment on her inn—she could see God's hand working in those blessings. But what good could be accomplished by his being in jail?

Her gaze swept his cramped confines. "I'm sorry Thad, but I can't see any good from your being in this dingy little cell."

"I can," he whispered. Taking her hands into his and giving them a warm squeeze, he brought her gaze back to his. "If this hadn't happened, I doubt I would have had an opportunity to spend nearly as much time alone with you these past two days."

Sheriff Lykins cleared his throat as if to remind them of his presence. Sounding embarrassed, he apologetically clicked the cell door shut. "You can use my desk chair to sit and visit if you'd like," he told her.

The back legs of the chair rasped on the bare floor as he dragged it across the room and set it near the bars. After locking the cell door, he mumbled something about an errand that needed his attention and slipped out the jailhouse door.

After asking a blessing for the food, Thad fixed Susannah with a worried frown. "Has that Macklin man bothered you. . .or been by the inn?"

Susannah shook her head and assured him she hadn't seen Mick since they saw him together at the post office. Only then did the tense lines in Thad's face relax a bit, and he dug into the basket of breakfast.

When he finished his meal, Thad set the basket aside and picked up the Bible. Thumbing through the pages, he stopped and began reading from the book of Acts, the account of Paul and Silas in prison.

"See," he said as he closed the book on his lap, "blessings can even come from being in jail." He reached his hands invitingly through the bars.

Susannah grasped his waiting hands and luxuriated in the wonderful warm tingles pulsing through her at his touch. She followed his example as he bowed his head in prayer. Hot tears pressed against her closed eyelids when Thad asked God to protect her, Georgiana, and Naomi and to give him patience and teach him what he needed to learn from this experience.

Susannah's heart throbbed with love for this man. Thoughts of what a life spent with Thad Sutton might be like teased the edges of her mind. She swatted them away. That could never be. Surely after this unpleasant experience, he would be eager to leave this place and never return.

~⚬~

For the next three days, Susannah divided her time between the inn and the jail. The times spent with Thad in conversation, Bible reading, and prayer were the sweetest of her days. As they shared stories from their childhoods and fond remembrances of George, Susannah felt the bond between her and Thad strengthen. Although she longed for his release, a part of her knew she'd miss these visits.

The Sunday following Thad's arrest, Susannah's heart throbbed with a familiar ache as she nestled a chicken pie in a linen-lined basket for his noon meal. Although the circuit judge arrived yesterday to hear the case, nothing had changed. The judge's sentence of forty dollars or forty days brought Thad no closer to freedom. Hopefully, the posts would run smoothly and he would soon receive a reply from the railroad board along with a promissory note in the amount of his fine.

As she covered the pie with a cloth, Susannah shoved aside the painful thought that when Thad secured his freedom, he would most likely leave Promise for good.

"Is Tad coming home today?" Georgiana tugged on Susannah's skirt and asked the same question she'd asked several times a day since Thad's arrest.

Helping her four-year-old daughter understand why her hero had been put in jail presented Susannah with a formidable task. The explanation Georgiana seemed to grasp best was simply that Thad was being punished for something he didn't do.

"Not unless the railroad sends him money to pay his fine," she said and saw her own feelings reflected in her daughter's pout. "Or if we could somehow come up with enough money to pay it."

"Tad could come home if we gave the sheriff money?" Georgiana's eyes widened in her upturned face.

"Yes," Susannah said, tucking a jar of sweet tea into the basket. "It's called a fine. But we don't have any extra money."

"Dolly has money."

Susannah couldn't help grinning at Georgiana's comment. She was glad that imagination still softened the hard realities of life for her little girl.

She brushed silky curls from Georgiana's forehead and gentled her voice. "Not the kind of money Miss Lacy uses, honey. Real money, like the money guests pay to stay here."

"Not Miss Lacy. Dolly. Dolly has real money. It's in her casket." Georgiana dragged out the puzzling words in a frustrated tone.

Susannah blew out an impatient sigh. She was already late taking Thad his dinner. "What on earth are you talking about, Georgiana?"

Georgiana grasped her hand. "Come on, I'll show you!"

Reluctantly, Susannah surrendered to her daughter's tugs, leading her out of the inn's kitchen and toward the garden.

"There, by the orange flowers." Georgiana pointed to the edge of the garden where Susannah had planted marigolds to help keep insects away from the vegetables. "That's where I buried Dolly in her casket, 'cause I—we—respect her."

Susannah caught her breath, afraid to believe the notion forming in her mind. Could it be? Could the cash box she'd thought stolen by Ruben and Lilly actually be lying buried here beside the garden? Dropping to her knees, she grasped her daughter by the shoulders. "Georgiana, did Lilly get the casket for Dolly?"

Georgiana shook her head. "Lilly just brought the pieces of Dolly to the garden. Then Ruben came and said they needed to go and they left. That's when I got the box. Thad said that we bury people in caskets to show re—respect. So I had to find a casket to bury Dolly in."

"Where, Georgiana? Where did you get Dolly's casket?" Susannah's heart pounded, praying Georgiana's answer was what she suspected.

"In the step. It's the box you keep in the step." She hung her little head and a tremor ran through her tiny voice. "Am I going to be punished?"

Susannah's heart melted at her daughter's tears. She understood that Georgiana's actions had been prompted by a sincere wish to honor her destroyed plaything. "Do you know what you did was wrong?"

Georgiana nodded.

"Do you promise to never take anything again without asking me or Grandma?"

Giving another nod, Georgiana sniffed and wiped her hand under her nose.

Susannah kissed her daughter's tear-dampened cheek. By admitting she'd taken the cash box, Georgiana had shown true courage in her desire to help Thad. "No, honey, you will not be punished."

Turning her attention to the mound, Susannah began frantically digging in the soft dirt with her bare hands. Her fingernails soon scraped against something hard. As she brushed dirt away from the object, she immediately recognized the oak cash box. Holding her breath, she exhumed the little casket from its shallow grave.

She lifted the hinged lid, conflicting emotions surging through her, then released her breath in a relieved puff of air at what she saw. "Oh, thank You, God," she whispered.

On a bed of bank notes, the pitiful broken pieces of Georgiana's beloved Dolly lay scattered among a dozen or so gold and silver dollars.

Guilt diluted Susannah's joy. She would need to write Ruben and Lilly, telling them of her suspicion and begging their forgiveness.

She looked at Georgiana's sad little face, and her heart constricted. Although it had been necessary, she'd disturbed Dolly's resting place. Taking her child's hand in hers, she looked Georgiana in the eye. "I will find another casket—a better one—for Dolly. And this time I will help you have a proper funeral for her.

We will even sing some hymns."

Georgiana ran the back of her hand across her wet cheek and nodded her agreement.

Rising, Susannah swiped at the dirt clinging to the front of her skirt. "But first, we need to get this money to Sheriff Lykins so Thad can come home."

Home. How wonderful if that were really true. Susannah's heart twisted, knowing Thad Sutton would never be making a permanent home here in Promise.

⋙

"Did you kill me to have my wife?"

Shaken, Thad sat up in bed. Breathing hard, he ran a trembling hand over his sweat-drenched face. Many times since the war, he'd been awakened by dreams of long-past battles. But this had been far more personal. The accusing specter of George Killion had seemed so real.

Since his release from jail yesterday afternoon, Thad had wrestled with the question of asking Susannah to be his wife. When she'd burst into the jail with the cash box and the fantastic story about Georgiana having buried it, she'd swept all doubt from his mind and heart. No other woman on earth would do for him.

Yet the old question that had tortured him since his arrival in Promise last April slinked again from the darkest depths of his conscience. Deep in his heart, he knew he had chosen to stay in Promise at the Killion House Inn while working on this stretch of the surveying job because of Susannah. Had he come here to meet and woo the widow of the man he sent to die? And what if he did? And what if by some miracle Susannah agreed to be his wife? Would he see George's accusing image gazing at him in the shaving mirror every morning for the rest of his life?

Thad knew that Susannah would always own his heart. Nothing would change that. But did his love for her make him a latter-day King David? The thought sickened him.

Throwing back the covers, he slipped from the bed and crossed the dark room on unsteady limbs. The pale glow of the moon shafting through the open window cast eerie shadows on his bedroom wall. They did nothing to dispel the dream-induced apparitions that had tormented his sleep.

The pitcher shook slightly as he lifted it from the washstand and poured some of its contents into the bowl. He splashed the tepid water on his face, allowing it to trickle down the front of his nightshirt.

He walked to the window where cool evening breezes fanned the wetness on his face, sending a shiver through him. Below, the canal—a silver slash in the moonlight—dissected Promise. Three months ago when he arrived from Cincinnati via the hapless ditch, he would never have imagined the effect it would have on his life. The good people of Promise despised him as if he'd come to assassinate a beloved family member. But oddly, the thing that had made Thad a pariah in Promise—the canal—had inextricably twined his life with Susannah Killion's.

And beyond his own concerns about his feelings for Susannah, there was the matter of his father's letter, which had arrived yesterday demanding that he return to Indianapolis. There had been no mention of Thad's request for money. The two letters undoubtedly passed in the mail. The words of his obviously irate parent had branded themselves upon his brain.

> . . . .*You will, and without hesitation, return to Indianapolis, forgetting this Killion woman and that mud hole with the ironic name, Promise. You should know that as of this date, your Union Railway expense account has been closed at Promise Bank. Also, you have been invited to the governor's ball to be held the evening of Saturday, July five, which I expect you to attend. There, you will ask the lovely Miss Olivia Vanderpohl to become your bride. Any deviation from my orders will result in your immediate dismissal from the employ of the Union Railway Company. . . .*

Thad trudged back to the bed, sinking with an agonized groan to the feather mattress. If he defied his father's orders, he would lose his job as well as his father's esteem. But if he did as Josiah Sutton demanded, he would lose all hope of having the woman he loved. Either way, Promise, the Killion House Inn, and Thad's hope for a happy life all seemed doomed.

Chapter 18

He will be back, daughter."

Susannah stopped folding napkins on the dining room table and jerked at Naomi's soft words and gentle touch on her shoulder. She turned away so the older woman would not see the renegade tear that had escaped the corner of her left eye.

"I doubt it," she murmured, not even attempting to pretend she didn't know who Naomi meant. She seemed able to read Susannah's mind. Although often irksome, that insightful quality in her mother-in-law felt oddly comforting to Susannah at this moment.

It had been more than a week since Thad Sutton simply disappeared from Promise. Yet his leaving without a word still stung. The only hint of where he'd gone had been the letter she'd found beneath the writing desk in his room. She felt a little guilty about having read a missive not intended for her eyes and now wished she'd dropped it, unread, into the lost-and-found bin behind the front desk. Obviously, he had bowed to Josiah Sutton's demands. In a few short days, Thad would be promised to Olivia Vanderpohl.

Susannah plopped a neatly folded linen napkin atop a pile of a dozen others and strove to affect a cool, detached tone. "It just seemed a cruel thing to do to Georgiana." Careful to keep her back to Naomi, she walked to the buffet and deposited the napkins in the top drawer.

Naomi smiled from the stove where she poured hot water from a whistling teakettle into a stoneware pitcher. "That's why I know he'll be back. Captain Sutton loves that child." She sent Susannah a knowing look. "And you know as well as I do, Georgiana is not the only person in Promise he holds dear."

Susannah's heart echoed Naomi's claim, and she wanted to believe them both. But Naomi had no knowledge of the letter. And even if Thad did love her, it didn't change the fact that his life belonged in Indianapolis with the Union Railway Company and Olivia Vanderpohl. Besides, as shabbily as he'd been treated in Promise, she couldn't really blame him for leaving after he'd been freed from jail.

Naomi hefted the steaming pitcher and headed toward the door to the hallway. Pausing at the threshold, she looked over her shoulder at Susannah. "I'll get Georgiana ready for the church's Independence Day picnic right after I take this shaving water to the drummer in room 204." She gave a little laugh. "That man is a true salesman. He even tried to sell *me* a plow."

"Thanks, Naomi." Susannah smiled as love and gratitude for her mother-in-law swept through her. What on earth would she do without Naomi? Susannah also appreciated the fact that Naomi had made no fuss or fanfare when she began joining her again each morning for scripture reading and prayer. She might not always agree with Naomi, but Susannah thanked God daily for George's mother.

"Are you sure you don't want to take Georgiana to the picnic? I'd be glad to stay and watch the inn." The kindness in Naomi's faded blue eyes caused tears to sting at the back of Susannah's.

"No, you and Georgiana go on." She grinned. "I don't mind missing a few patriotic speeches, and with everyone at the celebration, it will give me a good chance to catch up on bookwork and to inventory the supply room." Susannah's answer had been honest, but the real truth was that she had no heart for any sort of celebration.

A half hour after Naomi and Georgiana left for the church, Susannah sat behind the big oak desk staring unseeingly at her ledger book. The figures in the columns blurred, replaced by the image of Thad standing at the front of a church with Olivia Vanderpohl.

Susannah's heart constricted painfully, and a tear trickled down her cheek. She swiped at it impatiently. *And that is exactly where he belongs.*

She needed to forget Thad Sutton—forget how they'd worked side by side to save the inn from the flood, forget the time they'd spent together in Bible reading and prayer, forget the tender moments they'd shared in the blackberry thicket, forget the feel of his arms holding her as they prayed for Georgiana's recovery. And mostly, she needed to forget the sweet touch of his lips on hers.

Two large teardrops splat onto the ledger page, smudging the carefully inked figures. Sniffing, she wiped the back of her hand across her wet cheeks. Yes, the sooner she forgot Thad Sutton, the better. She must focus on her job—keeping this inn going. And that task had become all the more difficult in light of the coming railroad.

"Susannah."

Susannah's head jerked up at the masculine voice. Half expecting to see the man who'd dominated her thoughts, she blinked surprised into Garrett Heywood's face. Since it was Friday, she hadn't expected to see him until tomorrow.

"Didn't mean to startle you." He twisted his blue wool cap, his gaze not quite meeting hers. "I have a favor to ask of ya."

What kind of favor could Garrett mean? "You know you can rent a room on credit if you need to. . . ."

"It ain't that." He pushed his fingers through his russet hair as his brown-eyed gaze settled at last on her face. "It has to do with Sallie."

"Is Sallie all right?" Susannah had wondered if there was a problem with the *Flying Eagle* when Garrett and his boat hadn't appeared in Promise last

Saturday. Maybe Sallie had been sick, but surely he'd have simply found another cook until she recovered.

"Sallie's well." He cleared his throat loudly. "Thing is"—his gaze went skittering about the lobby again—"Sallie wonders if you might take her on here. You know, like you did Mick Macklin's girl."

His request puzzled Susannah all the more, causing her to blurt out the question that sprang into her mind. "Did you give her the sack?" she asked in a surprised whisper. Susannah couldn't imagine Garrett being so cruel to his longtime cook. And even if he had ended her employment on his canal boat, why would he be trying to find her another position?

Garrett's normally ruddy face deepened to an even redder hue, and he shook his head. "No, I didn't give her the sack. We kinda come to this decision together in Cincinnati." He cleared his throat again. "Sallie and me, well, we come to an understandin'."

"Understanding?" Perhaps Sallie had just decided she didn't want to work on a canal boat any longer. "What kind of understanding?" Susannah just wished Garrett would stop beating about the bush and say what he meant.

"Me and Sallie have an understandin' between us. But bein' Christian people, we don't reckon it'd be seemly to keep spendin' so much time together on the *Flying Eagle*. I suggested we just get hitched in Cincinnati, but she's got her heart set on a proper church weddin' here in Promise and—"

"Wedding? You and Sallie?" Susannah stared at Garrett and felt her jaw go slack. Since Sallie was such a devout Christian, Susannah had never imagined linking the two romantically. But now that she thought about it, since the church social in April, Garrett had attended every church service when he'd been in Promise on the Lord's Day. Susannah knew Garrett must have sincerely turned his life around or Sallie would never have agreed to such a match, even if she was in love with him.

He gave her a sheepish grin. "Funny how a man can't always see that what he really wants has been in front of him all along." His gaze dropped to his hands wringing the wool hat.

Unable to suppress a wide grin, Susannah rounded the desk to give him a quick hug. "Oh Garrett, I'm so happy for both of you!"

And she was.

Susannah sent up a silent prayer of thanks that God had not allowed her to become so lonely she succumbed to the charming canal captain's past overtures. Her friend Garrett would have a wife who truly loved him, not one who felt she merely settled for a convenient husband.

"It would only be until after the weddin'," Garrett said. "Sallie wasn't comfortable askin', seein' as how you and me had sorta. . ."

Sensing his unease at the awkward situation, Susannah rushed to Garrett's assistance. "Of course she can stay here. Though I can't pay her much, Naomi and I would be more than grateful for the extra help."

Garrett blew out a long breath and the tense lines in his face relaxed. "No pay is necessary. I'll see to it that Sallie has everything she needs." His brown eyes fairly danced, and an ever-widening smile marched across his broad, ruddy face. "Me an' Sallie appreciate it, Susannah."

After repeated thanks, Garrett left the inn, promising to return later with his intended.

Several minutes later, pencil and paper in hand, Susannah entered the storeroom. An annex of the kitchen, the storeroom jutted out from the inn's main structure between the kitchen and dining room. The earthy aromas of coffee, molasses, root vegetables, and flour assailed her nostrils as she made her way through the hodgepodge of crates, sacks, and kegs.

She couldn't help smiling again at Garrett's news and looked forward to Sallie's stay at the inn, however brief. Perhaps she and Naomi could even help the future Mrs. Heywood in planning her and Garrett's wedding.

A twinge of envy squiggled through Susannah. She couldn't help thinking that if not for the railroad and Olivia Vanderpohl, she, too, might have been offered a marriage proposal.

In her heart, Susannah knew Naomi was right. Thad Sutton had cared for her—maybe even loved her. But obviously not enough to defy his father.

Blinking back hot tears, Susannah tried to erase the image of Thad and Olivia from her mind by focusing on the work at hand. But after counting the kegs of molasses twice, she still had no idea what number to write on the scrap of paper.

Tucking the pencil behind her ear, she sank wearily to the top of a wooden crate and gazed at nothing.

And what if he had asked me to marry him? Would I have accepted?

The question she had avoided for months now demanded an answer.

No.

No. Even though she loved him, Susannah knew in her heart she would've declined an offer of marriage from Thad Sutton.

Why?

She knew the answer.

George.

Clearer than it had been for months, George's smiling face came into sharp focus before her mind's eye. Susannah knew that even if it hadn't been for the railroad or Olivia Vanderpohl, George's memory would not have allowed her to accept a future with Thad, or anyone else for that matter.

George was with God. Her heart was finally at peace with that. So why couldn't she let go?

Fear.

Here in the quiet of the storeroom, Susannah at last came face-to-face with the truth.

She couldn't remember when she hadn't known George. George was safe. George was familiar. Theirs had been a relationship formed in childhood, and, in a way, it never really matured. Since his death, she'd hidden behind George's memory, using it as an excuse to not subject her heart to the uncertainties of grown-up relationships.

Until Thad.

Despite her best efforts to keep it locked tight, Thad had opened her heart and allowed her to glimpse the hope of a future beyond widowhood.

Tears streamed down her face unheeded. Perhaps that was God's reason for sending Thad to Promise—to teach her heart it was capable of loving again.

Her gaze flitted toward the sound of a faint *squeak*. Sitting quietly, she watched a gray mouse appear from behind a molasses keg. Its tiny pink nose constantly twitched as it nibbled on a grain of corn. When the corn had been consumed, it sniffed the floor around the area where the corn had been. Seemingly satisfied that no other grains of corn remained, it scurried away behind the kegs. Even a mouse had sense enough to know when it was time to move on.

Susannah knew at last she was ready to move on, too. Ready to do the thing she had so long resisted. Ready to put the past behind her. All she needed was the courage to grasp whatever future God had in store for her.

The scripture verse from Psalm 31 that Naomi read before breakfast this morning sprang to Susannah's mind.

"Be of good courage, and he shall strengthen your heart, all ye that hope in the Lord."

Dropping to her knees, Susannah clasped her hands in prayer. "Dear Lord, help me know how to move on. I never want to forget George, but for Georgiana's sake as well as my own, give me the courage to live whatever life You have planned for me."

The image of a yellowed envelope floated behind her closed eyelids—the letter Thad had brought with him to Promise. By refusing to read George's last letter, she'd attempted to keep her marriage to George alive. She knew now it had been God's voice talking to her heart each time she'd felt a nagging tug to open the letter. Even though she had turned away from God, He had never left her. She'd just been too stubborn and angry to follow His direction.

Snuffling, she dried her eyes on her dress sleeve. "Thank You, Lord." She grasped the rough wooden lid of the crate in front of her and rose, knowing that she'd never be able to go on with her life until she'd read that letter.

"Ah, there ya be."

Susannah whirled at the slurred voice behind her.

A leering grin stretched across Mick Macklin's scraggly bearded face. He took a couple of unsteady steps toward her, bringing with him an overwhelming odor of stale sweat and whiskey.

"Don't seem to be anybody else in the place." Laughing, he gestured with upraised hands. "Maybe now that we're alone, you might be more in the notion to tell me where my girl is." His grin vanished and his eyes narrowed to cruel slits.

Susannah's mind raced as she fought the fear threatening to paralyze her. Normally she wouldn't have concerned herself with the drunken buffoon. But here, in the confined space of the dim storeroom, he presented a real menace.

Slowly stepping backward, she tried to assess her best hope of escape. She knew the door to the outside was locked. Her only way out of the storeroom was through the door that led to the kitchen, and Macklin had that route blocked.

Continuing to put more distance between them, she hoped to lure him farther into the room, distracting him with conversation. Then maybe she could slip past him back into the kitchen.

Though her throat had gone sawdust dry, Susannah forced a calm tone to her voice. "I will tell you that Lilly is safe. Beyond that, I think it's up to Lilly to let you know of her exact situation."

"Ya do, do ya?" His mouth twisted in an angry snarl as he advanced.

With a quick glance to her right, Susannah mentally mapped her escape route. *Around the potato bin, along the inside wall, and then follow the shelves holding the canned goods to the door that leads to the kitchen.*

She took another step backward and felt the calf of her right leg smack against something solid. Thrown off balance, she fell backward onto what she realized must be a pile of flour-filled sacks.

"Ahh!" She scrambled to right herself, but Macklin had reached her.

Grasping her shoulders, he pushed her harder against the flour sacks. "Mayhap if we was to get a little more friendlylike, you'd be more willin' to tell me what ya know about Lilly."

Raw terror grabbed at Susannah's insides. *God, help me! Please, help me!* She beat her fists against his disgusting bulk while rolling her head away from his yellow-toothed sneer and rancid breath.

Suddenly, she remembered that Garrett would be bringing Sallie back to the inn. *Dear Lord, please let them be in the inn!* Gasping for breath, she screamed as loudly as Macklin's bulk pressing on her chest allowed. "Garrett, help me! I'm in the storeroom! Please, help me!"

With eyes closed, she continued to beat futilely at Macklin until suddenly his weight lifted off her and she was beating at thin air. Opening her eyes, she gaped in disbelief as Thad's fist cracked against her assailant's jaw.

Chapter 19

Susannah shivered in the July heat, still marveling over her miraculous deliverance. The events of the past half hour played over in her mind, keeping her emotions and her stomach churning. While Thad guarded her subdued attacker, she'd hailed a passing reveler and asked the man to summon the sheriff. Then when the lawman arrived, she spent several uncomfortable minutes relaying to him Macklin's drunken attack on her.

From her seat on the bench beneath the oak tree, she expelled a ragged breath as she watched Sheriff Lykins shake Thad's hand before marching Mick Macklin away in handcuffs. With the ugly incident finally behind her, she sent up a bevy of thankful prayers.

"Are you sure you're all right?" Joining her on the bench, Thad took her trembling hands into his.

"Yes, just a little shaken up." Susannah forced a smile she couldn't quite hold steady. "I never imagined you'd be back—I mean—leaving in the night the way you did."

A penitent look clouded Thad's gray eyes before his gaze dropped from her face to their clasped hands. "I'm sorry," he murmured. "I know I should have said something." He lifted his face again, his gaze seeming to beseech hers for understanding. "But I had pressing business that required my attention in Indianapolis, and I didn't want to wake you or Georgiana."

Susannah couldn't help wondering if Olivia Vanderpohl constituted pressing business. She drew her hand from his. "You could have left a note. . .so Georgiana wouldn't fret."

A pained look crossed his face. "Did she fret?"

Susannah slowly shook her head. She almost wished she could say yes and punish him for sneaking off in the night. "No, she's gotten used to you leaving Promise and then later coming back. She just assumed you'd come back."

"But *you* didn't." There was no hint of a question in his voice.

"No."

The word hung in the air between them as they sat listening to the pop of distant firecrackers and faint shouts of "Huzza!"

" 'And a little child shall lead them.' " A smile traipsed across his face, setting Susannah's heart throbbing painfully.

Why does he have to be so handsome? Why does he have to be so good?

To hide the tears springing to her eyes, Susannah turned away, looking down the canal at a boat decked out in patriotic bunting. Somehow—she didn't know how—she must make her heart give up Thad Sutton. Whatever plans God had for her life, they couldn't include him. If not already promised, he would soon be affianced to Olivia Vanderpohl.

When she trusted her voice again, Susannah forced a light tone. "So, did you conclude your business?"

Grinning, he reached into his coat pocket and withdrew a folded paper. "Actually, yes." He held the paper toward her.

Puzzled, Susannah accepted the unexpected offering, unable to guess what it might be. Unfolding it did little to clear her confusion. It simply looked to be some sort of legal document peppered with lawyer jargon such as "whereas" and "wherefore."

"It's an agreement signed by every member of the railroad board to situate a depot in Promise when tracks along this stretch of the railroad are laid," Thad said in answer to her quizzical glance. "I, along with my father, successfully convinced the board that situating a depot in Promise would be a prudent decision."

Remembering Josiah Sutton's tone in the letter she'd read and his disdain for Promise, Susannah's confusion mounted. "But he said in the letter—" she blurted and then gasped, realizing her mistake.

It was Thad's turn to look surprised.

Unwilling to meet his gaze, Susannah stared unseeingly at the legal document in her hands. She hated having to admit her lapse in etiquette but knew she must explain her comment. "I—I found your father's letter in your room. I know I shouldn't have read it, and I sincerely apologize for doing so."

"Ah, I see." His quiet voice did nothing to douse the shame burning inside her. He cleared his throat. "When I returned to Indianapolis, I confronted my father concerning his demands, and we had a—discussion."

The pause before the word suggested to Susannah that it must have been a heated discussion.

His voice lowered. "We finally spoke plainly, man-to-man, as we should have done a long time ago."

"But your father seemed so—insistent." Susannah couldn't help believing there must have been more to it than simply Thad's powers of persuasion.

He fidgeted on the bench and rubbed his palms down the tops of his thighs, his gaze seeming to study the post office porch several yards beyond the National Road. "I let him know in no uncertain terms that I would not be bullied or blackmailed. I'm not especially proud of the fact, but I threatened to destroy the work I'd done unless the board agreed to my terms—a passenger depot in Promise."

Gratitude balled up inside Susannah. Thad had actually gone to battle for her inn. For Promise. She wondered at what cost. "Was your father angry?"

Thad shot her a grin. "Oh yes, very angry. But I think he actually respected me for the first time in my life. I was as surprised as anyone when he joined those voting in favor of placing a depot here."

"And Mr. Vanderpohl?" she asked in a near whisper, worried that Thad was now on unfavorable terms with his future father-in-law.

Surprisingly, Thad gave a soft laugh. "Old Vanderpohl was beside himself. I thought he might have a conniption fit right there in the boardroom. In fact, he gave me the sack."

Susannah emitted a soft gasp. Hot tears sprang to her eyes as regret twisted her heart. Thad had sacrificed his position—not only with the railroad, but with his father—for her. "But—but surely Miss Vanderpohl could intercede on your behalf. . . ."

Thad took Susannah's hands, folding his fingers warmly around hers. "I did not see Olivia, nor do I have any desire to see her, Susannah."

The soft, almost whispered tone of his voice sped Susannah's heart to a gallop. Holding her breath, she met his gaze and studied the serious intensity drawn on his face.

A quick twitch, like a wince, drew down his brows for an instant. "Susannah, I've been doing a lot of praying and soul-searching. That was another reason I needed to get away from Promise. Away from your nearness."

His throat moved as he paused to swallow. His gray gaze looked deeply into her eyes as if attempting to see all the way to the center of her heart. "I love you, Susannah. I love you more than I ever imagined I could love someone. But, because of George, I had to be sure that none of my past actions were dishonorable, which would taint the affection I have for you."

With his thumbs, he caressed the backs of her fingers while he blew out a long breath. "After much reflection, my heart is at peace and I am sure. And so, Susannah Killion, I ask you now. . .will you do me the honor of becoming my wife?"

During Thad's rambling and rather convoluted proposal, Susannah sat gaping at him, all at once astounded, mystified, and giddy. She'd barely recovered from the shock of his return to Promise. And now, he'd set her heart and head spinning again with a marriage proposal she could never have seen coming.

Having no idea what to make of his obscure references to soul-searching and dishonorable past actions, she fought the urge to laugh. Would she never get a normal proposal from a man?

George's best effort had simply been to say, "Well, Susannah, we're eighteen, so I reckon it's high time we got married."

Though she longed to say yes to Thad, Susannah knew she couldn't—not yet. Not until she'd read George's letter and put that part of her life to rest.

She gave his fingers a gentle squeeze and looked deeply into his hopeful eyes. "Thad, I care for you very much. But I cannot give you an answer just yet. There is something I need to do first. May I give you my answer tomorrow?"

A pained look flitted briefly across his face, but his quick, warm smile dispelled it. "Yes, of course. I understand. Take what time you need."

The sound of rockets exploding in the distance echoed the fireworks igniting inside Susannah. Though her every impulse clamored against her restraints, urging her to accept his offer without hesitation, she knew it would not be fair to Thad for her to leap into a future with him—this marvelous future God had opened up to her—until she'd closed the book on her marriage to George.

But her eager heart ached for the morrow.

~

It was long past dark when an excited Georgiana finally drifted off to sleep. All afternoon the child had danced and whooped at the return of her hero. Susannah's heart had joined in Georgiana's glee when Thad presented the little girl with a new china doll tea set he'd brought from Indianapolis.

Smiling, Susannah bent and brushed a golden curl from her daughter's brow, now serene in sleep. How happy Georgiana would be to learn that the man she adored would soon be her new father.

The night breeze fluttered the lacy curtains framing the open window. An occasional faint *hiss* and *pop* bore evidence to the continued Independence Day celebrations.

Susannah opened the top drawer of her dresser, her heart ready for its own emancipation from the past. She lifted out George's letter, sat on the edge of her bed, and broke the envelope's wax seal. In the sputtering candlelight, she began reading the left-slanted script of her late husband.

Dear Susannah,

It's comin' on to twilight now, and though there's a little chill in the air, it's right warm for February. We're holed up here in a mountain pass called Buena Vista. Santa Anna thinks he's got us on the run, but old General Taylor has other plans. He figures the Indiana Second and us in the Third, along with some Illinois boys and Jeff Davis's Mississippi Rifles, can give the old Mexican a run for his money.

Going to be a battle tomorrow for sure and it's shaping up to be a real ripsnorter. Captain Sutton, he don't feel right comfortable about our situation. That's the reason I'm writing this. He's asked me to head up a scouting mission soon as it gets dark to learn how close the Mexican line is to our flank. The Mexicans know this country, and finding them in the dark without them finding us could be a real trick. With you and our baby weighing heavy on my mind, I asked Captain if I might pass on this one. But he allows I'm his best tracker and the only man he trusts to head up this mission. Captain Sutton's a good man and I trust his judgment. But if you're reading this, then I reckon I didn't make it back. I want you to know I love you. Always have. You're the strongest, smartest girl I ever knew, and my heart is easy, knowing you will be able to see after Ma and the inn. Tell Ma I love her, too. If the baby's a boy, I'd be right proud if you'd name him after me. If it's a girl, well, you name her what you think is best. I sure would have liked to see our baby, but I reckon I'll see you both one day in heaven.

Love,
George

The words blurred through Susannah's tears, and she wiped her drenched cheeks. Suddenly, her gaze drifted to the date of the letter—February 22, 1847—and a cold chill slithered through her. She was sure that was the date Thad had noted as George's date of death. George had said the battle was expected the next day, and she knew few battles were waged at night.

Dropping the open letter, Susannah snatched the pewter candlestick from the top of the dresser and rushed to the trunk at the foot of her bed. She sank to the floor, the skirt of her nightgown splaying around her, and opened the trunk's metal latch. As she lifted the lid, the peculiar smells of the cedar-lined trunk tickled her nostrils.

In the flickering candlelight, she rummaged beneath a pile of Georgiana's baby quilts and dresses until her fingers touched the edges of an envelope. Pulling it out, her heart cinched painfully. Thad's now-familiar bold script was scrawled across the front of the yellowed envelope. She set the candlestick on the floor and slid out the folded missive.

Perusing the page, she fought sobs as the letter unleashed the same overwhelming sense of grief and loss that had caused her to faint when it arrived four years ago. Drawing a ragged breath, she corralled her feelings and searched for the information she dreaded to confirm.

Susannah gasped as her gaze fixed on the date of her husband's death. As she read Thad's words, her heart, along with any hope of a happy future with him, shredded against the cold, jagged edge of fact.

It is my unhappy duty to inform you that your husband, George, died valiantly this day, February 22, 1847, in service to his country. May God's grace and everlasting peace. . .

Susannah dropped the letter back into the trunk. Her heart echoed the dull thud as she closed the trunk's lid. On February 22, 1847, Thad Sutton had sent George on a dangerous mission. A mission from which George had requested to be excused. The mission that cost him his life.

She sat on the floor, hugging her shaking frame until her agony solidified to a rock-hard anger. Pressing her hand against her mouth, she battled nausea as a wave of revulsion swept over her. How could she marry the man who sent George to his death?

Chapter 20

All night Susannah tossed as sleep fled from her tortured mind and heart. Long before dawn, she surrendered any hope of rest and slipped quietly from bed. Praying Georgiana might sleep late this morning, she dressed and made her way down to the kitchen.

In the kitchen, she busied herself with her usual morning tasks, knowing this morning would be anything but usual. Thankfully, there were several guests who would need breakfast before the ten o'clock stagecoach arrived. Also, Sallie O'Donnell would have to be schooled in the care of the inn. Susannah feared none of these chores would be enough to crowd out the pain that last night's discovery had unleashed.

She opened the door to the side yard and closed her eyes as a morning breeze bathed her face. The gentle summer zephyr caressed her troubled brow with tender fingers.

Why, God? Why?

It was the only prayer her numbed mind could form.

Opening her eyes, she watched the dawn tint the canal, transforming it into a shimmering ribbon of pink. The sky had begun to lighten above the little woods. Somewhere in the distance, a rooster crowed.

She turned her gaze toward the woods, and a jumble of painful memories played before her mind's eye. She and Thad, with Georgiana on his shoulders, laughing together as they crossed the meadow, off to hunt mushrooms on a fine spring day. And then she saw the three of them wading through knee-high summer grass toward the blackberry thickets. Could she ever again look at the meadow and not see Thad's stalwart figure striding through the grass with his surveyor's tripod resting on one broad shoulder? Could she ever again pick blackberries and not feel his arms holding her, his lips tenderly caressing hers?

The shrill whistle of the teakettle pierced her anguished reverie. Turning back to the stove, she swiped at her tear-washed cheeks.

The time had come. Today, Thad would be expecting her answer to his marriage proposal.

She wrapped a piece of quilted flannel around the teakettle's handle and poured the steaming water into a stoneware pitcher. Her jaw clenched with her rekindled anger. With Captain Thaddeus Sutton's shaving water in hand, she started for the stairs.

Well, now he will get his answer!

Thad had just pulled on his second boot when three sharp raps sounded at his bedroom door. His heart sped to double-time cadence. This was the moment for which he'd waited through the torturously slow nighttime hours.

For the most part, sleep had eluded him. Different scenarios of why Susannah Killion might have postponed her answer to his proposal had chased endlessly around his mind.

The only viable answer had formed one name—Garrett Heywood.

Yesterday afternoon, when Thad had wandered through the inn looking for Susannah, it had been her frantic cries of Heywood's name that alerted him to the storeroom. But if she had her heart set on Heywood, why didn't she simply tell him yesterday when he proposed?

The moment he opened the door, Thad sensed something was terribly wrong. Susannah's grim expression sent warning bells clanging in his brain.

No hint of a smile softened the rock-hard lines of her face, and her gaze seemed intent on evading his. "Your shaving water, Captain Sutton," she mumbled as he took the pitcher from her hands.

"Susannah, what's wrong?" The impersonal frostiness of her tone slashed at Thad's heart like icy shards. He had fought in hand-to-hand combat on the battlefield, but he'd never felt the kind of fear that twisted inside him now.

Her chin quivered as it lifted, and she met his gaze. "George didn't die in the Battle of Buena Vista, did he?"

"No, he died in a skirmish the evening before the main battle," he said. As he carried the hot water to the washstand, Thad's mind raced. Hadn't he mentioned that fact in the letter he sent her four years ago? He couldn't remember.

At the washstand, he turned to face her and was stunned by the raw anger flashing from green eyes that glistened with unshed tears.

"You sent George on a dangerous mission—a mission he didn't want to go on—and he died. Isn't that right, Captain Sutton?"

The scorn with which she enunciated Thad's name felt like a dagger through his heart. Thad could not imagine how Susannah had only now learned the particulars of her husband's death. And it didn't matter. The incident that had haunted him for four years had been dragged from the dark dungeon of his conscience into the glare of daylight. And the woman he loved had become his accuser. He swallowed painfully. "Yes," he managed in a defeated, rasped whisper.

Her whole body trembled and one lone tear breached its lovely confines to slip unhindered down her rose petal pink cheek.

Thad longed to take her in his arms. He stepped toward her, arms outstretched.

Shaking her head, she wrapped her arms around herself and took a step backward. "Don't touch me!"

Thad blew out a sigh, and his heart deflated. Somehow, he must make her see the situation that faced him that February evening in 1847.

"Susannah, please, you must understand. I was responsible for a whole company of men. I had to know just exactly where the enemy was camped. George was my best tracker."

She narrowed her eyes at him, and her words sounded tight, as if shoved through clenched teeth. "And all you cared about was winning the battle."

Thad winced at the memory of George handing him Susannah's daguerreotype and a final letter for safekeeping in the event he didn't return. She would never know that he wept that night over the loss of Sergeant George Killion.

"Susannah," he told her somberly, "because of George, the mission was a success. George didn't make it back, but the two men he led on the mission did. Their information saved our company, and perhaps a large portion of our regiment."

Susannah's stiff demeanor showed no indication of softening or any sign that his words had made an impression. Her arms seemed to tighten around her body, and her chin lifted in a stubborn tilt. "I'm afraid I cannot have you in my inn another day, Captain Sutton. Please be good enough to vacate this room before breakfast." With this chilly proclamation, she whirled from him and fled down the stairs.

The July morning sun streamed through the window, bathing the room in a golden glow. But its warmth never touched the cold debris of Thad Sutton's shattered heart.

~

Susannah closed the pantry door after instructing Sallie O'Donnell on the different foodstuffs, their placement, and the amount of each that needed to be kept there. Earlier she'd done the same with the linen closets, shown Sallie the register and ledger books and how they should be kept, and gone over the rules having to do with the room keys, protocol concerning guests, and every other minute detail of running the inn she could think of. Anything that would take her mind off Thad.

"I'll never remember all this in one day." The look in Sallie O'Donnell's brown eyes reminded Susannah of a doe she'd surprised once in the little woods.

Susannah's conscience stung with regret. She touched Sallie's arm. "Oh, of course I never meant for you to get it all at once. I was just trying to acquaint you with. . ."

Susannah's voice faded at the half-truth. What she was really trying to accomplish was to clutter her mind until thoughts of Thad had no chance of slipping in. So far, her attempts had failed miserably.

It hadn't helped when she'd witnessed Garrett kiss Sallie's cheek before he departed for Cincinnati on the *Flying Eagle*. Although happy for Garrett and

Sallie, the joy of their newfound love seemed to underscore Susannah's pain at the loss of her own.

Naomi stepped into the kitchen from the storehouse, her apron laden with onions and carrots. "Sallie," she said, giving the woman a bright smile, "why don't you begin cleaning these. Later you can help me make a big pot of cressy soup."

The relief on Sallie's face smacked again at Susannah's conscience. It had never been her intent to overwhelm the woman.

Naomi emptied her apron of vegetables onto the worktable then turned a kind smile toward Susannah. "Come, daughter," she said while brushing her hands a couple of quick swipes down her apron. "Sallie tells me she's had her prayer and scripture reading time this morning, but I'm afraid we've been remiss in our own."

Susannah followed Naomi toward the lobby's sitting area. The knowing look on her mother-in-law's face told her the older woman had a specific subject in mind for their daily devotional. Naomi hadn't said a word to Susannah concerning Thad's hasty departure. But Susannah felt fairly certain that was about to change. She'd known Naomi Killion far too long not to realize her mother-in-law suspected there'd been a rift between her and Thad.

Naomi settled herself on the green velvet settee and patted the seat beside her, inviting Susannah to sit.

Susannah obeyed. Taking her mother-in-law's proffered hands, she closed her eyes. Other than unintelligible wailings of her heart, Susannah had not gone to God about her confrontation this morning with Thad.

Naomi's slight, work-roughened hands squeezed Susannah's. "Dear Lord, be with us this day and help us to see Your perfect will. I especially ask that You heal the contention that has come between my daughter and Captain Sutton. Salve their broken hearts and lead them in Your way of love and forgiveness."

Susannah yanked her hands from Naomi's and met the other woman's quizzical gaze. "Thad sent George on the mission that killed him, Naomi," she blurted. "George told me in the letter Thad brought last April." Shame dragged down her voice. "The letter I finally read last night."

Naomi cocked her head, a sad smile softening the deep lines of her face. "Susannah, George was a soldier, and Captain Sutton was his commanding officer. When Captain Sutton spoke to me of George, I could tell that he carries the burden of George's death with him still."

An incredulous breath puffed from Susannah's lips. "How can you defend Thad Sutton when he ordered George to his death?"

Naomi reached for Susannah's hands again and sighed. "Daughter, I am defending no one. Like you, when I learned my boy had been killed, it left a George-shaped hole in my heart. I knew I couldn't bear to live that way, so I asked God to fill it with love and forgiveness, and He did. I forgave the Mexican soldier who killed our George. I must also forgive Captain Sutton for any order that might have put George in the way of that Mexican soldier."

She paused as if considering her next words. "I don't think you ever asked God to help you forgive, Susannah, and I wonder if your anger at Captain Sutton has something to do with the argument you and George had before he left."

Susannah winced as her mother-in-law's gentle chide touched a raw nerve. What good did it do to remind her of past offenses? And what did it have to do with how she felt about Thad?

Naomi turned her attention to the Bible on her lap. Seeming to thumb purposefully through the whispering pages, she paused at last and began to read from the second chapter of Second Corinthians. " 'So that contrariwise ye ought rather to forgive him, and comfort him, lest perhaps such a one should be swallowed up with overmuch sorrow. Wherefore I beseech you that ye would confirm your love toward him.' "

The words convicted Susannah. During the past several months, she'd come to know Thad's heart. Despite her accusations this morning, she knew he was anything but uncaring. In her heart of hearts, she knew George's loss would have grieved him. Had her own pain and need to blame someone for George's death caused her to heap undeserved sorrow upon Thad?

Naomi moved her finger slowly down the page and continued reading. " 'To whom ye forgive any thing, I forgive also: for if I forgave any thing, to whom I forgave it, for your sakes forgave I it in the person of Christ.' "

She looked up from the book and fixed Susannah with an intense gaze. "Susannah, you love Thad. But this is tearing you up inside. It's just like when you found out he was surveying for the railroad. But in time, you came to care about him, so you looked past that. Unless you can find a way to forgive Thad, you will never have peace about this."

Susannah knew Naomi was right, but the wound on her heart from what she'd learned from George's letter was still too fresh. And somehow, her anger toward Thad felt like a shield. *Against what?*

"Mamma, Gwamma!" Georgiana came bounding into the sitting area, Miss Lacy tucked under one arm and her eyes grown wide. "It's really windy outside, and it's raining ice balls!" She opened her fist to display a dirty ice nugget melting across her grimy palm.

At Georgiana's announcement, Susannah stopped to focus on the sound of hail pinging against the inn's roof.

Susannah and Naomi turned in near unison toward the long, narrow window just beyond the lobby. Leaves ripped from their branches whipped past in an atmosphere colored a sickly green.

Naomi's face went ashen and she sprang from the settee. "Susannah, we need to get everyone to the storeroom. Now! I'm afraid a cyclone may be coming!"

Chapter 21

Thad leaned forward in the saddle and pulled his hat brim down lower on his face to fend off the wind and rain as his horse plodded along the muddy road. In the two hours since he'd left Promise, the weather, along with his mood, had markedly deteriorated.

Still numb from Susannah's rejection, he tried to focus on the sixty-mile journey before him. But he couldn't erase from his mind the hurt and anger he'd seen in her eyes. How she learned the details of Buena Vista remained a riddle. But he didn't blame her for her angry reaction. How could he expect her to forgive his decision when he hadn't been able to fully forgive himself for making it? He also knew that at some point, he would've had to tell her anyway.

He gripped the saddle's wet leather pommel until his hand hurt. *I should have told her. I should have told her right off before I let myself. . .*

A sardonic chuckle burst from his lips. Before he what? Before he fell in love with her? He knew that had been a *fait accompli* within the first twenty-four hours after he'd arrived in Promise.

The wind gusts had grown stiffer, driving the rain like wet needles against his face. Chieftain jerked his head up and down, neighing and snorting in protest at the inclement weather to which he was being subjected.

Squinting, Thad peered through the near deluge. He would need to avail himself of the next structure that offered shelter for him and his steed. It was bad enough being miserable on the inside. No sense in remaining miserable on the outside as well.

As he rounded a bend in the road, the brackish gray form of a hip-roofed barn came into view. Riding up to it, he saw that one of the barn doors had been left open. He guided Chieftain into the shelter, praying the farmer wouldn't appear and shoot him for trespassing.

The familiar barn smells of hay, wet straw, leather, and manure welcomed Thad to the rustic haven. Two milk cows mooed in their stalls at the intrusion, while a team of mules looked up from munching hay with only mild interest showing in their dark eyes.

Thad dismounted, tied Chieftain to a slat in one of the stall gates, and lowered himself to a somewhat clean-looking pile of straw. With his back against a rough-hewn support post, he blew out a long, weary sigh.

Gazing out at the rain-soaked vista beyond the open barn doors, he suddenly felt tired. So very, very tired. His lack of sleep last night, coupled with

Susannah's scathing rejection this morning, had drained his energy. The soft, pattering sound of the rain on the barn roof seemed to drag down his eyelids.

Oh, Lord, if she can never love me, please, just let her not hate me. The agonized prayer was his last conscious thought before sleep overtook him.

A sharp, jabbing pain in his side caused Thad to jerk awake, blinking.

Above him, a large, full-bearded face scowled down from beneath a black slouch hat. Thad was glad to notice that at least the pitchfork in the farmer's hands was turned handle down. He realized the blunt end of the tool handle must have inflicted the pain near his midsection.

Thad scrambled to his feet. "I'm sorry, sir. My intentions were not to trespass but only to seek shelter for me and my horse." He glanced toward Chieftain happily sharing hay with the two mules.

The big man raked a slow, suspicious look down Thad. At length, a satisfied smile lit his face like the sun that now streamed through the open barn door. He held out a beefy hand. "You're more than welcome, stranger. Thought mayhap you were a drunk or a bummer." The scowl returned for an instant. "Cain't abide drunks and bummers."

Thad accepted the farmer's firm handshake then brushed straw from his shirt and pants, hoping the man wouldn't change his opinion. "No, sir. I'm on my way to Indianapolis. Just came from Promise."

The farmer gave a long, slow whistle. "Reckon you're in the Good Lord's debt then." He cocked his head toward the opening in the barn. "A feller came by 'bout an hour ago and said a cyclone hit Promise. Flattened half the place and near emptied the canal."

The blood drained to Thad's toes. Dread gripped his insides at the thought of a cyclone tearing apart the Killion House Inn. Visions too awful to contemplate swam before his mind's eye. Had the inn been hit? Was Susannah all right? He had to know. "Were—were there any injuries?"

The farmer's shoulders lifted in a quick shrug. "Feller didn't say. Cain't imagine there wouldn'ta been though."

With an unsteady hand, Thad rummaged in his trousers pocket, brought out a couple of coins, and offered them to the farmer. "Thanks for the shelter," he mumbled, untying Chieftain.

The farmer accepted the coins, dragged off his hat, and scratched grimy fingers across his balding head. "Don't need to rush off. The wife's likely made plenty o' dinner. You're more'n welcome to stay."

Mounting Chieftain, Thad shook his head and wheeled the horse toward the open barn door. "Thanks for the invitation, but I have to go."

"Never get to Indianapolis tonight," the farmer hollered from inside the barn. "So where you headed in such an all-fired hurry?"

"Promise," Thad called back, praying God had seen fit to spare the Killion House Inn and the lives of those dear to him.

"Mamma, Miss Lacy don't like the dark."

At the whimper in Georgiana's small voice, Susannah hugged her child tighter, rocking her on her lap. Only precious, narrow shafts of light and air filtered down through cracks around the edges of the root cellar's ill-fitting trapdoor. Susannah was proud of how well her little daughter was handling the frightening, unexpected confinement. Neither did Susannah like the dark, dank hole that crawled with myriad insects and smelled of musty earth and rotting root vegetables. She forced a light tone to her voice. "I know, darling, and we'll be getting out soon."

Susannah prayed she was right. How long had it been since the seven of them sought shelter beneath the storeroom's floor—an hour, two hours? She found it impossible to judge. An interminable amount of time seemed to have passed since she and Georgiana, along with Naomi, Sallie, and the inn's three guests clambered down the short ladder to take refuge in the six-by-eight-foot cellar.

Moments after Susannah pulled the trapdoor over them, the most menacing roar she'd ever heard filtered into their little hidey-hole, making her ears pop. Clinging to Georgiana, she'd joined Naomi and Sallie in prayers for deliverance, though their words were swallowed in the din of the tumult.

After several terrifying minutes, the unearthly wailing and crashing sounds had abated, leaving only an eerie silence that felt worse than the cyclone's noise.

Eager to emerge from the dark, cramped space, Susannah had hurried to the ladder beneath the cellar's trapdoor. Standing on the third rung, she'd reached up and pushed against the little square door, but to no avail. Something seemed to be blocking their only escape route. Their refuge had become their prison.

The two men among the group, a young newlywed with his equally young bride and the dapper-dressed plow salesman, tried numerous times, without success, to free the group from their little dungeon.

But now, as the minutes dragged by, a general feeling of frustration had given way to a sense of unease that Susannah feared bordered on panic. Sallie clung to Naomi and muttered snatches of broken prayers while the young bride wept softly against her husband's shoulder.

The black-mustached farm equipment salesman, who seemed to have run out of stories to tell, became increasingly more fidgety. "Let me take another whack at that door," he said, making his way around the young couple huddled against the wall.

Susannah scrunched nearer Naomi to give the man room. Trying to ignore the strong smell of sweat and bay rum fanned by the drummer's movements, she prayed for his success.

After several fruitless shoves and a few mumbled words that caused Susannah to clamp her hands over Georgiana's ears, the drummer managed only to shower them with bits of loose dirt. Muttering his apologies, he returned in defeat to his previous spot behind the newlyweds.

Susannah watched the young couple embrace, the husband comforting his fretful wife. Suddenly, visions of Thad holding her and comforting her flashed before Susannah's mind's eye.

The words from the scripture Naomi had read this morning echoed hollowly inside Susannah. *"Lest perhaps such a one should be swallowed up with overmuch sorrow."* She remembered how she'd sent him away—swallowed up with sorrow—into the jaws of the storm. She'd sent him off in anger. *Just as she'd done to George!*

Now she understood what Naomi had meant when she'd said Susannah's anger at Thad had something to do with her argument with George all those years ago. Susannah realized she'd never forgiven herself for not making up with George before he left for the war. That was what she'd never faced. It had always been easier to be angry with someone else. First with God, and then with Thad.

Guilt, remorse, and an unfathomable sadness swirled inside Susannah like the cyclone they'd come down here to escape.

The cyclone!

Thad was out there, somewhere in the open, at the mercy of the storm. At the mercy of the cyclone. Fear grabbed Susannah's belly in an agonizing grip.

Oh, dear Lord, I did it again. I sent someone I love off in anger to die! Dear Father, please let him be all right. Please. . .

In the dim light, Naomi's gaze caught Susannah's, fixing on her teardrenched cheeks. A calm smile graced Naomi's lips. She reached over and caught Susannah's hand, giving it a quick squeeze. Then she turned to Sallie, who'd been softly singing hymns. "Wonderful idea, Sallie. Why don't you lead us all in song? It will lift our spirits and maybe someone will hear us."

For the next several minutes, Sallie and Naomi led them all in choruses of "Rock of Ages" and "Oh God, Our Help in Ages Past."

As the women began the first verse of "My Faith Looks Up to Thee," the words convicted Susannah's heart.

> *My faith looks up to Thee,*
> *Thou Lamb of Calvary,*
> *Savior divine!*
> *Now hear me while I pray, take all my guilt away,*
> *O let me from this day be wholly Thine.*

Susannah knew she would never be right with God until she asked Him to take away the guilt she still carried from her trespasses against the two men she loved. *Oh, Lord, do take away my guilt so I can be wholly Yours.*

Remembering the loving words of George's last letter, Susannah felt sure that her husband had, indeed, forgiven her for her anger at his departure. Now, with God's help, she would strive to forgive herself. The moment she emerged from this cellar, she would write to Thad and beg his forgiveness for her callous treatment of him this morning. She needed him to know that she no longer held George's death against him.

Her continued thoughts of Thad made him so real to Susannah that she imagined she heard his voice calling her name.

"Susannah? Susannah, are you here?"

The sound became clearer, convincing Susannah it was not her imagination. Her heart thumped so hard she gasped for breath.

"Stop. Stop!" she called, breaking into the song's chorus and even dousing the drummer's hearty tenor. She sprang to the ladder, climbed to the second rung, and pounded on the trapdoor. "We're here! We're down here!"

"Are you all right?" Thad's anxious voice, muted by the barriers between them, drifted down into their dark confines.

"Tad! It's Tad!" A gleeful Georgiana began hopping up and down, clapping her little hands.

"Yes, we're all right." By force of will, Susannah reined in the urge to follow Georgiana's example. "Please, get us out."

"Thank You, Jesus!" The words came out in a whoosh of his breath. "There's a tree limb blocking the door," he called down after a moment's pause. "I'll need to find something to use as a lever to get it off."

Susannah's own prayer of thanks lifted from her grateful heart. *Yes, thank You, Jesus! Thank You that he's here and unhurt!*

She wondered how much damage had been done to the inn. But knowing Thad was here and that he was safe negated all other concerns.

After several more minutes of scraping and grunting sounds, the trapdoor popped open.

The relief Susannah felt at the rush of light and fresh air into the stifling cellar was almost overwhelming. She immediately lifted Georgiana up to Thad's waiting hands.

Susannah's heart swelled when Georgiana, still clutching Miss Lacy, hugged Thad's neck and said, "I'm glad the storm didn't get you, Tad."

"Me, too, moppet," Thad said with a chuckle as he lowered her to the storeroom floor.

The guests were next to exit the root cellar, followed by Naomi and Sallie who voiced their hearty thanks to God and His servant, Thad Sutton.

At last, Thad reached down and grasped Susannah's hand, helping her up to the storeroom. Just to be near him and feel his hand in hers made the sight of the huge oak limb sprawled across the demolished room unimportant.

An awkward moment ensued until Thad broke the uneasy silence. "I heard about the cyclone. . . . I was afraid. . . ." His throat moved with a swallow, and he glanced around the room at the destruction. He turned back to her, his voice brightening. "The rest of the inn seems sound though," he said as they watched the others head for the kitchen, Naomi and Sallie taking charge of Georgiana.

Susannah only nodded, a knot of emotion choking off any answer. What could she say knowing he'd come back to check on their safety after she'd ordered him from the inn?

Love, gratitude, and shame bubbled up inside her until, with a sob, it all broke free. The floodgates opened and a deluge of pent-up tears spilled down her cheeks. "I'm sorry. I'm just so sorry. Please forgive me. I don't blame you for George's death. You have to know I don't blame you," she said between sobs as he engulfed her in his arms.

"Shh, it's all right, my sweet. It's all right, my love. There's nothing to forgive," he murmured, rocking her in his arms and muffling her sobs against his shoulder. "It's I who should be begging your forgiveness."

She pushed away and blinked back tears that blurred his dear face. "I think all that's left for us to do now is to forgive ourselves, and with God's help, I know we can."

He answered with a slow smile that crept across his handsome face. Further conversation was postponed as he gently nudged her head back with his chin and his lips sweetly caressed hers.

"I thought you were going to Indianapolis," she whispered at last, reveling in the feel of his warm breath against her neck.

"I don't have a job there anymore, remember?" he said, nuzzling his face against her hair.

"You think you can find one here?" Susannah teased, her heart singing as she gazed into his adoring eyes.

"I thought maybe I'd try my hand at innkeeping," he said with a grin.

Susannah stifled a giggle. Another odd proposal, but it was good enough for her. New tears sprang to her eyes, misting his features.

"Yes, I think maybe you should," she whispered before he silenced her with more kisses.

Epilogue

A golden shaft of sunlight slanted through the church's long, narrow window. It glanced across the strong, square jaw of Susannah Sutton's new husband, mildly surprising her.

She hadn't been aware of the moment when the rain stopped drumming on the church's roof or when the distant thunder had quieted its rumblings. She and Thad seemed wrapped in their own special sphere, apart from all happenings beyond their exclusive realm.

Gazing into his soft gray eyes, she had just now echoed the vows he had pledged to her moments before.

"You may kiss your bride," Pastor Murdoch told Thad.

A grin quirked the corner of Thad's mouth.

The instant before she closed her eyes to accept his kiss, Susannah caught a glimpse of the dimple she loved so much.

As his lips touched hers, the notion became real to her that she would actually be spending the rest of her life with this wonderful man. The thought sent a happy tear sliding from the corner of her left eye to her ear. Paradoxically, Susannah wished this kiss would never end yet at the same time was eager for her and Thad's new life to begin.

The church erupted in applause, and a giggling Georgiana bounced and clapped beside them.

Still wrapped in each other's arms, Susannah and Thad grinned down at their daughter's antics.

Swaying from side to side in her skirt of ivory lace over satin that replicated her mother's own wedding dress, Georgiana looked like a little lacy, tolling bell.

A beaming Josiah Sutton, who'd acted as his son's best man, clapped Thad on the back and kissed Susannah warmly on the cheek. Now his son's staunchest ally, Josiah had leveraged his influence with the Union Railway Company. His efforts had resulted in Thad being reinstated as the company's chief engineer and surveyor for the Cincinnati to Indianapolis project.

Through misty eyes, Susannah glanced at the front row pew. Sallie Heywood, clinging to her husband's arm, dabbed at her wet eyes with a linen kerchief. Susannah had been happy to learn that Garrett and Sallie would soon be selling the *Flying Eagle* and opening a dry goods store in Promise.

Shifting her gaze to her mother-in-law's face, Susannah returned Naomi's pleased smile. She'd read Naomi's mind too many years not to decipher the sentiments glistening from her brimming blue eyes.

Susannah gave her mother-in-law a nod of agreement. She, too, was sure that from somewhere in heaven, George was smiling down upon this happy moment.

Thad scooped up Georgiana then wrapped his other arm firmly around Susannah's waist. Together the new little family headed down the aisle and out the church's double doors.

There they paused, and Susannah caught her breath at the remarkable vista before them. A vivid rainbow arched across the slate gray sky.

"Look, a rainbow!" Georgiana pointed at the colorful scene from her perch on Thad's arm.

Susannah breathed in the fresh, rainwashed air, struck by the sense that for her, Thad, and Georgiana, God had made the world anew. The symbol seemed so personal, as if the Lord were reminding her to never again doubt His promises. And she knew she never would.

"Yes, my darling," Susannah said, leaning her head against her husband's shoulder, "it's the symbol of God's promise—His everlasting promise."

CHARITY'S HEART

Dedication

Special thanks to the Jennings County Historical Society of Vernon, Indiana; Ron Grimes, Archivist at the Jefferson County Historical Society of Madison, Indiana; and my husband, Jim, and daughters, Jennifer and Kelly, for their love, encouragement, and support.

Chapter 1

Vernon, Indiana
August, 1866

Are you a bummer, Mr. Morgan? Because I must warn you, my uncle Silas does not abide bummers."

Charity Langdon fought to keep her voice coolly aloof and to maintain her unflinching gaze on the man's dark eyes. She must not allow this Yankee—whose considerable height and broad shoulders filled the narrow doorway—the satisfaction of knowing his presence intimidated her.

"No ma'am." He stepped nearer her desk in the corner of the mill. The limp she'd noticed when he first walked in seemed even more pronounced, and she stifled a frustrated sigh. How many wounded Yankee veterans—transients really—had come through the doors of her uncle's grist and sawmill this past summer only to work a week or two and then disappear?

The man, who'd moments earlier introduced himself as Daniel Morgan, fished in the pocket of his faded blue calico shirt and pulled out a crumpled scrap of newspaper. He held it out. "I'm responding to the advertisement for a mill foreman Mr. Gant placed in the *Plain Dealer*."

Charity's gaze roved unbidden down the length of the stranger. Something uncomfortable twanged in her midsection. She had to grudgingly admit that with his strong, clean-shaven jaw, thick shock of dark hair, and muscular form clad in calico shirt and cotton work trousers, he was more than passably good looking.

The hint of a smile quirked up the corner of his mouth as his dark gaze smoldered into hers. He'd noticed her appraisal!

Heat leaped to her cheeks. Feeling like a cat that had just been caught with cream on its whiskers, she snatched the bit of grimy paper from his fingers. With an impatient whirl, she turned toward the open window as if to better catch the rays of the late August afternoon sun and pretended to read the small square of newsprint. In truth, she'd written the thing herself and knew its contents well.

When she felt her features had sufficiently cooled, she delicately cleared her throat and turned back to Daniel Morgan. "Have you any experience in the workin's of a grist mill, Mr. Morgan? The notice states plainly that the successful applicant must have at least two years'—"

"Yes, ma'am." For some reason, his eager answer, abruptly cutting short her caution, didn't bother her as much as she would have expected. "Before the war, I spent three years working at Kendall's Mill on Crooked Creek," he said without a blink. "It had a combination grist and sawmill operation, too. The last year I was there—in '61—I worked as foreman."

"I see." Charity didn't doubt the man could well fill the position of foreman, but the uneasy feeling he caused inside her made her search for a reason to send him on his way. "Well, Mr. Morgan," she said, her voice slightly diminished, "my uncle is not here right now, and I do not have the authority to hire."

She turned and rounded her desk, willing him to leave. Somehow, it was too easy to see this man in the dark blue uniform of a Union soldier. Why, he could even have been among General Sherman's army that forced her to flee her home in Georgia and take refuge up here in Indiana with Aunt Jennie and Uncle Silas.

Perhaps when he left, the tightness around her middle would relax and she could go back to ciphering the figures in her ledger book. She could always depend upon getting blissfully lost in the numbers. Seating herself behind the desk, she reached for a pencil and nearly jumped when he touched the back of her hand.

"How dare you, sir!" She jerked her hand away from his touch as if she'd been burned. For one awful instant, the vision of another tall Union soldier grasping her hand flashed before her mind's eye. She fought to control her erratic breathing.

"I beg your pardon." His face flushed a ruddy hue beneath his tanned skin. "I should have asked your permission. I meant no offense. I just noticed your wound and was concerned it might be infected."

She glanced down at the ragged-edged red streak running diagonally across the back of her hand. Yesterday, while walking past a pile of lumber, she'd raked her hand against the splintered end of a board and scratched it deeply. "It's just a scratch. It will heal." She managed to regain her composure but again felt heat tingle in her cheeks.

"You should bind it with a clean cloth soaked in a diluted carbolic acid solution."

At his odd suggestion, she swung her gaze up from her injury to meet his handsome face, which was full of concern. The caring look touched her and she tempered her voice. "Are you a doctor?" What kind of man comes into a mill looking for work then offers medical advice?

He shook his head, and she noticed how his hair looked almost blue black in the shaft of sunlight slanting through the open window behind her. "No, but my pa is a doctor. A few months ago, he read about an English surgeon who's been treating wounds that way to prevent infection. Pa's started using the treatment in his practice down in Madison and says it seems to work."

The *whoosh* of running water followed by the groaning of timbers and the sound of stone grinding against stone told her old Charlie Brewster had opened the sluice gate. The big wheel outside her window, which powered the mechanisms inside the mill, began turning. She was glad for the noise that hampered further conversation with this troubling man.

"Can I help you, sir?" Uncle Silas's deep, booming voice carried across the dusty mill, sending a measure of relief through Charity. Now her uncle could deal with the man.

The applicant gave her a cursory smile and nod of his head. Then he turned to her uncle, who ushered him outside, Charity assumed, to prevent their words from being drowned by the cacophony of the mill.

Despite Charity's efforts to concentrate on adding the debit column in her ledger book, her gaze kept drifting upward and out the open door where Uncle Silas stood talking with the tall Yankee.

A disquieting sensation tingled inside her. Anticipation? Trepidation? She wasn't sure which. This Daniel Morgan didn't look, talk, or act like any other mill worker she'd known. Well-groomed, well-spoken, and obviously intelligent, he seemed as if he would fit much neater into his father's profession of physician than that of a mill worker.

Thankfully, Uncle Silas was very choosy about whom he hired. Most likely, as he had done several times this past week, he would shake his head and send the man on his way.

But when she looked up again after trying unsuccessfully to add a column of numbers she could have normally ciphered in her sleep, Charity felt as if a swarm of butterflies fluttered about in her stomach. Uncle Silas was smiling and pumping the tall, dark-haired Yankee's hand.

❧

Gasping for breath, Daniel sat straight up in bed. His heart hammered like a triple-time drum cadence. He pushed his hair away from his sweaty forehead and willed his eyes to focus in the dim light.

Gratefully sucking in gulps of air, he realized he wasn't on the *Sultana* but in the neat little upstairs bedroom he'd rented at Essie Kilgore's boardinghouse in Vernon. His heart began to slow to a more normal speed, and he pushed away the covers. The mattress squeaked as he swung his unsteady legs over its side.

Rising, he half stumbled to the open window. He inhaled the warm, honeysuckle-scented evening breeze that gently rustled the leaves of the poplar tree outside his window. The pleasant, familiar smells and sounds calmed him, coaxing him more fully awake and distancing him from the terrifying images that had haunted his sleep.

Embarrassment, disgust, and anger tangled inside him.

He turned back to the moonlight-dappled room. His bare feet padded on the smooth, varnished floorboards as he crossed to the little washstand. With steadier hands than he'd had a few moments earlier, he lifted the water pitcher and poured himself a glass of the tepid liquid. There was something reassuring in knowing he was in control of the water flowing down his throat.

He returned to his bed and strove to discover what had initiated his latest nightmare. The dreams always carried sickening similarities. Watching Fred and Tom being beaten to death in the sewage-fouled mud of Andersonville. Reliving his futile effort to come to their aid. Feeling the whack of the iron rod against his lower left leg, snapping it like a matchstick. Hearing the hateful laughter of the prison guard who'd swung the rod. Then battling for his life in the dark, muddy waters of the Mississippi River and watching "Ol' Miss" swallow down the flaming ruins of the *Sultana* like a fire-eater at the circus.

It had been at least a month since nightmares forced him to relive the horrors of the Confederate prisoner-of-war camp and the explosion of the steamboat that had carried him homeward after the war. He'd come to Vernon to get a new start—to help put the nightmares behind him. So what had triggered this latest episode?

In an effort to scour the terrifying scenes from his mind, he tried to focus on more pleasant thoughts. The vision of an angelic face, hair the color of sun-ripened wheat, and pale blue eyes the shade of an August sky assembled themselves in his mind. Warmth spread through him. His new boss's niece and bookkeeper had been a delightful surprise. Knowing he would be seeing her each day, Daniel doubted Silas Gant would ever find him late to work.

Wishing he had a name to put with her face, he scrubbed his still-damp forehead with his hand. He was sure Silas Gant had mentioned his niece's name when he'd agreed to hire him.

"Glad to welcome you to Gant's Sawmill, son. I'll have Charity fill out the paperwork."

Charity. Daniel had a name to attach to her features.

He eased himself back onto the bed, pulled the covers to his chin, and expelled a soft sigh as he allowed his head to sink into the goose-down pillow.

"Charity," he whispered to the dark room, trying out the name on his tongue.

Suddenly, an uneasy feeling gripped his chest as he remembered her voice— slow and smooth as molasses. Her thick Southern drawl echoed the same enunciations as his torturers in Andersonville.

The smile that had touched his lips at the memory of the blond beauty at Gant's Mill evaporated. Daniel knew what had brought about his latest nightmare.

Chapter 2

"Pearl, please set an extra place at the dinner table as we will be having a guest."

Charity stopped stirring the pot of chicken and noodles when she heard Aunt Jennie's voice coming from the kitchen doorway. She turned from the stove in time to see the housemaid nod her dark, kerchief-clad head in obedience.

Charity was not surprised to learn that someone would be joining them for dinner. Aunt Jennie loved company, and a Sunday rarely passed without at least one guest at the table. She reached halfway up the stovepipe and gave the damper a quarter turn. With another diner coming, they couldn't afford to burn anything.

She turned toward her aunt. "Who are we entertainin' today, Aunt Jennie? Surely it cannot be our turn so soon again to host Reverend Davenport?"

Aunt Jennie gingerly lifted her black silk bonnet from her salt-and-pepper hair. "No." She smoothed back a few errant strands of hair that had pulled free of the chignon at the back of her head. "It's young Mr. Morgan—Silas's new mill foreman."

Charity's heart skipped a beat. When she found sufficient breath to speak, she strove to keep her voice casual. "Do you think that is wise, Aunt Jennie? After all, he is little more than a stranger." She went back to stirring and prodding things on the stove that required no attention.

In the four days since he'd come to work at her uncle's mill, Charity had continued to feel disconcerted when Daniel Morgan was near. So far, she had managed to maintain her distance from him, having only brief contact when he brought her the work orders from which she wrote customers' bills. Beyond murmured pleasantries, their conversation had been limited strictly to business matters. So the thought of exchanging dinner conversation with this former Yankee soldier was less than palatable.

An audible sigh heaved Aunt Jennie's plump, black bombazine-clad form. She fixed Charity with that patronizing, near-pitying look that always scraped down her last nerve. Aunt Jennie never seemed to take seriously any of the accounts of Yankee treachery Charity had shared with her aunt since Charity's arrival in Vernon, Indiana, nearly two years ago. "I'm sure there is nothing to fear from Mr. Morgan, Charity. Your uncle Silas is a great judge of character, and he has only praise for the young man."

Aunt Jennie turned her attention to her bonnet and brushed at some perceived blemish. "Besides," she added with a slight upward tilt of her chin, "I've come to learn that my dear friend Iris Pemberton's second cousin once removed has been a patient of Mr. Morgan's father for years now." Her gray eyes pinned Charity with a look as immovable as the granite they resembled. "Mr. Morgan comes from a *very* good family." As if to pronounce an end to the conversation, Aunt Jennie turned and left the kitchen.

Now Charity understood the invitation. Aunt Jennie was always alert to any connections that might serve to elevate her socially.

Pearl entered the kitchen from the dining room, a toothy grin shining from the midst of her dusky features. "Mmm, mmm! Haven't seen you this befuddled since Granger Hardwick showed up on yer mamma's porch with a fist full o' roses an' magnolia blossoms!"

"Pearl Emanuel! Don't you dare mention Granger in the same breath as that—that Yankee!" Charity whirled on her childhood friend and confidante. For once, she wished Pearl wasn't so attuned to her emotions.

Pearl cocked her head, obviously unfazed by Charity's rebuke. "Miss Charity, you know I can always tell what's goin' on inside you." She began scrubbing the kitchen worktable, washing away the remnants of her earlier noodle making. As she worked, her dark eyes flashed upward glances toward Charity. "I didn't breathe nothin' 'bout no Yankee and you know it!"

The familiar little pain stabbed inside Charity at the mention of her dead fiancé, but she was surprised at how blunted it had become. "You know very well what I mean!" She kept her face averted from Pearl's. "I just don't like the idea of a Yankee soldier—"

Pearl shook her head. "Mr. Morgan ain't no soldier no more. 'Sides, Jesus tells us we got to love our enemies."

Charity winced at Pearl's words. The Bible had been her primer. She knew Christ's teachings concerning forgiveness and turning the other cheek as well as Pearl knew them. Every Sunday from the pulpit, Reverend Davenport preached about healing, about "binding up the country's wounds," as Mr. Lincoln had said in his last inaugural speech.

And Charity had made a conscious effort to do just that. In April of last year, she'd wept when she learned of Mr. Lincoln's death at the hand of an assassin, sensing the slain president had genuinely cared for the suffering South as much as for those who'd suffered above the Mason-Dixon Line.

This past spring, she'd joined a sizable group of Christian ladies from the community to place flowers on the graves of Union soldiers. She hoped, in her absence, others were decorating the final resting places of Granger and her brother, Asa. But after all she'd seen, all she'd been through, all she'd lost, Charity had begun to wonder if complete forgiveness was even possible.

A mischievous glint sparked from Pearl's dark eyes. "Joy Rose Nash says she went with her man, Ned, to take a load o' corn down there to the mill a few days ago. Says she done seen the new foreman and he's a real looker."

At Pearl's comment, Daniel Morgan's image came into focus in Charity's mind, and her cheeks tingled warmly. She turned away from Pearl's teasing grin. "All I know is he once wore Yankee blue. And I find the thought of sittin' directly across the table from a man whose minie-ball might have killed Granger or Asa distasteful."

An hour later, as the party gathered in the dining room for Sunday dinner, Charity had to remind herself of her earlier declaration to Pearl. Indeed, she could find little distasteful about Daniel Morgan's appearance. Having seen him only in his coarse work clothes, she had to admit in his black serge suit, starched white shirt, and black silk string tie he cut quite a dashing figure.

Charity willed her hands not to tremble as she adjusted the folds of her blue-striped silk skirt around the seat of the cherry-wood dining chair. She managed to murmur her thanks as Daniel held her chair then helped her to scoot it up to the table.

With Aunt Jennie and Uncle Silas occupying the opposite ends of the rectangular table, she and Daniel were relegated to staring directly across its narrow breadth at one another. Thankfully, the moment Uncle Silas finished saying grace, he opened the conversation with talk of the mill.

Charity pushed her chicken and noodles around her plate and tried to avert her gaze from Daniel Morgan's hypnotically dark eyes. But she found herself repeatedly studying his handsome features. Invariably, whenever her gaze drifted to his face, she would be met by his gentle smile and a lingering look that set her heart fluttering.

During the main course, she managed to say little as her aunt and uncle peppered Daniel with questions about his family in Madison and his past experience in mill work.

Aunt Jennie sipped from her water goblet then daintily touched her linen napkin to her lips. "I trust, young man, that you are not related to the infamous General Morgan of the Confederacy who brought the war to our very porch steps?"

Daniel grinned and gave a little shake of his head. "Not as far as I know. My father's people hail from the Shay's Mill area in Washington County." He managed to sneak a bite between sentences. "My uncles and cousins still run the grist mill there that my grandfather built back in 1820."

Watching his impeccable manners and good-natured temper amid her aunt's and uncle's relentless barrage of questions, Charity noticed that her feelings toward Daniel Morgan had softened. Pearl's earlier comment pricked her conscience. The war, indeed, was over. So the man had fought on the side of the Yankees. Chances were he had never been near Asa or Granger.

Lost in her muse, Charity scarcely noticed Pearl enter the dining room bearing a tray laden with slices of the pie Charity had made yesterday.

Uncle Silas's voice filtered through Charity's thoughts. "Thank you, Pearl. I always save room for dessert. And there's nothing better than Charity's wonderful peach pie."

As Pearl served the pie, her glance flitted between Charity and Daniel, and her left eyebrow shot up. She sent Charity a sly, teasing grin.

The wings of the butterflies in Charity's stomach beat harder, fanning new flames in her cheeks. She sent Pearl a warning glare.

A mischievous twinkle danced in Pearl's eyes as she served Daniel a slice.

After a quick, murmured thanks to Pearl, Daniel Morgan's lips tipped up and his gaze turned to capture Charity's. "I do believe the best peach I ever ate in my life I had in Georgia on the Fourth of July in '64."

A quick anger stilled the flutters inside Charity. She thought of the times she'd seen Yankee soldiers stroll through the Georgia countryside picking fruit indiscriminately, as if such acts of trespassing were their right. Lifting her chin, she fixed Daniel with a stony stare and pasted on a stilted smile. "I wonder, sir, from whose orchard you stole that memorable piece of fruit?"

"Charity!" Aunt Jennie hissed from one end of the table, while Uncle Silas harrumphed from the other.

But Daniel never flinched. His gaze remained fixed to Charity's face. "Actually, Miss Langdon," he said, directing his reply to her as if Silas and Jennie Gant were not in the room, "the peach was a gift." He went on to tell how he and his troop of soldiers had passed a slave boy wheeling a barrow far too large for him to manage down a dusty road on the hot July day. The boy offered each soldier a peach, thus considerably lightening his load.

Shame burned hot on Charity's face. The words from the Gospel of Luke Reverend Davenport had read from the pulpit this morning replayed through her mind. *"Judge not, and ye shall not be judged: condemn not, and ye shall not be condemned: forgive, and ye shall be forgiven."*

Charity opened her mouth to speak and her voice squeaked. She cleared her throat and began again in a low, penitent tone, not quite managing to meet his eyes. "Please forgive my impertinence and bad manners, sir. I fear I have sinned against you and our Lord."

"Not at all, dear lady. I'm sad to say your assumption was far too often the situation. Our army did not always show respect for the property of the Southern citizens." His gentle smile and soft voice disarmed Charity, causing her to swallow the renegade tears threatening to well in her eyes.

But from somewhere back in her mind, an insidious voice rasped, *He was in Georgia in July of 1864.* Daniel Morgan could very well have faced Asa and Granger across the battleground of Peachtree Creek.

⥲

Daniel stood by the pile of freshly sawed lumber. Using the top piece as a writing surface, he scribbled figures on the customer's bill, but his mind refused to focus on his ciphering. The memory of Charity Langdon's blue eyes glistening with tears across the Gants' dinner table would not let him be.

Sighing, he lifted his gaze from the scrap of paper and looked out over the Muscatatuck River, winding its way through the dense woods that edged it. He'd come here to forget the war—forget all the trespasses committed against him as well as the trespasses he'd committed against others. But after three sleepless nights, he'd come to the painful conclusion that Charity Langdon would never allow him to do that.

He scrubbed his face with his hand. The girl had a hold on him. Her image owned his first thoughts upon awakening and his last upon repose. But to stay would only ensure deeper heartache, and that was something he could well do without. Her accusation at the Sunday dinner table had made it clear that she held a low opinion of those who'd worn the Union blue. Daniel wondered if it would be wise—or even possible—to attempt to bridge the chasm that seemed to separate them.

Daniel snatched the invoice from the piece of lumber. A quick anger shot through him. He liked this sawmill. He liked working for Silas Gant. And in the short time he'd been here, he, Silas, and Charlie Brewster had become an almost seamless working team.

His heart thumped harder with each step toward Charity's little office. She had crawled under his skin and bored into his heart like no other woman—even Phoebe.

He'd been surprised at how quickly after enlisting in the army his heartache over his former fiancée's rejection had dissipated. In hindsight, he'd seen that theirs would have been a miserable union. By breaking their engagement and marrying that banker, Phoebe had done them both a great favor.

As he neared Charity's desk, he saw her honey-colored head bent over the ledger book. She lifted her lovely face and Daniel's heart bucked.

What sin have I done that God should dangle one so fair, yet unobtainable, before me?

He swallowed, attempting to moisten his dry throat. He held the invoice out toward her. "Here is the invoice for the lumber we sawed for Ed Cochrane. He's waiting out front. Soon as you've recorded the amount, I'll take it to him."

"Thank you, Mr. Morgan." She accepted the invoice with a quick, almost shy smile. Since Sunday, he'd noticed her mood had turned markedly quiet and reserved. She scanned the invoice, and her delicate brow knitted together in a concerned look. Her pink rosebud lips formed an O.

Suddenly, the worry lines vanished from her forehead. She smiled up at him—a sweet smile that warmed him all the way to his heart. "You may go help Mr. Cochrane load up his lumber, Mr. Morgan, but don't quote him an amount. Just tell him I will be out with the invoice shortly."

Although a bit bemused, Daniel obeyed. Besides being his boss's niece, Charity Langdon was the prettiest thing he'd ever had the pleasure of gazing upon. He reckoned he'd do just about anything she might ask of him.

A few minutes later when Charity emerged from the mill, Daniel paused in loading Ed Cochrane's lumber.

With a bright smile, she handed Daniel a different piece of paper from the one he'd figured. "Mr. Morgan, I have prepared Mr. Cochrane's invoice as you asked."

Daniel scanned the invoice and his heart nearly stopped. His original figures would have shorted the sawmill by twenty-five percent.

He jerked his face up to Charity's, and their gazes locked. He swallowed hard at the unmistakable message he read in her pretty blue eyes. She would never breathe a word of his mistake.

With a less than steady hand, he passed the invoice to Ed Cochrane, who nodded and followed Charity into the mill to settle his debt. Daniel watched the two disappear into the building and knew that Charity Langdon had just saved his job.

Something squeezed hard inside his chest. Good sense told him it was folly to stay. But after what she'd just done for him, he knew he couldn't leave Vernon, or Gant's Mill. He would regret it for the rest of his life if he didn't at least try to win Charity's heart.

Chapter 3

Pearl's familiar three taps sounded on Charity's bedroom door, bringing Charity out of her bed.

When Charity opened the door, Pearl sashayed into the room carrying a steaming pitcher and humming a happy tune.

"What has put you in such a bright mood this mornin'?" Charity smiled as she quickly changed from her nightdress into bloomers and a camisole.

Though always a happy soul, Pearl seemed especially chipper. She set the pitcher of hot water on the washstand. "Miz Gant jist said I could take a few days off to go visit Mammy and Pappy down in Madison."

Pearl's news rasped against Charity's conscience. She knew Pearl missed her folks. Yet Charity was thankful that her childhood friend, who'd been more like a sister to her than a slave during their growing-up years in Georgia, had chosen to come work for Aunt Jennie and Uncle Silas instead of staying down in Madison with her parents.

She sent Pearl a sly look. "And could there possibly be somebody else down in Madison you'd like to see besides Jericho and Tunia?" Since her last trip to Madison, Pearl hadn't stopped talking about Adam Chapman. The son of Jericho and Tunia's best friends, Andrew and Patsey Chapman, Adam seemed to have his sights set on a ministry in the African Methodist Episcopal Church.

"Maybe." The apples of Pearl's brown cheeks glowed with a faint rosy hue. "Got another letter from Adam jist yesterday. He's been studyin' hard for the pulpit."

Charity was glad she had taught Pearl to read, write, and cipher when they were young, despite the fact that it was against the law. The two had simply made a game of the secrecy.

"He's gonna be a right-fine preacher in the AME Church one day." Pearl's chin lifted as she spoke of her friend's ambitions.

Charity wet a scrap of clean cotton material in the hot water and ran it over her face, neck, and bare arms. "And everyone knows," she said, forcing a serious tone to her voice as she finished dressing, "a preacher needs a wife."

"I got my eyes on that purty man, that's for sure." Pearl pulled a velvet-upholstered stool closer to the dresser and picked up Charity's hairbrush. "Now set yerself down and let me fix yer hair."

Smiling, Charity obeyed, allowing Pearl to brush her hair, then twist it into a knot, which she secured to the back of Charity's head with several pins.

Although Charity had repeatedly offered to do her own hair, Pearl insisted on continuing the morning tradition they'd started as young girls in Georgia. It was during these times they had opportunities to share thoughts, giggle, and generally chat.

"High time you found a man o' yer own," Pearl said as she stuck the last couple of pins into Charity's hair.

Charity's shoulders rose and fell with her sigh. "I had a man, Pearl. He died with Asa at the Battle of Peachtree Creek."

Pearl rested her hands gently on Charity's shoulders. "Been more'n two years since Granger Hardwick done went to his reward." Her voice softened with her caring tone but held no hint of pity. "Memories ain't gonna keep you warm at night or give you babies to rock, neither."

After Granger's death, Charity had abandoned all serious thought of marriage. No one since had caused her heart to skip.

Not until Daniel Morgan appeared at the mill two weeks ago.

Pearl rounded the stool to face Charity. With her arms akimbo and fists planted firmly on her hips, she fixed Charity with a stern stare. "If I was you, I'd be schemin' on snarin' that nice-lookin' Mr. Morgan."

Heat leaped to Charity's face. "Well, you're not me. For your information, I'm plenty warm at night, I am definitely *not* lookin' for a husband, and I wouldn't know what to do with a baby if I had one. And as far as Mr. Morgan goes, I'm sure he has no interest in me and I certainly have no interest—"

Pearl gave a little gasp and shook her finger in Charity's face. "Don't you dare start yer day with a fib, Miss Charity. Hard tellin' what might happen if you was to go off to that mill 'neath the Good Lord's frown."

Rising, Charity threw back her head and laughed. When would she ever learn she could more easily fool herself than Pearl? "Have it your way, Pearl. I will admit the man is passably decent looking. But it doesn't change the fact that he's a Yankee. And if I ever do marry, it will certainly *not* be to a Yankee!"

Charity headed for the door. Aunt Jennie would be cross if she was tardy for breakfast and made Uncle Silas late to the mill.

Pearl touched her arm, halting her. "Come down to Madison with me, Miss Charity. I'd really like for you to meet Adam. And 'sides, without you along, that train ride's gonna be pure tedious."

The girl's dark eyes shone with the familiar pleading look Charity had found irresistible since they were children. "Mammy and Pappy'd like it if you come, too. Adam says they been pinin' they ain't seen you for the longest time."

Guilt pinched Charity's heart as she thought of her parents' former slaves. Aside from her deep affection for the couple, she knew that she owed both her virtue and her life to the Emanuels. When General Sherman ordered Atlanta's people to evacuate then burned the city along with outlying homes like hers, only God's grace and Jericho and Tunia's protection had brought her safely past the Union army and on to Indiana.

Charity gave her friend a fond smile. "I do miss them desperately and would love to see them. If Uncle Silas can do without me at the mill for a few days, I surely would like to accompany you."

Later that morning as she rode beside her uncle in the buggy, Charity broached the subject of joining Pearl on her trip to Madison. She was surprised at how quickly Uncle Silas agreed. "I've already bought your train ticket," he told her with a wink and a grin, adding that he'd decided to close the mill for a few days prior to the corn harvest.

"When the corn comes in," he said, lifting his hat to run thick fingers through his thinning gray hair, "we shall scarcely have time to take a breath." Giving the horse a cluck of encouragement as he guided it down the dirt path to the mill, he shot her a sideways smile. "We'd best all rest up in preparation."

Charity nodded, remembering last year's harvest. For weeks on end, the extra work required them to arrive at the mill before daylight and stay until after dusk. So when Joe Simms quit his job as mill foreman and moved to Versailles at the beginning of August, her uncle had been desperate to find a replacement.

Thoughts of the man who had taken Simms's place sent tingles dancing over Charity's skin. She hadn't spoken at length to Daniel since she'd corrected his mathematical mistake last week. To her shame, she'd considered leaving it alone for Uncle Silas to discover. But remembering the admonition from the scriptures, *"Therefore to him that knoweth to do good, and doeth it not, to him it is sin,"* she knew she had to fix it.

Inside the mill, Uncle Silas joined Daniel and Charlie, who'd already begun preparing the machinery for sawing a load of lumber.

At her desk, Charity went about organizing her morning's work. So when a scuffing sound brought her face up, she was surprised to find Daniel standing before her.

His gaze skittered around the small area but seemed unable to meet her eyes. "I just wanted to thank you for what you did for me last week—with Ed Cochrane's bill." He rubbed his forehead—a nervous habit that had become as familiar to Charity as his limp.

Trying to keep her voice indifferent, she shrugged and turned her attention to the desktop, needlessly rearranging stacks of papers. "If you are referrin' to the adjustment I made to Mr. Cochrane's bill, checkin' for such mathematical. . . irregularities is just part of my job." It wouldn't do for him to think she'd done him a special favor.

She watched his Adam's apple move as he swallowed—hard. His dark eyes glistened while several emotions flitted in turn over his features. At last, his tender gaze settled on her face and melted into her eyes, snatching away her breath. "You are a mighty fine woman, Miss Charity Langdon."

With her heart pounding in her ears, Charity's gaze dropped to the desktop.

She could think of no intelligent response, which was just as well since she seemed to have lost the ability to speak. This man was indeed too troublesome by half! At least next week she would have a few days' respite from his disquieting presence.

"I was happy to learn from Silas that you will be joining Pearl on a trip to Madison next week." His statement yanked her attention back to his face.

Confused, Charity stared at the smile crawling across his lips. "I cannot see how my travelin' plans could be of any concern to you."

A red stain spread from his neck to his face. "I'd assumed your uncle told you. Knowing I was also planning a trip to Madison next week to celebrate my sister's birthday, your uncle purchased three corresponding tickets and asked that I escort you and Pearl." His smile widened. "The three of us will be sharing a train car, it seems."

Charity gaped at him. "I see," she managed to mumble. Irritation squiggled through her as she wondered if Pearl had known of the arrangement when she'd invited Charity to join her.

She stared at the retreating figure of Daniel Morgan's broad back. Watching his halting gait carry him away from her desk, she knew there'd be no peace for her troubled heart.

Chapter 4

Brightly whistling "Skip to My Lou," Daniel pulled the horse and wagon to a stop on Perry Street in front of Silas Gant's three-story brick home. He knew it was ridiculous to be so happy. The look of dismay on Charity Langdon's face when she'd learned he would be sharing a train car with her and Pearl had been plain. She clearly held him in disdain.

Yet he couldn't stop his heart from dancing as he jumped to the ground. Even the familiar stabbing pain in his leg caused by the jarring motion was eased by the thought of enjoying Charity's company for the twenty-five mile trip to Madison.

The wrought-iron gate gave a little squeak when he pushed it open. He crossed the neat little yard and stepped up to the porch, trying to ignore his pounding heart.

Pearl Emanuel answered his two quick raps on the door, a smile flashing from beneath the yellow calico bonnet framing her dark face. "We're all ready," she said, as he relieved her of two bulging carpetbags.

Charity, who'd joined Pearl in the hallway, greeted him with a silent nod and a stilted smile. She pushed a sizeable portmanteau toward the open front door while at the same time clutching a little carpetbag. Wearing a green dress and a becoming straw bonnet decorated with pink paper flowers, she reminded Daniel of a rose.

Not wanting her to find him staring, he turned his attention to depositing the luggage in the wagon. When he returned to the porch for Charity's carpet-bag, Mrs. Gant bustled breathlessly into the front hallway, waving a brown paper package tied with a gold cord.

"Charity," she said, the word puffing from her lips, "please deliver this small token of my regard to Miss Morgan in commemoration of her birthday."

A look of dismay flashed briefly across Charity's face. It fled quickly and she turned a weak smile toward her aunt. "Of course, Aunt Jennie," she mumbled.

Daniel couldn't guess why Charity might find the thought of delivering a gift to Lucy disquieting. But she clearly did not relish the errand. Charity had never struck him as particularly shy, but he did remember Silas mentioning that Mrs. Gant felt their niece should socialize more. Perhaps, like Daniel, Charity had simply allowed her social graces to grow rusty during the war.

Daniel smiled at Mrs. Gant and reached for the package. "A gift is entirely unnecessary, ma'am. But I would be happy to deliver your kind offering to my sister and relieve Miss Langdon of the chore."

Mrs. Gant shook her head as she opened Charity's carpetbag, tucked in the box, then closed the bag again. "No, no. As it is from the three of us—Silas, Charity, and me—I think it only proper that Charity deliver it personally. I will have it no other way." The solidity of her tone coupled with her uptilted chin suggested the futility of further argument.

Charity turned a genuine smile to Daniel. "Thank you for your offer, Mr. Morgan. But I look forward to meetin' your sister and personally wishin' her a happy birthday." Whatever concerns had sparked her earlier look of apprehension, she'd obviously set them aside and put both her aunt's and Lucy's feelings ahead of her own.

Daniel's heart clenched at the thought as he took the carpetbag from Charity's hands and deposited it in the back of the wagon. These glimpses of her inherent goodness—sweetness—left him frustrated. How he longed to discover what key might open her heart, allowing him to share in the wonderful treasures he sensed lay buried beneath the debris of bitterness and distrust left by the war.

He helped Pearl up to the backseat of the wagon then turned to do the same for Charity. Perhaps if Charity and Lucy met, it could help in his efforts to win Charity's favor. He could think of no abler ambassador of goodwill on his behalf than his bubbly, sweet-natured sister. The thought buoyed his spirit.

An almost intoxicating whiff of rose water tickled his nostrils, and his hands relinquished Charity's trim waist with regret. His heart ached. Would performing such courteous acts for her be the closest Daniel ever came to holding Charity Langdon in his arms?

Daniel climbed to the front seat of the wagon where Silas joined him and drove them the two and a half blocks to the Vernon railroad station.

The four-story hip-roofed brick station house jutted up against a hill of earth and stone nearly half the building's height. Three distant blasts of a train whistle announced that a locomotive would soon roll into view on tracks that ran along the top of the hill.

Charity, Pearl, and Daniel said their farewells to Silas on the station's long covered porch as the train rumbled to a hissing stop above them. Daniel paid two young boys to transport their luggage up to the baggage car as a porter's full-throated "Aa–a–all abo–o–o–oard!" wafted down from the tracks above.

Through a rolling cloud of acrid coal smoke, Daniel followed Charity and Pearl up the dozen or so wooden steps to the waiting train. He wished he could sit next to Charity for the hour excursion but knew Pearl would be sharing the bench seat with her.

They made their way down the car's narrow aisle, where the odors of stale cigar smoke and cramped humanity clung to the air. When Charity and Pearl were seated, Daniel slipped into the seat directly behind theirs.

A feeling of lighthearted anticipation filled Daniel as they chugged away from Vernon. As much as he'd needed to distance himself from his family's smothering care, he *had* missed them, especially Lucy. He was also eager to meet her fiancé. He'd been only mildly surprised to learn from her recent letter of her whirlwind romance with Pa's new apprentice.

He grinned. There was nothing remotely shilly-shallying about his little sister. When she made up her mind about something, it was full steam ahead.

Charity's mood showed marked improvement as well. She giggled and chatted gaily with Pearl as the train clacked and rocked over the tracks through open fields and shady glades. Daniel's heart thumped harder each time Charity cast a smile over her shoulder at him, inquiring about creek names and local landmarks. Perhaps his presence was not as odious to her as he'd feared.

When they passed over Graham Creek, Pearl gazed out the window beside her. "That creek reminds me of the time we caught yer brother, Asa, playin' hooky from school in the creek behind the cotton mill," she said with a laugh.

Charity's straw bonnet bobbed with her nod, and the soft pink curve of her profiled cheek lifted in a grin. "We made him do all our chores for two solid weeks in exchange for our promise not to tell Mamma and Papa."

Pearl chuckled. "Pappy couldn't 'magine what got into that boy to cause him to do such a power o' work."

Charity's giggle joined Pearl's. "And then when Mamma found out from the schoolmaster that Asa had been taking off from school, she made him do another two weeks of extra chores."

Their laughter trailed off, leaving a somber silence.

"I miss Asa." The sadness in Charity's quiet admission stung Daniel's heart.

Daniel's smile fell. A sudden urge to offer Charity a word of sympathy struck, but his better judgment counseled him to stay silent. According to Silas, Charity's brother died serving under the Confederate flag. He surmised any offer of condolence from a former captain in the Union army would not be well received.

"I miss him, too," Pearl said softly, making Daniel glad Charity had such a close, dear friend with whom to share her tears as well as her laughter.

At last, the train finally slowed and they pulled into the long, enclosed train shed depot just north of Madison's Ohio Street. A warmth spread over Daniel as the building's familiar shadows wrapped around him like a comforting embrace. It was good to be home.

As they disembarked, he scanned the crowd milling about the dimly lit shed for his family. Almost at once, he and Lucy spied one another and, with a little shriek, she bounded toward him, beaming. Daniel caught his sister in a hug, lifting her off the depot floor. A little more than five years his junior, his baby sister would always occupy a special corner of his heart.

"How mean of you to stay away for so long, big brother. You know how

I miss you." Lucy reached up to continue hugging his neck after he'd set her down.

"Hmm," he teased as he disentangled himself from his irrepressible sibling. "Now that you have a new man in your life, I doubt you've given me a moment's thought."

Lucy pinked prettily. "I can imagine your surprise at learning your spinster sister is finally getting married." Her bright blue eyes, so like their mother's, sparkled. "I can scarcely wait for you to meet Travis! You just missed him, leaving when you did for Vernon. He came the next week to apprentice under Papa. You two will get on famously, I just know it!" His sister linked her arm with his. "Papa and Travis are out calling on patients in Papa's buggy, so I brought the phaeton."

Suddenly remembering Charity and Pearl, Daniel resisted his sister's tugs and glanced over at the two women scanning the crowded depot, searching, he assumed, for Pearl's parents.

Heat marched up his neck. He would need to polish his rusty social skills so as not to embarrass his sister and mother when they dined tonight with Lucy's new beau.

He guided his sister to Charity and Pearl. "Lucy, I'd like for you to meet Miss Charity Langdon, my employer's niece, and her friend, Pearl Emanuel. They've come to Madison to visit Pearl's parents at Georgetown."

As the young women exchanged greetings, a middle-aged black man stepped toward them, dragging a battered felt hat off his graying head. Daniel recalled having seen him in the company of Andrew Chapman and surmised it must be Jericho Emanuel.

The man gave Pearl a warm hug. Then with a polite nod to the group, he mumbled something about fetching the luggage and headed toward the baggage car.

When Charity and Pearl turned back to Lucy and Daniel, Lucy's face lit with a look of revelation and she smiled at Pearl. "Oh, you are the young lady Adam Chapman is sweet on."

A sheepish grin stretched Pearl's lips and she cast a glance downward. "Reckon that road runs both ways, Miss Morgan. Jist glad he says so, though."

Then Lucy's look swung between Charity and Daniel. A mischievous glint in her eye sent warning ripples through Daniel. He held his breath, unsure what to expect from his outspoken sibling as Lucy settled her gaze on Charity.

"I hope we have an opportunity to visit during your time in Madison, Miss Langdon. I can see that Daniel's description of your beauty and grace was not in the least overstated."

Heat shot up Daniel's neck. He would tweak Lucy's nose for that comment on their way home.

A rosy hue suffused Charity's face, and then she gave a little gasp. "Oh,

Miss Morgan, I almost forgot. My aunt Jennie sent you a birthday gift." She cast a helpless look down the length of the train in the direction Pearl's father had gone. "But I'm afraid it is packed away in my luggage. Perhaps I can find Jericho—"

"Don't trouble yourself." Lucy shook her head. "I plan to open my gifts this evening at supper and would be most honored if you would attend and bring the gift with you."

Daniel's heart thumped quicker. He'd never imagined Lucy would invite Charity to supper, but he doubted she would accept.

"Miss Langdon'd be right pleased to join you, ain't that right, Charity?" Pearl turned to Charity, across whose deepening pink face flashed a look of alarm.

"I. . ." Charity shot Daniel a beseeching look, but he had no interest in assisting her in contriving a reason not to dine with him this evening. Her smile slowly widened as her gaze slid back to Lucy. "Thank you, Miss Morgan. I would be honored to attend."

Lucy clapped her hands, audibly expressing the glee silently bubbling up inside Daniel. "We will dine at six, so Daniel will pick you up at five thirty."

Chapter 5

Daniel's heart quickened, keeping pace with the trotting hooves of the sleek black gelding bearing him and the open phaeton down Mulberry Street toward Georgetown. In a few moments he would see Charity. This was a pleasure he hadn't expected to enjoy again until three days hence, when he would accompany her and Pearl on the train ride back to Vernon. Although he had soundly chided an unrepentant Lucy for embarrassing him in Charity's presence this morning, he silently thanked his sister for this opportunity to spend some time alone with Charity.

Daniel pulled up in front of the neat little white-washed shotgun house that belonged to Jericho and Tunia Emanuel.

The waning sun washed the late afternoon in a golden hue as he climbed down from the carriage and made his way up the porch steps. He hoped that despite her initial reluctant demeanor, Charity would enjoy Lucy's birthday dinner this evening. Indeed, the lovely warm September afternoon gave him courage to believe she might actually enjoy his company as well as the carriage ride to his parents' home.

Jericho answered his quick raps on the door, and Daniel noticed the man was dressed in his Sunday best. "Miss Langdon'll be along directly, Mr. Morgan. We're fixin' to head down to the AME Church for a hymn-sing this evenin'."

Daniel nodded. His uncle Jacob, who ministered at the church on Broadway Street, had mentioned that Andrew and Patsey Chapman's son, Adam, was studying for the ministry. He was about to comment on his uncle's joy in learning of Adam's choice of vocation when he glanced over Jericho's shoulder and saw Charity clutching Mrs. Gant's brown paper package.

Daniel felt as if he'd been punched hard in the midsection. Even in the common day dresses she wore to the mill, Charity Langdon was beguiling. He'd thought her enchanting when he saw her dressed in her Sunday finery the day he'd dined at the home of her aunt and uncle. But adorned in this pink silk evening frock, she was nothing short of stunning. Her golden hair, parted in the center, tumbled in long ringlets that brushed the white crocheted wrap covering her bare shoulders.

They made their parting salutations to the Emanuels, and Charity tucked her arm around Daniel's, sending a thrill through him. He hated that his game leg required him to grasp the railing to steady himself as they descended the porch steps. But even more painful was Charity's thick Southern accent that reminded him of why he limped.

"I suppose it was a good thing, after all, that my aunt insisted I bring an eve-nin' gown," she told him as he helped her into the carriage. "I hadn't imagined I would need one, but Aunt Jennie would not allow me to leave Vernon without a change of formal attire."

Daniel had never before heard Charity prattle on, especially about fripper-ies like women's fashions. He sensed she was nervous but couldn't discern if it was his company or simply the thought of dining with strangers that caused her unease.

"Thank you for attending Lucy's birthday dinner this evening," he said as he guided the horse onto Mulberry Street. "She and Mother are looking for-ward to your company. Normally, we would have a house full of women. Aside from my aunt Rosaleen, I have four female cousins who usually attend these affairs. But my aunt Rosaleen is tending my twin cousins, Rory and John, who are down with bad colds; my cousins, Lydia and Rose, have gone to visit their sister, Abigail, who attends a young women's academy in Cincinnati; and Lilly, my cousin Ruben's wife, is. . .in confinement and not socializing." Daniel's face warmed and he wished in his nervous blathering he hadn't mentioned his cousin who was awaiting the birth of her fifth child.

Charity fussed with the hem of her wrap, but he sensed her nervousness had nothing to do with his indiscretion. "It must be wonderful to have such a large family. You and your sister seem especially close."

The haunting, sad quality that tinged her words made him ashamed. He should have remembered she was an orphan before gushing about his large extended family.

"Yes, despite our age difference, Lucy and I have always been close." The memory of Lucy nursing him back to health after he returned from the war—refusing to leave his bedside for days on end—flooded his mind. He couldn't help thinking of Charity's lost brother and broached the subject he'd shied away from earlier that day on the train. "Were you and your brother close?"

His heart shuddered when she became quiet.

When she spoke, her voice was so soft he had to strain to hear. "Yes, we were."

"I'm sorry. Many good men were lost." He wished he had obeyed his earlier inclination and not asked. They spent the remainder of the trip down Main-Cross Street to his parents' home in silence.

Later in the family parlor, Daniel was happy to see Charity's mood brighten beneath his mother's gentle graces and his sister's friendly exuberance. While Lucy opened her gifts, she and Charity giggled together like schoolgirls.

"Aunt Jennie says a girl's hope chest is not complete without a fine set of doilies," Charity said, responding to Lucy's bemused look when she unwrapped the lacy white pieces of crochet work Mrs. Gant had sent.

Both girls glanced at Lucy's intended, who turned the color of a near-ripe strawberry.

Travis Ashby—whom Daniel liked immediately—was everything Lucy and his mother had advertised. During his service in the army, Daniel had learned to evaluate the character of a man very quickly. He soon found that a keen wit percolated beneath the young man's mop of curly, sand-colored hair. Travis's lively green eyes revealed a fun-loving nature Daniel could imagine was irresistible to his vivacious sister.

When she finished opening her gifts, Lucy led the way to the dining room, arm in arm with Charity. Seeing the two girls getting along so well ignited an inexplicable joy in Daniel.

After several minutes of Travis and Pa dominating the supper conversation with talk of medicine, Mother lifted an appealing look to Pa. "Please, Ephraim, no more talk of medicine. We must be boring poor Charity to death."

The corners of Pa's eyes wrinkled as he turned that familiar adoring look on Mother's face.

How he loves her still. The thought struck Daniel with heartwarming poignancy as he watched his father's gaze caress his mother's features. Though the years had streaked her chestnut hair with silver and etched fine lines on her face, his mother remained a stunningly beautiful woman. Her vibrant blue eyes, so like Lucy's, shone as brilliantly as ever. Could he hope to be as lucky as his father and find a woman who so completely captured his own heart?

His gaze drifted with the muse to Charity's face. Wreathed in candle glow, she looked absolutely celestial.

"Of course, my dear, you are right," Pa said, then turned toward Charity. "You have a lovely accent, Miss Langdon. From what part of the South do you hail?"

Charity blushed so prettily it made Daniel's heart ache. "Thank you for sayin' so, sir. I was born and raised in Peachtree, Georgia."

At her quiet declaration, a cold fist grabbed inside Daniel's chest. It had been just outside that town near Peachtree Creek that he, Tom, and Fred were captured by Confederate soldiers. Because of that capture, he spent six indescribably horrible months in the Andersonville prisoner-of-war camp, where his two friends and subordinates died.

Daniel noticed that the others around the table had grown quiet. Surely his family had guessed the ugly memories the mention of Peachtree, Georgia had evoked for him.

Blessedly, Travis piped up between bites of roast pork, filling the awkward silence. "Are you planning to return to Georgia sometime in the future, Miss Langdon? I hear much is already being done toward the restoration of the South."

The wistful look glistening in Charity's eyes pricked Daniel's heart. He remembered how acutely he'd missed his own home during the war. From the scraps of information he'd gleaned from Silas Gant and Charlie Brewster, Charity's family's property had been burned by General Sherman's troops.

"Yes, Mr. Ashby, I dream of the day I might return and reclaim my family's land and rebuild my home and cotton mill that was burned. . .durin' the war." She glanced at Daniel. The soft lines of her jaw seemed to harden slightly, and he glimpsed a flash of anger in her blue eyes. "That is, if some Yankee carpetbagger hasn't claimed it for his own."

After another stretch of uncomfortable silence, Mother wisely steered the conversation to the safer topic of women's fashion. The others, including Charity, grasped the subject like a lifeline.

But Daniel sat in miserable silence, tormenting a cooling heap of mashed potatoes with his fork. If he'd ever entertained a glimmer of hope that he might nurture a closer friendship with Charity Langdon, she'd just killed it.

Chapter 6

The tantalizing aromas of grits, coffee, and sausage coaxed Charity awake, dispelling the fog of sleep shrouding her consciousness. She squinted against the sunlight streaming through the long, narrow window of the sparse little bedroom she shared with Pearl. But when she turned to wake Pearl, she found the other side of the bed empty, the covers rumpled.

Scooting her legs over the side of the mattress, she lazily stretched and yawned. Her bare feet pressed against the nubby warmth of the rag rug that covered white-painted floorboards beside the bed.

She dressed quickly. Perhaps Pearl had gotten up early to help Tunia with breakfast. Tomorrow they would be traveling back to Vernon. Most likely, Pearl just wanted to get an early start on their last day here.

Pearl had spent much of the past two days visiting Adam and his family. Last night she expressed regret for having left Charity alone at the house so much and had promised that today they would go shopping together. The evening Charity visited the Morgans had been her only time away from Georgetown since arriving in Madison, so today's outing would be a refreshing diversion.

Thoughts of Lucy Morgan's birthday dinner caused Charity's skin to tingle and her face to warm. She remembered how her heart had skipped a beat when she first caught sight of Daniel waiting to escort her to his parents' home. Tall and handsome in his dress clothes, he had stirred even more deeply the disquieting feelings he'd evoked in her since first appearing at her uncle's mill.

The memory of his strong hands on her waist as he helped her from the carriage sent a renewed thrill through her. She tried to remember if she'd ever thought Granger so handsome or if his mere presence had caused her heart to flutter as it had the other evening with Daniel Morgan.

Shame sizzled inside Charity as she headed toward the kitchen. How could she be so disloyal to the memory of the man she'd planned to wed? She must not forget that Daniel Morgan could very well have looked across the battlefield, fixed Asa or Granger in his rifle's sight, and pulled the trigger.

"Done thought you was fixin' to sleep the day away, chil'!" Tunia glanced up from stirring a pot of grits on the stove, an ivory smile flashing from her dark round face as Charity entered the kitchen.

"Where's Pearl?" Charity returned the smile as she sat in a caned chair at the little rectangular table. Surrendering to another yawn, she smoothed a wrinkle from the red and white gingham tablecloth.

Tunia placed a plate of grits and sausage in front of Charity. "Adam come by early. Said his mammy's feelin' poorly today an' ain't up to helpin' Miz Hale down at the parsonage. Said Patsey was frettin' 'bout the rev'rend's wife havin' to manage two sick young'uns upstairs an' a parlor full o' church women by herself this afternoon. So she had Adam fetch Pearl down there to help." Tunia bustled about the stove, clearing away the breakfast remnants. "Reckoned I'd go see 'bout Patsey d'rectly, then head down to Rev'rend Hale's parsonage and help Pearl."

Disappointment pushed a sigh from Charity's lips. She understood Pearl wanting to help Adam's mother, but the situation relegated Charity to spending another day on her own.

A knocking at the front door sent Tunia padding through the house.

At the sound of Daniel Morgan's voice, Charity dropped her spoon back into the mound of grits on her plate. They'd planned to leave for Vernon tomorrow. What was he doing here today?

She jumped from her chair and hurried to join Tunia in the front room.

Tunia invited Daniel into the house then excused herself, mumbling something about the grits on the stove as she headed back to the kitchen.

At the sight of Daniel, that now familiar fluttering commenced in Charity's chest. "Daniel,"—she wished her face didn't suddenly feel so warm—"I understood we were not to leave until tomorrow."

"I'm not here to take you home." His large hands fiddled with the brim of his hat. "Lucy has planned a picnic for today and would like it very much if you would agree to join her, Mr. Ashby, and myself on the outing." He gave her a shy grin. "Lucy's dead set on a picnic at Cedar Cliffs." He cocked his head to the left. "It's a place a few miles east of Madison that overlooks the river."

Charity's heart pounded quicker, stoking the flames in her cheeks. Obviously Lucy and Travis required chaperones for propriety. Lucy must have decided making it a foursome was preferable to just having Daniel tag along with her and Travis.

Charity couldn't deny she liked Lucy very much. Daniel's sister was just her same age. Under other circumstances, she would relish a friendship with Lucy Morgan. But spending time with Lucy meant spending time with Daniel— something she'd hoped to avoid.

"If you would rather not, I'm sure Lucy will understand."

Charity studied Daniel's expression. Was that disappointment she saw in his eyes? And if so, was it disappointment for his sister or for himself?

Charity glanced back toward the kitchen. Since Jericho, Tunia, and Pearl would all be gone from the house, an afternoon picnic seemed preferable to spending the day alone. "Tell Lucy I thank her for the invitation and would love to attend."

A smile slowly traipsed across his handsome face, and his dark eyes that had dulled came alive. "We shall come by and pick you up about noon then." He gave a quick bow, turned, and headed toward his wagon. Even with his limp, there seemed to be an extra spring to his step.

Charity stood in the open doorway, watching until Daniel's wagon disappeared around the corner. She turned and headed to the kitchen, wishing she weren't so eager for twelve o'clock to come.

❧

Four hours later, as she bounced beside Daniel on the buggy's front seat with Lucy and Travis seated behind them, Charity still questioned the wisdom of accepting the picnic invitation.

For the past two years, she'd endured the company of Yankees simply because she'd had no other choice. Though cordial to her Vernon neighbors, she'd nurtured few close friendships there, especially among people of her own age.

Lucy Morgan's friendly effervescence had revived memories of lighthearted friendships Charity had shared with other girls her age in Georgia before the war. Hadn't Charity prayed for God to help her forgive the trespasses committed against her by the Yankees? Perhaps a promising friendship with Lucy Morgan was part of God's answer.

Daniel turned the buggy onto a winding wooded road that abruptly rose to a steep incline and angled a grin toward Charity. "Better hang on tight." His handsome profile made her heart skip, and she had to remind herself that she'd agreed to join this picnic as a favor to Lucy, not so she could spend an afternoon with Daniel.

At last, they emerged from a grove of evergreens into an open grassy expanse that overlooked the Ohio River, and Daniel pulled the buggy to a stop.

The pleasant smell of cedar scented the gentle breeze as Charity gazed down upon the river. The sight took her breath away. She'd seen the river up close several times. And two years ago, she and the Emanuels had crossed it as they neared the end of their perilous journey from Georgia. But from this height, the view of the river was nothing less than stunning. The wide, shimmering waterway was visible for miles, bending gently through woods tinged with the first golden touches of autumn's color.

After the men helped Charity and Lucy to the ground, Lucy gave Charity a hug. "Isn't this just the most delightful spot? I'm so glad you were able to join us, Charity." Bouncing with obvious excitement in her yellow linen-lawn frock, Lucy looked like an inverted buttercup in a stiff breeze.

"Thank you for invitin' me." The words left Charity's lips honestly and easily as she and Lucy each picked up one of the two quilts Lucy had brought and tucked it under an arm.

Lucy linked her free arm with Charity's. "Come. Let's find a good picnic spot while Daniel and Travis fetch the baskets."

Deciding on an area in the shade of a large cedar tree several yards from the buggy, Charity and Lucy worked together spreading the faded patchwork quilts over the grass. At last they seated themselves on the pallets, adjusting their voluminous skirts around them with care.

"Perhaps we should have chosen a spot closer to the buggy," Lucy said quietly, her tone edged with regret.

Charity stopped smoothing wrinkles from her green cotton skirt and followed Lucy's gaze. Daniel and Travis, with picnic baskets in hand, had just started in their direction.

A pained expression pinched Lucy's features as she watched her brother's halting gait. "He was always so big and strong, I sometimes forget."

"Was it a bullet wound?" Charity asked the question she'd wondered about since Daniel first limped into her uncle's mill.

"No. His left leg was broken. . .during the war," Lucy offered simply, becoming suddenly reticent.

Charity sensed Daniel's sister was holding something back, but good etiquette dictated she should not pry further.

The men arrived, bringing with them the wonderful aroma of fried chicken, and the conversation quickly turned to the picnic fare. Daniel and Travis sat cross-legged on the quilts, and Charity noted with interest that Lucy asked Travis, not Daniel, to offer grace before the meal.

Uncle Silas had mentioned that Daniel declined several invitations to worship with them at the little church on the hill overlooking Vernon. Yet his family seemed extremely devout. According to Tunia, Daniel and Lucy's uncle had long ministered at one of Madison's churches. Had Daniel rejected his faith? The thought made her sad. But when she sneaked a peek during the prayer, he had his head bent, his dark hair falling across his broad forehead.

Daniel Morgan was a puzzle, the pieces of which Charity told herself she had no interest in assembling. Yet she found herself eagerly listening as Lucy divulged incidents from his childhood.

"Daniel," Lucy said, pointing a chicken leg at her brother, "tell us about the time you saved Aunt Rosaleen when you were six."

Daniel squirmed and his face flushed. "I didn't save Aunt Rosaleen, Lucy. Uncle Jacob saved Aunt Rosaleen. And what would you know about it? You were just a baby." He shoved a forkful of potato salad in his mouth as if to put an end to the subject.

But Lucy would not be daunted. "I know plenty, because Mother told me," she countered, munching on a pickle. "Of course you saved Aunt Rosaleen. You told Uncle Jacob you saw that awful gambler abduct her."

"After Uncle Jacob shook it out of me," Daniel admitted with a self-effacing chuckle, then lifted his tin cup to his lips and took a long drink of the sweet tea Charity had made.

"Now you tell an interesting story about Lucy, Daniel." Travis's green eyes danced with fun as he reached over to tweak a glossy brown curl peeking from beneath his sweetheart's yellow bonnet.

Daniel shook his head. "Huh-uh! I'm smarter than that." His face took on a look of mock sternness when he turned it to Travis. "And I'd advise you not to ask about such things or my sweet sister just might shear those curls from your head like she did our neighbor's spaniel when she was five."

The mischievous grin he slid in Charity's direction set her heart prancing. This was a side of Daniel Morgan Charity hadn't seen. One she found both fascinating and endearing. It made her want to learn even more about him. A troubling thought.

Lucy smacked Daniel's arm. "Oh, you are horrid!" She joined the laughter around the quilt.

The playful banter between Lucy, Travis, and Daniel made Charity's heart ache. She remembered how Asa and Granger delighted in teasing her unmercifully. How she wished her brother was here to tease her about past escapades. Oddly, Asa's face remained vivid in her mind, while Granger's had faded to a blurry smudge.

The gentle look Daniel gave her suggested he sensed her sadness. . .and the cause of it. Was he remembering her admission the other evening on their way to Lucy's birthday dinner that she missed her brother? "I'm afraid we may be boring Miss Langdon with our silly reminiscences."

The kindness in his soft voice made Charity blink back hot tears. Why did he have to be so handsome, so charming. . .and so kind?

Renewed anger shot through her, stiffening her wilting resolve. She wouldn't accept compassion from a man who may have put Asa and Granger in their graves. Ignoring the thudding of her renegade heart, she brushed crumbs from her lap and lifted what she hoped was a cool, unaffected smile to him.

"Not at all, Mr. Morgan. In fact, I was about to ask if you and your sister recalled the occasion when Jenny Lind sang here in Madison in '51. My aunt Jennie still talks about how she and my uncle Silas traveled here to listen to the Swedish Nightingale sing in one of the old pork houses."

Lucy enthusiastically latched onto the topic, admitting that even at the tender age of six, she'd been awestruck by the sweet, pure quality of the woman's voice. "And I am convinced that at twelve, Daniel was entirely smitten by her. Why, I wouldn't be surprised if he doesn't still have that playbill with her picture on it tucked away somewhere in his room." Lucy grinned at her brother, whose tanned cheeks turned slightly ruddy.

They spent the next half hour discussing Miss Lind and her repertoire while devouring their picnic lunch.

While Daniel polished off the last piece of apple pie, Lucy began packing the lunch remnants and utensils back into the picnic baskets.

Charity followed her lead. She couldn't remember the last time she'd felt so carefree. . .so young. She'd actually shared a picnic with three Yankees and enjoyed it. Perhaps God was finally healing her heart and filling it with true forgiveness.

"Here." Lucy handed Daniel and Travis each a pie tin full of chicken bones. "Make yourselves useful and dispose of these somewhere in that grove of cedars."

With a salute from Daniel and a wink from Travis, they headed off to do her bidding.

Charity began helping Lucy fold up the quilts. "He's very handsome," she said, noting how Lucy blushed at Travis's wink.

"I've always thought so." Lucy glanced at the two men now several yards away as Charity transferred one end of a half-folded quilt into Lucy's hands. "Even if he *is* my brother," she added with a little laugh.

Heat leaped to Charity's face. "I was speaking of Mr. Ashby," she blurted breathlessly. How embarrassing to have Lucy think she found Daniel attractive!

Lucy laughed. "It's all right if you think Daniel is good looking. You'd have to be blind not to." She shot Charity a conspiratorial grin. "Oh, don't worry. I won't tell him. And yes,"—she gave a dreamy sigh—"Travis is so handsome he makes my eyes hurt."

What Lucy might tell her brother wasn't nearly as worrisome to Charity as her own feelings about Daniel. She wished her heart didn't race so when she was near him. And that his dark, smoldering gaze and handsome smile didn't snatch the breath from her lungs. She gazed at his tall, muscular form, his head thrown back, sharing a laugh with Travis.

Suddenly, a series of frightful images replayed in her mind. The ugly laughter of another tall, dark-haired Yankee echoed in her head. Again, she felt the soldier's fingers biting into her arm. Her kicking, flailing futilely as he dragged her to the cotton shed. The sounds of her dress ripping and her breathless sobs. The crack of Jericho's rifle butt on the soldier's skull. Then the blessed relief of being freed from the man's weight and sucking in grateful gulps of air untainted by the soldier's hot, whiskey-soaked breath.

A cold shiver shuddered through her.

What did it matter if Daniel Morgan had the ability to make her heart dance? It was also true that his mere presence could revive hideous memories for her. Agreeing to join this picnic had been a mistake. In the future, she must stay away from Daniel. . .and his family.

Chapter 7

Well, it's a fine pickle he's left us in, and no doubt about it!" Iris Pemberton paused in her indignation. With pudgy fingers, she lifted a china cup from the tray Charity held out to her and murmured cursory thanks.

Aunt Jennie shook her head and made tsking sounds as she leaned forward on the horsehair sofa to retrieve a cup of her own. "Why on earth would the schoolmaster leave without a word and the school term about to commence?"

Taking a seat beside her aunt, Charity pasted on a smile and groaned inwardly. Iris Pemberton's latest calamity seemed as punctual as her afternoon visits. Obliged to help entertain Iris, Charity wondered why she'd looked forward to the end of harvest.

Two weeks after she returned from Madison, the local farmers' corn harvest began arriving at the mill, and October had passed in a blur. Twelve hours a day, six days a week, the mill bought load after load of corn, ground it, and then shipped it to various buyers via the Jefferson, Madison, and Indianapolis Railroad.

Charity had been forced to work closely with Daniel as he provided her with information for bills of sales and lading. Though she'd begun each day resolving to steel her errant heart against his charms, it regularly disobeyed her. Daily her thoughts and affections were drawn toward him as if they were blossoms and Daniel was the sun. But at night, his sweet smile that lingered on her brain like a gentle shadow metamorphosed into the sneer of the soldier who'd tried to ravage her.

"Well, he won her affections, it would seem."

Iris's statement yanked Charity back to Aunt Jennie's front parlor with a gasp.

"My sentiments exactly, Miss Langdon!" Iris dropped her teacup to its saucer with a punctuating *clink*. "No one I'm aware of even knew the schoolmaster was keeping time with the young Widow Foster. But whatever possessed them to elope to Cincinnati is beyond my understanding."

"Surely there must be someone else in Vernon who could fill in as teacher— at least until a permanent replacement can be found." Aunt Jennie offered Mrs. Pemberton the hopeful thought along with the plate of iced tea cookies.

"You would think so." Iris daintily plucked a cookie from the plate. "But my poor Cletus has scoured the town and can find no one willing or able to step into the position." She paused to wash down a cookie with a sip of tea.

Heaving a sigh, she dabbed at her mouth with her linen napkin before dropping it back into her ample lap. "Cletus had so hoped to win reelection to the office of school board president. But with this embarrassment, that buffoon Atwell will most likely beat him out."

"Perhaps if we put our heads together and listed all the relatively clever, unmarried young women in Vernon, we could think of someone," Aunt Jennie suggested.

Desperate to escape the parlor before the discussion digressed into a gossip session, Charity hefted the china teapot from the mahogany table beside the sofa. "Oh, the pot is nearly empty," she said, rising. "If you ladies will excuse me, I'll go brew—"

Suddenly Aunt Jennie and Iris Pemberton both looked at Charity as if they had never seen her before, halting her words in midsentence.

Aunt Jennie's face bloomed with inspiration. "Iris," she addressed her friend while gazing directly at Charity, "now that the harvest is over, Silas only requires Charity's services in the office one or two mornings a week. Silas could easily bring home what little bookwork there is for her to do now."

Hope flickered anew in Iris Pemberton's despair-dulled eyes. "Why yes, Miss Langdon. Your aunt has on more than one occasion remarked upon how well-read you are. I understand you have an amazing grasp of mathematics, and you are a spin—" Iris's face flushed at her *faux pas*. Any woman who'd reached Charity's age of twenty-two and remained unmarried was considered a confirmed spinster.

"Me, a teacher?" Charity sank back to the sofa, her knees suddenly wobbly, and plunked the teapot down on the table. She had never entertained the idea of becoming a teacher.

"You do like children, don't you?" Encouragement laced Iris's voice.

Aunt Jennie rushed to answer for Charity. "Well, she doesn't *dislike* them, I'm sure."

"No, of course I don't dislike children. I just don't know. . . ." The notion seemed so foreign. Charity strove to let it sink in. When she first came to live with Uncle Silas and Aunt Jennie, her work at the mill had seemed a natural transference of her role at her family's cotton mill. But this. . .this was something she'd never considered.

She suddenly found herself engulfed in Iris Pemberton's smothering embrace. "Oh, you are a godsend, my dear. A true godsend!"

"Thank you, Mrs. Pemberton, but since Pearl decided to stay in Madison after our recent trip there, I'm sure Aunt Jennie will need my help around the house." Charity worked to extricate herself from Iris's lavender-scented grasp.

Aunt Jennie gave a dismissive wave of her hand. "Iris has given me the names of several women who might be interested in a domestic position. I'm sure we'll have someone to take Pearl's place in no time."

Any further thoughts Charity might have regarding her teaching at the common school seemed to have been rendered immaterial. While Iris Pemberton and Aunt Jennie chatted excitedly about the upcoming school year and how they'd saved it, Charity sat in stunned silence.

The thought struck her that this might be God's answer to her prayers. For weeks, she'd entreated the Lord to take away the uncomfortable feelings Daniel Morgan evoked within her. In her mind, she'd imagined Daniel moving back to Madison and taking a job nearer his family. But she would not question God. This was obviously, at least in part, a divine solution to her troublesome problem.

So why didn't she feel happier about it?

On Monday morning two weeks later, Charity trudged up Perry Street at the crack of dawn, her arms full of books and her heart full of trepidation. The November wind sliced through her light wool shawl, making her wish she had opted for her heavier one. Before the children began arriving, she would need to start a fire in the stove.

But as she neared the school, she was surprised to see wisps of light gray smoke curling skyward from the building's chimney. Charity hastened her steps. How would she garner the students' respect if one of them had arrived ahead of her?

When she approached the schoolhouse door, she noticed the wagon and mule parked outside the building. Her heart quickened. It was the mule and wagon Uncle Silas had given Daniel to use.

She hurried up the steps and pulled the door open. The schoolroom's inviting warmth met her. The place smelled of chalk, coal oil, and burning maple wood. She also noticed that the floor had been swept clean—another job that should have been hers.

Daniel knelt, feeding kindling into the black potbellied stove in the center of the room. He pivoted a quarter turn and cast a smile at her over his shoulder. "Thought you might enjoy a warm room for your first day of school."

"Yes. . .thank you." Charity hurried to close the door and keep out the chill.

Daniel rose, and it pricked Charity's heart to see him have to grasp a nearby desk to stand. "Well, I suppose I'd better be getting on to the mill." He took a couple of halting steps to the wall and plucked his hat from one of the pegs.

When he turned back to her, the shy look in his dark eyes melted her insides. She'd thought by taking this job, she'd escape Daniel Morgan and the uncomfortable effect he had on her. She hoped he wouldn't make this a daily ritual.

Charity hung her shawl on one of the wall pegs and strove to compose herself. How handsome he looked, even in his work clothes and that rumpled brown corduroy jacket.

She pasted what she hoped was a cool, aloof smile on her face. "Thank you very much, Mr. Morgan. I appreciate you preparin' the room for my first day. But as those tasks are part of my job as teacher, I will perform them from now on."

A hurt look flashed across his face for an instant before his smile dispelled it. "I wish you a good day, Miss Langdon." He plopped his brown felt hat over his head and slipped out the door.

Trying to put Daniel Morgan out of her mind, Charity moved behind the large desk at the front of the schoolroom and sank to the seat of the sturdy, well-worn oak chair. Suddenly something red caught her eye, and she picked up a shiny Winesap apple from the desktop. The ache in her heart burrowed deeper. Ridding herself of this worrisome feeling might be more difficult than she'd thought.

Thankfully, the children soon began arriving. After the brief introductions, Charity's lessons, which she'd spent hours preparing, demanded her full attention.

Charity found the eight boys and eleven girls, ranging in ages from six to thirteen, curious, attentive, and eager to please her. She suspected they enjoyed a change from the previous schoolmaster.

Happily, none of her students proved unruly or disagreeable. But she found one little fellow especially endearing. With his earnest attitude, sharp mind, and a Georgian accent to match her own, seven-year-old Henry Porter quickly claimed a special place in Charity's heart.

At noon, Charity was surprised to see the boy remain at his desk rather than join the other children in the schoolyard. A glance at the floor along the wall beneath the coat pegs told her all of the lunch buckets had been claimed.

"Henry, didn't you bring a lunch?" Charity walked to his desk where he sat marking on his slate with his chalk.

Henry shrugged his narrow shoulders. "I didn't wake up in time to fix anything."

Anger flared inside Charity. What kind of mother left her child to fix his own lunch? "Why didn't your mother fix you something?"

"Ma's dead," he said matter-of-factly. "And Pa was still asleep."

At his desk, she looked down at his slate, expecting to see a childish drawing. Instead, she saw a division problem. "Henry, the division problems are for the fifth grade students, not the second grade."

He shrugged again. "I know, but I like trying to figure them out."

Charity's heart went out to this little motherless son of the South who shared her love of numbers. "Very good," she said, picking up his slate to examine his work. "But look, you must carry this number forward." She picked up his piece of chalk to make the correction. "But that is enough work for a while." She put down the slate and chalk and took Henry's hand, urging him up. This child would not do without lunch if she had to forfeit her own. "Why don't you come and share my lunch with me. I know I've packed more than I can eat."

"Henry." The man's voice that accompanied a brief gust of cold air stopped Charity and Henry, turning them toward the doorway. "I brought your victuals." The scraggly bearded, thin-framed man stepped into the schoolroom and held out a battered dinner tin.

Charity noticed that Henry accepted the lunch bucket with muted enthusiasm. Not having a mother, he'd probably thought it would be fun to share his new teacher's lunch.

Turning his attention to Charity, the man dragged his hat off his head, revealing a shock of sandy-colored hair the same shade as Henry's. "Forgive me for intrudin' ma'am, but I didn't want the boy to do without." His silky Georgian drawl caressed Charity's ears with the sound of home.

"Not at all—Mr. Porter, I presume?"

He dipped a deep bow. "Sam Porter, if I might be so bold as to introduce myself." His green eyes sparked. "I do believe I detect the accent of a Southern lady."

"Charity Langdon," she said. "I was born and raised in Peachtree, Georgia."

Sam Porter's face lit. "Why yes. I know the place very well. Before the war, my family owned Willow Grove Plantation just north of Atlanta."

Charity gave a little gasp. She could hardly believe her ears. Her family had done considerable business with Willow Grove Plantation. "You're one of the Willow Grove Porters? My family owned the Peachtree Creek Cotton Mill. We milled your cotton!" Her words came out in an excited rush.

"My, my." He shook his head and chuckled. "Fancy us meetin' up North like this. I'm surprised we didn't become acquainted at one of my mother's famous soirees." His eyes twinkled. "For if I had met you, I surely would have remembered."

Charity's face warmed. Though she found his gallantry admirable, surely he knew such an invitation would likely not have been proffered to the daughter of a mill owner. "I'm afraid I was affianced by the age of seventeen and didn't attend many soirees, Mr. Porter." At least her answer was true.

"And your young man?" The cautious tone of his question suggested he had guessed the answer.

"He fell at Peachtree Creek." She found herself relishing the attention of this Southern gentleman.

Sam Porter nodded somberly. "Please accept my sincere condolences. The South lost many a good man."

"Did you serve then, Mr. Porter?" The conversation had whisked Charity back to the Georgia that used to be. She smoothed her hands down the folds of her skirt, almost imagining she was entertaining a gentleman caller back home in her mother's parlor.

He straightened, standing a little taller. "Why yes, ma'am. I'm proud to say I fought under General P.G.T. Beauregard until I took gravely ill and was returned to my home." The muscles along his jaw hardened. " 'Bout the time I got on my feet, that devil Sherman's minions swooped down on our fair state, and me and my family had to run for our lives."

Sam's eyes exhibited the same distant, empty look she'd seen in countless pairs of Southern eyes since the war's end. His voice lowered to barely above a whisper and his shoulders sagged. "It's all gone now—Willow Grove, all our slaves, and even my parents. All gone." He cocked his head to the left. "We took refuge a few miles south of here in Clark County, Indiana, with my late wife's elderly cousin." He shook his head sadly. "Now they're both gone, too."

Charity offered an understanding nod. She was not surprised to learn that like her, Sam and his family had fled north as General Sherman's army poured into the South.

Then he gave her the lopsided grin she'd seen replicated on Henry's little face. "This past summer, I got work as a night watchman for the Jefferson, Madison, and Indianapolis Railroad. That's what brought us to Vernon."

Charity understood now why Henry's father had been asleep when Henry left for school. The war had displaced so many people from her native state. She wondered how many times a similar scenario had played out among her fellow Southerners. "At least the Lord has blessed you with a fine son." She smiled fondly at Henry, who opened the dinner pail, releasing the smell of bacon.

"Yes, I suppose He has." Sam Porter seemed eager to linger while Henry quietly ate his lunch at his desk. "I've been thinkin' I need to get Henry back to church. My Bess—God rest her soul—would want that." Sam's face brightened as with sudden inspiration. "What church do you attend, Miss Langdon—it is *Miss*, I presume?"

"Yes, it is." There seemed to be something almost too smooth about Sam Porter, but Charity found herself drawn to these fellow refugees from her home state. "I attend the little brick church just up the road here at the top of the hill. I would like to extend the hand of Christian fellowship and invite you and Henry to worship there with our congregation this Sunday."

Sam's gaze held Charity's for a long moment. "Why, thank you, Miss Langdon." He lifted her hand and brushed his lips gently across the back of it. "May I say it's been a true pleasure to make your acquaintance? I very much look forward to seein' you at church this Sunday." His lingering gaze left little doubt that he would like to become better acquainted with her.

He tousled his son's hair. "You be good for Miss Langdon now, you hear?" Though lightly said, Sam's parting admonition seemed lacking in warmth.

Munching his bacon sandwich, Henry nodded mutely.

When Sam had gone, Charity walked to her desk and sat in the oak chair. She gazed at the boy who'd remained curiously quiet during the entire conversation between her and his father, then picked up the apple from the desktop and took a bite. The fruit filled her mouth with sweetness and just enough tartness to tingle the inside of her jaw. Sam Porter, she reflected, was not a bad-looking man. And he had displayed the same impeccable manners she had observed in the most refined Southern gentlemen. So why wasn't she more excited by the fact that he had shown a decided interest in furthering their acquaintance?

She took another bite of the apple Daniel had left for her. Looking at the fruit in her hand, she knew the answer.

Chapter 8

J ust a couple of Rebs. They deserve each other!"

Daniel stood at the mill's window and mumbled the disparaging sentiment, which he immediately regretted. The words didn't relieve the pain in
his heart. Nor did the sight below amend his opinion of the mill's new employee.
He didn't like Sam Porter one little bit.

Scowling, he watched Porter drive one of the freight wagons into the mill
yard with Charity at his side. Since the war, he'd seen many men like Porter—
spoiled sons of Southern planters. Deprived of their lavish, indolent way of life,
they'd found themselves with few skills and little ambition and ill-equipped to
carve out a decent living.

It hadn't pleased Daniel to learn that it was Charity's urgings that prompted
Silas Gant to hire the Southerner to haul grain to the train depot and lumber
to paying customers. Ironically, it was Daniel who'd suggested they needed to
hire an additional man in order to free him and Charlie Brewster from the time-
consuming tasks. But when he learned that Porter had been sacked from his
night watchman's job for the railroad, Daniel had questioned the wisdom of
Gant's choice.

Also, Daniel had to admit that the man's thick Southern accent was an
added daily irritant he could well do without. As he'd done with Charity, Daniel
had fought the repugnant feelings Porter's accent evoked. The war was over. It
was patently unfair to scorn people simply because of their speech. But unlike his
reaction to Charity, Daniel had sensed an innate meanness in the man.

He'd witnessed no particular act that would deem Porter unfit to work at
the mill. But he'd seen a series of troublesome incidents that he felt revealed a
base, malicious nature in the man. To Daniel's mind, Porter was far too quick
with the whip when driving the mules. On more than one occasion, he'd seen
him kick the cats that prowled the mill. And yesterday, when Charlie Brewster
smashed his thumb while tightening the tension on the idler pulley, Porter actually sneered.

Daniel jerked away from the window, his scowl deepening. Last week,
he'd overheard Porter offering to squire Charity to Sunday services. A flash of
jealousy shot through Daniel. He feared that since Porter was a Southerner, it
might blind Charity to the man's true character.

The tight frown in Daniel's forehead relaxed only a bit when Charity
entered the mill, a serene smile gracing her lovely lips. The expression on her

face caused a painful stab in his chest. Was her happy mood the result of having been in Porter's company?

Even now in the midst of November's chill, her presence felt like a warm spring breeze against his heart. Since she'd begun teaching, he hadn't seen nearly as much of her. He found himself looking forward to these Saturday mornings when she came in to bring the mill's weekly paperwork up to date.

"Good morning, Daniel." Her smile widened to a bemused grin. "You look as if you had pickles for breakfast," she said with a chuckle. Her twinkling eyes set his heart frolicking like a colt in an April pasture.

"Sorry," he mumbled, "I suppose I just have things on my mind."

Why did she have to be so beautiful? He tried to think of something he might say to warn her about Porter. But however he might fashion such a warning, she was sure to dismiss it as nothing more than his bias against Southerners.

She brushed past him, leaving his heart aching and the scent of rose water tickling his nostrils.

Later, as Daniel worked to grind a load of grain to be shipped to Indianapolis, he couldn't get Charity and Porter off his mind. Several times he'd noticed Porter slip away to Charity's little office.

A scripture from Proverbs flashed into Daniel's mind. *"A sound heart is the life of the flesh: but envy the rottenness of the bones."*

It must be true. His heart felt anything but sound, and he ached all the way to his bones.

When Daniel went to close the sluiceway gate above the overshot wheel to stop the operation, he noticed Porter heading once again toward Charity's office. Irritation bristled through him. At least he had a reason to go chase Porter away from Charity. The ground corn needed to be bagged, loaded on the wagon, and taken to the depot before two o'clock.

What he saw when he reached the open doorway of Charity's little cubbyhole-sized office made his blood boil. Sam Porter was bent over Charity's hand, kissing it.

"Porter!" He barked the man's name, causing both Porter and Charity to jump. "The corn is ready to bag." He fixed the man with a glare. If Porter wanted to court Charity, he would need to do it away from the mill. That thought, however, offered Daniel's heart no ease.

An icy animosity glinted from Porter's eyes. "I'll be right there, *boss.*"

The emphasis the man put on the last word skated very close to insubordination, straining Daniel's temper to its limit.

Porter turned back to Charity, whose cheeks had turned a deep rose color. "I will see you Thursday then. Henry and I are both lookin' forward to it." With that, he turned and headed out of the office. When he passed Daniel, his knee bumped against Daniel's bad leg. Although he mumbled an apology, Daniel had the distinct feeling the man had done it on purpose.

When Sam had gone, Daniel ignored his better judgment and blurted out his thoughts. "Miss Langdon—Charity,"—since their time together in Madison, Daniel felt relatively comfortable calling her by her given name, hoping to encourage her to continue reciprocating in kind—"your personal relationship with Mr. Porter is none of my business, but—"

"Mr. Porter is the parent of one of my students. Nothin' more." Charity's face reddened. Her back stiffened, and her chin lifted a good inch.

Heat raced up Daniel's neck. "I never meant to suggest anything improper. . . ." What a mess he was making of things! If he'd set out to make her detest him, he couldn't be doing a better job.

Her features relaxed and her sweet smile returned, warming him all the way to the center of his heart. "I'm sure you didn't, Daniel. I cannot expect you to be familiar with Southern traditions of etiquette. I simply invited Mr. Porter and his son to Thanksgivin' services at our church and dinner afterwards."

Charity's gaze dropped for an instant to her desktop before returning to his eyes. Was that a look of shyness that flitted over her face? More likely it was embarrassment that he'd caught Sam kissing her hand.

"We—that is, Uncle Silas, Aunt Jennie, and I—would like very much to extend the same invitation to you. Unless, of course, you have plans to travel to Madison to visit your family on Thursday."

Her obvious disconcertion sent ridiculous shivers running through him. He would like to think that her nervousness was caused by his nearness. But more likely it was because she found extending the Gants' invitation to him distasteful.

"No, I hadn't planned to go to Madison. A train trip doesn't seem worth it for one day. I reckoned to do with whatever repast Mrs. Kilgore offered at the boardinghouse."

"Then can we expect you for dinner Thursday after church?" Was he imagining the hopeful gleam in her eyes?

Daniel's first inclination was to decline the offer. But maybe better to accept the invitation and keep an eye on Porter than to lie on his bed in the boardinghouse and stew all day Thursday. "I would be honored—and thankful," he said with a small laugh, hoping the reply didn't make him sound as much of a dunderhead to her ears as it did to his.

Daniel returned to work with a conflicted heart. The joy of knowing he would be spending Thanksgiving Day with Charity Langdon was dulled by the realization that they'd be sharing the day with Sam Porter.

Chapter 9

As their buggy crested the steep incline leading up to the church, Charity scanned the churchyard. She, Uncle Silas, and Aunt Jennie had made arrangements to meet Sam and Henry there before the Thanksgiving service. But Charity knew her sweeping gaze wasn't seeking out the Porters.

Last week, the look in Daniel's dark eyes when he agreed to come to Thanksgiving dinner had set her heart bouncing in her chest like an India rubber ball. But he'd made no promise to attend worship services.

Uncle Silas guided the matched pair of sorrels to the hitching post beside the church. Charity saw no sign of Daniel, and her heart sagged with her shoulders. Of course it was her Christian duty to hope others would worship in the Lord's house and to encourage them to do so at every opportunity. But she knew there was more to her disappointment at Daniel's absence. Somehow, despite her resistance and denials to the contrary, Daniel Morgan had become important to her.

When Uncle Silas lifted her from the buggy, the sight of Henry Porter's little smiling face buoyed her heart. Standing with his father near the church steps, he waved his hat to get her attention.

Sam Porter chastised his son's exuberance with a quick cuff to Henry's ear. Charity gasped at the sight. Though sorely tempted to express her disapproval at the man's harsh action, she exercised restraint. Sam did lack the gentling presence of a wife to help raise his son.

Sam strode toward her, wearing a smile as wide as the one he had, a moment earlier, squelched from his son's face. "Miss Langdon," he drawled out her name and dipped a deep bow. His too-tight, outdated gray wool coat stretched taut across his shoulders as he bent. The garment was clearly from his youth, before his shoulders had broadened.

Two weeks ago, when Henry had come to school in tears saying his father had lost his job with the railroad and that they might have to go to the poorhouse, Charity knew she at least had to try to help.

At first glance, it had seemed unfair to her that the railroad should sack Sam for only one instance of falling asleep while on the job. But last month, two brothers named Reno brazenly robbed a moving train a few miles east, near Seymour. So considering the extraordinary recent event, she better understood the railroad's heightened interest in security.

Unable to bear the thought of Henry suffering from his father's mistake, she'd convinced Uncle Silas to hire Sam as a teamster. The moment Sam began working at the mill, his attentions toward her intensified.

Pearl had told her some time ago it was high time she found a man. Sam was a fellow Georgian with the kind of Southern manners that made Charity feel at home. But despite her attempts to talk her heart into doing so, it refused to swoon for Sam Porter.

Henry tugged at her skirt, his hopeful face tilted up toward hers. "Will we have turkey for dinner, Miss Langdon?"

Charity laughed lightly. Although Sam had not managed to capture her heart, his son definitely had. She smoothed the boy's sand-colored hair away from his face. Today's Thanksgiving feast would be a rare treat for this mother-less child. "Yes, Henry, we have a huge one baking in the oven right now," she said, taking his little hand in hers as he licked his lips in anticipation.

She was still smiling when Sam offered her his arm. Just as she tucked her free hand in the crook of his elbow, the *clip-clop* of hooves on gravel turned her toward the lane leading up to the church.

Daniel's gaze met hers, but no smile touched his lips. From atop his bay stallion, he gave her a stony look and a terse nod.

Her heart performed its now familiar little flip in response to Daniel's presence. A feeling akin to resentment squiggled through her. If not for its stubborn insistence on being shackled to that Yankee, her heart would be free to care for Sam.

Jerking her head around, she tipped her face up to Sam's and gave him a wide smile. Perhaps if she just put her mind to it, she could divert her affection to a man more suited to her—a man whose son she adored.

Throughout the service, Charity's attention continued to drift unbidden across the aisle. More often than not, her look was met by Daniel's dark, piercing gaze.

Following the sermon, Reverend Davenport entreated the congregation to stand and join in singing the hymn "Come, Ye Thankful People, Come."

Charity glanced over at Daniel to see his scowl slide in turn from Sam's face to Henry's and then to hers. Aggravation prickled along her spine. Daniel's dislike of Sam had been obvious from the man's first day at the mill. To her understanding, Sam had never been late to work or missed getting a load of grain or lumber to its destination in a timely fashion. She surmised Daniel's disapproval of the man sprang from the fact that he was a Southerner. She could hardly blame Sam for responding negatively to Daniel.

Outside in the churchyard after the service, the two men regarded one another with an icy formality. Charity hoped their animosity toward one another wouldn't mar the day's enjoyments for Henry.

Several minutes later, the group arrived at the Gants' home. A cornucopia of savory and sweet smells greeted them as they all filed into the front parlor.

Henry licked his lips and his eyes grew large as he took in the elegant room. "It looks like a king's house," he said with a long, low whistle then looked up at his father. "Is this like the house you grew up in at Willow Grove?"

Sam frowned and thumped the back of his son's head soundly. "Mind your manners, boy!"

Charity had been about to follow Aunt Jennie into the kitchen to assist her and the hired girl Aunt Jennie had found to help with today's big meal, but seeing Henry's eyes well with tears, she stayed. "That must mean I'm a princess," she said, hoping to divert his attention from his father's chastisement.

"You look like one." He gave her a shy smile, and his little ears turned bright pink.

"I agree." Daniel's quiet voice drew Charity's attention across the room. His gaze caught hers in a tender grasp and she suspected her warm cheeks matched Henry's ears in color.

Glowering at Henry, Sam muttered something about children needing to be seen and not heard.

At his father's withering look, Henry took two quick steps backward. Before Charity could warn him, he knocked into the little mahogany table beside the sofa. It teetered, sending Charity's favorite picture of her mother crashing to the floor.

"Henry!" His son's name exploded from Sam's mouth, and his features turned nearly purple. He jerked Henry by the arm toward the picture on the floor. "You pick that up!"

Sam turned to Charity and cleared his throat. The embarrassment registering across his red face suggested he wished the floor would swallow him up. "I must apologize for the boy's clumsiness. Don't know what's got into him."

Henry seemed unable to move, a look of horror distorting his frozen face, and Charity's heart broke for him. "I'm sorry, Miss Langdon." The barely audible words shook from his tiny voice while tears slipped down his tortured face.

Ignoring Sam, Charity crouched and gave Henry a hug and wiped the tears from his cheeks. "Why, it's just a little ol' picture, Henry. Don't you give it another thought, you hear?"

Uncle Silas, looking uncomfortable, waved his hand to dismiss the incident. "That's right, Porter," he told Sam. "No real harm done."

Turning her attention to her mother's picture, Charity saw that although the photograph itself seemed undamaged, the glass covering it had shattered, and a large chunk of the walnut frame's corner had chipped off. But determined not to let Henry see her dismay, she hurried to deposit the damaged picture in the little drawer at the front of the table.

"I never really liked that frame, anyway," she told Henry with an indifference she didn't entirely feel and shoved the drawer shut. As she started to rise, strong fingers gripped hers, helping her up. She thought Sam had stepped forward to assist her, but straightening, she met Daniel's gaze and her breath caught. The look in his dark eyes could only be described as admiration.

Once again, she wished Daniel Morgan's presence didn't always make her feel off balance and breathless. To hide her disconcertion, she turned, took Henry's hand, and led him into the dining room.

Aunt Jennie and the hired girl were loading the long cherry table with a tantalizing array of delicious-smelling dishes. Charity hoped Henry would forget the accident and enjoy the meal. But even the huge roasted turkey steaming from the center of the table and its tempting aroma did little to brighten his demeanor.

After Uncle Silas gave the blessing, the conversation among the adults turned to such topics as the price of grain and the weather.

Charity glanced across the table at Henry's long face. Her heart wept for him as she watched him poke unenthused at the sweet potatoes on his plate.

Sam, seated beside Henry, seemed oblivious to his son's suffering. Between bites of corn bread dressing, he regaled Aunt Jennie with anecdotes of sumptuous dinner parties given at the plantation home of his youth.

It bothered Charity that Sam paid no heed to Henry's discomfort. But she knew a father couldn't be expected to take notice of a child's feelings like a mother would. She was again struck by the notion that the two desperately needed a woman's presence in their lives.

She prayed God might give her something to say that would lift Henry's spirits. But before she could think of something, Daniel—seated next to her—spoke up.

"You know, Henry," he said, causing the boy to raise his drooping chin, "when I was about your age and visiting a neighbor's home, I did something far worse than breaking a picture. And my offense was compounded by the fact that I did it on purpose."

Charity almost choked on her bite of mashed potatoes. Daniel's words seemed anything *but* an answer to her prayers. How callous of him to humiliate Henry further by bringing up the embarrassing incident! She shot him a sideways barbed look which, if he noticed, he chose to ignore.

But Henry gave no indication that the comment bothered him in the least. In fact, he looked surprised and pleased that an unfamiliar adult had addressed him at the table.

"Once when I accompanied my father to the home of Mr. Lanier, the richest man in town," Daniel went on, "I was fascinated by the crystal drops hanging from one of the table lamps in his front hall." Daniel paused to take a bite of turkey and wash it down with a swig of tea. "Well, sir, I noticed how the baubles made little rainbows on the wall, and I decided Mr. Lanier, being so rich, would never miss a couple. So when Pa wasn't looking, I stuffed two in my pocket."

The reactions to Daniel's confession were as varied as the diners around the table. Henry's mouth gaped, and Aunt Jennie gave a little gasp. Uncle Silas guffawed, while Sam became sullen.

Daniel grinned. "When Pa found out what I'd done, he marched me right back to Mr. Lanier's house. After I apologized and gave him back the glass baubles, I, at my father's urging, promised Mr. Lanier that I'd pull all the weeds from the acre of fencing around his considerable yard."

"Did you get a belt-tannin'?" Henry asked, his eyes growing wide.

Daniel shook his head. "No. Whenever I or my sister did something wrong, Pa wanted us to learn a real lesson from it. And he always said little was ever learned at the end of a belt." He finished the sentence with a pointed look at Sam, who responded with a sarcastic snort.

Remembering Sam's rough treatment of Henry, Charity pressed her napkin to her mouth, stifling a smile. She hoped Sam might take Daniel's father's opinion to heart.

"So what did you learn?" Henry asked around a bite of sweet potatoes, now fully engaged in both the meal and the story.

Daniel stabbed a piece of turkey, and his gaze slid from Henry's attentive face to Charity, setting her heart thumping. "I learned never again to take anything that wasn't mine, the Ten Commandments forward and backward, and that after pulling an acre of weeds, even lye soap won't get all the grass stains off your hands."

Everyone around the table laughed appreciatively except for Sam, who remained dour faced.

Charity sent up a special prayer of thanksgiving that God had found a way to restore Henry's joy.

But no joy shone from Sam's face. Instead, he glowered at Daniel. For an instant, the two men's steely glares crossed like rapiers over the Thanksgiving table.

As much as she would like to deny it, for Charity, there was no question as to the hero of the silent duel. He had raven black hair, hypnotically dark eyes, and no Southern accent.

Chapter 10

"Perhaps I should just go to church with Uncle Silas and Aunt Jennie as I always do." Pushing the lace curtain aside, Charity gazed out of her bedroom window on the courthouse square below, knowing full well she could not change her plans at this late hour. In doing so, she would disappoint little Henry and embarrass Aunt Jennie.

She felt as drab and cold as the winter scene outside her window. Since Thanksgiving, she'd made a concerted effort to deepen her relationship with Sam Porter. But as she waited for Sam and Henry's arrival, something closer to dread than joy filled her chest.

She'd told herself that God, in His infinite wisdom, had gifted her with the affections of a Southern gentleman—something rare this side of the Mason-Dixon Line. Obviously, Henry—whom she adored—needed a mother's gentle touch. And Sam needed a tempering influence in his life, especially in regard to his parenting of Henry. Since Sam and Henry had begun attending church, she'd made every effort to encourage them to continue the practice. So when Sam offered to escort her to church this morning, she'd agreed without hesitation.

Frowning, she allowed the curtain to fall across the window, obscuring the dismal view, and turned away, rubbing her arms. Regret ached in her bones like the early December chill. It all seemed so perfect. So why didn't it *feel* perfect?

Perhaps that was why she liked numbers. When it came to ciphering, there was no murkiness. Her father's old saying concerning arithmetic flashed to the front of her mind. *"Figures don't lie."* Through proper calculation, one came to the correct answer, and that was the end of it. Pure and simple. Sadly, other facets of life lacked the clarity of mathematics.

The bedsprings creaked in gentle protest as she sank to the edge of her bed with a sigh. She glanced up at the ticking clock on the fireplace mantel, and a tiny stab of panic attacked her midsection. In less than fifteen minutes Sam would be pulling up in front of the house.

Slowly, she forced herself to her feet and lifted her dark woolen cloak from the foot of her bed. "Dear Lord, if Sam and Henry are to be my future, then why do I feel so miserable?"

The answer to her prayerful, mumbled plea came like a rasped whisper, echoing from somewhere deep in her tormented brain. . . .

Daniel.

An elusive ache she didn't want to investigate throbbed in her chest. She thought again about how he'd attempted to alleviate Henry's distress at breaking her mother's picture by recounting an embarrassing story from his own youth. That simple act of kindness toward the boy had touched her deeply.

Yesterday at the mill, she'd noticed the disapproving look on his face when she accepted Sam's invitation to church. Although reason argued she shouldn't care one whit about Daniel Morgan's opinions, the memory remained vexing. And neither the cheery fire crackling in the fireplace nor the weight of the wool cloak enveloping her could dispel the dampness from her spirit.

She lifted her mother's worn Bible from the table by the bed and pressed it to her bosom. "Lord, take this feeling from me. Clear the way so that I might grasp, unencumbered, the future You have planned for me."

The prayer had no sooner left her lips when the distant sound of metal-banded wagon wheels crunching on gravel jerked her up with a start. She glanced out of the window and down on Perry Street. Sam and Henry had arrived. Her heart, which should have perked with gladness, sagged with resignation. Expelling another deep sigh, she plodded out of her room and down the staircase.

Charity's discomfiture intensified over the course of the morning. The more time she spent in Sam's company, the less she enjoyed it.

The subject of Reverend Davenport's sermon was peace. When he read the scripture from Isaiah 32:17, the words smote Charity's conscience as if God had breathed them directly into her ear.

" 'And the work of righteousness shall be peace; and the effect of righteousness quietness and assurance for ever.' "

She glanced down at Henry seated next to her in the pew, and a deep sadness gripped her. Her spirit felt neither quiet nor assured. If the effect of righteousness was peace, then what she was doing must not be right. In all good conscience, she could not allow the boy to believe she would one day become his stepmother when she felt no true affection for his father. With this thought in mind, she resolved to rebuff any future attentions from Sam, including accepting his offers to squire her to church.

So the following Tuesday when the invitation to Lucy Morgan and Travis Ashby's engagement party arrived in the mail, Charity was torn. If she accepted, it would mean she'd most likely be traveling on the train to Madison with Daniel Morgan and spending a considerable amount of time next weekend with him and his family. A disconcerting thought. But at the same time, it would effectively distance her from Vernon—and Sam Porter.

Beyond that, she would get to see Pearl again. Although not entirely unexpected, Pearl's decision not to return to Vernon after their trip to Madison in September had come as a blow to Charity. Yet knowing Pearl and Adam Chapman were on the verge of becoming engaged and would probably soon marry, she fully understood her friend's desire to be closer to her loved ones. But with Pearl's departure, Charity had felt acutely the loss of daily talks with her childhood friend.

Wednesday afternoon when she closed the schoolhouse door for the day, she still struggled with her decision about Lucy's party. Heading to the street, she hugged to her chest the little leather satchel filled with papers she would be grading this evening. The December wind bit her cheeks and whipped at her cloak as she trudged toward the apex of Perry Street. A sense of loneliness dragged her spirit down with her shoulders.

Squinting, she lifted her face to the gray sky. Icy crystals, which were not quite sleet yet not quite snow, pelted her cheeks. Ahead on her left, the little church loomed. Its sturdy brick facade beckoned, promising a haven for both her body and her spirit. As she did every Wednesday afternoon, old Annie Martin would be tidying the sanctuary in preparation for next Sunday's services.

Charity glanced down the hill. Uncle Silas and Aunt Jennie's home sat across from the courthouse, no more than fifty yards ahead. The weather was not so inclement that she needed to take immediate shelter. But looking up at the church, she knew it was the thought of Annie Martin's company more than the shelter that drew her.

She longed for a female confidante. Although she knew her aunt cared for her, Charity had never been especially close to her mother's sister. Aunt Jennie's personality so differed from her own that they rarely shared intimate conversations.

She turned toward the church, climbed the four stone steps, and pulled open the heavy front door. Slipping quietly inside, she was met by the smell of linseed oil, old books, and wood smoke.

"*Faites attention!* Be careful, *ma chère*. I have just swept the floor." Annie Martin poked her head, covered by a black wool bonnet, above the tall back of the front pew. "I would like to keep the mud out until everyone tracks it in Sunday morning." The crevices at the corner of her light brown eyes etched deeper with her smile.

"I'll be careful, Annie." Charity grinned as she slipped into the back-most pew.

Annie's coarse, dark wool skirt swayed with her ambling gait as she made her way to the back of the church, glancing down each pew as she passed. Charity knew she was checking to see that each held its allotted number of hymnals. When she came to the pew where Charity sat, she scooted in beside her.

The old woman cocked her head and fixed Charity with a curious look. Wispy curls of silver hair that still showed traces of auburn peeked out from the bonnet framing her aged face.

"So, ma chère, are you here to talk to me or to God?"

Charity smiled. She always loved listening to the woman's accent, which she'd inherited from her French fur-trapper father. "Maybe both," Charity said with a sad smile. She began telling her about Daniel, Sam, and Henry Porter, and her quandary concerning whether or not to accept Lucy Morgan's invitation. "I've tried to care for Sam for Henry's sake, but—"

"But your heart bends toward Mr. Morgan instead." Annie's eyes, cinnamon brown and flecked with amber, studied Charity's face.

Charity started to open her mouth to object to Annie's accurate deduction but shut it. There was no use in denying it. Annie Martin was far too astute. "Yes." The admission puffed out in a weary breath. It felt good to finally release the truth from its prison deep within her heart. Unwilling to meet Annie's gaze, she looked down at her hands clasped in her lap.

"And Mr. Morgan? He shows you no interest, ma chère?"

"Oh, no—I mean yes—yes, he does. In fact he. . ." Charity looked up, and heat leaped to her face at the knowing grin lifting the corners of Annie's mouth.

Annie took Charity's hands in her gnarled fingers. "Then why, ma chère? Why spurn the man your heart desires and try to force it toward one it rejects?"

Charity felt her jaw go slack at the absurdity of Annie's question. Surely Annie could guess the reason. "Because Daniel Morgan is a Yankee," she blurted. "He fought in the Union army!"

Annie's brows knit together in a frown, making Charity feel obliged to expound upon her explanation.

She met the old woman's narrowed look. "Sam is a Southerner like me, and he wants to go back to Georgia." She shook her head sadly. "I couldn't marry a Yankee. I just couldn't! They burned my home, killed both my brother and the man I was goin' to marry. And. . .and I can't even say in church what one of them tried to do to me!" She blinked back the hot tears springing to her eyes. That was the truth. And if Annie thought ill of her for saying it out loud, it couldn't be helped.

A kind, sad smile softened the wrinkles around Annie's mouth and eyes. "Ma chère, the war is over. Our Lord tells us we must forgive those who sin against us seventy times seven." Annie paused and breathed a deep sigh. Her knobby fingers gave Charity's a gentle squeeze. "I do not know who you should marry, or even *if* you should marry. But I *do* know one thing. You've got to scrub your heart clean of the past."

"The past."

Those two little words conjured up scenes so terrible and so vivid they still assaulted Charity's every sense. Irritation chafed up her spine. She had tried to forgive—ever since Jericho prayed with her the evening he saved her from that Yankee soldier. But how could she forgive when she couldn't forget?

She slid her hands from Annie's grasp. "I don't know, Annie. I don't know if I can."

Annie reached into her skirt pocket and pulled out a little black Bible. She thumbed the pages, then stopped and began to read the verse from First Corinthians Charity had committed to memory when she was but a small girl.

" 'And now abideth faith, hope, charity, these three; but the greatest of these is charity.' "

Annie closed the book, slipped it back into her pocket, and stood. "You must live up to your name, Charity. Unless your heart is scrubbed clean of all malice, it won't be a fit place for God's love to grow."

Charity rose and picked up her satchel. She followed the old woman out of the pew and gave her a wan smile. "I will try, Annie."

When Charity stepped out of the church, the cold wind smacked her face like the truth in Annie's words. She headed down the steep slope of Perry Street toward home, her heart heavier than when she'd left the schoolhouse. Had she truly tried to forgive? She thought she had. Wasn't shoving thoughts of the war out of her mind and settling into a life here the same as putting the past behind her? Wasn't that a kind of forgiving?

Charity knew the answer. There was a part of her heart that had refused to relinquish the hurt and the rancor.

By the time she reached her aunt and uncle's home, she knew what she had to do. Lucy Morgan had been kind enough to invite her to her engagement party. It was a small step, but perhaps a step in the right direction. Charity would attend the party, even if the thought of attending another social event with Daniel Morgan made her heart tremble.

Chapter 11

Lucy's doll."

At his aunt's quiet voice, Daniel straightened suddenly from lounging against the piano in his parents' parlor. With the considerable crowd milling around the room, he hadn't noticed Aunt Rosaleen settle herself on the stool in front of the instrument's keyboard.

He and his aunt had always enjoyed a special relationship since the role he played in her rescue from a riverboat gambler when he was six. But following the *Sultana* disaster, the bond between them had grown even closer with their common experiences as survivors of separate steamboat explosions.

His aunt nodded, her look directed across the room where Daniel's gaze had been fixed for the past several minutes. "Miss Langdon—she reminds me of the china doll Lucy had when she was little. Don't you remember? The one with the blond hair."

Daniel did remember. The doll had been as delicate looking as Charity. He even remembered it having a fancy blue dress—not so different from the blue party frock Charity was wearing this evening.

Daniel's gaze followed his aunt's. "Yes, I guess she does look something like that doll—except Charity is much prettier."

"Charity, hmm?" Aunt Rosaleen's teasing tone sent heat marching up Daniel's neck, making him wish he hadn't used Charity's given name. "I'm planning to play another waltz. Why don't you ask her to dance?" She gave his arm an encouraging pat. "You're supposed to be her escort, and the girl has danced with every male here but you, including John and Rory, who seem to find dancing with Charity far preferable to dancing with their sisters or cousins." She added the last with a laugh as she glanced over at her fifteen-year-old twin sons who were helping themselves to the punch bowl.

Daniel cleared his throat. In truth, he didn't particularly care for social events and would have preferred to forego this one if he hadn't feared it might tarnish his sister's joy. That, and knowing Charity would be attending. "I don't know, Aunt Rosaleen." He tapped his bad leg. "I never danced well before I limped. Now. . ."

"Nonsense! If you can walk, you can waltz." Aunt Rosaleen's blue green eyes flashed. Daniel had learned through the years to heed his uncle Jacob's oft-expressed warning, "When Rosaleen gets her Irish up, beware!"

Aunt Rosaleen's slender fingers slid expertly over the piano keys, executing a musical scale. She glanced across the room at Charity, who stood near the front window, chatting with Lucy and Travis, then gave Daniel's back a gentle shove. "Now you go over there and ask her for the next dance before one of your cousins beats you to it."

Daniel gave his aunt a grin of surrender. "As you please, Aunt," he said with a chuckle and started across the parlor. He had no idea how his invitation might be received, so he was glad Aunt Rosaleen had begun playing a few scales to nimble her fingers. Hopefully, the sound would drown out the thumping of his heart.

He and Charity had exchanged only a handful of words since they boarded the train for Madison this morning. Though polite and cordial, her demeanor toward him had remained decidedly cool. Beyond the obligatory pleasantries common etiquette demanded, she'd opted to spend the train trip engrossed in a penny magazine rather than conversation with him. Upon their arrival, she'd spoken to him only to confirm the time of the party before Jericho escorted her to his home where Charity would be staying the night.

He would ask for the dance to please Aunt Rosaleen, but Daniel crossed the room with low expectations and high trepidation.

Suddenly Charity turned from talking to Lucy and Travis and looked directly at him. Her mouth wore the remnants of a smile—probably in response to one of his future brother-in-law's famous jokes.

In that instant, Charity's beauty simply took his breath away.

Before Daniel could find his voice, Lucy piped up. "Daniel, you old stick-in-the-mud, you really must try to be more sociable!" Her brows pushed down into a perturbed V, but a light giggle danced through her words.

He hunched his shoulders and gave his sister the most innocent look he could muster. "Talking to Aunt Rosaleen doesn't count as being sociable?"

"Oh, you know what I mean," Lucy said with a huff. "Sometimes you act positively ancient, standing around talking to the old folks."

Charity's lips pressed tight together as if to stifle a giggle. The twinkle Daniel glimpsed in her blue eyes before she glanced away caused his heart to throb and his face to burn. Did she, too, think him stodgy?

Daniel looked toward the piano where his uncle Jacob had joined Aunt Rosaleen. Standing close behind her with his hands on her shoulders, Uncle Jacob bent forward. With his cheek against his wife's and his blond head pressed against her reddish brown hair, they seemed to be studying the sheet music together.

"Old folks? I don't know, sis. They look pretty spry to me."

This time, Charity's giggle burst free.

Daniel garnered his courage and turned his attention from Lucy to Charity. "Speaking of my aunt Rosaleen, Miss Langdon," he began, "I have it on very good authority that she is about to play a waltz. Would you do me the honor of partnering me for the dance?"

A look akin to panic flashed briefly across her face and his heart pinched. Perhaps she did find him distasteful. But then a sweet smile bloomed on her features, and it was as if the sun had risen inside him. "I would be honored, sir," she said with a demure dip of her head.

A moment later, the melody of the waltz filled the parlor, and couples began twirling and gliding over the polished wood floor to the three-quarter tempo of a Strauss waltz.

Daniel's first few movements were stiff and unsure. He hadn't danced since before the war. He prayed he wouldn't tread on Charity's toes or step on the hem of her dress and rip it. He could feel beads of sweat break out at his temples. What a clod she must think him!

He felt compelled to voice an excuse in advance of any possibly embarrassing faux pas. "I hope you will pardon my clumsiness. It's been a long time since I've danced." He was acutely aware of her hand in his and the warmth of her tiny waist against his arm.

"You're doin' fine." Her encouraging smile filled him with relief. Perhaps his feet couldn't dance, but that smile of hers set his heart waltzing.

For a while they danced without further conversation. Having slipped more comfortably into the rhythm of the steps, Daniel simply enjoyed holding Charity in his arms. He silently blessed his aunt for prodding him toward this blissful moment.

As the dance entered its final movement, Charity's uptilted face held both surprise and appreciation. "Why Mr. Morgan, you were bein' far too modest. Your dancin' skills are superb. How long has it been since you last waltzed?"

"I suppose it was at my engagement party five years ago."

An odd expression crossed her face, and Daniel regretted having divulged that information.

Just then, the waltz ended, forcing him to reluctantly release her. He bowed deeply toward her, his heart feeling as bereft as his arms. "Thank you for the dance, Miss Langdon. I enjoyed it immensely."

She dipped a quick curtsy. "Thank you," she murmured. Before she could say anything more, John and Rory appeared, plying her with cups of punch and each begging her for the next dance. One on either side of her, they bore her off toward the refreshment table.

Feeling oddly out of place, Daniel glanced around the room. Lucy and Travis had gone to sit together on the settee against the east wall, where they seemed to be engaged in intimate conversation. Mother and Pa were chatting with Uncle Jacob and Aunt Rosaleen by the piano. They were soon joined by his cousins, Lydia and Rose, and their husbands. Everyone seemed to have someone.

Perhaps it was the mention of his failed engagement, but for whatever reason, a wave of melancholy rippled through Daniel, and he found himself longing for a few moments of solitude.

Slipping out of the room, he headed for the hallway.

The library's open doors invited. He stepped into the darkened room and paused to light the oil lamp on the desk just inside the door. The warm, golden glow infused the space, illuminating its familiar comforts.

His gaze roamed the many bookshelves that lined the walls. How many blissful hours had he spent here as a boy, escaping to the exciting and wondrous worlds of Robinson Crusoe, Moby Dick, and Gulliver? But tonight he found no escape from the dispiriting feelings gripping him. This room, filled with so many memories, served only to accentuate his loneliness.

Crossing the braided rug that covered the center of the floor, he peered, unseeing, through the darkened window that divided the southern wall. A parade of memories marched before his mind's eye.

His spirit further deflated with the long, slow breath he expelled through his nostrils. Maybe Lucy was right. Maybe he was growing old and stodgy after all.

The sound of light footfalls along the hallway dragged him from his glum reverie. Lucy or Mother must be coming to fetch him back to the party.

But when the footsteps continued down the hall and he heard the door to Mother's sitting room squeak open, he breathed a relieved sigh. Lucy had probably gone to find the latest edition of *Godey's Lady's Book* to share with their cousins.

In another moment, the footsteps resumed then stopped at the library's open door. He turned, resigned to be dragged back to the party by his determined sibling. But it was Charity, not his sister, he saw framed in the wide doorway, and his heart did a quick flip.

"I forgot and left my reticule on the table in the sittin' room when Lucy was showin' me and your cousins pictures of the latest weddin' gown styles." She held out her arm to display the little black beaded bag dangling from her wrist.

Struck momentarily mute, Daniel stood gazing at her, his eyes unable to get their fill of the sight. In the soft light of the oil lamp, Charity Langdon looked like a golden, satin-clad angel.

Just as she made a motion to turn, seemingly poised to head back to the parlor, she turned back to him, lingering. "Lucy was wonderin' where you had gone."

"Tell Lucy I'll be along shortly," he managed, finally finding his voice. He tried not to think of how wonderful Charity had felt in his arms during their shared waltz.

She nodded and sent him a shy smile, and his heart galloped. "Well, Jericho should be along directly to fetch me, so I should be gettin' back. . . ." Suddenly, her smile evaporated, and she seemed to focus on something past him near the floor. "My mother had a trunk just like that one." As if drawn to the thing, she stepped into the room and walked to the trunk beneath the window.

Daniel glanced down at the dome-topped spruce trunk. "It's just full of old keepsakes." He remembered when Pa had bought it in '47 for the family's trip to Promise, Indiana, to visit his aunt Susannah, Mother's younger sister. He thought again of the fun he'd had playing around the Whitewater Canal near his aunt's inn while the family awaited the birth of his cousin, Georgiana.

"Ours held keepsakes, too—Mamma's weddin' dress that I'd planned to wear and things for my hope chest."

Something in Charity's voice told him her mother's trunk no longer existed. Her sad smile nearly broke his heart. "It was lost in the fire."

"I'm sorry." The two words seemed so insipid. . .so inadequate. But it was all he had to offer.

"Who was she—the girl to whom you were engaged?"

Daniel blinked at the unexpected question. "Phoebe Saunders—Bryant now."

"She's still alive?" Charity's confused look caused him to smile. Surely she didn't find it so incredible to imagine a young lady breaking off an engagement to him.

"Oh yes. Very much alive, married, and, to my understanding, the mother of four children." His grin widened. "Phoebe seemed to come to the conclusion that it would be far more prudent to marry a banker too nearsighted for the army than a man with perfect sight, who might not return from the war."

"I–I'm sorry." Charity's flustered demeanor thrilled Daniel more than the sentiment.

"Don't be. I've come to realize she did us both a favor." Daniel wished he could add that he'd only fully understood that truth since he'd met Charity.

"I was engaged once, too." Her quavering smile accompanying her admission suggested that unlike Phoebe, her intended was no longer living.

"And your intended. . . ?" The words crept out cautiously. He was sure he knew the answer but thought it only polite to inquire.

"He fell alongside my brother, Asa, at the Battle of Peachtree Creek."

"I'm sorry." This time when he muttered the trite condolence it chafed against his conscience. He was indeed sorry for the grief she'd borne. But he couldn't make his heart sorry that circumstances had rendered her unattached.

She nodded mutely, her gaze sliding back down to the trunk. "So many times I've wished we could have at least saved Mamma's trunk. But we—Jericho, Tunia, Pearl, and I—had only enough time to save ourselves and grab a few keepsakes and essentials before the fire took the house. I saved my mother's picture and her weddin' ribbons, but the rest. . ."

Charity's delicate chin quivered as tears welled in her eyes and spilled down her cheeks, obliterating Daniel's restraint. He drew her into his embrace, muffling her soft sobs against his chest. As he rocked her in his arms, he sensed her tears were for far more than an old steamer trunk and its contents.

"I'm sorry. I'm so very, very sorry," he murmured against the sweet-smelling softness of her hair. Wishing he could offer her more in the way of comfort than the ridiculous sentiment, an unexpected prayer lifted from his heart.

Dear Lord, just help me know how to comfort her.

The next moment, she gently pushed away from him and lifted her tear-streaked face to his. Her long, honey-colored lashes still glistened with moisture while her petal pink lips beckoned. A look of sweet understanding passed between them, presenting Daniel with a temptation he felt powerless to resist. He lowered his head, and her soft, sweet lips welcomed his.

In the midst of their tender kiss, Daniel found a joy beyond any he'd ever known—and with it, a new purpose and a new prayer. From this day forward, all he wanted from life was to love, comfort, and care for Charity Langdon.

Suddenly, she pushed hard away from him, ripping his heart asunder along with their embrace. She said nothing, but the look of horror and disgust on her face spoke agonizing volumes.

Watching her flee the room, Daniel was left in tortured confusion, his head spinning and his heart writhing.

Chapter 12

I cannot imagine what possessed me!" Charity stabbed the needle into the red wool material with unnecessary ferocity. "I should have known such a bright color would hurt my eyes when I chose it."

Aunt Jennie looked up from the tatting work in her hands. "You said red is the boy's favorite color. And red *is* traditional for Christmas."

Charity dropped the half-finished coat she was making for Henry into her lap and rubbed her eyes. Lately it seemed everything set her nerves on edge. And she didn't like the feeling one bit.

"I could have Sarah Kerns finish it." Aunt Jennie's offer tiptoed out tentatively. "According to Iris, she does excellent work, and—"

"No!" Charity felt ashamed when her barked word made Aunt Jennie jump. She quickly tempered her tone. "I'm sorry, Aunt Jennie. This is my Christmas gift to Henry, and I should finish it myself. It's just that it gets dark so soon now, and this color is hard to work with in the lamplight."

Aunt Jennie narrowed her eyes at Charity and pursed her lips. "I must say, I don't know what to make of you these days, Charity. You've been in a sour mood ever since you returned from Madison. I trust Dr. Morgan and his family were in no way inhospitable to you."

"No. No, of course not. Dr. Morgan and his family were most congenial," Charity muttered.

Hoping to put an end to Aunt Jennie's troubling questions, Charity popped up from her sewing chair, draped the wool material over the chair's arm, and walked to one of the room's twin fireplaces. She picked up the iron poker and jabbed at the glowing maple logs in the hearth, feeding them oxygen and coaxing a renewed blaze from them. The smoke filled her nostrils and lungs, making her cough. But she welcomed the fire's heat scorching her face and giving her a reason to have flushed cheeks.

In truth, she knew all too well the cause of her ill humor. She'd been unable to get Daniel Morgan or their shared kiss off her mind in the week since she'd returned to Vernon. That she'd allowed such a thing to happen constituted only part of her shame. The fact that she'd enjoyed the kiss—had welcomed it—compounded her mortification. The night Jericho bashed that Yankee soldier in the head, saving her from an unthinkable fate, she vowed she would die before letting another Yankee touch her in such an intimate way. It had been the sudden memory of that vow washing through her on a wave of humiliation that had propelled her from Daniel's arms.

The pain she'd glimpsed in his dark eyes still gouged at her conscience. His intentions had been chaste, she had no doubt. In that brief moment of forgetfulness, she'd experienced a flash of unimagined joy. But the next moment, the past had intruded, rising between them like a dark and sinister specter.

And so it would always be. As kind, gentle, and caring as Daniel Morgan was, she feared there'd always be a part of her heart that would find him contemptible.

She'd stayed an extra day with the Emanuels so she wouldn't have to travel back to Vernon on the same train with Daniel. Thankfully, since her return to Vernon, she'd been too busy with her teaching job and helping Aunt Jennie around the house to spend any time at the mill. After Pearl left Uncle Silas and Aunt Jennie's employ, they'd had a series of housemaids, each staying only a few days. At present, they were once again without domestic help.

Aunt Jennie's voice penetrated her reverie. "I know it will be a lot of extra work, but I'm glad you invited Mr. Porter and his little boy for Christmas. Having a child here will make the day more festive, don't you think?"

Charity hurried to agree, glad that her aunt had abandoned the subject of Charity's latest trip to Madison.

"I actually enjoyed the little lad's company at Thanksgiving, despite the unfortunate accident with your mother's picture," Aunt Jennie said with a soft laugh.

"I'd nearly forgotten." Charity crossed to the little mahogany table. "I want to buy a new frame for Mamma's picture."

She opened the table drawer and gave a little gasp. The picture, frame and all, was gone. Down to the last shard of broken glass.

"Aunt Jennie. Did you move Mamma's picture?"

Her aunt craned her neck around, her face full of surprise. "Why no, dear. It's not there?"

"No," Charity breathed the word softly. She continued to stare at the empty drawer, as if by looking hard enough she might cause the picture to materialize.

Aunt Jennie's brow puckered. "I recall asking Deloris. . .you remember Deloris, don't you? She was the second housemaid after Pearl left."

Charity gave an impatient nod, and Aunt Jennie resumed her disjointed thought. "Anyway, I had the woman pack away several pieces of bric-a-brac to make room for Christmas decorations. She must have found the picture in the drawer and packed it away in one of the boxes."

Aunt Jennie's shoulders rose and fell in an unconcerned shrug. "I'm sure that's where it is, but I'm afraid we must wait until after Christmas to look for it. Silas would not be well pleased to have to fetch those boxes down from the attic then carry them back up again."

Charity's heart ached. She could only pray her aunt was right. The thought of losing such a dear memento was crushing. She returned to her sewing, determined to climb to the attic and search for herself at first opportunity.

Exhaling a soft sigh, Charity took her work back upon her lap, then reached across the table beside her chair and turned up the wick on the kerosene lamp. She wasn't even half done with Henry's coat. And with school and helping Aunt Jennie with Christmas preparations crowding her days, Charity would have little time for snooping in the attic.

As she worked the bright thread around a buttonhole, Charity's mood lifted with her smile. Like Aunt Jennie, she looked forward to Henry's presence at Christmas. Although she'd stopped accepting Sam Porter's attentions, she could not bear to distance herself from the little boy who'd become dear to her. Having noticed the ragged state of his patched coat, she'd decided to make him a new one. It warmed her heart to imagine his shrieks of glee when he discovered his new red coat on Christmas Day. She was smiling at the thought when several sharp raps at the front door yanked both her and Aunt Jennie's attentions across the parlor to the hallway.

"I'll get it." Once more, Charity rose and set her needlework aside. Hopefully, it was the woman Iris Pemberton most recently recommended as a possible housemaid.

But when Charity opened the door, her heart shot right to her throat. Daniel stood on the porch, the December wind batting the brim of his slouch hat.

"I just returned from taking a load of corn to the depot. As it is the end of the day, I thought I'd bring by the bill of lading." He looked everywhere but her face.

Charity reached for the square of yellow paper he held out to her, careful not to allow their hands to touch during the transfer.

"Might I come in? I'd like a word or two with Mr. Gant, if he's here." At last, his gaze settled on hers.

"Yes—yes, of course," she murmured, embarrassed by her lapse of manners. "Uncle Silas is in the library." She shuffled backward a couple of steps, making room for him in the cramped space. Her pulse raced. She hadn't been this close to Daniel since that evening in the library at his parents' home.

He dragged off his hat and twisted it in his large hands. His gaze skittered away from hers again, and she suspected his mind, too, had returned to the moment of their warm embrace.

"Charity. . ." Her name drifted out on a slowly exhaled breath, and his dark eyes looked deeply into hers. "I want to apologize—"

"No apology needed, Mr. Morgan." Her heart throbbing, Charity feigned a light tone. "I'm sure Uncle Silas will be glad to talk with you." She then whirled around and led him down the short hallway. She knew well he wasn't referring to his unannounced appearance. But she couldn't bear to hear him say he was sorry he had kissed her.

After leaving Daniel in the library with her uncle, Charity rejoined her aunt in the parlor. Unable to concentrate on her sewing, she managed only a few stitches while keeping her ears perked for footfalls in the hallway.

A few minutes later, she heard Uncle Silas's and Daniel's unintelligible voices and their footsteps moving toward the back of the house. A thread of disappointment wove through her. What was the matter with her? Why should she long for another glimpse of Daniel Morgan when she'd been avoiding him at all costs since her return from Madison?

She jabbed the needle into the wool. When its point struck her finger, she emitted a soft cry of pain.

"Be careful, my dear," Aunt Jennie chided gently. "Perhaps you should use a thimble."

Charity continued her work in sullen silence, wishing there was such a thing as a thimble for the heart.

Chapter 13

W here do you go, Daniel, when you look off into that place the rest of us can't see?"

Uncle Jacob's quiet words pulled Daniel back to his parents' parlor. Grinning, he turned to his uncle and accepted the mug of hot apple cider he held out to him. He inhaled the fragrant steam spiraling from the mulled drink. "Sorry," he murmured, wishing his uncle wasn't so perceptive.

Uncle Jacob settled himself on the sofa across from Daniel's chair and breathed a contented sigh. "You've been staring at that Christmas tree for ten minutes, and I'll wager you couldn't tell me if Lucy got her way and topped it with an angel or my Rose won the argument and a star sits on its highest branch."

Unwilling to admit that his mind had indeed been absent, traveling unbidden back to Vernon, Daniel decided an evasive maneuver was the best tactic. "I didn't think preachers were supposed to gamble, Uncle Jacob," he said and sipped the warm, spicy cider.

"You know very well I meant it only as an expression. Don't change the subject. And no fair peeking." Uncle Jacob's blue eyes sparkled with fun.

Daniel averted his eyes from the spruce tree in the front corner of the parlor. He, Pa, Uncle Jacob, and Travis had spent the better part of the morning scouring the wooded hills on the north side of Madison for the two best-looking young spruces they could find. One now graced the front parlor of Uncle Jacob and Aunt Rosaleen's parsonage. The other stood across the room, being adorned in festive splendor by Lucy, Travis, and Daniel's cousins. From an adjacent settee, Mother and Aunt Rosaleen offered the enthusiastic young workers suggestions as to how they might best proceed.

"Why, it's an angel, of course, Uncle." Daniel gave Uncle Jacob a sly grin. "You know Lucy always gets her way."

A rich, throaty chuckle burst from Uncle Jacob's lips. "That she does," he admitted, his attention turning to Lucy, who stood laughing with her intended across the room. "The poor fellow had no idea his fate was sealed the moment your sister set her cap for him."

Daniel watched Lucy and Travis argue playfully over the placement of a brightly colored glass bulb. At another time, his uncle's comment might have brought an easy grin to his face. But not now. Not with the rich smell of pine in his nostrils, the taste of spiced cider on his tongue, and the dazzle of Christmas brilliance all around him. Instead, his mouth drooped with his heart. To his shame, he felt a wave of envy swell up in his chest.

He wrapped both hands around the warm cup of cider and gazed into its amber contents. "Oh, I don't know, Uncle. I'd say Travis is one lucky man."

"That he is, Daniel." The smile in Uncle Jacob's voice faded, and Daniel could sense his elder's gaze. "Hmm," he murmured in that knowing tone that warned Daniel his thoughts had been breached. "That brings us back to where we were, doesn't it?"

Daniel said nothing as he studied the tiny brown specks of grated cinnamon floating in his cider. There was no use in trying to evade Uncle Jacob's dogged curiosity.

"You know," Uncle Jacob's voice lifted, "just this past week I joined two couples in marriage. And each of those four people had either passed a fortieth birthday or was nearing it. You are still a very young man, Daniel. I have no doubt there is someone out there for you."

Daniel's mouth twisted in a wry grin. If only his problem was as simple as desiring to find a wife. Such an obscure longing didn't approach the anguish of having lost his heart to one who considered him repugnant.

"Ah, I see." Uncle Jacob dragged out the words in a low tone of enlightenment. "Miss Langdon, I presume?"

Daniel nodded. His jaw jerked with a feeble smile. "I'm afraid she finds me. . .distasteful. I assume because I wore the Union uniform."

His uncle reached over and tapped the knee of his bad leg. "Does she know about Andersonville?"

"No." Daniel's scalp prickled at the name of the place. He didn't like to think about it, let alone hear the word spoken. Daniel's spirit ebbed with his sigh, and he shook his head. "Maybe it's just as well, Uncle Jacob. There are so many memories—bad ones—on each side. I don't know how it would ever work."

"Daniel,"—Uncle Jacob reached over and patted Daniel's knee—"with God, all things are possible. God allowed this girl to set your heart alight for a reason. Maybe it's to be your helpmate, and maybe it's for an altogether different purpose. Let God guide you, Daniel. Don't close your mind, or heart, to any possibilities."

Daniel noticed Aunt Rosaleen had gone to the piano and begun softly playing a carol. A shuffling sound in the hall drew his attention to the parlor doorway. Pa, who had left sometime earlier to deliver a Christmas Eve baby, stood smiling at his family. Snowflakes still clung to his hat and caped shoulders. His arms were filled with several brightly wrapped packages.

Amid squeals from the girls, Mother rushed to give him a tender kiss and divest him of some of the colorful bundles.

At the sight, Daniel's heart throbbed with a sense of loneliness. How was

Charity spending her Christmas Eve? Would she like the gift he made for her, or would she take offense?

When he joined his family around the piano to sing "It Came Upon the Midnight Clear," Daniel marveled at how such an idyllic scene could seem incomplete. How he longed to have Charity by his side, gazing up at him adoringly as Lucy was doing to Travis.

As he sang the words of the song's third verse, they convicted his heart.

Yet with the woes of sin and strife
The world has suffered long;
Beneath the angel strain have rolled
Two thousand years of wrong;
And man, at war with man, hears not
The love-song which they bring;
O hush the noise, ye men of strife
And hear the angels sing.

Charity cared for him, he was sure of it. He'd felt it in her kiss. He'd seen it in her eyes. The war was over. If he could put it behind him, so could she. He vowed to return to Vernon with a renewed resolve to win her heart.

Chapter 14

For me?" The light in Henry's wide eyes as he unwrapped the red wool coat and cap Charity had made for him set her heart aglow.

"Of course," Charity said with a laugh. "It certainly wouldn't fit anyone else here."

Henry wasted no time in shrugging on the coat and plopping the cap on his head.

Charity, her aunt and uncle, and Sam and Henry had just moved from the dining room to the parlor following a sumptuous Christmas dinner. Thankfully, two weeks ago, Aunt Jennie had hired a widow and her fifteen-year-old daughter to help with the cooking and other domestic chores.

It had thrilled Charity to watch Henry enjoy the meal. In fact, all morning her heart had warmed seeing the wonder and joy glowing from his little face. Several times during the Christmas service at church this morning, she'd questioned the wisdom of encouraging the child's attachment to her. Clearly, he had begun to see her more as a mother figure than simply a teacher.

And it wasn't just Henry. Sam, too, had shown signs of having been emboldened by her invitation for him and Henry to join her and the Gants for Christmas. She'd done her best not to encourage him, addressing him only by his surname and keeping Henry between them in the church pew. And she'd been adamant that she would ride to and from church with Uncle Silas and Aunt Jennie. But despite her efforts to dampen his ardor, Sam's attentions toward her had intensified.

But looking at Henry's happy face, she knew she'd made the right decision. She'd had the power to make the little boy's Christmas a delight instead of the dismal day he would have most likely spent otherwise.

"Look, Pa, look at my new coat and hat!" Henry scampered over to Sam then pulled up short as if remembering himself.

"That's mighty fine, boy. Mighty fine." Sam's eyes held little warmth when he spoke to his son, a reaction Charity had noticed several times before. It also bothered her that she'd never heard Sam call Henry "son." His distant demeanor seemed to keep the child at arm's length. "Now show some manners, boy, and thank Miss Langdon for her gift." The odd look on Sam's face sent warning bells clanging inside Charity. Did that little smirk suggest he saw Henry as a way to her heart?

Henry proceeded to do just that, throwing his little arms around Charity's waist in an affection-starved hug. Although Henry received several other gifts, including marbles and two school tablets from Uncle Silas and Aunt Jennie and a Barlow knife from Sam, his favorite present was clearly the new coat and hat. He refused to take them off, even when beads of sweat popped out on his forehead.

As evening approached, sending shadows stretching across the parlor, conversation waned. Only the crackling and popping of the fireplaces and Uncle Silas snoring in his chair disturbed the silence.

At length, Aunt Jennie daintily stifled a yawn with her fingertips and rose from her chair. "Come, Henry." She reached a hand out to the child playing with his marbles on the floor. "Let's go ask Mrs. Akers and Matilda to wrap up some of those iced cookies for you to take home."

Henry quickly stuffed the marbles into his new coat pocket then scrambled to Aunt Jennie's side and took her hand.

Charity found herself in the uncomfortable position of sitting alone on the sofa beside Sam with only her sleeping uncle as chaperone. Rising, she gave a nervous little laugh. "Perhaps I should go help Aunt Jennie and Henry with those cookies."

"I would rather you not." He grasped her arm, compelling her to sit back down. "I'd like a few words with you."

The serious look on Sam's face filled Charity with trepidation. Feeling like a rabbit cornered by a fox, she forced herself to not bolt for the kitchen.

He reached inside his coat and pulled out a pamphlet. "There's a new South bein' built, Charity." He waved the paper beneath her nose. "Land can be bought for a fraction of what it would have cost before the war. We could go back—you, me, and Henry—we could start anew."

Charity leaned farther away from him, repelled by his suggestion. She, too, had seen the advertisements—publications put out by carpetbaggers looking to profit from selling stolen lands back to displaced Southerners. "Sam, I–I'm not prepared to speak of such things."

The scowl drawing his brows into a V disappeared as quickly as it had come. He stuffed the pamphlet back into his coat. "I understand. I'm gettin' ahead of myself. First things first."

Brightening, he reached back into his coat pocket and pulled out a small pewter box. "I have somethin' for you that I saved until. . ." He glanced at Uncle Silas, whose bottom jaw sagged as he continued to snore loudly. "Until we were somewhat alone."

Charity's heart quaked. As much as she would like to be Henry's mother, her every instinct rebelled against becoming Sam's wife. "Really, Mr. Porter, I cannot—"

"Nonsense. Of course you can. You and your kin have been more than generous with me and my boy. At least allow me to give you this little token of my affection." He flipped open the hinged box to reveal a gold locket necklace.

Gazing at the piece of jewelry, Charity felt only one emotion—anger. It was obvious that Henry didn't eat as well as he should. He wore tattered and patched clothes to school, and his boots looked a half size too small with soles worn nearly paper thin. How dare this man allow his own son to go wanting while he bought expensive trinkets for the object of his affection?

Charity took the box, snapped it closed, and handed it back to Sam. "It's a lovely gesture, and I do appreciate the thought. But I can't accept it. I would much rather you return the necklace and use the money to buy Henry a new pair of boots."

Sam's face reddened. His jaw hardened, and anger flashed from his eyes like barbed lightning. For a moment, Charity feared he might strike her. He shoved the box back into his coat pocket and shot to his feet. "I doubt you would have turned it down if that Yankee, Morgan, had offered it!"

Charity opened her mouth but could think of nothing to say that might calm him.

Sam's hands balled at his sides in fists. "Forgive me, ma'am. I mistook you for a Southern lady. I see you're nothing but a Yankee-lover," he said, grinding the words through his clenched jaw.

Just that moment, Aunt Jennie and Henry appeared in the parlor.

Sam glanced at Henry who was lugging a linen-covered basket with both hands. "Gather your things, boy. I fear we may have overstayed our welcome." Although he seemed to make a mighty effort to temper his tone in Aunt Jennie's presence, his voice still grated with a hard edge.

By the time Charity had Henry's new coat all buttoned up, Sam managed to get control of his voice. Aunt Jennie woke Uncle Silas and they all bunched in the front hallway. There, Sam delivered his thanks and good-byes in the smooth, sugary tones of a Southern gentleman.

But all the while, fear, anger, and disgust knotted in Charity's chest. Now she understood the look of fear she'd seen in Henry's eyes when Sam spoke to him. She'd experienced it firsthand.

"Miss Langdon." Sam's voice was sweet as his head bent to brush a kiss across the back of her hand, but the look of smoldering fury in his eyes stunned her.

She quickly pulled her hand away and crouched to give Henry a warm hug. "Be a good boy, Henry," she whispered in his ear. "And don't forget to say your prayers. Remember, if you're ever afraid, just pray and ask Jesus to take care of you, and He will."

Henry gave her a solemn nod and Charity's heart twisted.

She stood at the open door and watched the mule-drawn wagon bear father and son down Perry Street through the purple-tinted winter dusk. Would Sam take out his anger toward her on Henry? She fought down the panic bubbling up inside of her at the thought.

Dear Jesus, just protect him. Protect little Henry.

When she finally shut the door, a tap on her shoulder turned her around. Uncle Silas was holding a flat package wrapped in brown paper. "I forgot, niece, there was one more gift for you," he said with an odd smile as he handed her the package.

"Thank you, Uncle Silas." She tried to force a smile. Whatever the gift was, it seemed unimportant after sending that sweet little boy off with an angry father who was capable of. . .what? She didn't like to imagine.

Uncle Silas held both hands up, palms forward. "Don't thank me. I'm only playing St. Nick." Uncle Silas's rosy cheeks above his graying mustache plumped up with his smile, bringing an easier grin to Charity's face. If anyone looked the part, it was certainly Uncle Silas.

He lifted his overcoat and hat from the row of wall pegs. "Now, I must hitch up the buggy and take Mrs. Akers and her daughter home. Probably with enough food to keep them through the next week, if I know Jennie." With a little laugh, he sauntered off toward the kitchen.

Charity followed her uncle around the L-shaped hallway toward the stairs. She could hear Aunt Jennie, Sadie, and Matilda Akers chatting as they worked in the kitchen. She would take the gift—most likely a token from the school board—up to her bedroom and open it later.

Up in her room, she dropped the wrapped package on the table by her bed and started to turn and head back downstairs. But in the dim, flickering light from the fireplace, the name "Daniel" on the right top corner of the package caught her eye.

She lit the oil lamp on the table, sat down on the edge of her bed, and picked up the package. Sure enough, clearly penciled in Daniel Morgan's handwriting was "To Charity from Daniel."

She tore away the brown paper, and her heart nearly stopped. In her hands lay her mother's picture she'd feared had been lost. But now it was encased in new glass and a beautifully hand-carved walnut frame.

Charity ran a finger lovingly over the rose and leaf design delicately etched in the wood. He'd done this. She didn't doubt it for an instant. She couldn't begin to guess the hours it must have taken him to create this stunning piece of art—all for her.

Charity's eyes stung, and her mother's image blurred. Sam was right. She loved Daniel Morgan. She could no longer deny it. Yet her mind stubbornly rebelled against the notion of a romantic relationship with a former Yankee soldier. The tears that had slowly welled suddenly became a torrent, and she sobbed. She held her mother's picture to her heart and rocked herself on the edge of her bed as tears streamed down her face.

"Dear Lord, what am I to do? What am I to do?"

Chapter 15

T hank you."

Charity's soft voice behind him caught Daniel up short in midstride. He'd been on his way to shut the sluice gate in preparation of closing the mill for the day.

"For the frame you made for my mother's picture, thank you. It's beautiful." It wasn't so much her words or quiet voice as the way her gaze drifted shyly away from his that caused Daniel's heart to pound.

"I'm glad you liked it. I was afraid you might—might take offense. . . ." Daniel found himself almost mesmerized by the condensation of her warm breath in the cold mill. The misty clouds puffed from her rosy lips with her every breath—the essence of her. His arms ached to embrace her—to hold her close and warm against him.

"Not at all." The surprise on her face that told him such an idea had never crossed her mind set a surge of relief rolling through Daniel.

Her gaze continued to glance away from his. But he sensed her avoidance of his look was not generated by disdain. Indeed, the relief in his chest mingled with the sweet notion that her demeanor sprang from attraction rather than revulsion.

She seemed to study the fringes of her shawl, rolling one short length of wool thread between two fingers. "Had I known beforehand, I would have reciprocated in kind. . .in some small way. . . ."

Daniel prayed—something he'd been doing more of lately. Just this moment, he prayed that his throat wouldn't tighten up, strangling his voice to a croak. He shook his head and bought himself another second or two of time. "But don't you agree that if a gift is paid back, its value is made null, robbing the giver of the joy of having given the gift in the first place?"

She looked up at him. An appreciative smile, as slow and languid as her Southern accent, crept over her lips, and then a musical giggle bubbled from between them. "Why, Mr. Morgan, I had no idea you were such a philosopher."

"I've been called worse, I suppose," he blurted and silently upbraided himself for the stupid reply.

"Still, your thesis aside, I hope you will accept an invitation to dinner this Sunday." She pulled the dark wool shawl closer around her, forcing him to, again, resist the impulse to wrap her in his arms.

"I will agree on two conditions. You call me Daniel and allow me to escort you to church."

The words had flown from his lips before he realized his blunder. Since Christmas, Porter had been crowing about having spent Christmas Day with the Gants and the particular attention Charity had been giving his son, Henry. It was even possible Charity and Porter had an understanding. The thought raked across Daniel's heart like a briar.

To his utter relief, she gave him a smile and a nod, allowing him to breathe again. "I would be honored. . .Daniel."

She held out her hand to him and he enclosed it in his. It was the first time they had touched since the kiss.

Realization flickered in her eyes. Yet her gaze didn't waver from his, nurturing the hope growing in his heart.

"I will see you Sunday morning then." He held her hand a moment longer than convention allowed and felt the loss acutely when she slipped her fingers from his.

"This Sunday," she repeated, but her smile had faded. A troubled look flashed across her face. It seemed directed toward a point past his shoulder.

She turned abruptly and headed out of the mill. Her quick footsteps clicking against the wooden floor echoed his racing heart. Silas Gant wasn't here. And Charity hadn't gone to her little office. She had come to the mill for no other purpose than to thank him for the picture frame.

Through the window, Daniel watched her climb into the buggy and turn it toward the little gravel path. Was it indeed possible she could care for him? Could he trust this tiny glimmer of hope flickering inside of him?

He remembered the scripture from the Gospel of Mark Uncle Jacob reminded him of Christmas Eve. " *'For with God all things are possible.'* "

During the war, he'd prayed daily. His connection with God had sustained him through the horrors of Andersonville. When he survived the sinking of the *Sultana* without being burned or suffering any other serious injuries, he'd considered it nothing less than a miracle from God. But oddly, the moment he reached the safety of home, he'd stopped praying, reading his Bible, or even going to church. He'd pushed God away along with all other recollections of the war. Uncle Jacob had reminded him that his need for God didn't end with the war. And suddenly, that need never seemed greater than at this moment.

Dear Lord, forgive me for neglecting You.

"The last grind has been bagged. So, with your permission, sir, I will be leavin' for the day." Sam Porter's voice behind Daniel was as chilly as the mill's interior.

Daniel turned to meet the man's scowl. He wondered if it was Porter's disgruntled look that had withered Charity's smile moments earlier.

"Thank you, Sam. . .and good evening." Daniel fought to push his mouth into what he hoped was a pleasant expression. Did the man actually see him as a possible contender for Charity's affection? Oddly, the thought buoyed his spirits.

He watched the Southerner swagger past him, ignoring the man's scornful snort. During his time in Andersonville, Daniel had learned that allowing an adversary to goad him into anger invariably handed his opponent the advantage. And Daniel had no doubt that in a contest where Charity Langdon's affections were the prize, he had a committed adversary in Sam Porter.

        ~

"Daniel, I need your help." Charity glanced over at Daniel's profile beside her in the rented buggy. The ride to church was a short one, so she didn't have the luxury of leading up to the subject gradually. The surprise mixing with concern on his face would have caused her to smile if the situation weren't so serious.

For the past week, she had agonized over the bruises she'd noticed on Henry. Convinced that her worst fears on Christmas night had come true, she was desperate to save the child from further injury.

"Of course. I will help you in any way I can if it is within my power to do so." He kept the horse to a slow walk, which she sensed had less to do with the snow-covered streets than allowing extra time for their conversation.

"I think Sam Porter is beatin' Henry." There, she'd said it. In one awful rush of breath, she'd impugned the man she'd not so long ago considered marrying.

"What?" Daniel shot her a sidelong glance, his knuckles whitening around the leather reins. "Do you have any proof of this?"

Charity wadded the ends of her shawl in her hands and wished for Henry's sake she didn't have so much proof. She told Daniel about the bruises on the boy's face and hands. "He always has an excuse when I ask him what happened." Charity blinked back tears remembering how Henry had shrugged off her questions about an ugly purple bruise on his right cheek last Thursday. "He said he fell against a rick of wood when he went to fetch fuel for the stove."

"And you didn't believe him?" Although a frown continued to line his forehead, the doubt in his voice sent ripples of panic through Charity. If she couldn't find an ally in Daniel, where could she turn?

"Fallin' doesn't leave marks that resemble a man's fingers on a child's wrist!" she blurted, barely able to contain both her anger and her tears.

Daniel blew out a long breath. "No, it doesn't." The anger snapping in his dark eyes gave her hope. "Have you spoken to Mr. and Mrs. Gant about your concerns?"

"I tried." The words rolled out on a puff of frustration. Charity held out her hands to demonstrate her helplessness. "I could tell Aunt Jennie was concerned, but she shrinks from anything controversial. She simply said it is not our place to dictate how a father should deal with his son. And Uncle Silas just laughed and said boys are rambunctious and are always gettin' hurt."

Charity rested her hand on Daniel's arm. "I was hopin' that perhaps you could have a word with Sam. Mention how glad you are that you had a kind father. . . somethin'." She shook her head. "I'm worried sick about Henry, and I don't know where else to turn. And I think Sam might respond better to another man."

Transferring the reins to one hand, Daniel covered her hand on his arm with his free hand. His smile sent warm encouragement radiating through her. "Don't worry. I'll talk to Sam."

When they reached the churchyard and Daniel parked the buggy, he turned and took Charity's hands in his. His gaze caressed hers. Deep, dark pools of bottomless kindness she could get lost in. Could these be the eyes of one who'd glared in hatred at her loved ones across a battlefield? The thought seemed impossible.

The January wind tugged at her shawl and nipped at her cheeks, but she didn't care. She wanted to continue sitting there, soaking up the strength, the warmth, the security that flowed from Daniel's hands to hers.

"It will be all right," he said, and the assurance in his voice made her believe it. "In the meantime, let us pray that God will soften Sam's heart, or at the very least stay his hand if raised in anger against the boy."

And Charity did pray.

Throughout the church service, she found her attention constantly drifting from Reverend Davenport's sermon to Henry Porter's plight. It alarmed her to see that Sam and Henry were not present at services. She made a mental note to offer Henry a ride to church whether or not his father chose to attend. The thought that she could somehow protect Henry if she were to become his mother still tortured Charity.

She glanced at Daniel sitting next to her in the church pew, and her heart rebelled against such a sacrificial notion, however noble. It seemed a vile sin to vow to love, honor, and obey a man capable of injuring his own flesh and blood while her affections twined ever tighter around the good, decent man beside her.

Monday brought Charity no relief from her worries. Henry didn't show up at school, leaving her to wonder if he lay too sick or injured to attend. Something was wrong. He was always one of the first to arrive in the morning and the last to leave in the afternoon.

Although frantic to learn of the boy's situation, Charity had a school full of other students to teach. She would have to wait until after school to check on Henry.

The day dragged as she spent every spare moment praying for Henry's safety and glancing at the excruciatingly slow-moving hands on the wall clock. When three thirty finally came and the last student had left, Charity rushed through the routine chores of closing the school for the day. She knew she wouldn't be able to sleep tonight if she didn't stop by the Porters' home and assure herself Henry was all right.

She'd just reached up to turn the damper on the stovepipe, cutting off the oxygen supply to the smoldering coals in the stove's iron belly, when she felt a draft of cold air behind her. One of the students must have forgotten something and returned.

She whirled around, her every muscle tensing with impatience at the shuffling sound near the door. "Yes, what is it—" The sight of Daniel in the doorway snatched the breath from her lungs. And the somber look on his face made her tremble.

"He quit." The two words rang hollowly in the empty room.

Charity could only stare at him. She didn't need to ask, "Who?"

"I'm sorry." He twisted his hat in his hands and shook his head. "I made a mess of it. I told Sam you were worried about the bruises you'd seen on his boy. He said he didn't need Yankees or Yankee-lovers telling him how to raise his son." Daniel's Adam's apple bobbed with his swallow. "He told me he was quitting, dropped what he was doing, and just walked out."

A new and terrible fear gripped Charity. For one awful moment, she couldn't move. She couldn't breathe. Sam would have been furious. And if Henry was home when Sam returned from the mill, Henry would most likely have borne the brunt of Sam's anger. What was worse, Charity knew she had brought it about. "Daniel." His name croaked from her frozen throat. "Henry didn't come to school today."

Daniel's face blanched. His gaze locked with hers in a grim, mutual understanding.

Chapter 16

L et's go." Daniel snatched Charity's heavy wool shawl from the wall peg and draped it around her shoulders.

He felt sick. Porter had a hair-trigger temper, and Daniel had witnessed the man take his anger out on whatever hapless creature had the misfortune to be in his way. If he thought the boy had gone to Charity and Daniel for help. . .it didn't bear thinking.

"Daniel, it's not your fault. I asked you to talk to Sam. If it's anyone's fault, it's mine." Charity's words, puffing out in the cold air as he led her across the snowy schoolyard, touched Daniel deeply but did little to ease his guilt.

He helped her onto the wagon seat then climbed up beside her. Watching her fingers convulse, wadding handfuls of her skirt, he winced. He couldn't bear to see her blame herself for Henry's welfare. "Charity, if Sam's hurt that boy, it's nobody's fault but Sam's."

Charity nodded as he took off the brake and grasped the reins. Her delicate chin trembled, and Daniel vowed to make Sam pay if he'd hurt Henry.

They made the trip across Vernon in silence.

Perhaps Charity was wrong and Sam was lovingly caring for his son who'd woken up with a fever or a bellyache or. . .the quivering in Daniel's stomach told him that scenario wasn't likely.

At last, he pulled the wagon up in front of the little dilapidated hovel at the south end of Posey Street Sam and Henry called home. Daniel had learned from his landlady, Essie Kilgore, that few in Vernon had cared to rent to a Reb. But for the boy's sake, old man Gossman had rented Sam this empty shotgun shack not much larger than a summer kitchen.

Before Daniel could help her down, Charity clambered from the wagon and hurried to the house. Her sharp raps on the weathered front door went unanswered.

Daniel walked to the back corner of the house. He could see Sam's unsaddled horse munching on hay in the three-sided shed. He doubted the man had walked any distance through the several inches of snow cover.

He rejoined Charity at the front of the house. Her drooping shoulders as she turned from the door spoke of her disappointment at finding no one home. Daniel seriously considered trying the door, just to check on Henry and ease her mind.

Suddenly the door opened, releasing a stench composed of several foul odors, not the least of which were whiskey, rancid lard, and kerosene.

"Whatcha want?" Sam swayed unsteadily in the open doorway. He was shirtless with the top half of his dingy underwear unbuttoned at the throat. His sagging galluses hung off his shoulders.

"I want to see Henry." Charity's plucky challenge made Daniel smile. Many women would have fled, scandalized by the man's condition of undress.

"He's not here. Ain't seen 'im since he left for school this mornin'. Dawdlin', most like."

Sam's bleary-eyed gaze drifted from Charity to Daniel and back to Charity again. He gave a soft snort. "So, Miss Langdon, you and your Yankee—"

"Stop right there, Porter!" Anger stiffened Daniel's spine and he stepped toward Sam. He would not allow this man's whiskey-soaked tongue to embarrass or impugn Charity in any way. "Your boy never showed up at school. Miss Langdon just came by to assure herself he is all right."

To his credit, Sam Porter seemed to sober slightly. "He wasn't at school?"

"No." The word quivered from Charity's lips, and she turned horror-widened eyes to Daniel.

The color drained from Porter's face, softening Daniel's opinion of him. Daniel gripped Sam's arm. "Do you know where your boy might have gone? Maybe to one of the neighbors'?"

Sam gave his head an emphatic shake. "No. I tanned him right good for doin' that once without tellin' me. He wouldn't do it again."

Daniel's voice rose. Trying to drag useful information from Sam's whiskey-soaked brain was beyond frustrating.

"Georgia," Sam suddenly muttered and looked like he might be sick. "I—I gave him a tannin' last night for sassin' me. He said he was goin' to leave and go back to Georgia." His gaze that swung from Daniel to Charity pled for understanding. "He's seven. I never thought he'd try. . ."

Daniel strove to keep the disgust from his voice. "Get your clothes on, man. It'll be dark soon. We need to go after him." Drunk or sober, Sam Porter would have the best idea where to start looking for Henry.

Five minutes later, Sam, now fully clothed, led Charity and Daniel behind the house. He gave his head a quick jerk to the south. "Henry likes to play back here in the trees a lot."

Among dog and rabbit tracks that marred the snow cover, they could make out small human footprints leading to the narrow wooded area between the house and the river gorge. Beyond the tree line, the footprints were no longer obvious, obliterated by deepening shadows and myriad animal tracks. Daniel and Charity followed Sam's lead, dodging bare tree limbs and briars until they emerged at an open space overlooking the Muscatatuck River.

But they found no sign of Henry.

Just when Daniel was about to suggest they question the neighbors who lived a few yards behind them along East Jackson Street, Charity's excited voice stopped him.

"Here. Over here," she called from where she'd wandered westward along the edge of the woods.

Daniel rushed to join her with Sam close on his heels. He followed Charity's gaze to a stretch of snow-covered ground streaked with the evening's lengthening purple shadows and the gold of the setting sun. There in the snow, he could make out a line of small footprints heading west and running parallel to the woods.

Charity repeatedly called the boy's name as she followed the trail of footprints.

Suddenly, a small figure dressed in red appeared from behind a large bush several yards ahead of them. The boy stood silhouetted against the snow, between the woods and the river gorge.

Sam took quick steps toward the boy. "Henry! Henry, you come here right now, boy, or I'll wear that strap out on you!"

When Henry took off in the opposite direction, Daniel couldn't blame him, but his heart quaked at the sight. The boy was running straight for the bluff where the land sloped steeply down to the river's edge. Recent rains had swollen the usually shallow, languid river, making it a rushing torrent. If Henry slipped and fell down the ten-foot slope and into the river, the current could easily carry him away before they could ever reach him.

The next moment, Daniel's worst fear was realized when Henry stumbled and fell and with a yelp, slid over the embankment and out of sight. An instant later, Daniel heard a *splash*.

Charity screamed Henry's name, and to Daniel's horror, he watched her follow Henry, disappearing down the incline.

Shouting Charity's name, Daniel raced to the spot where she and Henry had gone over the edge of the bluff. Beside him, and sounding just as frantic, Sam called for his son.

Daniel's heart sank when he saw no sign of them. Then the sound of splashing and fractured cries for help drew his attention to a spot several yards downstream. Squinting westward against the setting sun, he could make out Charity's head and upper torso. She seemed to be clinging with one hand to a partially submerged tree limb. With her other hand, she amazingly grasped something red from which poked a sputtering little head.

His mind numb with fear for both Charity and the boy, Daniel followed Sam down the slippery bank and along the narrow strip of rocky ground that edged the river.

Daniel watched helplessly as the rushing water swirled around Charity and Henry. He felt frozen in place as the memory of that terrifying April night two years ago flashed through his mind. The deafening explosion. The other-worldly sense of being hurled from the hurricane deck of the *Sultana* as if shot from a cannon. Plunging into the dark, swirling, muddy currents of the Mississippi. His lungs burning while he frantically fought to reach the surface of the river, unable to discern what was up and what was down. Breaking through to the surface and pulling life-giving air into his lungs, while the sounds of hundreds of men dying around him filled his ears.

Although the temperature had undoubtedly dipped below freezing, beads of sweat broke out on Daniel's forehead. For nearly two years, his fear of drowning had exceeded even what he'd felt at his baptism of fire on the battlefield. He had a vague sense of Sam beside him, shucking off his boots and coat and wading into the neck-high water.

A sharp cracking sound split the air, followed by Charity's screams. The limb she was holding on to had broken, sending her sluicing farther down the stream and leaving Henry clinging alone to the fallen tree.

Charity's arms reached up, thrashing wildly at the fast-moving water. Her intermittent screams turned to desperate garbled wails. Twice, her head went completely beneath the surface.

Charity was drowning.

Daniel's body jerked with a mighty shudder as if he'd been struck by lightning. A fear, far greater than any he'd ever experienced, shot through him, thawing his frozen limbs. With his gaze fastened on Charity's flailing figure, he ripped off his boots and coat and strode into the cold river.

Dear Lord, just give me the strength to save them.

Chapter 17

Gasping for air, Charity struggled to stand as she fought against the frigid current that dragged her down while pushing her westward. But her left leg buckled, refusing to support her. When she slid down the steep bank after Henry, her leg had smacked into a large rock just as she went into the river. She vaguely remembered hearing a sickening *crunch* and *snap* as a searing pain shot up her lower leg to her hip. But the icy water had quickly washed away the pain, and her mind, focused on wrenching Henry from the lethal clutches of the Muscatatuck, had ignored her injury.

Her only thought had been to hold on to Henry, keeping his head above the roiling water that was shoving them both downstream. Blessedly, as she and the boy slid past a fallen tree, she'd managed to grab a limb and hold them fast, while alternately screaming for both Daniel and Sam.

But amid her prayers for deliverance and her cries for help, the branch that had been her and Henry's lifeline snapped. At the same time, she'd lost her grip on Henry.

Henry. She couldn't see Henry! An overwhelming sense of grief and panic seized her. Then out of the corner of her eye, she saw Sam towing Henry toward a snow-covered sandbar—a tiny icy island jutting up from the center of the river.

Thank You, Jesus!

But her relief gave way to a new terror. Glancing at the shore, she saw Daniel wade into the river only to be knocked off his feet by the strong current. He immediately disappeared beneath the river's surface. She tried to scream his name, but her throat refused to make a sound.

A silent sob tore from deep inside her. Her arms that burned with exhaustion felt leaden, sapped of their last ounce of strength. With Daniel gone, the will to fight left her.

When she'd learned of Granger's death, she'd cried. Yet that grief had not extinguished the life-spark within her. But now that the Muscatatuck had taken Daniel, she was content to let the river take her, too. With one last, sweet gulp of air, she stopped fighting to keep her face above the rushing water and slipped beneath it.

Suddenly, an iron-tight grip around her chest propelled her upwards, into the winter gloaming and life-giving air. How had Sam, in such a short amount of time, managed to get Henry to the sandbar and still get back to help her?

But when she cocked her head, she saw that her rescuer had jet black—not sandy-colored—hair.

Daniel!

Thank You Jesus, thank You! Her silent prayer winged its way heavenward as she rested against him.

When they reached the riverbank, he helped her to her feet. But blinding pain exploded in her left leg, and it collapsed under her.

She felt her body being lifted in Daniel's strong arms then gently lowered to the snow. She wanted to tell him how glad she was that he was alive. But her eyes kept closing and her mouth wouldn't open. Icy numbness gripped her.

A flurry of commotion swirled around them. Many voices. People running. Shouting.

Daniel's quick, warm breaths caressed her face. His hands shook as he wrapped her in his wool coat, ordered someone to make sure she didn't fall asleep, and then headed back into the river.

"Daniel! Daniel!" Sobs convulsed from her shivering body.

"Shh, shh, ma chère, you are safe. You will be all right," Annie Martin's voice soothed. The old woman crouched beside Charity in the snow, rocking her in slender, wiry arms. "It is a good thing you have strong lungs, hey? I reckon everyone along East Jackson Street heard you hollerin'."

Charity could only repeat Daniel's name. Why had he left her? Why had he gone back?

A cacophony of voices around her barraged her frozen brain. The only thing she heard clearly was an unidentifiable voice saying, "They found him. He's drowned."

A mind-numbing, spirit-crippling anguish gripped Charity. Her last conscious thought was that Annie was wrong. Daniel was gone, and she would never be all right again. Then a blessed blackness engulfed her.

⤳

Charity's first sensation was one of warmth as she struggled to emerge from the dense fog shrouding her mind. Next, she noticed a dull, throbbing pain in her left leg. A low moan sounded, and somehow she realized it had come from her own throat.

She rolled her head on the soft down pillow, inhaling the familiar scent. She was home. Aunt Jennie had all of her bed linens washed in lemon-verbena-scented lye soap.

Although her lips felt thick and numb, she strained to enunciate the beloved name screaming through her heart. "Daniel."

"I'm sorry, Charity. He's gone." Aunt Jennie's soft voice hovered above Charity. Her words sent a new wave of crushing sadness rolling through Charity's chest. Tears stung her eyes then slipped from their corners to course down her cheeks to her neck. How she wished she'd told him that she loved him.

Aunt Jennie patted Charity's hand. "Now, now, dear. He will be back soon."

Charity blinked at her aunt's astounding statement. What could she mean?

"He went to the railroad depot to telegraph his father. He insists we allow Dr. Morgan to attend you," Aunt Jennie said, answering Charity's bewildered gaze. "I told him he should rest after such an awful ordeal, but he insisted—"

"Daniel's alive?" Unspeakable joy burst like Fourth of July fireworks inside Charity. *Thank You, Jesus! Thank You, thank You.* Then she suddenly remembered the words someone had muttered on the riverbank. "He's drowned."

The image of Henry bobbing in the icy river appeared before her mind's eye. She'd seen Sam put Henry on the sandbar. Could the child have slipped back into the river?

"Henry!" Frantic, she tried to push up with her elbow.

Aunt Jennie gently pressed her shoulders back against the pillow. "Henry is all right. He's asleep in the spare room down the hall."

"But someone said—they said. . ." Charity had to force the grim words from her lips. "Someone said, 'He's drowned.' "

Aunt Jennie made soft tsking sounds as she tucked the wool blankets and quilt snugly beneath Charity's chin. "I'm sorry to have to tell you, Charity, but Mr. Porter perished."

"Sam?" A jumble of emotions Charity didn't have the strength to untangle balled up inside her.

Sadness laced Aunt Jennie's somber tone. "Daniel said that when he went to rescue you, he saw Mr. Porter put Henry on a sandbar. He assumed both father and son had made it to safety. But when he got back to Henry, Sam was gone." Both her voice and her gaze lowered. "They found Sam's body about a half mile downstream."

Aunt Jennie glanced through the open doorway to the short hall, sniffed, and pulled a handkerchief from her sleeve to dab at her nose and eyes. "Poor little Henry. Poor little orphaned mite. Had to watch his own papa drown." She shook her head and dabbed at her eyes again.

Although sad to learn of Sam's tragic death, Charity was consoled by the knowledge that Henry was well and safe—at last. However harsh Sam's previous treatment of his son, he'd died heroically, sacrificing his life for his child's. At least Henry's last memory of his father would be a positive one.

Charity shifted in bed, and the throbbing pain in her leg increased, causing her to moan.

Immediately attentive, Aunt Jennie fussed with Charity's pillow and covers. "I'm sorry, dear, but it's too soon to give you more of the laudanum Dr. Grayson left."

Another puzzle. Charity groaned, wishing her mind didn't feel so foggy, as if in a perpetual state of half-sleep. If their family physician, Dr. Grayson, had already attended her, why would Daniel feel it necessary to call his father to come all the way from Madison?

"Aunt Jennie, if Dr. Grayson has been here and seen to my injuries, why did Daniel go. . . ?"

A stricken look creased Aunt Jennie's forehead and she twisted the handkerchief in her hands. "Charity, dear, I'm afraid your leg is terribly, terribly broken." Her throat moved with a hard swallow, and her gaze slid to her lap. "Dr. Grayson suggested an extreme procedure to which Daniel violently objected."

A new alarm brought Charity's head up from the pillow. "Aunt Jennie, tell me plainly. What did Dr. Grayson suggest?"

"Amputation." The word left Aunt Jennie's lips on a quavering breath.

Charity sank back against the pillow. A blessed numbness gripped her, not unlike what she'd felt while in the Muscatatuck River. What if Dr. Morgan came to the same conclusion? What kind of altered life lay ahead for her?

Sam Porter had lost his life. She felt almost ashamed to grieve the potential loss of a limb. But she'd seen the pity in the eyes of many who looked upon war amputees. Perhaps she, too, had cast pitying looks at those unfortunates.

Aunt Jennie's head bowed as she squeezed Charity's hand. She'd gone to Christ in prayer.

She followed her aunt's example. But her prayer was not one of self-pity but praise. Daniel was alive!

Her leg might be irreparably damaged, but her heart lightly skipped in her chest. Even in her semiconscious state, the spark of life that had sputtered and gone out inside her when she thought Daniel had died flamed anew. Any lingering doubt that she loved him had been extinguished tonight in the icy Muscatatuck River.

Sleep dragged at her eyelids, and she could feel consciousness slipping away. As she struggled to fashion a coherent prayer, she found little room for self-pity.

Dear Heavenly Father, I pray that You will allow me to keep my leg. But if not, give me the strength to face what's before me. Grant Sam mercy and comfort Henry. And thank You for saving Daniel. Just take care of Daniel.

"Daniel. Daniel. . ."

She drifted off to sleep with the sweet taste of Daniel's name on her lips.

Chapter 18

"Charity. Charity, are you awake?" The voice sounded distant, as if she was at the bottom of a well and someone was at the top, calling down to her.

She squinted, struggling to open her eyes fully. But the glare from the window stabbed painfully at her eyes until a large form moved, blocking it.

"Are you in much pain, my dear?" When the face first came into her field of vision, she thought it was Daniel's. But then she noticed the streaks of gray in the older man's black hair. Dr. Morgan's dark eyes were full of concern as they peered into hers.

The morning's events pieced themselves together like a crazy quilt in Charity's mind. She remembered Dr. Morgan walking into her room and examining her injured leg, his expression guarded. The last she recalled was Aunt Jennie holding her hand and praying over her while Dr. Morgan pressed an ether-laced cloth to her mouth.

"Only a little," she mumbled. The sunlight streaming through her window told her it was early afternoon. Her insides shuddered at the thought of what might have transpired while she was unconscious. But she had to know.

"Is it. . ." Charity couldn't bring herself to say the word *gone*. She was well aware that the sharp, stinging pain assailing her lower leg offered no assurance that she'd kept the limb. During the war, she'd helped nurse wounded soldiers when her church served as a makeshift hospital. Many times, those who'd lost limbs remarked that they still felt pain in a leg that was no longer there.

Dr. Morgan moved the covers to expose her left side.

She hitched up her courage and looked down at the place where her limb should be. A dizzying wave of relief rolled through her. Wrapped tightly in white bandages, her leg—still attached to her body—was encased in a wire and wood apparatus that protruded beyond her nightdress.

"I must admit yours was a complicated injury, and setting the bones was a real challenge. Both the tibia and the fibula are broken, and the fibula—the small bone in your leg—is broken in a couple of places. I don't fault Dr. Grayson. Amputation would have been the simpler and arguably safer choice of treatment." He shook his head. "But at your age, I felt it was worth trying to save the limb if at all possible. I managed to set the bones, and with proper care, I believe there is a very good chance that you will regain full use of the leg." Dr. Morgan's kind smile helped to further ease her anxiety. "I have it wrapped and fitted with a Hodgen wire cradle extension splint. The apparatus will exert the right amount of pull on the muscles so they won't draw up, shortening the leg as the bones heal."

He gently draped the quilt back over her injured leg. "If diligently attended, your leg should heal soundly in a couple of months. About the time the first crocuses bloom," he added with a grin.

"Where's Daniel?" Charity was aghast that the question traipsing about the confines of her mind had escaped her lips. The fact that Daniel had refrained from visiting her since he'd pulled her from the river pinched her heart painfully.

Dr. Morgan smiled fondly. "He's asleep—for the first time in over twenty-four hours from what I understand."

The doctor shook his head. "I still find it hard to believe he entered that river twice of his own volition. Since nearly drowning when the steamboat *Sultana* sank, I haven't known him to so much as dip a toe into any substantial body of water."

"Daniel was on the *Sultana*?" Charity felt her eyes widen. She remembered reading in the spring of '65, the horrifying account in the local newspaper, the *Plain Dealer*. Most who'd lost their lives in the disaster were Union soldiers returning from the war. Although a Southerner, she recalled thinking how awful it must have been for the victims' families to learn that their loved ones made it through the war only to die in a steamboat explosion on their way home. The full recognition of Daniel's courage yesterday struck her a reeling blow.

Dr. Morgan nodded as he carefully straightened the covers back over her leg. "Thankfully he was thrown clear of the boat and didn't suffer the burns experienced by most of the survivors of the calamity. But I think nearly drowning in the Mississippi River scared him more than anything he experienced during the war—including the time he spent in Andersonville."

Charity lay stunned, trying to assimilate what she'd just learned. Even among Southerners, the name of the infamous prisoner-of-war camp at Andersonville, Georgia, was often whispered in shame, so hideous were the stories that came out of that place. That Daniel had endured both the horrors of that awful camp and the terror of the *Sultana* disaster was almost beyond comprehension.

She turned a helpless look to Dr. Morgan. What could she say as a Southerner? But as upon her previous visits to his home, she found no guile in his kind face. A Christian in the truest sense, it appeared Dr. Ephraim Morgan's only enemies were the myriad physical ills that afflicted God's children.

The doctor bent to retrieve his medical bag from the floor. When he straightened, he fixed her with a serious, knowing look. "Miss Langdon," he said quietly, "I've never questioned my son's courage or inherent goodness, but it took a very strong emotion—stronger than those I've mentioned—to propel him into that river."

Charity's heart thudded painfully in her chest. Was he trying to tell her

Daniel cared for her—loved her?

He plucked his hat from a hook on the wall, plopped it on his head, and gave it a quick tap. His smile—that reminded her so much of Daniel's—returned.

"Weather permitting, I shall come weekly to check on your progress. I'll have your aunt send up a light meal, perhaps some good, rich chicken broth and bread, to help knit those bones back together. Beyond that, I prescribe rest."

"Thank you, Dr. Morgan." The words seemed inadequate for someone who had just saved her leg. Charity's lashes beat back stinging tears and she gave him a faint parting nod, although she doubted she could eat anything. The lingering taste of ether in her mouth had robbed her appetite and left her nauseous.

Heaving a sigh, she listened to the doctor's footfalls fade down the stairs and clamped her lips tight together. As for his instruction to rest, it seemed she had little choice in the matter. She'd never been one to loll about, and the thought of being confined to bed for two months felt like a prison sentence.

That thought reminded her of what Dr. Morgan had shared about Daniel. The notion that Daniel could care for her—a Southerner—after being incarcerated in Andersonville was overwhelming.

New tears slipped hotly from the corners of her eyes to puddle in her ears. She remembered Daniel's kiss at Lucy's engagement party and how she had pulled away from his embrace. She rolled her head on the pillow until her mother's picture, encased in the frame Daniel had made for it, came into view.

The groan that welled up from the depths of her insides did not reflect the pain in her leg. Regret pressed like a stone on her chest. For months, Daniel had reached out to her. Yet time and again, she'd responded by rebuffing his attentions. And then he'd faced his worst fear to save her.

Charity stretched out her hand, trying to touch the picture frame Daniel's hands had fashioned. But it sat just beyond her reach. With a sigh, she sank back against her pillow, allowing her arm to fall across her chest. Forlornness draped heavily around her spirit. Was Daniel, too, just beyond her reach now? Why hadn't he come to see her? Had she squandered the last drop of his goodwill?

Charity welcomed the encroaching slumber tugging heavily on her eyelids. But before the last bit of consciousness seeped away, she whispered one plea to the darkening room.

"Dear Lord, let Dr. Morgan be right. Let Daniel love me."

Chapter 19

Y
ou're bound 'n' determined to give that Dr. Morgan a conniption fit, ain't ya?"

From her perch on the bed, Charity looked up to see Pearl march into the room. The girl's brown face was pruned up in a scowl that foretold a scolding as she plopped a bundle of letters on the bed beside Charity.

"The biznus mail," Pearl said unnecessarily.

To help fill Charity's long days, Uncle Silas had begun having Pearl pick up the mail from the post office each day and have Charity sort through it, separating the bills from other correspondence.

Charity gave the bundle of envelopes tied with a string a cursory glance and grunted in answer. She continued to ease her leg encased in the cumbersome Hodgen splint over the side of the bed. It had taken her a full ten minutes to untie the sandbag weights that normally kept a constant tension on her foot.

Pearl crossed her arms over her chest and glared at Charity. "Do you wanna limp fer the rest o' yer life? Dr. Morgan said them weights'll keep the muscles in yer leg from drawin' up so yer leg won't heal shorter'n it oughta be."

Undaunted, Charity allowed gravity to drag her limb imprisoned in the heavy metal brace over the side of the bed. "Surely takin' the weights off for a few minutes won't do any harm, Pearl. I just get so terribly tired of lyin' in that one position."

Though thrilled her friend had come to nurse her, Charity sometimes wished Pearl didn't take her job so seriously. It still made her smile to remember how two days after the accident, Pearl strode into the sickroom with all the authority of an army field general and declared, "Ain't gonna let nobody see to ya 'cept me an' Dr. Morgan. 'Specially not that sawbones that wanted to lop off yer leg!"

With Pearl's help, Charity maneuvered herself into a sitting position on the edge of her bed. She wiggled her bare toes sticking out from the wire cage-like restraint. Tingles pricked at her foot as the blood rushed into it, and she grimaced. But even a few minutes of respite from lying on her back would feel good.

Crouching beside her, Pearl carefully arranged Charity's cotton skirt to completely cover her bare legs.

"School'll be out in a few minutes, so young master Henry'll be along d'rectly. Got to git you decent." Finishing her task, Pearl rose and flashed a fond

331

smile. "You know that chil' don't knock, holler, nor nothin'. Jist rushes in here like a cat with his tail afire!"

Charity chortled at Pearl's accurate description. She thanked the Lord for Henry's childlike resiliency. The week following his father's funeral he'd seemed sad and withdrawn. But then the grief lifted like a somber fog, and Henry emerged his former cheerful self. Yet he still talked of his desire to return to Georgia.

Charity had no idea if the boy still had relatives there. And even if he did, she didn't have the first notion how she might go about locating them. But she understood Henry's desire to return to his native state—a desire she shared. But lately she'd begun feeling a tug to stay in Indiana. And she knew why.

Daniel.

As if reading her mind, Pearl shot Charity a teasing grin over her shoulder before crossing the room to her sewing chair. "An' Henry ain't the only feller comin'. You *know* Mr. Morgan'll be along, jist as sure as I'm sittin' here," she said, plopping herself into the chair.

Warmth infused Charity's cheeks. To cover her blush, she turned and reached for the bundle of envelopes beside her. Thankfully Daniel had quickly banished her worries that he wanted nothing more to do with her. In fact, he'd proved a faithful visitor, daily bringing by the mill receipts and discussing everything from the price of grain to the subject of Reverend Davenport's latest sermon.

Although she had thanked Daniel repeatedly for saving her and Henry from drowning, she never mentioned what his father had told her about Andersonville or the *Sultana*. It had seemed a gift from God that Daniel still wished to spend time with her. She'd lacked the courage to mention anything that might tarnish their relationship that grew increasingly closer and warmer. Indeed, as the winter days passed, fusing her broken bones, Charity realized they were also fusing her heart—her spirit—with Daniel's.

She looked over at Pearl working on a piece of tatting that would decorate her wedding dress. Guilt rasped against Charity's conscience. In a few weeks, Pearl would be getting married. She should be in Madison, working on her wedding dress with Tunia and helping to fix up the house in Georgetown Andrew bought for them.

"I'm sorry, Pearl." Charity gazed at her friend who sat humming a hymn as she focused on the work in her hands. "You shouldn't be here. You should be in Madison, gettin' things ready for your weddin'. In fact, I'm mendin' well. You really don't need to stay—"

"'Course I need to stay!" Pearl's face yanked up, but her stern look quickly dissolved into an appreciative smile.

"Mammy says it'll do Adam good to miss me some 'fore the weddin'. 'Sides, I git a letter from him pert-near every day." She dropped her gaze back to her needlework but not before Charity noticed a telltale glistening in her friend's dark eyes that sent new thorns of guilt pricking at her conscience.

Charity undid the string Postmaster McClelland had tied around the handful of envelopes. Pearl was right. She would have little time to complete her task before Henry arrived. She reached for a pencil on the bedside table to mark each missive according to its contents.

Suddenly her hand froze. The first envelope in the stack had originally been addressed to Sam Porter, but the postmaster had marked through his name and written "The Gants" above it.

The return address in the upper left corner read, "New South Investors, Atlanta, Georgia." It was the same name and address she'd seen on the pamphlet Sam had shown her at Christmas. This was probably a reply to Sam's inquiry about Southern land for sale. A letter would need to be sent to the company informing them of Sam's tragic death. And since Uncle Silas disliked writing letters, Charity had no doubt the errand would fall to her.

She broke the envelope's seal with her thumb and slipped out the single sheet of folded paper. As she perused the letter, her heart thumped harder and her eyes widened. It offered, for five dollars per acre, land in her home county of Fulton, Georgia, along Peachtree Creek. It was signed, "Armand Dubois, Esquire, New South Investors."

Charity had no doubt the man was a carpetbagger. But the notion that land near her childhood home could be obtained so cheaply tempted her imagination. Also, if Mr. Dubois was acquainted with the area, he might be able to help her discover whether Henry still had relatives in or near Fulton County. Sam's words echoed tantalizingly in her ears. *We could go back—you, me, and Henry. We could start anew.*

Pearl eyed Charity over her needlework. "Sump'un wrong? You look like you done seen a ghost!"

Charity ran her tongue over her dry lips as she quickly folded the paper and tucked it back into the envelope. Something restrained her from divulging to Pearl all of her thoughts on what she'd just read. "Just carpetbaggers tryin' to sell Georgia land to Sam," Charity said, trying to sound unaffected even as tempting possibilities swirled through her mind. The moment she left Georgian soil nearly two and a half years ago, Charity had vowed to return. During her time here in Vernon, she'd saved nearly a hundred dollars from both her job at the mill and her wages teaching school, hoping to one day use it to return to Fulton County and try to reclaim her parent's land.

At the quick, staccato-like sound of Henry's footsteps running up the stairs, Charity jerked. She hurriedly slid the letter beneath the stack of other envelopes, which she moved to the table beside her bed. If Henry happened to see his father's name on the envelope, it might rekindle the boy's grief.

"Miss Charity!" Henry blew through the open doorway like a miniature whirlwind. His enthusiastic hug nearly knocked her sideways on the bed.

He unceremoniously dropped his schoolbooks held together by a leather belt beside her on the quilt top.

"Daniel let me ride home in his wagon," he said breathlessly. "He said I could help at the mill this Saturday if Uncle Silas says it's all right. Do you think Uncle Silas will say it's all right?"

In his exuberance, Henry bumped against her metal splint. "I'm sorry. I didn't mean to hurt your leg. When will your leg get out of the cage anyway? Daniel says he misses you at the mill. Are you going to go back to work at the mill or are you going to be our teacher again?"

Charity laughed at Henry's barrage of questions, but a squiggle of joy shot through her learning Daniel missed seeing her at the mill.

"You didn't hurt my leg, Henry. And let's take one question at a time." She brushed back the shock of sandy hair falling across Henry's forehead. "You'll have to ask Uncle Silas. But if you promise not to make a nuisance of yourself, I imagine he will allow you to help at the mill. And," she added, "you must get all the lessons done Miss Gannon has assigned to you." After her accident, Charity had worried that her students would be left without a teacher. So she'd been greatly relieved to learn that a soon-to-be-graduated student of the normal school had taken over her teaching duties.

"I will." He fiddled with the loose end of the belt that girdled his books. "But if I learn how to work in a mill, I can work in one when I go back to live in Georgia."

Charity shared a concerned glance with Pearl. A day never passed that Henry didn't remind them he wished to one day return to Georgia. It made the thought-provoking letter from New South Investors even more enticing.

"So when are you gettin' the cage off your leg?" Childlike, Henry reiterated his earlier question. "'Cause Daniel made you crut—" He clapped his hand over his mouth just as Daniel appeared, filling the open doorway.

"You little scamp! You let the cat out of the bag, didn't you?" Daniel's good-natured laughter sent a thrill rippling through Charity.

With a quick greeting to both Charity and Pearl, a grinning Daniel brought from behind him two oak crutches, the tops of which were padded with a bright blue and yellow calico print.

Henry hopped down from the bed and bounded to Daniel like an eager pup. "Miss Charity says she thinks Uncle Silas will let me help you at the mill."

Daniel gave Henry a fond smile, and it struck Charity how easy it would be to imagine the three of them making a little family.

"Well, he's downstairs. Why don't you go ask him?" Daniel tousled Henry's hair as the boy rushed past him, out of the door, and down the stairs.

Daniel stepped into the room and held the crutches out for Charity's inspection.

"Thank you, Daniel." Charity pushed the words past the lump in her throat. This was the second time she'd benefited from his excellent handiwork.

He leaned the crutches against the wall beside her bed. "When Pa takes that iron thing off your leg, I'll help you learn to walk with them."

Smiling, Charity nodded. But her smile faded when her gaze slid from the crutches against the wall to the stack of envelopes on the bedside table, reminding her of Mr. Dubois's offer.

She looked at Daniel's handsome face stretched in a sweet smile and winced inwardly from the pain of having her heart tugged hard in opposite directions.

Chapter 20

Charity glanced for the umpteenth time at the clock above the mantel. It was not like Daniel to be a half hour late.

Needing to do something, she reached for the crutches propped against the wall beside her bed. Three weeks ago, Dr. Morgan had removed the cumbersome Hodgen splint, replacing it with a more ambulatory set of splints. Since then, she'd been practicing maneuvering around her room with the help of the crutches Daniel had fashioned for her.

She shoved the cotton and calico padded tops of the crutches under her arms and hobbled to the window.

"Quit yer frettin'. He's comin'. Don't he always come?" A teasing giggle rippled through Pearl's chide. Seated in the wingback chair beside the fireplace, she grinned up from the knitting in her hands.

Yes, he always did come. Charity gazed down on Perry Street as if she might make him appear. When, she wondered, had Daniel's daily visits become as vital to her as the air she breathed?

Suddenly she noticed the halting, uneven footfalls on the staircase—a sound now dear to her. Her heart thumped harder and she turned from the window.

"See, I told ya." Shooting Charity a smug grin, Pearl gathered up her knitting, plopped it in the basket beside her chair, and headed for the door.

"Where are you goin'?" Charity swung her crutches out in front of her and planted them solidly on the carpet, propelling herself forward. Never once had Pearl left her unchaperoned.

"I have to help Mrs. Akers with somethin' in the kitchen." Pearl mumbled the vague excuse on her way out of the room, nodding at Daniel on his way in. "Afternoon, Mr. Morgan."

The sly grin Pearl shot Charity over her shoulder irked her. Charity knew Pearl Emanuel too well not to know when she was up to something.

"I'm sorry I'm late." Even in his dark wool work shirt and trousers, he looked so handsome that, as Lucy had once said about Travis, it made her eyes hurt.

An odd, almost caressing look in his eyes sent Charity's heart pounding painfully against her ribs. How embarrassing if he should guess she'd worried he might not come.

"Why Daniel, is it past time for your usual visit? I hadn't noticed," she drawled in her best, slightly bored Southern-lady voice.

Attempting to hide the blush she felt flaring in her cheeks, she turned quickly away from him on her crutches. But with her abrupt movement, the tip of one crutch caught in the rug and she pitched forward with a decidedly unladylike yelp.

About the time she expected her face to smack the carpet, it was cradled instead against the soft wool of Daniel's shirt. She could feel the low rumble of his laugh bubble up inside him before it burst forth.

"Oh, Charity. You really shouldn't try to lie. You are so terrible at it."

He turned her gently in his strong embrace until she faced him. Neither spoke as he drew her closer, their locked gazes uttering in unison the soundless sentiments of their hearts.

Resting in the secure circle of his arms, she tipped her head back, closed her eyes, and welcomed his kiss. This time she didn't pull away. No ugly specters from the past popped up to spoil her joy. This was Daniel. No one else. Good, sweet, beloved Daniel. The man who owned her every heartbeat. The man she loved.

"Sweetheart," he whispered warmly against her hair. "I was late because I have some very important things to discuss with you, and I wanted to rehearse them so I'd say them just right."

He gently helped her over to the edge of bed then pulled up a chair so he could face her. "Charity, you have become exceedingly dear to me," he began. Leaning forward, he took her hands into his and shook his head. "No. More than dear. Beloved."

He paused, and the tip of his tongue peeked out to moisten his lips or perhaps taste the lingering remnants of their kiss. "The day I walked into your uncle's sawmill I found a job, but I lost my heart. I've known for months that you are the woman I want by my side for the rest of my life."

His gaze dropped to their linked hands. "For the past several weeks I feel we've grown even closer. That the past—things that once might have been impediments to our mutual happiness—no longer matters—"

"Daniel." Amid the cacophony of the wild, joyful celebration his words triggered inside her, a small, rasping voice of foreboding slinked out to squelch her bliss. The war might be over, the past behind them; but just since her accident she'd learned things about Daniel she hadn't known. About the *Sultana*—and Andersonville. She couldn't bear the thought of worrying each day of their lives that some obscure memory might suddenly emerge, souring their sweet love.

She gave his fingers a gentle squeeze and fixed him with an unflinching gaze. As tempting as it was to lightly dismiss the fact that they'd been on opposite sides of the war, she couldn't risk it. "Your father told me you were in Andersonville."

Daniel paled slightly. "That was in the past. It doesn't have any bearing on—"

"It might." She shook her head and prayed for courage. They had to get it all out—everything. They had to get past this. "Daniel, we need to talk about it. All of it. We can't just pretend it didn't happen, shove it back until one day it's grown into a monster that pounces from its hidin' place to rip our love to shreds."

His body heaved with a mighty sigh, and he shook his head somberly. The muscles working in his angled jaw spoke of his dread.

Charity screwed up her courage and began. "Andersonville. I heard it was—"

"Yes. It was. Everything you heard and more." An anger so intense it frightened her flickered in his dark eyes.

"Tell me. Tell me all of it." Charity stiffened her back and prayed God would give her the courage to bear all she was about to learn.

Daniel drew in and blew out a deep breath, scoured his face with his unsteady hand, then obliged her request. Over the space of an excruciating half hour, he shared with her the horrors to which her countrymen had subjected him and many of his compatriots.

She learned how a guard had broken his leg with an iron bar when he'd attempted to intervene in the beatings of two of his friends. She wept as he described how he'd had to set his own leg, making a splint from the broken lengths of a lean-to pole. By the time he finished with the frightening recounting of the *Sultana* tragedy, Charity's cheeks were drenched.

"I'm sorry. I'm so sorry." The words sounded woefully inadequate.

At last, a gut-wrenching breath shuddered through Daniel as if he were expelling the last of his demons. His features looked weary—drained of energy. But the angry flame in his eyes had been quenched. "Your turn," he murmured with a nod, his expression somber.

Charity felt spent. As bad as her experiences had been, they didn't compare to what he'd described. But just as she needed to know of his sufferings, he needed to know of hers.

She hugged herself to still her shaking body and tried to determine where to start. "Papa died of dropsy just as the war broke out. Asa was seventeen and itchin' to join the Confederate army. But havin' just lost Papa, Mamma forbad it. She told Asa he had to stay and help run the cotton mill." Charity grimaced, remembering the terrible argument between her mother and brother. "But Asa had no interest in millin' cotton, and it was really Jericho and I who ran the mill."

Daniel nodded. The concerned interest on his face encouraged her to continue.

Charity blew out a frayed breath then forged on. "Mamma never got over losin' Papa. Her health failed, and a year later she succumbed to lung fever." She paused to get a better grip on her emotions, focusing on her hands wringing in her lap. If she looked at Daniel now, she'd fling herself into his arms and sob. "The day after Mamma's funeral, Asa joined the army."

Daniel reached out and clasped her hands warmly in his. "And you never saw your brother again?"

Charity sniffed and forced a smile, remembering her last conversation with her brother. "I saw him once more, briefly. It was July 19, 1864. The day before he died."

Daniel let go of her hands and an odd look crossed his face. Taking his action as a cue to resume her narrative, Charity continued. "Asa stopped by the house to tell me he was camped less than a mile away with General Hood's army." Charity's words tumbled out more quickly as she remembered her frantic attempt to keep her brother safe. "I told him I feared there'd be a battle, because I'd just come from the creek and had spied three Union soldiers there fillin' their canteens. Asa kissed my cheek then took off like the devil was after him. That was the last time. . ."

Charity suddenly sensed an odd tenseness in Daniel. An ominous stillness fell between them like the foreboding quiet before a storm. She looked at his face that had gone chalk white.

He rose slowly. Deliberately. Without a word, he simply turned and walked out of the door.

Charity sat stunned and bewildered, listening to his familiar halting steps descending the stairs. What on earth could she have said that would have caused him to react so?

"Daniel." His name came out in a pitiful croak when she finally found her voice.

The sound of his steps paused for an instant then resumed, finally fading away.

Charity sat as if paralyzed, a terrible dread gripping her chest like an icy fist. Although she couldn't begin to guess why, she knew with excruciating certainty that Daniel Morgan would not be back.

Chapter 21

I won't allow it."

Lying on his back in bed, Daniel stiffened at his mother's voice. Why couldn't everyone just leave him be? Was a little solitude too much to ask?

The bed creaked in protest as he slowly pushed himself to a sitting position on the quilt top and swung his legs over the side. He strove to shove down the resentment rising inside him. In his twenty-seven years of life, he'd never shown disrespect to his mother, and he wouldn't start now.

Daniel heaved a sigh and looked up at his mother's resolute figure in the doorway. "Won't allow what, Mother?" he asked in a leaden tone.

"You know very well what!" She planted her fists atop her hips on either side of her still-trim waist. The all too familiar signal that he was in for an extended siege evoked an inward groan from Daniel.

Mother stepped across the threshold into his room. "I won't allow you to cloister yourself away day after day—"

"Three days, Mother. I've only been back home for three days." His words that seemed not to faze his mother struck Daniel full force. It felt like three lifetimes since he'd learned that Charity—the woman who'd won his heart—had been responsible for his and his men's capture.

Mother took another step closer. "What is going on, Daniel? You simply appear at the house, say only that you've quit your job at the mill in Vernon, and closet yourself up here like a recluse. You don't eat. Don't sleep. Oh yes," she answered his surprised glance, "we hear you pacing your room, tromping up and down the stairs at all hours—"

"Is there something you require of me, Mother?" Daniel sprang to his feet and strode to the window. If activity would bring an end to his mother's and Lucy's constant nagging, he'd happily chop firewood for the whole of Madison! "If there is something you would like for me to do for you, I'd be glad to do it."

Mother's weary sigh gouged at Daniel's heart. Her voice softened, which was so much harder to bear than her earlier scolding tone. "Yes, Daniel. I need—we all need—to know what happened. Why you left Vernon. Daniel, whatever it is that's troubling you, you shouldn't let it fester."

Stifling a sardonic snort, Daniel stuffed his hands into his pockets and looked out of the window, seeing nothing. He'd never understood the notion that laying a wounded heart open, exposing its injuries to the harsh light of day, somehow promoted healing. Even animals knew enough to crawl off to a dark, secluded place to lick their wounds.

"Does it have to do with Miss Langdon?" Mother's gentle, coaxing voice did nothing to relax Daniel's shoulder muscles that tensed at her touch. "Because if it does, you recovered from Phoebe's rejection and you shall recover—"

"Yes, Mother, it has to do with Charity!" Daniel whirled to face her. His mother's words had finally managed to lance the festering sore on his heart. So she must deal with the ugliness her determination had freed. "It has to do with Charity. . .and me and Fred and Tom!"

At her puzzled look, he recounted what Charity had told him. At last, Daniel fashioned into words the hideous truth that had haunted his brain like a shapeless, dark apparition these past three days. "It was Charity who put me, Fred, and Tom in Andersonville. I limp because of Charity. Fred and Tom are dead because of Charity."

Only the long silence that stretched between them indicated his mother's shocked surprise. But in truth, he never expected his stunning revelation to evoke any outward sign of dismay from his unflappable parent. Years of training her countenance to remain serene before seriously ill patients had given his mother a poker face to rival that of the most skilled gambler.

"My darling, it was the war. I'm sure she had no idea the consequences of telling her brother that she'd seen the three of you."

His mother's sweet smile made Daniel want to bury his head in her shoulder and sob as he did when he was young. But he wouldn't allow her—or anyone— to manufacture excuses for Charity's actions.

"What difference does it make why she did it, Mother?" Daniel rubbed his forehead. "The fact is she did it."

"And what was her response when you told her you were among the men captured?"

Daniel turned back to the window. This was the question he'd most dreaded. His abrupt departure—that he'd simply walked away from Charity—had bothered him since he left Vernon. "I didn't tell her. I just left."

"Oh, Daniel." The disappointment in Mother's voice stung worse than if she'd slapped him. He knew his parents prided themselves in having raised him and Lucy with exemplary manners.

He turned and forced himself to meet his mother's look of dismay, his gaze pleading for understanding. "I couldn't stay in that room, Mother. Not another moment. Not after I learned that two of the best friends I've ever had—men who saved my life more times than I care to count—lay dead because of the woman I. . ." He couldn't bring himself to finish the thought.

"The woman you love?" Mother softly finished it for him.

Daniel nodded, not trusting his voice.

After a long pause during which Daniel assumed she was weighing her next words, Mother blew out another soft sigh. "Have you asked God's guidance in this?"

This time, Daniel didn't even try to stifle his sarcastic snort. "Why would I ask God for guidance when He allowed me to fall in love with the woman who has the blood of my friends on her hands?" He rubbed his hand across his forehead so hard it hurt.

"You'll never rub it away, you know." Mother's voice had taken on a hard edge. "Ever since you returned from the war, you've been rubbing your head like you're trying to rub away the images there. You won't talk to your father, or me, or even Lucy about what happened to you. And you won't let us talk about it."

She folded her arms over her chest and cocked her head. A small smile tipped up her lips. "Do you remember the time when Lucy was little and I asked her to sweep dirt from the parlor carpet?"

Daniel couldn't imagine how that incident—one of Lucy's many childish acts of mischief—could have anything to do with his current situation. But eager to steer the conversation in another direction, he nodded. "You praised her for doing a good job of it and even gave her a penny and had me take her down to the drugstore to buy a stick of candy." He chuckled at the memory, in spite of himself. "Come to find out, the little swindler had swept the carpet all right but had hid all the dirt under it."

"That's you, Daniel." Mother's gaze bored into him. "The hate you still carry in your heart from things that happened in the war are like the little piles of dirt Lucy swept under the rug. Just because you don't talk about them, don't bring them out where they can be seen, doesn't mean they are gone."

Daniel bristled. "No amount of talking is going to change anything, Mother."

"Maybe talking to us won't, but talking to God can." She gave his arm a little squeeze. "Give the hate to God, Daniel. All of it. It's the only way you'll ever get rid of it."

Mother finally slipped out of the door, and Daniel was glad. He had no intention of doing any more talking to God. He'd *been* talking to God and had gotten only heartache in return. Instead of talking, he'd like to rail at God for playing such a dirty trick on him. Of all the women who could have attached themselves to his heart, why this one?

What Charity told him should have killed any affection he had for her. But it hadn't. Instead it flourished, resisting his every effort to eradicate it. Her sweet, angelic face framed by honey-blond curls teased and tortured his every thought. Her visage vied with the gray, bloodied faces of Fred and Tom, their gory lips fashioning one accusing word, over and over.

"Traitor."

In Andersonville, the guards had mongrel dogs they abused in order to make them mean. When one dog would find a bone or morsel of food, another dog would grab the loose end in his mouth, and they'd snarl and fight until the prize was ripped asunder. Daniel felt as if there were two angry, fighting dogs inside him, pulling in opposite directions and ripping his insides to shreds.

He sank back to his bed. Bending forward, he pressed his face in his hands. Charity put him in Andersonville. But his love for her had sentenced him to a prison more awful than Andersonville—and one from which he feared he would never emerge.

Chapter 22

"Write to 'im."

Charity looked up at Pearl from the library's mahogany desktop. "I will not!" She reared back in the leather chair as if the sheets of Aunt Jennie's stationery Pearl held out to her were red hot. "Have you lost your senses entirely, Pearl Emanuel?"

Pearl slammed the paper down on the desktop beside the mill's debit book. "Reckon I'm as sound in mind as most and better'n some!" Her dark eyes pinned Charity with a glare that dared her to break the gaze. "Adam said in his letter that Daniel's been mopin' aroun' like all the life's been plumb sucked outta him. Anyways, that's what Daniel's aunt Rosaleen told Adam's ma."

"And why should I care in the least little bit if Daniel Morgan is mopin' or not?" Charity pretended to study numbers in the debit book, although her brain refused to register the figures on the page. As fond as she was of her friend, sometimes Pearl could irritate the hide off a mule!

"'Cause you love 'im."

At Pearl's quiet declaration, Charity puffed out a breath of surrender and grabbed the edge of the desk to help push herself up. She couldn't bear to hear the truth that screamed day and night from her heart put into words, even by Pearl, whom she loved like a sister.

She gingerly shifted her weight from her injured left leg. Although the leg grew stronger every day, she was still reluctant to exert much force on it. Last week, Dr. Morgan removed her splint, examined her leg, and declared her healed. Before he left, he apologized for his son's rude departure. He went on to explain that Daniel had been in the group of Union soldiers whose whereabouts Charity had alerted her brother to the day before the Battle of Peachtree Creek.

While Dr. Morgan's explanation had resolved the mystery of Daniel's sudden leave-taking, the implication of his words hit Charity like a body blow. Remembering how Asa had raced out of the house that day, she had no doubt her brother precipitated Daniel and the other Union soldiers' capture. That knowledge collided with the awful images of Andersonville Daniel had painted in her mind, making her physically ill.

Charity took a few halting steps toward the hat tree beside the library door that opened to the hallway. The day was unusually warm for mid-March, and if Pearl insisted on pestering her, she might as well enjoy the sunshine.

Pearl rounded the desk in pursuit. "Maybe you can run away from me, but you cain't run away from yer heart."

Charity reached for her shawl then turned and gave Pearl a hug. "I know you mean well, but there's nothin' I can do or say to amend what I did." She shrugged her shoulders in defeat. "It doesn't matter how I feel about Daniel. He hates me—and I can't blame him."

"If he hated you, he wouldn't be mopin'." Pearl stepped between Charity and the doorway. "You got to tell him, Miss Charity. You got to tell him that you promised yer ma you'd take care of Asa an' you was feared Asa would run right smack into Daniel an' them other Yankee soldiers."

"Daniel doesn't care why I did it, Pearl. Andersonville crippled him and killed his friends."

Ignoring Pearl's scowl, Charity wrapped her shawl around her shoulders and limped out of the library, down the hall, and out of the front door.

Today, school was letting out for the summer, and in a half hour, Henry would be returning home. Dr. Morgan had suggested short walks would strengthen Charity's leg, and she knew it would please Henry for her to meet him at the crossroads of Jackson and Perry streets on the last day of school. Perhaps Pearl was right. Maybe she couldn't run away from her feelings for Daniel. But during the past week, she'd used her growing affection for Henry to help plug up the hole Daniel's leaving had gouged in her heart.

On the porch, she gripped the handrail alongside the two stone front steps and haltingly descended to the gravel walkway. It felt good to be outside again—to breathe in fresh air and feel the ground beneath her feet.

Beside the steps, she noticed yellow and purple crocuses blooming. Spring would come. Life would go on. Charity found little joy in the blossoms' silent proclamation.

She needed to get away—away from Vernon and the mill, places that evoked thoughts of Daniel. She was glad she'd saved the letter the New South Investment Company had sent to Sam. Tonight she'd write to Mr. Armand Dubois and inquire if the land in Fulton County, Georgia, was still for sale.

Since the accident, the bond between Charity and Henry had grown even stronger. He increasingly looked to her as a mother figure, and she couldn't love him more if he was her natural son. Aunt Jennie and Uncle Silas had grown attached to the child as well, and Charity had no doubt Uncle Silas would be willing to become Henry's legal guardian.

But Henry needed a new start, too, and he still talked about returning to Georgia. Yesterday, Charity had read with interest an article in one of Aunt Jennie's penny magazines that told of churches recruiting missionaries to help with reconstruction of the South. They were especially looking for Christian teachers. She could join one of the groups traveling to Georgia. While there, she could search for any kin Henry might still have living in the state. It would also give her an opportunity to investigate the land New South Investment was selling in her home county. . . .

"Ah, Charity, ma chère. It is good to see you up and walking." Annie Martin's voice filtered through Charity's musings.

Charity looked across the yard to where the old woman stood outside the front gate, a large market basket on her arm.

Annie grinned from the shaded depths of her dark wool bonnet. Her quick, studying gaze seemed to miss nothing as it slid over Charity.

"That evening last January down by the river, I wasn't sure I would see you again this side of heaven."

Charity limped toward the wrought-iron gate separating the two. "Now I distinctly remember you tellin' me I would be all right," she teased, responding with a grin of her own. Unlike Aunt Jennie or many of Charity's other female acquaintances, Annie would not take offense at such a contradictory rejoinder. Indeed, the sprightly old woman seemed to delight in friendly verbal sparring.

"And so you would have been—either way." Annie's agate-colored eyes sparkled and her chin lifted. "Like the apostle Paul said, 'For to me to live is Christ, and to die is gain.' In Christ our souls are safe, wherever God decides they should dwell."

Charity gave a little laugh—the first that had passed her lips since Daniel left Vernon. Annie Martin was good medicine for her. "Of course you are right, Annie, as always."

Annie cast a glance across the street to the courthouse lawn. "I have been waiting all winter to sit on that bench beneath that old catalpa tree. Would you like to join me?"

Charity nodded. "I would love to." After weeks of Pearl and Aunt Jennie's doting, Annie's company was as refreshing as the spring breeze.

They ambled haltingly across Perry Street. Charity didn't doubt that the spry septuagenarian could have easily out-distanced her. But she appreciated Annie slowing her steps to accommodate Charity's infirmity.

They sat on the bench, and Annie placed her linen-covered basket on the spring grass at her feet. She reached beneath the linen cloth covering the basket and pulled out a square of blue knitting with two wooden needles attached. After a moment, she settled back against the bench and inhaled deeply. "Smell that? That's the smell of promise. . .of hope."

Charity followed her lead and sniffed the air filled with the earthy scents of sod, budding vegetation, and the unidentifiable fragrance of newness.

Sitting quietly with her hands clasped in her lap, Charity made no response. The words "hope" and "promise" held little meaning for her now. Those words had walked out of her life two weeks ago with Daniel.

"Funny how we're always surprised when they come back." Annie's words jerked Charity's attention back to the woman beside her.

"What?" Her mind never far from thoughts of Daniel, Charity's face warmed and her heart thumped harder.

"The spring bulb flowers." Annie nodded her bonneted head toward a row of little green spikes poking up along the base of the black iron fence. In another couple of weeks, the daffodils would decorate the fencerow with a solid line of sunny yellow blossoms. "Each spring, we're always just a little surprised to see them come up, do you not agree?"

"Yes, I suppose so," Charity mumbled. Her heart slowed to a more normal rhythm. She had no doubt that Annie was well aware Daniel had left Vernon. Little happened in this town that escaped Annie's knowledge. But Charity had just left the house to avoid a conversation with Pearl about Daniel. She had no interest in taking up the subject with Annie.

"It is like love, yes?" Annie gave her an innocuous smile as her nimble fingers worked the yarn around the clicking needles. "You may not see evidences of it for a season," she said, "but all things planted by God in the heart or in the earth do not die. They sleep and wait for God's hand to stir them awake, reviving our faith and reminding us that God, who makes all things new, is still in control."

Charity blinked back bitter tears. She understood Annie's little parable had to do with her heartbreak over Daniel.

When she could trust her voice, she faced Annie. "But if you dig up the bulbs—destroy them—they will not come back."

"Ahh." Annie stopped her work long enough to wave a wrinkled hand. "A few years ago, I dug up a clump of bluebells that grew behind my barn. I wanted to plant them instead under the tree by my front porch," she said with a grin. "I dug and dug and was sure I had them all."

Her fingers stilled again and the kind smile she turned to Charity smoothed the wrinkles around her mouth. "Yet every spring, bluebells still bloom behind my barn. We cannot destroy what God intends, ma chère."

Charity met her seatmate's knowing look, her eyes widening. Annie could not have known why Daniel left, yet somehow, the astute old woman must have guessed it had something to do with Charity.

They sat quietly for a time, watching robins peck for worms in the damp earth. Charity allowed the cheerful songs of the birds and the *clickety-click* of Annie's knitting needles to fill the silence that stretched between them.

"You do not believe me, ma chère?" Annie said at length, a smile embroidering the edges of her voice.

Charity shrugged. Let Annie think what she liked, but Charity had seen the look on Daniel's face before he walked out of her room that afternoon two weeks ago. Whatever love he'd had for her, she'd irreparably destroyed.

Charity rubbed her unadorned left hand and glanced at the little brick church perched on the hill above Jefferson Street, overlooking Vernon. Then her gaze slid to the large brick and stone courthouse to their right. If she had never forced that discussion with Daniel—if neither of them had learned of her part in his capture—the two of them might have been procuring their marriage license in that courthouse. Reverend Davenport might be performing their wedding ceremony. . . .

A renewed sense of loss seized Charity in an almost suffocating grip. The sooner she left Vernon, and Indiana, the better.

"I've decided to go back to Georgia," Charity blurted. "I thought perhaps I could search for some of Henry's kin. Uncle Silas and Aunt Jennie have been very generous concernin' Henry—as they have been with me—but if the boy has family there, it's only right that they learn of his situation." She fixed her gaze on a robin tugging a fat worm from the black earth but could feel the heat of Annie's scrutinizing gaze.

The clicking of Annie's needles slowed a beat or two. "It is a kind thing you and your kin did for the boy—taking him in. But from what I understand, the South is still very unsettled after the war. I would not have thought your aunt disposed to visiting a place in such turmoil."

Charity readjusted her shawl around her shoulders, wishing she had some knitting of her own to keep her hands busy. "My aunt and uncle and Henry won't be going. . .not at first, anyway. Just me."

Annie sat up straighter, and her knitting needles fell silent. "That is a long way for a young woman to go alone, do you not think, ma chère?"

A giggle burst from Charity's lips. A trip to Georgia paled in comparison to the harrowing stories Annie had told of her youth. "How can you say such a thing when you were dragged across the country by Shawnee during a war while in the family way?"

The clicking began again, and the smile returned to Annie's voice. "Well, it was not by choice. And I was only seventeen—too young to know just how frightened I should be. But you should know better than to travel alone—"

"But I won't be alone. I plan to join one of the missionary groups that are helpin' rebuild the South. I have an address of a group that is askin' for teachers to join them."

Annie's concerned scowl suddenly changed to one of startled enlightenment. "Oh, I almost forgot." She dropped the knitting to her lap and reached into the basket. "That's what happens when you get old. You get forgetful," she added with a little laugh. "I stopped by the post office to mail a letter to my son Jonah and his wife, and Jim McClelland asked me to bring this by. He missed gettin' it in the bunch Pearl picked up earlier for you." She held out a little square envelope to Charity.

The sound of children's voices drew their attentions to the crossroads of Perry and Jackson Street. "Here comes your young charge now," Annie said.

Eager to reach Henry, Charity stuffed the envelope in her skirt pocket. The letter would have to wait. She rose stiffly, half wishing she had used the time to exercise her leg.

Annie grasped Charity's hand and angled her face up, her narrow auburn brows knitted together tighter than the rows of yarn she'd been working.

"Just be sure you're runnin' toward God's will and not away from it. Pray for God's guidance before you do anything, Charity. And give God time to do His work. *Qui vivra verra.* What will be, will be. But remember, 'A man's heart deviseth his way: but the Lord directeth his steps.' "

"I will pray, Annie," Charity promised. Eager to get to Henry and hear of his day, she slipped her fingers from the old woman's.

Annie's face brightened like the sky when the sun breaks through the clouds. "Thank you for keepin' me company for a while. I think I'll sit here in the sun a bit longer and warm up like an old lizard on a rock," she said with a cackle.

With a parting smile and nod to Annie, Charity limped as quickly as her leg allowed toward Henry, who'd nearly reached the house. She would say nothing to him yet of her plans to travel to Georgia. She would take Annie's advice and pray about it.

But her heart wailed night and day in lament at the loss of Daniel's love. The only respite she could see was escape from this place and all that reminded her of him.

For some reason, God had seen fit to separate them with this unbridgeable chasm. Obviously, they were not meant to be together. Her only prayer now was that God would give her the courage to do what she needed to do for both her and Henry. And somehow fill Daniel's heart with enough mercy that he wouldn't spend the rest of his life despising her.

That evening after supper, she passed the library and noticed Uncle Silas had left the light burning. Suddenly remembering the envelope Annie had given her, she reached into her pocket and pulled it out. When she examined the return address her heart raced. It was from Lucy Morgan.

Surely Lucy had learned of Charity's involvement in Daniel's capture. Could she be writing to vent her anger? The notion evaporated the moment it was formed. From what Charity had seen of Lucy Morgan, she doubted the woman capable of harboring even a speck of guile.

She broke the seal and slipped out the single sheet of fine stationery. Quickly perusing the missive, she realized it was an invitation to Lucy and Travis's wedding to be held in April, the Saturday following Easter.

Beneath the formal invitation, Charity noticed Lucy had written a postscript.

I pray you will find it in your heart to grace us with your presence.
Daniel's spirits have been so very low since returning to Madison, I am more
than confident your attendance would be a positive tonic for his melancholy.

The words blurred before Charity's misty eyes. Was Daniel grieving, too, over the lost joy they might have known together? Charity was not at all sure she shared Lucy's optimism. In all probability, her attendance would only serve to cause her and Daniel added pain.

On the other hand, perhaps this was an answer to her prayer. She had no hope of reclaiming Daniel's love. But perhaps attending Lucy's wedding would provide her with an opportunity to beg his forgiveness, hopefully freeing both her and Daniel from a life sentence of anger and guilt.

Chapter 23

"The whole family has gone mad!" Daniel muttered the sentiment he'd held for the past several days as he limped across the wide expanse of Main-Cross Street. Everyone but him, it seemed, was not only actively involved but obsessed with Lucy and Travis's coming wedding. As the date neared—now only two weeks away—the one advantage Daniel found amid the craziness was that the family's collective attention had shifted from him to his sister's nuptials.

Like a formidable army general, Mother led the campaign for a flawless wedding, daily assigning chores to each family member and household employee.

Daniel had no clue what errands Uncle Jacob had waiting for him at the church, but this morning when Mother consulted her wedding preparation notes and relegated errands, he welcomed the fact his assignment required a walk across town. After his discussion with mother concerning Charity, the sympathy heaped upon him had been next to smothering. So the mad dash to finalize the wedding plans had granted him a respite from his family's well-meaning but exasperating pity.

However, Daniel's own mind and heart had not granted him any such respite. The sound of Charity calling his name as he walked away from her, down the Gants' staircase and out of the house, continued to echo torturously through his mind. The memory of the hurt tone in her voice slashed at his heart. He remembered the strong, painful tug on his heartstrings that had momentarily halted his descent, urging him to turn back and retrace his steps. But pride? Anger? Perhaps both had propelled him down the stairs, out of Vernon, and out of her life.

More than once since his return home, he'd been tempted to gather up a few necessities and leave Madison—maybe even Indiana—and become the bummer Charity had accused him of being that first day at Gant's Mill. But deep down, he knew he could travel the world over and never escape his love for Charity Langdon. And that realization was gradually killing him.

He slowed his pace as he headed down Broadway. Easing down the sharp slope, he stretched out his longer leg first to accommodate his uneven gait. Thoughts of his own infirmity reminded him of Charity's injury. Was she walking now without the crutches he'd made for her? How carefully, how lovingly he'd fashioned those crutches. And when he'd presented them to her, his heart had swelled at the tears of appreciation he'd seen glistening in her blue eyes.

Daniel paused at the edge of Broadway while a wagon and mule team rumbled past, sending up gray puffs of gravel dust. He scrubbed his face. Then he remembered what Mother had told him and knew she was right. He could scrub his forehead raw and never erase the torturous images that lay behind it.

He gazed at the greening lawns coming alive with vivid colors of spring flowers. Yellow blooms covered the large forsythia bush on the east side of Uncle Jacob and Aunt Rosaleen's parsonage. The cheerful chirping of birds tickled his ears. The scents of greening vegetation filled his nostrils. From every direction, the newness of spring bombarded his senses. It all felt like an insult to his withered spirit. Two weeks ago, his heart had blossomed like the burgeoning spring, joyfully anticipating joining his life with Charity's. But God had played a cruel trick, turning his sweet joy into souring resentment.

Daniel neared the church, not at all liking the wad of scorn and anger building inside him at the sight of the building. Uncle Jacob had helped to build this church with his own hands. Daniel had attended services here since the building's completion when he was six years old. It was in this church at the age of fourteen that he'd made his confession of faith and given his heart to Christ. Yet at this moment, as he gazed on the building's brick and stone facade, Daniel felt only anger.

Had he lost his faith entirely? Facing the enemy's rifles across the battlefields of the South, through the unspeakable horrors of Andersonville, when the *Sultana* hurled him into the Mississippi's unforgiving waters, he'd kept his faith. He'd clung to it like a lifeline. Even after the war when he'd ignored God, he'd felt no animosity toward his Maker.

But knowing that God had allowed him to fall helplessly in love with the woman who'd trespassed in the worst way against him and the men he'd loved like brothers was something he could not bear. He imagined the Almighty sneering down upon his misery, and a terrible, frightening rage boiled in his belly.

By the time he reached the church's steps, he had to summon every ounce of his sense of duty in order to mount them and enter the building. He'd come here to help Uncle Jacob, not to commune with God. The sound of wood clacking against wood greeted Daniel as he passed from the vestibule into the sanctuary.

Dressed in work trousers and rolled-up shirt sleeves, Uncle Jacob knelt on the raised stage at the front of the church, prying up flooring planks with an iron crowbar.

Daniel made his way up the aisle between the rows of pews, half wondering if his uncle had taken leave of his senses. "Uh, do you think it's a good idea to be tearing up the church just before Lucy's wedding—not to mention Easter?"

Uncle Jacob looked up and grinned. He ran the back of his hand across his sweaty forehead. "When that storm tore a hole in the roof last fall," he said, glancing upwards, "rain damaged this floor. We had enough to do just getting the roof patched before winter. But now," he shifted his gaze down to the pile of ripped-up boards beside him, "this floor is beginning to warp." His grin widened. "I wouldn't want to be preaching—or about to proclaim your sister and Mr. Ashby man and wife—and suddenly disappear beneath the stage."

Chuckling at the picture, Daniel nodded and took in the situation. This was something he could do. The past two weeks of idleness had driven him to near distraction. He relished the opportunity to busy his hands working with tools and wood.

For the next several minutes, the two worked together with little talk. After determining the subfloor was undamaged, they began fitting new boards in place to close the gaping hole in the stage. Daniel picked up a fragrant, newly planed oak plank from the pile of replacement wood Uncle Jacob had assembled. Taking hold of one end while his uncle held the other, Daniel smacked the edge of the board with the heel of his hand, shoving it flush against the existing old flooring.

"Ouch!" Uncle Jacob shook his pinched finger then popped it into his mouth.

"Sorry, Uncle. I should have made sure your fingers were out of the way." Remorse smote him. Minor accidents were a common occurrence in woodworking, but he regretted that his inattention had caused his uncle an injury.

Uncle Jacob shook his head. "Don't wor—" He suddenly stopped and narrowed his eyes at Daniel. "What would you say if I said I don't forgive you for pinching my finger, Daniel?"

Bewildered and a little hurt, Daniel rocked back on his heels and met Uncle Jacob's look. It was not like his uncle to hold any kind of grudge, especially for something as trivial as a hurt finger.

Daniel gave a nervous chuckle. "I guess I'd say you need to get another helper."

"Of course I forgive you, Daniel." The kind smile Uncle Jacob gave Daniel swept him back to his childhood. "Do you feel better for having been forgiven?"

An uncomfortable feeling squiggled through Daniel. Exactly what point was Uncle Jacob trying to make? "I suppose I do," he mumbled.

"And I feel better for having forgiven you."

Avoiding his uncle's gaze, Daniel lifted another new board from the pile beside them. "Is this one of your famous lessons, Uncle?"

Uncle Jacob gave a little shrug. "Just working out this Sunday's sermon. The theme is forgiveness and is taken from the fourth chapter of Ephesians. 'Let all bitterness, and wrath, and anger, and clamour, and evil speaking, be put away from you, with all malice: And be ye kind one to another, tenderhearted, forgiving one another, even as God for Christ's sake hath forgiven you.' I hope to show that by obeying Christ's commandment to forgive, both parties are blessed."

Daniel decided it might not be prudent to tell his uncle he didn't plan to be in the audience.

Uncle Jacob grunted and popped his finger into his mouth again. "Although forgiving you has lightened my soul, it's done nothing to stop this finger from bleeding," he said with a little laugh. "I'm afraid I'll have to have your aunt Rosaleen bandage it. I'll be back directly." Stepping down from the stage, he headed toward the front door.

Daniel grinned. "I know you, Uncle. You just welcome an excuse for Aunt Rosaleen to dote on you."

"Don't need an excuse," his uncle shot over his shoulder before disappearing into the vestibule.

Daniel turned his attention back to the work at hand and pounded a nail into the new board, securing it to the subfloor. Uncle Jacob was a wily old fox. He didn't doubt for a moment his uncle had the situation between Daniel and Charity in mind when he made the point about forgiveness.

Daniel blew out a deep breath and ran his hand over his face. After the war, he'd convinced himself he'd forgiven the Rebs for what they'd done to Tom and Fred. And to him. But he hadn't. Learning the part Charity had played in his capture had dredged up the foul, rotting hatred he'd buried in the dark recesses of his soul. Mother was right—simply not thinking about it didn't constitute forgiveness.

He pounded another nail into the board so hard the hammer's head dented the wood. He wasn't sure he *could* forgive his captors. Or that he wanted to.

And Charity shared their guilt. Her only thought had been to help the Confederacy, not caring what lives might be lost as a result. To continue loving her meant he had to forgive her. And forgiving her complicity in the matter felt dangerously close to treason. So somehow, some way, he had to stop loving her. And if that meant his soul must remain burdened, then so be it!

A sound near the vestibule yanked him from his troubling thoughts. Uncle Jacob must have returned. But when Daniel glanced up, he didn't see his uncle but was greeted instead by a dark, smiling face. For an instant, he thought it was Uncle Jacob's old friend, Andrew Chapman. But he quickly realized it was Pearl Emanuel's father, Jericho.

Daniel knew Uncle Jacob and Aunt Rosaleen enjoyed close acquaintances with the free blacks at Georgetown. He also suspected they remained deeply involved in the continued work of the Underground Railroad. He gave the man a smile and nod. "Jericho. If you'd like to talk to Uncle Jacob, he's gone to the parsonage. . . ."

Jericho shook his graying head as he continued walking toward the stage. "You's the one I wants to talk to, Mr. Morgan. Has to do with Miss Langdon."

Fear leaped in Daniel's chest. Strength drained out of him and he dropped the hammer with a clatter. Had something happened to Charity? "Is—is she ill? Is she hurt?"

Jericho shook his head, sending a wave of relief swooshing through Daniel.

"My girl, Pearl, she writes reg'lar to Andrew Chapman's boy, Adam." He flashed a gleaming smile up to Daniel. "Pearl and Adam, they's promised, ya know."

Daniel nodded, wishing the man would get to the point.

"Well, sir. . ." Jericho paused and twisted his black felt hat in his hand. As with many of his race who'd been reared in slavery, Jericho's gaze tended to slide downward when talking to white folks. "It ain't in my nature to interfere, but my girl begged me to talk to you. Seems Miss Charity's got a crazy notion in her head to go back to Georgia with a bunch o' missionary teachers 'n sich. The South ain't no safe place to be these days, Mr. Morgan."

Jericho's comment set Daniel back on his heels. But at second thought, he didn't find it all that surprising. He'd heard Charity mention on more than one occasion that she dreamed of returning to her home state. But Jericho was right. From what Daniel had heard, the South swarmed with carpetbaggers and rogues of every stripe. All points south of the Mason-Dixon Line were nearly as dangerous now as they'd been during the war.

As Daniel headed for the steps connecting the stage with the main sanctuary floor, one thought tamed the fear rearing up inside him. Silas and Jennie Gant would never agree to allow Charity to set off on any venture they'd deem unsafe.

Daniel settled himself on the top step and motioned for Jericho to join him. "Georgia? Surely Mr. and Mrs. Gant would never allow—"

"They don't know. Miss Charity made Pearl promise not to tell 'em." Jericho's jerky movements as he gingerly perched himself on the bottom step spoke of his unease. "But Pearl never promised not to tell anybody else. She thought maybe you—"

"I'm afraid Miss Langdon and I didn't part under friendly circumstances." Daniel's cheek twitched with the forced smile. Now it was his turn to feel uncomfortable.

"Pearl tol' me 'bout you bein' one of the soldiers Miss Charity saw at Peachtree Creek 'fore that battle in '64." For once, Jericho looked Daniel directly in the eye. "If you don't mind my sayin' so, I think there's somethin' you need to know."

Daniel cocked his head and sat up straighter, his spine stiffening. He wasn't sure he cared to hear any more about the incident, but he'd let the man have his say.

"Miss Charity—well, she's like one of my own." Jericho's reddening eyes glistened with unshed tears. "Me'n Tunia, we b'longed to the plantation that bordered Miss Charity's pappy's place. We'd jist jumped the broom when the man who owned us took a notion to sell Tunia. Well, sir, Mr. Langdon got wind of it an' offered to buy us both. It liked to ruined him, but he done it." Jericho paused, cleared his throat, and dropped his gaze to his hands wadding his hat.

Daniel sat quietly, allowing the man to get a better grip on his emotions.

Jericho snuffed and swiped a weathered hand under his nose. "Miss Charity's pappy treated us more like fam'ly than slaves." He looked up at Daniel and flashed a grin. "We stayed, had our Pearl, and raised her 'longside Miss Charity and her brother, Asa. Then when Massa Langdon passed on, he left it in his will that we be freed. But we stayed and worked the mill, 'cause Miz Langdon was poorly and couldn'ta managed without us."

Although unsure what all this had to do with Charity's part in his capture, Daniel found the information fascinating and nodded for Jericho to proceed.

"Miss Charity, she was more like her pappy. Solid. Good head on her shoulders." He chuckled and shook his grizzled head. "That boy, though. . .he was a wild one. Wilder'n a deer. Always outta one scrape and into 'nother! After Massa Langdon passed on, it was all Charity's ma could do to keep that boy reined in. So when she knew she was 'bout to foller Massa Langdon through the pearly gates, she made Miss Charity promise to watch out for her brother—try to keep him safe."

Jericho's dark gaze pierced Daniel's. "That's what she was tryin' to do that afternoon. Nothin' more. Nothin' less. Jist tryin' to do what she promised her ma." He shook his head sadly. "Didn't do no good though. Asa fell next day in battle, less than a half mile from where he was born and raised."

Daniel swallowed hard. He wouldn't have thought knowing the reason Charity had disclosed his and his men's location would make any difference to him. But it did.

With a groan, Jericho planted his hands against his knees and rose slowly. "Ol' bones don't move so fast these days," he said with a grin. "Sorry to take up so much of your time, Mr. Morgan." Then he narrowed his eyes at Daniel, his dark forehead wrinkling. "Jist thought you ought to know why she done it, that's all." He poked his chest with a finger. "Ain't never seen a better heart than what beats inside that girl." With that, Jericho turned and ambled down the aisle and out of the church.

The scripture Uncle Jacob had quoted about forgiveness talked about a tender heart. When Jericho explained Charity's actions, Daniel had felt his heart soften in his chest. He felt mean. Regret draped his spirit like a wet overcoat. If not for his capture, he would have participated in the Battle of Peachtree Creek. A minie-ball from his own gun might have killed Charity's brother. How many times had he sighted down his rifle barrel at a faceless Confederate soldier, held his breath, squeezed the trigger, and watched his target fall lifeless before him?

Yet for the past two weeks, he'd done nothing but feel sorry for himself and rail at God like a sanctimonious idiot. The sour taste of hypocrisy rose up in his throat like bitter bile. How Charity must despise him—and he didn't blame her.

Daniel stood and gazed around this sanctuary he'd known since childhood. Why should he be surprised that it was in this place his heart finally heard the whisperings of God's still, small voice?

A new, terrible sadness took hold of him. It was too late. God had given him a chance to have Charity's love. And because he was too proud to forgive, he'd thrown it away. He wished with all of his heart he could do something to stop her from leaving for Georgia—to somehow protect her. But after walking away from her the way he did, he couldn't imagine convincing her to accept his apology, let alone to stay in Indiana.

He blinked back the emotion misting his sight. "Dear Lord, forgive me. I know I can never win back Charity's affection. I just ask that she not hold me in the basest contempt. And take care of her. Please, Lord, take care of her."

Chapter 24

"I still think it's a bad idee!" Pearl huffed out the words as she walked beside Charity.

The considerable incline of Madison's Mulberry Street taxed Charity's lungs as well as her legs. Only now did she fully realize how much the weeks she'd spent convalescing in bed had weakened her constitution.

"I thought you wanted pearl buttons for your weddin' dress." Charity knew it was useless to act ignorant of Pearl's meaning, but she hoped to postpone the argument as long as possible. She wished now she hadn't told Pearl about the letter she received last week from Mr. Dubois, telling her of his plans to be in Madison.

"You know good an' well I ain't talkin' about shoppin' fer buttons." Pearl clutched Charity's arm to steady her when she stumbled slightly at a dip in the road.

"No good's gonna come from talkin' to that man. An' if Mammy knew we was goin' to that place, she'd rail and pray over us for two solid hours, then make us scrub with lye soap till our skin was raw!" A mixture of fear and aggravation flickered in Pearl's dark eyes. "In fact, I been prayin' the Good Lord'll send an angel to stop you right in yer tracks, 'cause heaven knows, I ain't been able to."

Charity stopped and drew in a restorative breath. She was glad they'd finally reached Main-Cross Street, but Pearl's words had dampened her earlier bravado. Indeed, she'd spent countless nights praying for God's guidance in the matter. But no good reason had presented itself to dissuade her from going forward with her plans.

"You act like it's a saloon or somethin', Pearl. It's just a hotel, and we'll only be in the lobby." She reached in her skirt pocket and fingered the letter she'd received two days ago from Armand Dubois.

"I jist don't like lyin' to Mammy. And that Madison Hotel is full of all kinds of dangerous gamblers an' such off them riverboats."

The quiver in Pearl's voice raked at Charity's conscience. Pearl and Adam's wedding was only two days away. She shouldn't be tarnishing her friend's joy with her own concerns.

Charity blinked back tears as she turned and gave Pearl a quick hug. She didn't like to think about starting a new life in Georgia without her childhood friend by her side. "We haven't lied to Tunia. We *are* goin' button shoppin'. Right after I talk to Mr. Dubois. And if you don't want to go in with me—"

Pearl gasped. "I ain't 'bout to let you go in the Madison Hotel by yerself! Hard tellin' what that carpetbagger and his scalawag friends might do."

Charity turned her attention to the traffic along the main thoroughfare. She waited for a farm wagon and two buggies to pass, then started across the street's wide expanse. The sooner she got this meeting over, the better. "I'm just goin' to talk to Mr. Dubois about the land back home, Pearl. That's all."

Safely on the south side of Main-Cross Street, Pearl grasped Charity's arm and pulled her up short. "I ain't got a good feelin' 'bout this. 'Sides, you take off all suddenlike an' you knows it'll throw Miz Jennie into all kinds o' conniptions an' vapors. Massa Gant won't have nobody to do all his mill figurin', an' it'll send poor li'l Henry into another fit o' grievin'."

Pearl's indictment rubbed sorely against Charity's raw conscience. Her aunt and uncle had been good to her. They'd taken her in and given her a nice life after she lost everything. And the way they'd accepted Henry after Sam's death had warmed her heart. She knew Pearl was right. Yet she couldn't turn her back on this chance to return to Georgia. . .and maybe find Henry's family in the bargain.

Charity pushed a long, weary sigh from her lips. "I promise I will tell them when I return to Vernon. The thought of hurtin' them truly pains me, but—"

"Charity? Why, it is you, isn't it?"

Lucy Morgan's voice spun Charity around. Heat filled her cheeks as she turned to face Daniel's sister. She hadn't replied to Lucy's wedding invitation, having not fully decided whether or not to attend the couple's nuptials.

The oversight seemed not to bother Lucy in the least. That musical little laugh Charity remembered bubbled from Lucy's lips as she trained her irrepressible smile on Charity. "I'm so glad to see you walking so well. I could hardly detect a limp."

Charity's burdened spirit lightened in the face of Lucy's infectious cheerfulness, and she experienced an unexpected flash of regret. It would have been nice to have this happy woman as a sister. She gave Lucy a heartfelt smile. "Please tell your father that I shall always be indebted to him for savin' my leg."

Lucy reached out and patted Charity's hand. She cocked her bonneted head, and her lips curved up gently. "Oh, what a sweet thing to say. Of course I will relay your sentiment to Papa. But just knowing that you are doing well is all the reward he requires." Then an impish grin replaced Lucy's kind smile. "Well, that and your uncle's generous payment of the bill," she added, sending out another melodic giggle to dance gaily on the spring air.

Lucy glanced down at the basket on her arm. "Speaking of financial matters— which I'm loath to do—I've just finished another shopping errand for wedding notions." Her slight shoulders rose and fell with her resigned sigh. "There seems to be no end to what a proper wedding requires, and the bills are adding up."

She grinned at Pearl. "At least I still have a week to prepare. I understand your big day is only two days away."

Eager to end the conversation and proceed on to the hotel and her meeting with Dubois, Charity piped up before Pearl could answer. "Actually, Pearl and I are goin' shoppin' for buttons—for Pearl's weddin' dress." The half-truth chafed against Charity's conscience. But she couldn't very well divulge to Daniel's sister her other appointment.

Lucy gave a dismissive wave of her hand. "No need to buy buttons, Pearl. I bought far more buttons than I needed for my dress. You are welcome to as many as you'd like. Consider it an additional wedding present." Her azure eyes lit with rekindled enthusiasm. "Come, and I'll show you both my wedding dress while you pick out your buttons, Pearl."

Panic seized Charity. Her heart was not yet prepared to face Daniel. Perhaps when she'd solidified her plans to return to Georgia the thought of facing him would be less painful. "I—I don't know if we should—"

"Why, thank you kindly, Miss Lucy." This time it was Pearl who cut Charity off in midsentence. "Me an' Charity'd love to see yer dress. Wouldn't we, Charity?" Not allowing Charity the space of a half-breath to answer, Pearl turned back to Lucy. "I really appreciate you offerin' me the buttons. Like you said, the weddin' bills are addin' up." Pearl shot Charity a smug grin then stretched it into a brilliant smile which she slid toward Lucy. "You are an angel, and that's a fact, Miss Lucy."

Outnumbered, Charity cast a longing glance toward the Madison Hotel. According to Armand Dubois's letter, he should be in Madison for the next couple of days. There would be ample opportunity to meet with him.

But as Pearl dragged her down the boardwalk behind Lucy Morgan, Charity knew the quivering inside her had little to do with missing her appointed meeting with the carpetbagger. It had everything to do with the probability of another meeting—one she dreaded.

⌒

Daniel pulled on the reins to slow the pair of horses as he neared the intersection of Main-Cross and Mulberry Streets. Ignoring angry comments by drivers forced to maneuver around him, he brought the team and wagon to a complete stop.

He glanced northward where Mulberry sloped gently downward toward Georgetown. The war Jericho Emanuel's words loosed inside him last week raged more fiercely. According to Aunt Rosaleen's friend and housekeeper, Patsey Chapman, Charity had come to Madison to attend Adam Chapman and Pearl Emanuel's wedding.

The muscles in Daniel's arms twitched, wanting to turn the wagon toward Georgetown. How many times in the past week had he started to the train depot to buy a ticket to Vernon, only to turn around and walk back to the house?

He scoured his face with his hand. What would he say if he did confront

Charity? Would he beg her forgiveness for walking away from her like a cad and a coward? Would he demand she not leave Indiana for Georgia? Would he warn her of the dangers she might face traveling alone to the South?

And if he did, how would she respond? Daniel was sure he knew. In his mind's eye, he'd seen it played over and over in excruciating repetition. She'd laugh in his face—a sour, scoffing laugh. Then she'd gore him with a glare sharper than any bayonet and demand he remove his pitiful Yankee carcass from her sight.

At least that was the response he expected—the response he knew he deserved.

And even if he did manage to screw up his courage enough to beg her forgiveness and attempt to persuade her from leaving, what would it accomplish? It would only make her hate him even more. If that was possible.

He despised his cowardice. Even though he deserved them, he dreaded the thought of experiencing Charity's scathing recriminations.

Daniel snapped the reins down sharply against the horses' rumps, causing them to bolt. The wagon lurched down Main-Cross Street, and he pressed the soles of his boots hard against the angled footboard to steady himself. As the wagon bounced over the gravel street toward home, he gripped the leather lines so tightly his fingers cramped.

With effort, he forced his thoughts from Charity and back to the errands Mother and Lucy had assigned to him for the day. Later this afternoon, he would need to fetch Aunt Susannah and Cousin Georgiana from the depot when their train arrived from Indianapolis.

Daniel parked the wagon in front of the house and climbed down. At least the endless tasks preparing for his sister's wedding helped to fill his days and offer a diversion from agonizing over Charity. He didn't care to think beyond Lucy's wedding.

~⁓~

Charity stood transfixed in Mrs. Morgan's upstairs sewing room. Her gaze refused to budge from the breathtaking beauty of Lucy's wedding dress. Displayed on a dressmaker's form, the frock was a full-skirted vision of pale ivory silk satin overlaid with Honiton and net bobbin lace. It shimmered with hundreds of crystal and mother-of-pearl beads that adorned its V-shaped neckline, elbow-length sleeves, and voluminous skirt.

Moments ago, Charity and Pearl had literally gasped with awe when Lucy carefully removed the protective sheet from the dress. But they'd barely gotten a glimpse when Mrs. Morgan appeared in the open doorway. Apologizing for the interruption, she'd requested Lucy's help with something in the kitchen. She also informed Pearl that Patsey Chapman, Pearl's future mother-in-law, had stopped by and would like a word with her.

Tears dimmed the wedding gown's glory. Charity couldn't help imagining herself wearing this beautiful creation and standing beside Daniel as they exchanged marriage vows.

She blinked back her tears and turned to the button box Lucy had placed on a little round table. That dream had died when Daniel walked out of her sickroom three weeks ago.

She'd been relieved to learn from Lucy that he was out on an errand and wasn't due back for another hour. Hopefully she would be gone long before he returned.

The sound of footsteps on the stairs buoyed that hope and she reached for the button box. The sooner Pearl chose the buttons for her dress, the sooner they could leave.

"Lucy, what time did you say Aunt Susannah's train is due in at the depot?" Daniel's voice shot through Charity like a lightning bolt.

Charity's heart bounced painfully against her ribs. She whirled toward the open door and dropped the button box, scattering its contents over the room's floral carpet.

For a long moment they just stood staring at one another across the threshold.

Daniel's dark eyes were as wide as silver dollars in his pale face, and his unshaven jaw hung slack.

Charity suspected her expression mimicked his.

"I'm sorry." They said the words in near unison, and incredibly, Daniel's eyes grew even larger.

Frozen in place, Charity felt powerless to move. In almost detached fascination, she watched his Adam's apple bob in his throat as he stepped into the room.

The afternoon sun slanted through a long window on the west wall and glinted on his raven black hair. It reminded Charity of that first day he entered her uncle's mill last August. He was dressed much the same—a faded blue shirt, rolled up at the elbows, and black cotton work trousers.

He took another couple of steps toward her, and her heart crimped at his halting gait. Seven weeks ago, she'd begun dreaming of becoming his wife. She remembered how she'd smiled, imagining them limping together down the aisle of the little brick church in Vernon.

Amazingly, Daniel reached out and took both of her hands in his, sending a jolt through her body. His eyes, now hooded with a look of pain, glistened with unshed tears. "I'm sorry. I'm so sorry, Charity."

His unbelievable words jarred her free from her paralyzed state. Why on earth was he apologizing when it was she who'd injured him?

"Sorry for what?" Charity reared back but allowed him to keep her hands captive in his.

A bewildered frown wrinkled his broad brow. "For walking away from you—from us—like the cad and coward I am."

Images of unspeakable suffering her actions had brought upon Daniel flashed in Charity's mind. Shame seared her soul, and her heart throbbed with an unfathomable, aching love. "It is I who should be beggin' your pardon." Charity allowed the tears to stream unmolested down her face. "If I hadn't told Asa—"

Daniel shook his head, and his strong fingers gripped hers tighter. "Jericho told me. . .about the promise you made to your ma. I have no right to fault you for trying to save your brother." The corner of his mouth jerked in a failed attempt at a smile. "I thank the Lord I was not allowed to take part in that battle at Peachtree Creek. I don't have to wonder every day for the rest of my life if it was my bullet that—"

"Oh, Daniel!" The agony in Daniel's voice was more than Charity could bear. She threw herself against his chest and sobbed. "Please forgive me. Please say you forgive me."

"I forgive you, my love. I forgive you," he murmured against her hair. "Do you forgive me for walking out on you like a coward?"

A burst of indignation pushed her away from the sweet sanctuary of his embrace. She lifted a stern face to his. "You are not a coward, Daniel Morgan, and I won't allow anyone—not even you—to say you are! You are my good, sweet Daniel. The man I love."

Suddenly, his arms tightened around her, his head lowered, and his lips captured hers. The world could have crumbled around her and Charity wouldn't have cared. At last she knew she was where she belonged—where she needed to be for the rest of her life.

Without warning, Daniel released her and dropped to one knee. Keeping her hands in his, he gazed up at her, his dark eyes glistening. "Charity Langdon, I told you once, and I'll tell you again. You've owned my heart since last August. Will you put me out of my misery and agree to be my wife?"

A deluge of new tears washed down Charity's face. Her head bobbed with fierce nods until she finally managed to push the word between her sobs. "Yes."

A twittering sound near the door intruded into their private island of happiness. Lucy's voice, embroidered with her sprite laugh, skipped into the room. "Well don't stay down there like a dunderhead, Daniel! Get up and kiss her!"

And so he did.

Epilogue

W e'll miss you." Uncle Silas's gruff voice in the little foyer was thick with emotion, and his eyes glistened with moisture.

Charity reached up on tiptoes and kissed his weathered cheek above his grizzled beard, then patted his arm linked with hers. "We will just be in North Vernon, Uncle Silas. And since you've made Daniel part owner in the mill, we'll both be seein' you there nearly every day."

He cleared his throat. "Still, it will be different."

Surprised at her uncle's display of sentimentality, Charity couldn't help a giggle. "Remember, you and Aunt Jennie will have Henry for the first month while Daniel and I settle in. I have no doubt he will be company enough."

Remorse smote Charity's conscience. Pearl's assessment had been right. If God had not intervened and changed Charity's plans, her leaving would have indeed shattered her aunt's and uncle's hearts. It seemed incredible that only three weeks ago, God had reached down, saved her from her folly, and shifted the course of so many dear lives.

She suddenly remembered her missed meeting with Armand Dubois and had to suppress a giggle. After Daniel's marriage proposal, she hadn't given the carpetbagger another thought. It tickled her to imagine his continually checking his watch while pacing and fuming in the lobby of the Madison Hotel.

None of that mattered now. Here in the foyer of the little church overlooking Vernon, Charity's heart was at peace. Her future sparkled like the morning sun glinting off the myriad beads that adorned her wedding dress—the same dress her future sister-in-law wore two weeks ago to wed her dear Travis.

The first strong notes of "Blest Be the Tie That Binds" filtered into the foyer, sending nervous butterflies flitting in Charity's stomach.

She tightly gripped her nosegay that silently exclaimed, in the language of flowers, all the emotions throbbing in her chest. Deep purple violets spoke of her undying love and faithfulness, wild yellow irises proclaimed her faith in God and hope for future happiness, while sprigs of yarrow pledged final healing of all past wounds. Glancing down at the faded ribbons that bound the bouquet, she was struck by their symbolism as well. Violet ribbons from Daniel's mother's wedding bonnet twined with the yellow ribbons Mamma had worn in her hair when she married Papa. Two families, one from the North and one from the South, were uniting. Perhaps, in some small way, she and Daniel were part of God's larger plan to heal the nation.

As Uncle Silas escorted her into the sanctuary and down the church's center aisle to where her darling waited, all other thoughts fell away.

Daniel took her hands in his, enfolding them in his warm, strong fingers.

As they pledged their vows to one another, his dark gaze melting into hers held no hint of regret or lingering rancor. Only love.

And when the Reverend Davenport pronounced them man and wife, Charity could almost feel God fusing her and Daniel's hearts and spirits into one.

The soft whispering of her mother's voice filtered through the celebration of joy bursting inside Charity.

"And now abideth faith, hope, charity, these three; but the greatest of these is charity."

At last she understood the full meaning of that scripture and the power of God's grace and forgiveness.

As her husband bent to brush a tender kiss across her lips, a bevy of grateful prayers lifted heavenward from Charity's heart.

A Letter to Our Readers

Dear Readers:

In order that we might better contribute to your reading enjoyment, we would appreciate your taking a few minutes to respond to the following questions. When completed, please return to the following: Fiction Editor, Barbour Publishing, Inc., P.O. Box 719, Uhrichsville, OH 44683.

1. Did you enjoy reading *Freedom's Crossroad* by Ramona K. Cecil?
   ❑ Very much. I would like to see more books like this.
   ❑ Moderately—I would have enjoyed it more if _____
   _____
   _____

2. What influenced your decision to purchase this book?
   (Check those that apply.)
   ❑ Cover   ❑ Back cover copy   ❑ Title   ❑ Price
   ❑ Friends   ❑ Publicity   ❑ Other

3. Which story was your favorite?
   ❑ *Sweet Forever*   ❑ *Charity's Heart*
   ❑ *Everlasting Promise*

4. Please check your age range:
   ❑ Under 18   ❑ 18–24   ❑ 25–34
   ❑ 35–45   ❑ 46–55   ❑ Over 55

5. How many hours per week do you read? _____

Name _____

Occupation _____

Address _____

City_____ State_____ Zip_____

E-mail _____